Played

Bad-Boy Storyteller

ISBN: 1479369667

ISBN 13: 9781479369669

*"Sometimes you never know who is playing who
until the damage is done."*

Acknowledgments

To my numerous friends and family members who stood by me during the creation of *Played*—even Blueberry.

Prologue

As it plays out in his mind, he can see a rickety, wooden chair holding her motionless body far from anything normal. Consciousness has mostly abandoned her, leaving her at the whims of her captor, who moves patiently, circling his work. The windows are boarded, and the only light glows from a shaded table lamp, alone in a remote corner. Hope is long forgotten for the young woman as she slumps naked, exhausted, drained, and resting from her torments. Standing behind her he studies her body, leaning lasciviously close to her neck, whispering to her in the silent room.

"Ugly…shameless…deserving."

A deliberate smile creases his lips as he examines his labors. The bleach-soaked ropes binding her wrists are now taking their toll, eating into the exposed flesh fashioned from her struggling. Her mouth is pulled tight and wide, held with a thin, black belt. Again he whispers.

"No one, not your lying prayers either, will save you…miss you…or ever care."

Positioned still by her side, partially blocking the light, he pulls something from his pocket, a chosen implement. With a pop he removes the orange cap from the filled syringe, and a tiny squirt of liquid shoots into the air that is teeming with revulsion and excitement.

"You're a liar…fake."

Containing his attack and savoring what is next, he sees himself placing the needle into a crudely positioned IV taped to her arm and pushing the plunger down. The shot of adrenaline will awaken her suddenly—but not from a bad dream, rather to more unthinkable nightmares.

"I…I am justified."

Methodically he has prepared; now he envisions. Her heart pounds from the drugs and fear. Her body twists and contorts in pools of sweat. For the last time, she will fight against the restraints, making her final pleas for mercy, begging through the choking leather, her blood-drenched eyes desperately striving to read his thoughts. But nothing she can possibly imagine will prepare her for the hatred within him, driving him. He then stands immobile, clearing his broken mind of any sanity, putting in order his final assault.

Chapter One

"We are going to take a short commercial break, but stay tuned to Seattle's KDEX 103.7 FM: talk radio that listens." An after-Christmas liquidation advertisement begins as Sarah Michaels turns down the feed into the well-lit studio. It's her place of refuge, where she's worked for the past seven years covering all the hot topics of the day from the recession and health care to obesity in America. For Sarah it also serves as an outlet, an alternative home where she can disgorge all of her built-up opinions and views of the world's problems—her true calling in life. And the success of the show has brought about not only her picture riding along the bus lines, displaying her short, brown hair styled around a tiny-featured face, but the renovation of the entire studio. It's built like any other, packed with stacks of high-tech components, all emanating little flashing lights. A large stained-wood desk sits in the middle with a hefty chrome microphone suspended above it, hanging down from the ceiling. Underneath she sits in her new leather chair, staring at her schedule for the day and refreshing her lip gloss.

"T minus ten seconds," says Howard, the set manager, over the intercom, waiving his hand, gay as can be, through the glass wall that separates the operations room from the studio. Sarah smiles through newly glossed lips and nods her head, assuring him she has it all under control. And in control she is. Her understanding of the world's controversial topics is superior to most, sometimes even surpassing that of the experts that come on her broadcast. And today, so far at least, her self-confidence is evident in her quick wit and sexy-smooth voice—the same voice that has elevated ratings to the current estimated audience of over a million listeners. A red, flashing number three pulses on the equipment… two…one.

"Welcome back to the Sarah Michaels Show. I hope you missed me," she says, and follows with a flirty laugh. She then swiftly announces the time, 11:35 a.m., and gets to the topic of the day. "Our national debt is currently over sixteen trillion dollars; is this sustainable?" she asks. "Can we really continue to borrow from China and spend without any foreseeable limits? I think not," she adds, offering an answer to her own question while looking at the teleprompter that displays a name and city. "But we're going to find out what Eldon Jacobson from Whidbey Island thinks." She pushes a little green button and says, "Eldon, welcome to the Sarah Michaels Show; what are your thoughts?"

"Hi, Sarah, and thank you for taking my call. The way I see it is that big government is out of control, which everyone agrees, but the problem is as soon as we start talking about cutting back on programs everyone starts yelling, 'Not my program!' It seems everyone really wants to be socialists; they just don't want to pay for it."

"Well that's fascinating Eldon, but do you think that maybe—just maybe—there are many who don't want all these entitlement programs, that there's actually a force out there working against the status quo?"

"Yes, I definitely agree. And not only that—I think of myself as part of that movement, and at the same time, the thing no one seems to understand is that we're not going to solve these problems with words. The only way we have ever solved these problems throughout other times in history is revolution! We need to take this country back and take the power from government and make them work for us!"

"Interestingly put," Sarah replies, crunching her lips together while musing over his statement. Then the teleprompter lights up again with name and city—UNKNOWN, Seattle. Howard, the always-happy set manager, circles his finger behind the glass, telling her to move it along. Sarah agrees and thanks Eldon for his input. "Okay, let's take another call." Again she pushes the green button. "Okay, caller 'Unknown' from here in Seattle, what are your views?"

Silence.

"Caller, you're on the air, and we would like to hear your analysis concerning our huge national debt. What say you?"

Still no response, only what sounds like light breathing. Sarah gives a quizzical glance to her producer, sitting next to Howard, and once again attempts to get her seemingly reluctant caller to talk. "Caller, you are on—"

"I'm going to kill her." The voice comes across the line in a slow violent murmur. The man's malevolent tone, more than his words, sends a chill through Sarah, tightening her legs.

"I am sorry, caller. I'm not sure what you mean," she replies, in an effort to remain composed.

"I am going to kill this bitch!" the unknown caller replies, more loudly and angrily.

Sarah shudders, feeling a shock of terror shoot through her body. "Who are you going to kill?"

Caller Unknown from Seattle returns to silence, an eerie silence that raises the hair on the back of Sarah's neck. Howard and her producer, behind the glass, are on full alert while Sarah scrambles for a pen. She has had her share of prank callers in years past, but her instincts tell her something about this is real, very real. "*Who* are you going to kill?" she inquires once more.

Again, silence.

"Caller, are you still there?" she asks, her voice cracking. A tense moment of stillness follows.

Then a calm and unnatural *yes* comes across the line, leaving her no doubt this is something she needs to handle with the utmost scrutiny. Howard gives her the signal to cut the call, but she holds up a finger, demanding some extra time. She pulls herself together and gets down to what she does best—getting her subjects to reveal their core feelings to her, to bare their souls.

"Caller, you're giving me very little info about who you are, who you wish to kill, and most importantly why you believe this person needs to die. I want to hear, in detail, all you have to say; leave nothing out." She hears only heavy breathing in response. "Caller," she says more forcefully, "I presume you called this show because you have something to say, a message you would like the world to hear; is that the case?"

"Yes, I do want the world to hear. I want the world to hear her die!" caller Unknown blurts out furiously.

"Who?" Sarah asks, backing off her tone, trying not to piss him off.

"My fucking filthy wife. She's playing me. She thinks she can get away with it. I have her tied up in a chair and a knife in my hand, and if you even *think* about taking me off the air, I promise I will torture her first. I have a drill and eight-inch wood screws I will bore into her legs."

The thought wrenches Sarah's stomach. "Okay, okay, let's settle down. I've listened to what you've said, but I want to know more," she replies, waving off her producer who is tapping insistently on the glass. Then in attempt to relate to the caller, she reveals some fictitious personal information. "I want you to know that I know your pain; my ex-husband cheated on me constantly; I *know* how you feel."

Her plan backfires, opening floodgates of wrath. "You have no idea how I feel, bitch! You are *all* the same. You think you can do whatever you want and then cry your way out of it. You make excuses for all that you do."

Sarah can sense an unadulterated evil mounting in his voice with every word, and she gets the sense he's doing all he can to hold it back.

"I've given her every chance to tell the truth. She cannot tell the truth. She is a lying, cheating whore, and she *is* going to die!" The audio over the line changes. Sarah realizes he has put the call on speakerphone, and before she can respond, he begins screaming out his hatred in the background. "You fucking fantasy! You think you can fuck my friends and get away with it! You believe I do not have the *power* to do something!"

Then for the first time, Sarah can hear the woman in the room. "Mmm... mm...mm."

"I have the power! I have all the power from God to make you suffer!"

Between his screams all kinds of other noises fill the studio: some Sarah can make out, like a chair being thrashed about and the strained sounds of struggling.

"Mmmrr...mmrrr...mrrraahh!"

More thrashing, and caller Unknown roaring, "Die, you fucking lying, disgraceful whore—die!"

"Mmmraghh! Mmmrr! Mmmrr!"

Then suddenly it all comes to a stop. There's mostly silence on both ends of the line, only heavy breathing coming from caller Unknown.

"Caller, talk to me. Caller!" she shouts, panicked and disarrayed. Fear surrounds her, and she's not even sure she wants his answer.

Before she can discern her thoughts, she hears him taking in a deep breath and exhaling the words, "She got what she deserved. They all did!"

The line goes dead.

Chapter Two

Thirty-five minutes earlier.

"Eleven..."

"Okay."

"Seventeen..."

"Uh-huh."

"Twenty-four..."

"All right, come on baby."

"Thirty-two..."

"Damn."

"Thirty-seven..."

"Damn."

"And the power ball number is forty-two..."

"Ah, to hell with it anyway!" he grumbles to himself, sitting alone at the breakfast table. It's a small table, cramped for two, that's placed in front of his apartment window with shades pulled. Staring back at him sits a glass jar full of change, a half-eaten plate of eggs covered in Tabasco, a gun, and a badge that reads, "Detective Cools." Again he glances to the loser lottery ticket, lying crinkled and helpless atop the table, and flicks it away. For another brief moment, he counts his loss and then finishes the eggs while ignoring the mid-morning news playing in the adjacent room. Nothing of interest catches his ear, just the ordinary blah-blah-blah bullshit and the weather.

Today will be cold and rainy—characteristic of Seattle.

The sound of a two-cup coffee pot on the counter means his morning fix is brewed. He pours a cup and lights the second cigarette of the day.

By and large he's a hostile man, but wasn't always so. He began his life in a prominent, middle-class family, schooled and raised in the peaceful, mountain suburbs of Redding, California. There he benefited from a good, old-fashioned upbringing that catapulted him into a world ripe with opportunity and optimism. And optimistic he was. He set out to save the world—full of intentions to promote his youthful liberal approach to life.

But then he became a cop. And the years observing people at their worst have taken their toll. All of them—from petty thieves to diseased crack addicts, pedophiles to woman beaters—his job, his life is to take them off the streets only for them to be placed into a corrupt justice system where everyone spends their every breath lying. As a young child, Bradley Cools was taught to always tell the truth, and then into adulthood he took oaths to uphold his integrity. But it's all been downhill from there.

Now his days teem with untruths from every player in the game. The criminals lie their way out of trouble; once that is accomplished, he and his coworkers lie them back in. Then in the courtrooms, the prosecutors and defense lawyers tell more lies. Enough to rival those told in the jailhouse full of snitches, or even the girlfriends who come during visiting hours.

He finishes his cigarette, drinks the last of the coffee, and rinses the cup in the sink before heading to the bathroom.

Passing the living room, decorated in functional boring, he steps into view of the bathroom mirror, where a smile is forced across his face. The glass reflects a hard, handsome man with strong features that serve as a foundation for frustrated age lines. Cools is, and always has been, good-looking. At six feet tall, sporting wavy black hair, light brown eyes, and a muscular build, he has never gone without attention from the opposite sex. Currently, and for the past two years, he has been dating Chelsea, a pretty woman who has a bit of an insatiable desire to be with him. Together they make the ideal fit. Being something of a wallflower, she thrives on his daring stories, while at the same time soothing his angry and sometimes sarcastic view of the world. And, although he doesn't realize it, he needs her more than she needs him, and he is lucky to have her.

He finishes his daily grooming with an electric shave that leaves a hint of stubble. Then, already three hours late for work, he makes his way to the front door, checking things off his list: gun, badge, wallet, and so forth. Little does he know that the events soon to take place will offer him two paths, either saving him or plunging him alone into a final downward spiral where even the notion of escape is clouded.

Chapter Three

At the Seattle Police Department's downtown precinct, Michelle Robertson, Brad Cools's partner, sits properly just inside an open cubicle, doing her nails while occasionally glancing at her fellow policemen as they come into view. Everything about a man in uniform keeps her warm and safe inside. Her desk/office for the most part is out in the open for all to see upon entering the station; only one wall separates, and her glamour-magazine look contrasts with the pale, cement-walled ambiance. As viewed by others, she is overaccessorized (even were it the '80s), wearing multiple earrings and thick makeup over tanned skin. If taken all away, what would be left is a beautiful, married woman with brown highlighted hair, a curvy shape, and metallic-blue eyes, metallic not only for their shimmering blue-gray tint but also for their steadiness.

Today, as the clock is nearing noon, the police station hums lightly with all the usual—boosters in search of their sunrise fix and daytime prostitutes coming in. Going out are the line of last night's highly inebriated problems that will soon return. Michelle studies them, looking for the ones she's busted before while her computer grinds away, crunching the new data entered concerning a cold case file assigned to her: one of those all-too-common cases where everyone knows who did it but failed to find enough evidence to prove it in a courtroom. She could care less anyways—it is only a theft, albeit a large one; still, not the kind of case she became a detective to solve. Then annoyingly her desktop phone rings.

"Detective Robertson," she answers. Right away she can tell the 911 operator is rattled. Stating in a lightning-fast pitch that someone has just killed his wife on a live radio broadcast. Michelle drops her nail polish and springs into action, listening intently to the nervous operator, who recounts that KDEX 103.7 FM's *The Sarah Michaels Show* has traced the call, and reports the local number to her. Quickly, while holding a pen in a handful of wet finger nails, she writes down the number then types it into the computer. Immediately her P.C. comes up with a name: Joshua Siconolfi. The police station now becomes still, leaving only the sounds of the keyboard clicking away as she punches the name into the department's data-base. The name seems somehow familiar; she's heard it before but cannot place it. And after a few moments, the screen unfolds his lengthy history.

Joshua P. Siconolfi

Height: 6' 1"

Weight: 185 lbs.

Age: 27

Date of birth: 05/07/1985

Eye color: Hazel

Last known address: 2018 Crestwood Ln., Seattle, WA 92443

Marital status: Married; Kimberly Siconolfi

Then his picture pops up. It's a six-month-old mug shot of a bronzed and very fit *GQ* type. "Oh, you are a handsome boy," she says softly. But who are you? she wonders. Then the page begins to fill.

Convicted Felon—Violent Criminal—Gun Restricted

05/20/2012: First Degree Arson, St. Luke's Parish: dismissed due to lack of evidence

06/16/2011: Disorderly Conduct: thirty days in jail

04/02/2006: Violation of No-Contact Order, Sherry Hill: charges dropped

06/22/2005: Third Degree Vehicular Assault, Sherry Hill: plea bargain, one year

11/12/2003: Domestic Violence, Sherry Hill: trial/not guilty

04/04/2003: DUI: deferred program, completed

01/27/2003: Domestic Violence, Sherry Hill: dismissed

09/15/2002: DUI: dropped to reckless driving/probation

08/29/2001: DUI: dismissed

Now Michelle remembers Joshua, and it doesn't have anything to do with three DUI's, rather everything to do with Sherry Hill. Suddenly the picture of the good looking man on the screen morphs into a monster. A cold chill enters her and runs its course through her veins; her palms dampen. She whips in her chair to check anything or anyone creeping from behind. Then leaving the 911 operator on hold, she dials her partner. She holds the phone away as not to smear her sweating make-up and speaks loudly into the handset. "Brad, listen...Joshua Siconolfi...do you remember him?"

"Of course I do," he replies, with a hint of exhilaration in his voice.

"Well, someone just called a radio show from his residence, and the situation seems to be that he's killed his wife."

Cools, driving down a busy street, can tell her voice is shaking but doesn't comment. "Give me an address."

She relays the information.

"I'm on my way!" he yells. Then, using his years of experience, he skillfully cranks the wheel and taps the brake pedal, spinning the cruiser one hundred eighty degrees, in heavy traffic. His cell phone slides across the seat, dropping to the floor mat. And soon he is speeding, shouting to the windshield, "I always said this creep would kill somebody someday!" I should have set him up years ago.

"Brad...Brad, are you there?" Her worried voice bounces around the floorboard amid sounds of her partner's car being pushed to its limits and his screaming in the background. "Brad...Brad!" she shrieks, now concerned as to what he might do. Giving up, she calls in other responding officers over the radio. Moving pictures flood her mind of him recklessly steering through busy downtown streets, yelling for shoppers to clear the way. She says a quick prayer and finds a moment of relief to hear other units are on the way. Then noticing the 911 operator line still flashing, she picks it up for more information, only to hear the previously recorded *Sarah Michaels Horror Show*.

On the other side of the city, the late-morning traffic travels along at 55 mph, bearing unhappy faces that curse the assholes they follow. Most of them almost spill their coffees—startled by a cop-car speeding by at nearly 95 mph. Joshua has eluded his grip before, but today opens a new page. Today he'll receive the justice he deserves.

Taking a hard right, his phone slides back within a reachable distance. He picks it up and snaps it shut just as it rings again.

Michelle's voice shakes over the air like an early-morning bed wetter discovered by an abusive father. "Brad...oh...Brad, you need to listen to this!" She plays the recording.

At first, even he is held frozen in disbelief. "That's fucking it!" he shouts. He's heard all he needs to hear, stood by more than he should have, and he knows what must be done. Today someone who's had it coming for a long time is going to get what they deserve; today Brad Cools is going to kill an evil. His reasoning is simple: an eye for an eye, a tooth for a tooth, and a life for a wife!

And wanting to know what his chances are of pulling off a successful, well-executed accident, he asks, "Michelle, are there any other officers on the scene?"

"Brad, don't!"

He slides the cruiser sideways around a tight left turn. "Tell me now. Are there other officers on the scene?"

She replies in haste, "Fine then...how far away are you?"

"I'm about ten minutes away."

She leans close to her desk, covering the phone to speak privately to him. "Be careful, Brad. Don't do anything you don't have to, okay?"

"I won't," he replies, not assuring her. "Now tell me, are there any other officers?"

A short, uncertain silence follows. Michelle lets out a frustrated sigh. Then she hears some news from dispatch. "Well, it sounds like there are a few closer than you," she says, sensing relief.

Not getting the answer he wanted, he snaps his cell phone shut, cutting her off. Then he switches his radio over to dispatch and, in a calm voice, says, "This is Detective Cools. I need to have immediate contact with all officers en route to the Siconolfi residence."

"Give me a second," dispatch replies. There's a pause. "Okay, Detective Cools, I have you connected to the lead officer closest to the scene."

"Who am I speaking to?" Cools asks forcefully.

"Officer Renker. And I'm four blocks from the Siconolfi residence, on Applewood Street, waiting for backup."

"Don't move! I need you to hold back. The suspect is armed and dangerous, and is *not* to know you are there until I arrive. Do you understand?"

"Affirmative. And I know this neighborhood well. I can set up in the alley to protect against any escape from the rear."

"Okay," Cools agrees, "but take another car with you, and remember, he's to be considered extremely dangerous; be fully prepared to take him out if you have to!"

His cruiser angles the corner onto Applewood, where he finds two other squad cars waiting and another coming in from the opposite direction. Attempting to keep a low profile, it's his first turn without squealing tires in the past seven minutes. He switches off the overhead lights and exits the car expediently. The other men do the same, and without any words, and as if trained for this specific scenario, they assemble into a football huddle in the middle of the street. The officer to his left is a short man; to his right, a young pale rookie—probably on his first call—and in front of him, a bony redhead donning a frightened smile. It's a motley crew, but the only thing Cools cares about is that they all seem eager to be involved.

Curtains from curious onlookers are pulled aside as homeowners watch their every move. Cools shoots them long, serious stares until they retreat deep within their homes. Then after a few short and sweet introductions, he uses his hand-held radio to call Officer Renker in the alley. "Officer Renker, are you in position?"

"That's affirmative; we have the rear sealed."

"Okay, I need you to remain silent and wait for further commands."

"Detective, what's the plan?" asks the rookie.

"Okay, here's the seriousness of the situation. The suspect is Joshua Siconolfi. I put him away once for almost beating his girlfriend to death; he spent eight months, although he deserved twenty years. And now it seems he's not only murdered his new wife, but this creep did it on a live radio show. We are dealing with a real sick and twisted individual that at this point has nothing to lose except spend the rest of his life behind bars. So we're not taking any chances—do not hesitate to take him out! Does everyone understand?"

The officers, now realizing the full scope of the situation, look to each other, mustering courage as his words sink in. Cools makes one final attempt to weed out anyone not 100 percent sure. "Is there anyone who for any reason isn't ready to go?" Silently they all shake their heads no. He then systematically looks each of them in the eye until he is satisfied all will do their job. "Okay, you," he says, pointing to the short officer. "You flank my right." Then he gestures to the rookie and the redheaded officer, ordering them to flank the left, while lifting his radio to his mouth. "Officer Renker, we're going in; are you ready?"

"Affirmative."

Cools begins walking backward to his cruiser, saying, "Okay, let's go; safeties off and follow my lead." A moment later, in his vehicle, he lights a much-needed cigarette. He takes in thick, full drags while waiting until everyone is lined up. He envisions what he might find or, rather, more what he hopes to find. In his mind's eye, he sees a bloodied, dead girl tied to a chair and Joshua going for his gun. A flood of endorphins ignites his brain as he envisions his response, unleashing all his skill and fury with the quickness of a rattlesnake, which will equate to two bullets in Joshua's chest and one to the head. Joshua will then slump to his death against the wall, taking a good look at his executioner as he dies, and he will know that Detective Cools was the wrong guy to piss the fuck off.

Cools is then pulled back to reality by a flash of a thumbs-up from the officer in the patrol car now positioned beside him. Cools tosses his cigarette out the window, then takes a deep, fresh breath before leading the charge up Crestwood Lane. He doesn't even see the road—only his gun firing—until they reach the driveway. They enter promptly at 2018. The other patrol cars, flanking his sides, tear into the lawn, lights flashing. One of them running over a row of Japanese maples bordering the perimeter of the yard. Then they all come to an abrupt stop and exit their cruisers, assuming tactical positions. Cools crouches behind his door, gun in his right hand and cell phone in the other. He dials the number and pushes send.

At the fourth ring, Joshua answers smoothly, "Hello?"

Cools's first impression is that he sounds drunk as well as seemingly unaware of being ambushed. It gives him poise, and in a low, commanding voice, he states, "This is Detective Cools from the Seattle Police Department. You are surrounded. You need to come out the front of the house holding your hands in the air; if you attempt to go out the back, you *will* be shot! And if you do not come out immediately, we are coming, in full force! Do you understand?"

He pauses a second for Joshua's response but only hears breathing and then—click.

Oh, you're fucking dead! "Okay, is everyone ready?" Cools calls over the radio. Everyone confirms, and he wastes no time. "Follow me!" He starts for the door with his Ruger 40 Auto leading the way and his makeshift team of street cops moving in on all sides. The rookie and the redheaded officer to his left have AR-15s and are gradually creeping across the lawn. Maybe I'll get lucky, and one of these guys will also shoot him. Swiftly and cautiously and low to the ground, he sprints toward the large, heavy wooden door while surveying the structure. It's a large, single-story home with wrought-iron security bars over the outside windows—the kind only the wealthy and crack dealers have installed. His head sways back and forth, collecting information—curtains and shades drawn tight, no sign of a dog—and then he sees movement. "Halt!" he yells, holding his left arm high. Everyone crouches into combat positions as the front door slowly opens.

Cools and the other officers would never have expected what happens next. Joshua just casually walks out the door onto the colored concrete walkway,

Chapter Seventy-Eight

The next and final evening, reporters and the paparazzi leap from there vans as Joshua unexpectedly comes into view at his front door. He stands still, casually waiting for them to assemble around him; then he feeds them a prepared speech. "Antisocial!" He lets the word dangle in the breeze. "Antisocial is a conspiracy slogan from the psychological-propaganda machine, intended to make us all drones!"

"Are you and Kimberly having a baby?"

"Was this all a scam?"

"We want to talk to Kimberly!"

Ignoring their questions he steps back through the doorway, silencing the crowd by shutting the door. Then a few minutes later, the red Lotus revs its engine, squeals out of the garage, and speeds away. Alone Joshua does some late-night shopping from one store to the next until once again he sees the black Mustang. Earlier this morning he had a loyal fan that works at the DMV run a check. And sure enough, one Bradley Cools owns the same car.

He drives around until after one in the morning, when he pulls out onto an abandoned dock. It's dark and cloudy, with only a faint glow of moonlight shimmering on the waters. He exits the car and walks to the edge of the pier—passing a little, red light—and leans over the rickety railing, listening to the peaceful sounds of the waves splashing the pier. And there he waits.

Chapter Seventy-Nine

Cocaine travels at one hundred seventy miles per hour through a straw and into the nostril of ex-detective Cools, who then bellows, "It's time to get it on!"

He eases the slide back, chambering a round in his 9 mm Berretta, and slips out of his car. The weight of the loaded gun feels powerful in his hand. These are the little pieces of metal that will put an end to Joshua once and for all. Cautiously he moves up behind the Lotus; it's empty. And now he knows where Joshua stands, as he has followed him here before. Gradually and warily he steps alongside the broken-down warehouse—the only thing blocking his view of his target.

It begins to rain, as memories of the past few months serve as a backdrop to his thoughts: top cop...Kimberly isn't real...she deserved it...live on forever, of no evil...sometimes these things go off, punk...Sherry Hill...Amberly ... car club...Vitalisep...stealing the kilo of cocaine...now I've got your DNA... William Siconolfi...Joshua, will you forgive me for my sins...guilty...crooked cop...has-been...lawsuit...liar...addict!

He shakes away the burning sickness in his mind to concentrate on the task at hand, edging nearer. He peeks around a building, and he can see Joshua's unsuspecting outline. This is all too easy, he thinks to himself, creeping slowly up the dark pier. Closer and closer he makes his way until he can distinguish almost every approach around him. There is not a person for at least a mile in all directions, and he has an easy shot. He sniffs some more of the cocaine and raises his weapon. It's time to settle our score. You took my life; now I'm taking yours! He levels an expert aim, inhaling deeply, exhaling evenly, skillfully locking in his target.

Bang! Bang! Bang!

Bullets rip into the night, all hitting their mark with precision. He drops to his knees, reaching for his chest, gasping for oxygen. Blood covers his hands among the smells of burned flesh and gunpowder. Confusion engulfs him as his life fades. And his eyes are fixed on a silhouette that turns; the moonlight illuminates the smile on his face, standing next to a little red light. Suddenly Kimberly emerges from the darkness, wielding a smoking gun. In midstride she shoots again.

Bang! This one blasts Cools's kneecap into a bloody mess. He squirms in agony. "You bitch! You fucking bitch!" he screams, using the last of his conscious breaths. Then with all his might, he attempts to lift his gun and pull the trigger, but only succeeds in squeezing off one round. A stray bullet ricochets off the abandoned building two hundred yards away.

Kimberly doesn't flinch, only approaches faster. Joshua bursts out into evil, dominating laughter, glorifying his victory, the winning of the game.

Bang! This one rips into Cools's stomach just as Kimberly reaches him. He tries to curse her more, but only blood comes out of his mouth. His open eyes ice over.

Joshua looks up and starts howling into the night, "I know you can still hear me, you fucking loser. I want you to wait for me... Wait for me in hell... Because when I get there, we are going to play again. We are going to play forever!"

Then he notices Kimberly standing over the lifeless body. She's in shock. He grabs her. "Okay, let's get out of here! Kimmy, we have to go. It's over, so let's go. Let's get out of here—now!"

In an instant they flee the scene, leaving Cools to the darkness. Everything returns to silence. With his last glimpse of reflection, he sees her; with his final escape of air, he utters her name... Chelsea.

Then Joshua adds to her excitement, saying, "Yeah, I can see it now: little Joshes and Kimmys running around here playing. We could guide them and teach them."

"So do you think it's a good idea then?" she asks anxiously.

"Yes, it's a great idea! It's such a great idea in fact, I'm going to call some reporters right now and tell them the news!"

"I love you so much," she shouts, jumping out of bed and dancing about the room.

They make love. And later they're spotted shopping about the malls. Kimberly is absolutely beaming, like a woman who has all of life's problems solved. And she loves being seen publicly, totally in love, spending the day with her husband shopping for new maternity clothes. Before they left, they'd decided not to call and report their impulsive decision to have a baby; rather, they will let the media figure it out on their own.

Joshua plays his part flawlessly, given that he's not nearly as excited about the plan as he pretends to be. There's a voice of wisdom that speaks to him, whispering what he must do.

Chapter Seventy-Seven

A couple of days whirl by in deep slumber as they come off the heroin and alcohol. Joshua wakes in the late afternoon but doesn't get out of bed. Instead he watches Kimberly sleep for a few quiet minutes. He likes that her hair is starting to grow back nicely. And he loves her immensely. Still there's the nagging thought that she's a liability. I want to trust her, but can I? Can I trust her to never say a word about what we've done and do what we need to do?

She begins to wake. He just stares at her, grinning, and says, "I want to tell you something. I want to tell you who little Frankie is."

"Is that the name you were saying in your sleep?" she asks curiously.

He then tells her everything—sharing also that he believes the good nature of the boy somehow balances his inner wickedness.

"That is beautiful, Joshua. But I love your inner wickedness. And why didn't you ever tell me about this before?"

"I don't know. I thought you'd think it was silly."

She holds him lovingly. "I don't think it's silly at all. And actually I just realized something about you." She searches his eyes. "And that is what a wonderful father you would make." His reaction is unresponsive. Kimberly presses forward, revealing her desires. "You know I said I wanted to open a French restaurant, but what I really want is a little Frankie...a little Joshua. And I would be a good mommy, and the world would love our child. We could get off the drugs and start acting normal."

Joshua slumps quietly in his chair amid plenty of unwanted noise inside his head. His anxieties elevate as he struggles to restrain the images of Trace and Kimberly from his mind. It's been itching at him for some time now. So he smokes some more of the heroin off of a piece of tinfoil and gazes through the hotel room's skylight. It loosens him into a state of bliss. Then he smokes more than he should and closes his eyes. There his feelings and symbolic thoughts meld into pictures—stories of joy and boyhood fun.

It's summertime in Idaho. The heat drops down upon the Clemsen farm by day, and The Andy Griffith Show *plays on their color television set at night. It's a world that is safe and fulfilling—an open meadow for the grand adventures of little Frankie.*

Ever since hillbilly Abe and Sally stole him away from a life of inopportunity and left him with his new family, he's finally been able to be a normal young boy. He spends his days playing in the sun with Billy, his new brother, and Trixter, the family dog. The two boys have in a short time formed an unbreakable bond. And although neither of them realizes it, they both benefit from being followed around by their sister, Bobby-Sue, who asks them countless questions. The three of them are inseparable in doing their chores around the farm and helping Mrs. Sue Clemsen prepare homemade meals. And Jake Clemsen even gets little Frankie his own calf, which he names Moo-Moo and tends to daily.

On weekends they go to baseball games at the high school, where Mrs. Clemsen retells her favorite story to her friends: the day her little Frankie, the boy who wouldn't speak, said, "I love you," to her—his first words since the incident. And how she'd responded with a burst of tears and hugs, how she held him firm, not letting go for five minutes straight, only releasing her clutch to call the fellow members of her church to report the miracle—their gift from Jesus. And that how, in just a few short weeks, he was speaking well, like he'd never had a problem. Except for some occasional crudeness, she would add in a lower tone; you know...his past learned responses that Jake and I had to deal with in short order.

Occasionally she tries learning of his past. And even though he hasn't yet opened up to her, she finds no need to rush him. She simply trusts that someday, when he's ready, he will share his secrets. But little Frankie isn't holding out on her; he really cannot remember much of anything, since most of his past is hidden from him as well. He's only left with a haunting and vivid likeness of a beautiful woman who wears long, flowing, blond hair. Though he believes the image comes from the preaching at church, the figure in his mind is that of what a worldly woman would look like.

Suddenly, he, like looking directly into a camera lens, turns to Joshua within the dream and says something. It's something Joshua knows to be of great importance; however, he cannot understand the boy's utterances.

Then the imagery shifts—days turn to months and years. Joshua speed-dreams, seeing little Frankie attending school, where he makes many friends, particularly with the girls in his class, and is adapting well to his new environment by getting good grades, becoming a valued member of the Clemsen family, as well as proving himself a role model for Billy and Bobby-Sue.

And now at the age of twelve or so, his voice begins to change—a voice that's full of energy and optimism. And no one would ever believe he had a speaking problem before. Nowadays the only trouble is that no one can shut him up. He speaks out about everything from politics to social issues to Jesus. He tells of his aspirations and love for life, counsels his siblings, and quotes scripture. Some think he'll be a great preacher someday. And little Frankie believes this as well. He also believes he will see the woman in his mind someday.

Joshua stirs to the sounds of Kimberly rummaging loudly through her purse. He sits up, rubbing his face.

"Who's little Frankie?"

"What?"

"The name you keep saying in your sleep, little Frankie—who is he?"

Joshua doesn't answer. He gets up; his stomach feels sick—needing more of the smoke from the tinfoil. He has some and shares it with Kimberly. Tranquility once again surrounds him. He lies back with his eyes closed and, in a malleable voice, says, "Maybe I'll tell you about him someday...But for now, I just want to go home."

She thinks about it for a second, then replies with a concession. "Sure...We can leave now if you want, but on one condition...When we get home, we need to clean up some and quit drinking all the time." She slaps him on the shoulder.

Joshua just nods and lies back, enjoying the heroin now coursing through his body, when she adds, "I'll call and make the arrangements at the airport...You need to get ready to play your part." There's no response. "Are you listening to me? Joshua, are you listening to me?"

"Yes. What? Yeah, you said I need to play my part...my part in what?"

"What we talked about...or don't you remember? Our plan to make a scene at the airport on our way out...Remember, we want everyone to know we were here getting high, and then we are going to cause a disruption in the terminal?"

Two and a half hours later, at Amsterdam's Schiphol Airport, the young, high, drunk, missed, and apparently distraught couple makes a spectacle of cursing and belligerence—a performance played well enough to make headlines throughout the world.

There's something about the "trouble in paradise story" everyone gravitates to.

Chapter Seventy-Six

At the Seattle Police Department, the next morning, Detective Michelle Robertson puts down her morning paper, complete with aligned photographs of what the editor refers to as the "Siconolfi-Amsterdam-Connection." Rumors are they were caught trying to board the plane carrying a large amount of illegal drugs. But it is all of little concern to her now, as she stares at her cell phone resting on her desk. What should I do? Should I warn him? God, why is he such an asshole?

Grudgingly she pushes send, somewhat hoping he won't answer. Four rings, five, six—

"Hello."

She can clearly hear a hung-over and beaten voice on the other end—wherever that may be. "Did you know that your name came up in today's morning briefing?"

"Oh yeah?"

"Yeah, and I'm to pick you up on assault charges if I see you. What did you do?"

"I...I was working out some problems."

"And how's that working out for you? I'll tell you how it's working out," she yells over the line. "It's gotten you some felony charges—that's how!" Then she hears a distinct noise. "Are you...did you...just snort something?" He doesn't answer. "Brad, are you doing drugs? Tell me."

"Did I ever tell you I really miss you?" Now it's Michelle that doesn't answer, only sighs on the other end. "Well, I do…I miss you a lot, Michelle…and…And I want my life back." She can hear the desperation in his voice. "Can you help me?" he begs.

She breathes hard into the phone, rendering her frustration. There's a moment of silence. They can feel each other over the airwaves. "I'll talk to Captain and see if we can take down the guy you beat half to death. He went to the hospital you know. He had broken teeth, a broken nose, and needed many stitches for his eye socket."

"He was a street punk!"

"Oh, you're so tough, aren't you?" Cools says nothing. "And you're right; he is a street punk. His name is Ramon Jaurez, and he's a gang member. And if you can promise me…promise me, Brad, that you're going to stop this rampage of yours, I…I will think about picking him up and have him drop his charges against you for me dropping whatever charges I get on him."

"I love you, Michelle…I fucking love your sweet ass."

"Don't give me your bullshit, Brad! Promise me this bullshit is going to stop."

There's a pause as he considers the commitment. Then he replies, "I promise."

"Okay…good. Also answer me this: have you been following the Siconolfis?" Again he doesn't answer. "Brad, have you? Because I'm sure you've heard they returned last night from Europe."

Click.

for him in prison. They're now calling her the Sister of Mystery, as they repeatedly dub in segments of her interview with Tabatha Sterns, in which she vaguely insinuated some possible girl-on-girl escapades at the getaway.

Finally one evening Joshua confronts her about it. He asks softly, "Kimmy, when you were at the ranch did you…you know, did you fool around with any of the other girls?"

She smiles to him with a luster.

"Did you?"

"Well…There was this one silky woman there named Paloma. A tall, thin black woman from Georgia, she was always touching me and lauding over my figure. She made me feel warm and sexual, the way you do. And whenever I would go to her room, she would dress in my presence—she wore browns and purple lace." Kimberly stares off, continuing, "I often felt myself wanting to touch her skin. Then one night we were up late, peering through a provocative lingerie book—it was from France or somewhere. And the girls in it were young and fresh. Paloma kept telling me how delicate I would look wearing them, and I was starting to fantasize of what she wanted from me. So I began touching the girls in the pictures, my fingers brushing over their flesh. She asked me if that's how and where I liked to be touched, and I said—"

She then stops due to his peculiar reaction. She would have normally expected him to be turned on, but instead he appears to be preoccupied. She asks him what's wrong.

"Nothing."

"No, something's wrong. Are you jealous over what Paloma and I were doing?"

"No…well, no…But is that the way Trace would touch you?"

Kimberly instantly becomes infuriated. "Do not do this, Joshua! It was your plan, remember? You're the one who told me to do it. I did it for you. I did it for us!" She pauses for a time. With each passing moment, her emotions rise, while he feels increasingly guilty for bringing it up.

She stands over him. "I can't believe you would ask me this when it was all your idea! This is all your fault Joshua. And now you want to ask me things. What do you want to know? How good a lover he was? Did I like fucking him? Did he make me come? I don't even want to think about. It's over—done!" She starts crying. "I only love you, Josh…you and only you." Then she runs to the bedroom, and before the door slams shut, she yells, "You know I would do anything for you; then you take advantage of me like this!"

Chapter Seventy-Five

Hiding away in Europe, the renowned duo hasn't a care in the world. They fritter away their days without rule, blowing money like spoiled children and taking in all the sights. Joshua whisks her away to Paris on a fairytale romance. Then off to Monaco to gamble with their ill-gotten fortune, followed by a tour of Egypt's pyramids and other ancient sights—never staying more than a night in any one place. They spend an evening in a villa off the coast of Italy, and then to Prague, where they meet another young couple who suggest they must experience Amsterdam. And the next morning they're off and running, eating and drinking their fill of the local delights—one of them being the unrestricted Afghan heroin.

In their hotel, as they lie in bed, skin pressed to skin, and high, Joshua mumbles his love for her. He tells her how he would be forever lost without her and that if she were to die, he'd commit suicide to be joined with her once again. Kimberly, so loaded she cannot reply with words, tells him all he needs to hear with her caress. And there they stay for the next few nights, doing the drugs of the heavens and making love, bothered by no one, not even the maid who obeys the "Niet Verstoren" sign hanging outside their door.

Each day they pay careful attention to all news broadcasts. Joshua dribbles over every word, good or bad. But underneath the surface, he holds some jealous sentiments concerning the growing popularity of his new wife. Everyone is beginning to seem more interested in what life was like for her on the ranch than

Chapter Seventy-Three

The next week sails by as Joshua and Kimberly hole up in their home, planning their future and catching up for lost time. Outside the reporters are still on twenty-four-hour watch, and inside their Facebook page is blowing up with prospective magazine photo-ops, limitless interview offers, lawyers that would like to handle their potential lawsuits, agents who are begging to represent them, and one woman who even requests to have Joshua's seed, so she can bear his child. They only venture out at night for expensive dinners and drinks in some of Seattle's finest restaurants, to make their appearances, using every opportunity to make sure one of them says something that borders profoundness and/or insanity, to maintain the public's involvement. They're living the high life with no end in sight and cherishing every morsel of their stardom. At home they cuddle and play and discuss all they're going to do with their lives, as well as working on the final stages of their scheme.

It's not long, and the money starts pouring in, fueling the lifestyle they've longed for. Nearly nine hundred thousand dollars is awarded to them, via MTV, for the exclusive rights to film their upcoming wedding, with a few reality twists of course. And they begin spending it right away, making many purchases off the Internet: expensive guitars, jewelry, clothes, and a black, almost see-through, wedding dress. And the dope man now visits on a daily basis. They have a nine-thousand-dollar hot tub put in, where they discover new ways to make love in the evenings. And by day Joshua thrives on the fascination of the paparazzi. He greatly enjoys speeding away from their vans in his Lotus and has even more fun ditching the black Mustang. Although he's never actually seen its driver, he knows it to be Cools. And in the back of his mind, he presumes he'll have to deal with him at some point—he just doesn't realize how dangerous he is.

Subsequent to their R & R, they get down to business, hiring an agent and giving interviews on all the top shows—*The View*, *The Ellen DeGeneres Show*, *Nancy Grace*, and *Piers Morgan Tonight*—never revealing much of their story, only hinting at the book, soon to be on the stands. Every show pays them generously as well as setting them up in premium hotels and flying them first class to new cities and awaiting limos. High-end clothiers and jewelers even pay them to wear their latest designs, and the flood of laughter never runs dry. While on the road, and in between gigs, they negotiate other deals, like the million-dollar offer for Kimberly to pose in *Playboy*. And the nearly two million proposed by an adult film producer for a full-length video of them. Kimberly consults with the attorneys representing the Seattle Police Department, who are suggesting a backdoor settlement of five million to leave certain aspects of the interrogations out of their book. And another company, which sells novelties, wants them to pose for a hot, romantic, cultish calendar for 2012, to run from January 1 to December 21, representing the Mayan calendar—the Doomsday Count beside the Doomsday Countess. They release their wedding vows on MTV and commence shooting film for their new reality show pilot. The world literally falls for the young couple, seeing the true love they hold for one another.

Finally the demand for them gets so intense they decide to go away for a while on a well-deserved vacation. So in the dead of night, they slip out the back of their hotel and, with fake passports, sneak off to Europe. There, with a couple of wigs and oversized clothes, they tour around undetected for weeks. They can do no wrong; even their abrupt disappearance gains them more notoriety.

"Where did they go?"

"Whatever happened to Joshua and Kimberly?"

And these headlines only overshadow the more aggressive commentators who are curiously asking why all of Joshua's poems were previously copyrighted, why he was so arrogant, and how convenient it has all worked out for them. And even the tougher questions, alluding to the fact that they may have scammed, tricked, and manipulated the media, add to their intrigue.

Together they are becoming demigods.

Chapter Seventy-Four

Cools again awakes in his car. This time he's in a superstore parking lot, where within the mind-numbing fog of a hangover he tries to revisit the night before, remembering only transitory pieces.

I was at the Shelter.

Sitting alone in the dark, spiritually weary…

Phone rings…I'd thought she'd given up.

I switched to coffee, put away the coke, ate part of a meal.

I knocked on her door. She was waiting with open desire; soon we were naked, united, loving.

We were resting under a thin sheet. I told her everything. It felt good to let go. For a moment I sensed another path, another destiny. She seemed to understand; her words were soft, but they held insinuations, scoffing at my feeling sorry for myself. I began to argue, hinted at future atrocities. The cocaine and anger were calling. I exploded into a scathing torrent of words—words I wish I could take back.

Then I was barreling down the highway, snorting cocaine from the palm of my hand, mad at the world, mad at Joshua, mad at Chelsea, mad at myself. I started screaming, "Fuck him! Fuck her! Fuck my life! I'm going to find some piece of shit and beat the pain into him. The only one who can stop me is the devil himself."

I realized I was only a few blocks from the El Rancho, a drug-infested billiards bar. My tires skidded over the curb. I snorted another handful. Every cell in my body was raging. I stepped in, prepared for war. Loud music blared; women were dressed scantily; the natives were watching. I wore the stare of death, sniffed the cocaine in my nose, demanded the bartender to give me a bottle of tequila, slapping a hundred on the counter.

"I can't give you the whole bottle, man."

"Then take a fucking bottle and pour the whole fucking thing into as many shot glasses as it takes!"

He began to pour. I swallowed three in a row. This caught the notice of the regulars. Unsociable behavior moved my way.

"Hey! Hey, aren't you that cop?"

I didn't acknowledge him or even turn around, only took another shot.

"Hey! I'm talking to you. Aren't you that cop? Mr. Cool or something?"

"And what if I am!"

"Yeah, I knew it was you." He looked around at the other men, speaking loudly, "So how does it feel to waste your life framing an innocent man?"

I spun off my stool and punched him in the nose. Crack! Blood spurted all over his cheeks. He staggered back. I advanced, grabbed his shirt collar, and landed four more heavy blows to his face. I forced him to the ground, yelling, "Say something stupid—I dare you! Say one more stupid fucking thing!"

"Go fuck yourself, dirty cop!"

Then I cannot remember anything more. Why can't I remember? What did I do?

Chapter Seventy-Two

Not understanding why his son won't answer his calls, William starts to question what has happened and if he's been used. He also fears that if certain ones conclude that Joshua compromised the car club all over some scam, he and his brazen little whore may be excommunicated—a word that, within the tenets of the car club, takes on a whole different meaning than it does in Catholicism.

wearing leather sandals, long baggy khaki shorts, and a designer button-up shirt, untucked. He looks freshly tanned and at ease, extending both hands in the air, one of which appears to be clutching a cocktail. His eyes squint against the sun peeking through the cloud cover, and he begins to say something. "What's the big fucking idea—"

"Drop the drink and turn around," Cools demands, as he steadily advances closer. Make a sudden movement—anything!

Joshua smiles and replies, "This is very expensive scotch."

Bang! Cools shoots a warning shot into the ground, blasting a hole the size of a tennis ball in the driveway, then aims his weapon back at Joshua's upper left chest. The noise scares even the other officers. "I said put the drink down and turn around! Do it now!"

"Whatever, top cop," Joshua replies, before leisurely placing the drink on the walkway. The other officers scattered about the yard look in amazement at each other. The rookie seems relieved while the other two look disappointed. Cools's feelings coincide with the latter.

"Now interlock your hands behind your head and drop to your knees!" Cools commands, although in his mind he wills him: please do something; make a sudden move. His wish goes unanswered, as Joshua nonchalantly slumps to the ground. Frustrated, Cools runs up, pulls the suspect's arms behind him, plunges a heavy knee onto his neck, and as roughly as he can, cuffs him tightly. He pats him down, finding nothing, and places him in a white, bamboo chair situated outside the doorway.

The officers all wipe the sweat from their brows and relax a bit. But not Cools, he's still running in the red. Wasting no time he instructs the rookie to watch over their suspect and directs the other two to assist him, ordering, "Okay, let's do a search of the house." Then he storms into Joshua's well-kept home, or his music studio—he's not sure. The living room is packed with amplifiers, and at the far wall rest three very polished guitars, all neatly in a row below framed pictures of swimsuit models. A leather sectional couch is placed around a flat-screen television and stacks of stereo equipment. And built into the wall is an enormous fish tank, home to many colorful fish. To Cools it doesn't look like a married man's home, more like a playboy's bachelor pad. Moving through, he comes upon a film poster of *Scarface* and passes into a stainless steel kitchen where everything is remarkably clean and organized. Nothing is out of the ordinary: no dead woman, signs of a struggle, or evidence of a murder. So he makes his way down the hallway as the officers enter rooms at the other end of the house. He feels a bit childish; nevertheless, he wants to find her first. Then, as expected, he finds something: a locked door. Endorphins rush in his mind; he promptly kicks in the door. The wood frame splinters. And the officers come running at the commotion. They stop short, staring at Cools, who is carefully making his entry. His eyes widen. Inside are many computer screens monitoring the entire outside perimeter of the property. Cools turns to the others standing in the broken doorway. In their faces he finds more disappointment. "Anything?" he asks, with a hint of desperation.

"The front area of the house is clear; we haven't found anything, Detective... What's all this?"

"I'm not sure, looks like home surveillance."

"Wow, he's better equipped than us."

"Keep looking!" Cools demands. But another search of the home yields the same results. On the various monitors he can see the patrol cars on the front lawns, the rookie standing over Joshua, and Officer Renker waiting in the back, clear as day. Irritated he blurts out for all to hear, "Time to get the info out of the perp—old school!" He then strides hastily out to the front entryway, fully prepared to beat a confession out of the suspect if he has to.

There Joshua sits with legs sprawled out, looking quite comfortable. His head is rested back, and he looks like he could take a nap. Cools snatches him to his feet and marches him out to the front of his squad car. "Where's your wife?" he demands.

"Oh...Is that what you're looking for?" Joshua replies, acting surprised.

"Where is she? Tell me right now!"

Joshua pauses, curiously observing the bulging blood vessel on Cools's forehead. Then he calmly replies, "She's at work. So would you please take your hands off me?"

Cools pushes him, letting go of his grip, thinking how everything seems upside down. I'm the cop, yet I'm the one sweaty and agitated, while Joshua, the killer, is composed—almost too composed. He tries to get his head around it while continuing his questioning. "Where does she work?"

Joshua starts acting a little more human and says, "Fuck you, Officer Cools. What the hell is this all about?"

"You know exactly what this is about; you called the radio station. I heard the tape."

"Oh, that."

"Yeah, that," Cools replies sarcastically.

"It was just a joke."

"A joke? You call that a fucking joke?"

"Yeah, man, I thought it was kind of funny. I was just fucking around."

"Where's your wife, asshole?"

"I told you, top cop; she's working."

"Where?"

Joshua smiles, pauses, then answers, "She's working the noontime show at the Kitty Club in Everett."

Cools gives him a look of disbelief and pulls his phone from his pocket, noticing that even his hands are shaking from agitation. He dials 411. "I need Kitty Club in Everett." The prompter gives him an option; he pushes another button and is shortly connected, expecting to learn momentarily that it is just more bullshit. And what's more nauseating to him is the fact that Joshua slouches back on his heels, unconcerned, maybe even enjoying the charade.

"Thanks for calling the Kitty Club; this is Candy. What can I do for you?"

"Is Kimberly Siconolfi there?"

"Well...yes...she is," Candy's amorous voice replies.

"I'm Detective Cools from the Seattle Police Department; I need to speak with her."

"Oh...I'm sorry, Detective; she's dancing. Would you like some Candy instead?"

"No, I need to talk to Kimberly," he replies, growing strangely frustrated by her sexy talk. "Are you *sure* she's there?"

"Oh, well let's see...I'm looking at her fine, round ass quivering in the air. Wait—she's turning...Yep, those are her big, beautiful tits straddling the pole... Oh and now she's crawling across the stage, and I can see her face. It's definitely Kimberly. Why don't you come over, Detective, and we can watch her together."

"Maybe another time, Candy," he answers sharply, and hangs up. "What kind of sick fuck are you?"

Joshua doesn't respond, only grins while peering around his yard full of cop cars and police officers snooping about his home. Cools does the same, seeing the whole thing beginning to slow down. Then he gets a call from his captain and, with a hand gesture, motions the rookie, who is now simply loitering nearby, to watch over Joshua. Passing him off like a baton on the track course, he moves to the other side of the yard, so he can privately talk to his boss, Captain Jackson.

He and Cools have been friends for many years; they make it to the basketball court two or three times a month and go deep-sea fishing in the summer.

They even share the same temperament. Socially and mentally they are equals but physically quite different—mostly because Captain Jackson is a large black man, a bit older, who wasn't even pretty when he was young. Cools reports the entire situation, and then there's a long silence. "What should we do?" he asks.

"Hold tight; do nothing; I'm gonna call you right back."

Cools, feeling it all slipping away, lights up a cigarette and glares at Joshua. "Pretty boy punk," he mutters under his breath. Then the phone rings; "Jerome Jackson" shows on the display.

"Cools, I have in my office assistant prosecuting attorney Levits, and she's telling me, unless you can find some evidence of a crime, we have to let him go."

"Let him go! Are you fucking kidding me?" He knew it could come down to this, but he doesn't plan to cave without a fight. "I am not just going to let him go!"

Captain Jackson snaps back sternly, "You know who his father is, and when you break it all down, we got nothing. If we try to arrest him for a prank, they'll…they'll have our balls on a platter!" Then in a more affable voice, he says, "Cools, you *do* remember who his father is don't you?"

Cools answers with a long and exasperated yes, while briefly running a couple details through his mind: William Siconolfi, one of Seattle's greatest trial attorneys and head of the legal team representing the Roman Catholic archdiocese.

Then Captain Jackson adds, "That's just the way it has to be: no crime, no time."

"Fuck! Fuck! Fuck!" He holds the phone in the air, shooting daggers at it with his eyes for a time, then slowly pushes the end button, trying to quiet his nerves. He scans the scene of cops standing around aimlessly at this midday false alarm, gathered about a tall, tanned playboy without a care—smiling like a kid at the circus. Maybe I should get him some cotton candy.

Then, as if it couldn't get any worse, other cops, followed by two news vans, begin pulling onto the scene. "Damn, they're fast," he says just before recognizing a familiar face. It's Tabatha Sterns jumping out of her van, microphone in hand, and he's not the only one to take notice of her easy, blond hair and dark blue, inviting eyes. She carries with her that innocent, Midwestern, good-little-girl way about her, the kind you want to dirty up. "Hold 'em back!" he yells to some of the fresh cops now on-site. Soon a collision between cops and reporters forms a mob of noise and questions. Cools shakes his head in disbelief, making his way back to his cruiser, where Joshua stands smiling for the cameras. He has no choice but to accept defeat. There he excuses the officers of their duty, and once again they are alone.

"Like the street party, top cop," Joshua says, almost as if making small talk to a friendly neighbor.

Cools doesn't answer, only glances around to make sure no one is within ear-shot, then positions himself up close, locking eyes with a cold stare that would strike fear in most men, but has little noticeable effect on Joshua. "I have to let you go for now, but first...I do not like you—you sick fuck!" Next he breaks his eye contact to guide Joshua's attention to the gun he's holding; he moves it side to side and says, "These things accidentally go off sometimes, punk. It's rare, but it happens. Next time...next fucking time!"

Joshua's relaxed grin is his only reply. Outwardly he appears to be nothing more than an adult delinquent; though on the inside, he's strategically laughing his ass off, picturing it all: a courtroom, a jury, a HD home surveillance clip, and an expert witness on the stand gaining the trust of the twelve while rambling off his credentials as a lip reader, telling the jury exactly what Detective Cools is saying.

Chapter Four

Cools struggles through the rest of his day, stumbling at every step down a steep and rocky hill. The first hurdle presented itself, as he was parting the cluster fuck of a call, when Tabatha Sterns asked for an interview. Not meaning too, he apparently shrugged her off, which she responded to by calling him an asshole. Tabatha Sterns, his favorite news reporter—not to mention the one he's had a boyhood crush on for years, the one he watches every night—now hating him. Then to the station where Captain Jackson balled him out and informed him that he'll soon most likely be sued for shooting the hole in the driveway, in addition to emotional distress brought on by an overzealous cop. All of which is followed by an earful from his partner, Michelle. And Joshua goes back to sipping expensive scotch in his khakis. The rest of his afternoon is spent alone in his office, brooding over the morning call and catching up on all things Joshua Siconolfi.

His phone rings. It's an attractive woman, a persistent sweetness, who seems to have forgotten he's an asshole. Twenty minutes later she sneaks in the rear entrance of the station. "Thank you for meeting with me on such short notice," she says, holding out a slender hand. They've met a few times through the years, yet he can never get over the fact that she appears thinner in person. Their last meeting took place at the Deistali Restaurant, where after a few drinks, he got the impression she wanted him to give her more than just information on the latest, high-profile arrests.

"Have a seat," he says, presenting an empty chair. She sits and crosses her long legs, her movement wafting her fragrance through the air. Then playfully cutting to the chase, he asks, "So do you still think I'm an asshole?"

"Yes," she quickly and matter-of-factly replies. Cools's eyes tighten, showing rigid lines while processing her sharp, confident answer. Then she cuts to some chases of her own tactically ignoring his frustrated puzzzlement, "Do you have a complete rap sheet on Joshua, and do you think he's a danger to the community?"

Cools's thoughts shift to the demented person of interest. "You didn't get to interview him?" he asks, somewhat surprised.

"No, but he sent me a text. I'm not even sure how he acquired my number." She slips her phone from her bag, keys in a few buttons, and reads it proficiently. "Today I will retire within the sanctuary of my dwelling, relishing in my endeavors, forcing the media to beg for my story in tomorrows."

They sit quietly pondering his objective, both coming to the simple conclusion that he plans on giving a statement tomorrow because he considers himself worthy of some sort of celebrity status. Cools breaks the silence, saying, "Well, I can tell you this: this isn't his first run-in with the law by any means."Tabatha's ears perk up. She fumbles out a recorder while he reads from the computer screen. "2001: DUI: dismissed. 2002: DUI: dropped to reckless. 2003: domestic violence, Sherry Hill: dismissed. A few months later another DUI: deferred program, completed. And later that year, another domestic violence again Sherry Hill; this one goes to trial, and he's found not guilty. Then he snaps, and in mid-2005 he gets a third degree vehicular assault on his battered girlfriend Sherry Hill... His father is William Siconolfi—you might have heard of him?"

"Yes, yes, I have; he's a high-dollar trial attorney, isn't he? And didn't he represent some Catholic priests a few years back?"

"That's him, and every time his insane son gets into it, Daddy gets him out. So it turns out that he was released on good behavior in February of 2006, doing a grand total of eight months, three in a minimum security, the remaining five in a work-release unit where he worked as an assistant manager at a strip club—Chloe's Paradise. He gets picked up six weeks later for violation of a no-contact order against, once again, Sherry Hill. This time Daddy gets the charges dropped on a technicality. After that he goes off the Doppler radar for a few years. Then in 2011 our records show he's married to a Kimberly Sharons; he was arrested for disorderly conduct...served 30 days. And another little misunderstanding when he's arrested for the first degree arson of St. Luke's Parish in Aberdeen, Washington, but charges were dropped due to lack of evidence."

"Arson? So there was enough evidence for an arrest but not enough for a trial?"

"Well...money can make a lot of problems go away in this town. Besides it turned out that the parish was insured for double what the property was worth. And after some further investigation by a private investigator, paid for by William, it was later reported that it was a distinct possibility that the maintenance man could have forgotten a can of gasoline in the basement earlier that day."

"So was it arson or an accident?"

"Arson...accident...It doesn't fucking matter. This guy probably could get away with murder."

Tabatha raises an eyebrow and makes a notation. Then their attention is diverted by some noise coming from a small group of officers who've gathered outside Cools's office window to watch the two of them as they interact, most likely paying more attention to her. Cools throws them a quick a glare before shutting the blinds and denying them anymore fun. Tabatha looks down to her legs and blushes a bit. Cools pretends not to notice and returns to the task at hand, adding, "Now here's another curious tidbit. Our records show that twice within the past year, 911 calls were made from a woman, claiming to be Kimberly Siconolfi, reporting to have been physically abused by her husband. But no contact with her was ever made, other than the initial calls."

Tabatha writes on her pad and asks, "Are there going to be any charges filed concerning the events of this morning?"

"No, most likely not. But I'll tell you this: this freak has jumped a step."

"What do you mean?"

"I mean, not only does he escape any real punishment, but each time he advances to the next level of violence against women. Just the fact that he's fantasizing about it, especially in this much detail, would mean he's getting closer to actually doing it."

"So he *is* a danger to Kimberly, in your opinion?"

"Let me show you something." He navigates his keyboard to revisit an old case; a picture of a young, pretty girl lights the screen. He swivels the monitor, giving Tabatha a better view. "This is Sherry Hill before what he did to her."

Tabatha sees his facial muscles tense; she then looks jealously to the picture of the teenage girl in her cheerleading uniform; the insignia across the bottom reads, "Senior Year 1984." She is tiny, looking as if she weighs a hundred pounds, with eyes bright and full of life, and light brown hair partially hanging over her delicate features.

"She's as cute as a baby kitten."

Cools waits until Tabatha has taken her in before pressing forward. "And this is what he did to her." Another quick click of the keyboard, and a horrifying picture of a dead-looking girl appears on the monitor; she is nearly unrecognizable. Her left cheek is busted, exposing bone; one of her eyelids is entirely swollen shut, the other not far behind. Her nose is smashed and discolored, and dried blood cakes her once ivory-white skin. Cut marks, bruising, and broken blood vessels cover most the rest of her body. A couple of close-ups then reveal that two of her finger nails had been completely snapped off and clumps of hair had been ripped out of her scalp, as she fended off her attacker.

"Oh God, she's a mess. But wasn't this a car wreck?"

"No!" he yells. Then he opens a drawer, fumbles through a few files, and hands her an unofficial report he'd written years earlier. Tabatha begins to read in silence. Her first impression is that Detective Cools is a gifted writer. As she reads, the story comes alive.

Joshua walks into a dealership and begins the process of a new purchase. Then, when left alone in the salesperson's office, he sneaks a look at the monthly sales sheet until he finds what he's looking for—2013 Cadillac Escalade sold to Ronald and Anne Hollister just five days earlier. He shuts the door to the office and makes a call.

It takes seven rings before Anne, because of her age, can check the caller ID ("Jenkins Cadillac") and answer. "Hello."

"Hi. Is this Anne Hollister?"

"Yes."

"Hi, Anne. I'm David Ellis, the shop manager, down here at the dealership. And I'm sorry to inform you that we have to recall your Escalade. I shouldn't bore you with the details, but there's a relay switch that needs to be replaced—one that I was supposed to have done before it was sold. So I'm in a bit of a bind here. I'm a married man, Anne, with three kids, and I cannot afford to lose my job. So what I would like to do this afternoon is send a man over to pick it up, and I can have it back to you, fixed, fully gassed, and cleaned inside and out, in under two hours."

"Well..." She pauses. "Well, I don't think that would be a problem, David. I wouldn't want you to get into trouble with your work."

"Okay, great, Anne. I'll send my guy over. You're a real sweetheart."

Thirty-two minutes later Anne Hollister is handing over the keys to her new Escalade to Joshua, who's now wearing a mechanics uniform.

Tabatha turns the page, and the story moves forward.

Joshua is in his home. He's drunk and ranting at little Sherry Hill. Then he begins smacking her around, beating her until she's unconscious, then dragging her limp body into the garage. He sits her up in the front seat, and soon they are driving down the interstate. He reaches over and turns off the airbag for the passenger side and starts speeding recklessly through the night's traffic. He veers over the white line and onto the drunk bumps. He looks at her. She doesn't wake, even as the truck continues to speed faster and faster. Then he moves his gaze back through the windshield, still steering off the road. Up ahead there's an underpass embankment. He aims the vehicle and closes his eyes. They crash into it at full speed. The Escalade flips, end over end, crashing upside down. There's nothing left but twisted metal, broken glass, and smoke.

Tabatha's mouth falls open as she turns the page.

Now Joshua is in the ER, being treated for some light abrasions and a dislocated shoulder, while Sherry is in an adjacent room on the operating table, looking like Hannibal Lecter was playing with her.

When Cools sees that Tabatha has finished his report, he adds, "But Daddy convinced the prosecutor otherwise, and Joshua was allowed to plea to the lesser crime of vehicular assault due to negligent driving."

"And what about stealing the car?"

"It's not a theft when the owner hands you the keys."

Tabatha gasps, springs from her seat, and stands facing the wall for a moment. Cools lets it sink in. She stiffens visibly in anger. "You fucking asshole; why did I never hear of this before?"

Her reaction catches Cools off guard. But the detective quickly realizes her logic. The story, for her, always comes first. He raises his hands in defense. "You know we cannot let information like that leak. We couldn't prove it, and no one wants to look incompetent in the face of the public."

"You let him off because you didn't want to look bad?" she wails.

"Remember, William was representing him; we had to make certain concessions."

"Concessions? Concessions!"

"Look, Tabatha," he says, holding out his hands, gesturing for a truce, "it makes no sense to try a man for something we cannot prove." Tabatha doesn't reply. "We have a responsibility not to supply ideas to the public; they're much better served believing that forensics, that CSI will uncover any crime."

Then silence. They both linger for a minute, cooling down. "Okay, I see your point," she says, retaking her chair, switching gears. Between a few smiles and soft eyes, she apologizes for her outburst. They talk for a while until their emotions subside and a bit of playful flirting finds its way back into their little chat. Wanting more, she invites him to her apartment for some late-night conversation and a few drinks. He responds to her advances in a way Tabatha has only experienced a few times in her life: he refuses the offer. Disappointed she leaves as sassy as she came, thinking that whoever the woman is in his life, he must really love her.

Chapter Five

At 9:58 p.m., at The Shelter, a dark, quiet bar in Pioneer square, one of the oldest parts of the city, Cools sits in a round booth all to himself. It's a place where nobody asks any questions. An ashtray and a bottle of Jameson are resting in front of him—the usual routine. Already feeling the alcohol he replays in his mind the interview with Tabatha, mostly thinking about what information he'd given her and how she might weave it into a lead story, mixed among a few innocent thoughts of ravishing her on his desk. A slight wave of guilt enters his mind, as he admires the treasured details of the barroom. Everything is either dark brown or black. The walls are covered in wood veneer that reflects only dim light coming from behind the bar. And the steady rhythmic shadows from the ceiling fan mounted high above provide tranquility—the ideal place to meditate. There, in deep thought, he stares into the bottle, watching the liquid roll round and round. It comforts him more than the thick leather cushions of the booth—his booth. He's actually never seen anyone else in it—his private harbor from the rest of the world. Even the sounds in the bar are kept low to his liking; no music plays; only muffled conversation makes its way back to where he is perched alone, judging humanity.

The Shelter is not a cop bar, actually more the opposite; it is a private club owned and operated by the Khruschev's, an old-school gangster family from the Ukraine. And even though the Khruschev's are no longer the organized crime organization they were in the '80s and '90s, they aren't exactly the Boy Scouts either. Most everyone—including the family themselves and, certainly, Cools's coworkers—finds it odd that he drinks here.

But then again few know the real tale.

Eighteen years ago, while a young Officer Cools was leaving the scene of a shoplifting—the usual grab and run by a couple of local youths—something caught his attention. It was his first year on the force. And for reasons he can no longer remember, he was without his partner on that bright and sunny day. So as he walked alone past a dirty alleyway filled with overflowing dumpsters and newspapers blowing in the wind, he saw what appeared to be three big guys roughly escorting a fourth into the remote back entrance of The Shelter.

The man being tossed inside had obviously been severely beaten and didn't look to be visiting for drinks and laughs. So Cools dropped his paperwork and unsnapped his holster before quickly making his way down the stinking alley. He was a lot faster in those days and probably entered the bar less than twenty seconds behind them, not realizing he'd lost his radio en route. They were no slouches either; they already had the guy in a chair, and one was beating him in the face while the other waited his turn, gun in hand. The guy delivering the assault was a stout man wearing a black leather jacket and low-cut T-shirt over thick chest hair and gold chains. The other, holding the 9 mm, was taller and dressed in basically the same attire. The victim in the chair was bloodied and bruised to the point his own mother wouldn't have recognized him. And the fourth man, a much older and heavier man, stood behind the bar, holding a cannon of a gun. The only light seemed to come from the open door Cools was now standing in, wielding his service revolver. He locked on and yelled, "Freeze!"

Everyone suddenly turned to him, and in that second, for the first time in his life, he felt panic—even more so when he reached for his radio only to find it missing and began to realize none of them seemed ready to comply. Adding to his predicament, he'd never actually pulled his weapon before, much less on three tough-looking and armed men in a dark bar. His face said, "Oh shit," and they read it plain as day. "Put your weapons down now!" he tried again, more forcefully. But no one moved an inch.

Hastily he formed a rudimentary plan. It was simple: if anyone raised their guns, he would shoot at the two younger men first and then dive behind the cigarette machine. It was one of the old-fashioned ones with the pull levers and looked bulky enough to slow some bullets. Again he shouted, "Put your guns down *now* and your hands in the air!" Still no one moved a muscle, and out of fear, neither did he.

He entertained the idea of slipping back out the door and making a run for it; probably his best idea thus far, just not anything that was likely to happen. Instead he stepped forward; keeping his weapon fixed on the taller man. "Put your hands in—"

"No!" yelled the older man behind the bar. "You do not understand as much of our situation we share." A response in broken English Cools hadn't prepared for in training. Neither was he prepared for the desperation in the man's eyes, a man with nothing to lose. Still he stood his ground, not budging, not knowing what to do.

"Help me!" cried out the man in the chair, in strained echoes of pain.

"You shut the fuck up!" the short man said, as he hit him in the face, leaving a fresh red mark on the man's forehead from his gold ring. Then he turned and scowled at Cools like he didn't have a care in the world.

"Everyone fucking freeze!" Cools stepped in closer, feeling it all about to go down, trying to keep one eye on the older man behind the bar while considering shooting first.

The taller man with the 9 mm stood, unmoving; Cools's had a bead on his thinning hairline. The shorter man looked coldly into his eyes and said, "I think you should put down your gun, Officer, before someone gets hurt."

Cools, awestruck by the man's statement and demeanor, was coming up short of any real response, when the old man spoke again. "Why don't we sit to table? We drink together. You can…eh…hear our plea."

The old man spoke slowly with an assuring and honest tone, giving Cools the odd sense he was a man to be trusted. His request hung in the air as Cools considered an option not yet measured. All of a sudden, he felt no immediate danger. He ran the scenarios through his mind, which also was a little quicker in those days, and came up with two options: either shoot it out with these three guys, most likely getting killed, or do as they've suggested and learn why the man was in the chair in the first place.

"Okay, okay, but I'm keeping my gun!"

"Has…eh…anyone asked you to surrender to us your gun, officer?"

No, no one has asked for my gun, he thought, before gradually lowering his weapon. He cautiously walked over to the dimly lit bar and sat down. Behind him the taller of the two toughs moved to the backdoor and set the deadbolt.

"Don't! Don't do it!" screamed out the guy in the chair, just before getting belted again.

"What is it of mine you wish to drink?"

"Jameson," Cools replied, wondering what this is all about, wondering if he had made the right choice.

"Do you...eh...know who you are speaking?" asked the old man, while pouring a glass.

"No," Cools replied, speculating as to why he would. The man's face was wrinkled with hardness and age, sagging of sadness, and the home to soft, soul-filled eyes, yet a face he'd never seen.

The old man took in a steady breath and ran his broad fingers through his thick black hair, combing it back, and stated, "I didn't think so. Eh...you must be new, so I will fill you in with words and drink...You, drink." He motions for Cools to start sipping. "My name Sergey Khruschev; I own this bar." With that he slowly gestures his hand toward the other two and says, "These...eh...are my boys: Jorge and Koladiva."

His words end in silence, just long enough for everyone to strangely look upon the obvious question in the room.

"And the guy in the chair?" Cools asks.

Sergey points to him accusingly. "He...eh...is a cockfuck. He needs taken care of! He's done unthinkable thing; he...he..."

Then, before the old man could finish his words, he broke down, lowered his head, and wept in his hands.

Cools turned his attention to the guy in the chair. What did you do? Even through the guy's bloodshot eyes, he could see guilt and shame all over him, and Cools knew this was more than an unpaid debt. He finished his glass and asked Sergey to pour him another, partly because he needed one and partly in an attempt to get down to it; it had always made him nervous to watch another man cry. Sergey complied like a generous servant and waited patiently for him to drink it down; he then composed himself and began to explain.

"His name Reuben. He is a Jew," Sergey said in a crackling tone, pointing with an old shaking finger. "And he is kind of bum. So he marries my daughter, Sasha, and she is...eh...how you a say?—non-attractive of a woman. So we accept him as one of us. We think him as family, treat him all the same. Then also Sasha has my grandson, Nico, from previous marriage...eh...she is widower from. So my Nico is four years in age, and he complains of this, so we go Sasha's house. We find videotape...videotape of *him* and Nico! He molests! And not just touch...I mean, eh...this motherfuck puts his cock in my Nico, and for this he will die today!"

With that Koladiva hit the child molester again.

"No!" Sergey yelled at his sons. "This officer needs a quiet time to think his mind through."

"You can't kill him! I can't let you kill him!"

Sergey just shook his head, assuring Cools he is not a man to be told what he can and cannot do. "And who are you to stop me?"

"Then, what…are you going to kill me? I'm a police officer!"

"What I have set to do…I will do today, my friend. But only…eh…the guilty needs to be punished." Sergey's words reverberated in the room, followed by a moment of disoriented stillness, confusion.

Cools, trying to process everything, picked up the bottle of Jameson and went to a learned comfort zone—staring into the bottle, watching the brown liquid move back and forth. Sergey offered him a cigarette, but he didn't respond. Rather he slowly reached into his pocket and pulled out his own, never taking his gaze from the swirling fluid. He lit up and took a deep drag, searching the bottle for answers. "We have to take him in. With the video, he'll go to prison for a long time," Cools pleaded, offering the better solution for both himself and the child molester in the chair.

"No!" Sergey yelled. "So he can live his days…eh…jerking off to my Nico. No he has to die. Today he will die!"

"You cannot be serious. I'm a police officer. I can't…I can't just let you beat this man to death—whether he is a pedophile or not!"

"Yes, you a can, and you will, and I want you…eh…to remember: I will beat this cockfucker! You can only arrest an old man to jail."

"I *will* have to take you to jail and your sons along with you. Is that want you want?" he asked, raising his voice, raising the tension in the room. Sergey answered with his stare, pleading with him—threatening him.

"We're not going to any stinking fucking jail, officer!" Jorge said, pointing his gun in Cools's direction.

"No, you hold it down; we do not kill the police, nor do we have to kill this officer. I see it in his eyes. He only needs…eh…some time to make this choice…this only one choice."

Cools opened his mouth, but nothing came out. There was no point to argue. He returned to the bottle, studying the flowing solution. Like the brown liquid, the moment rolled in slow motion. He could sense Jorge lowering his gun behind him and a slight humming in his ear. Are you actually considering this? Another drink, another cigarette, as he surveyed the room again, trying to get a fix on the situation, but nothing had changed. It was still a dark, empty bar with one child rapist bleeding in a chair and two other guys standing by with guns, all opposite an old hopeless man somehow making sense of it all. Then, more ringing in his head—this time an old television commercial slogan, he couldn't recall what product only the catchphrase: "It sells itself." It sells itself. Sergey wasn't pushing any product; he'd simply made his pitch then set back to let it sell itself. Cools turned for a long look at Reuben, estimating his value. The man had dead eyes, no soul; and the gruesome imagery of him raping the young boy ran briefly in the young officer's mind. What if it was my sister's kid? My grandson? He was under no real pressure to make a quick decision; he was being fully respected and given all the time needed to process everything. Cools took one more look into Sergey's hurting eyes, seeing his pain was genuine, his truth was real, and his intentions were justified. His thoughts began to scream. Fuck this guy! If he did this to anyone in my family, I would want to do the same—I *would* do the same! He now looked about the room through new eyes. All the men saw his transformation. Koladiva and Jorge knew they would soon return to their business, and Rueben slumped even farther into his chair, deeper into hopelessness.

"I was..." He pulled in a cleansing breath. "I was never here."

Sergey nodded in confidence, reached out, and held Cools's hands, saying, "We share this occasion for life."

Then, with true clarity, Cools cleanly rose to his feet. He took a last look at the soon-to-be tortured to death child molester in the chair, who'd abandoned every wishful thought of being saved. Then, for Koladiva and Jorge, he slowly holstered his weapon. The deal had been struck: the simple notion that justice is far greater than any law had won the day. And there was nothing left for him to do except to simply walk out of the bar, back into a sun-shining world, with nothing except the occasional shoplifter to worry about.

A few days later, he returned to the bar. He couldn't ignore the realization adhered to the memory of that day. It was calling him to revisit the place where he had become a man—a man of courage, of nobleness, a man who could make the tough decisions for the right reasons, one who had passed the test. He didn't experience any guilt or remorse, only a warm sense of backdoor justice. It was a philosophy he would carry to his end.

When he walked into the dark bar, Sergey welcomed him as family, with a long embrace and an esteemed kiss to the cheek. He then led him to a round table near the back, facing the spot where just days before a monster met his end. They shared no words of the incident as was the custom. A short spell later, a pretty young girl brought him a bottle of Jameson, leaving him alone with his thoughts. It became his place of solace, his shelter, a place he could visit anytime and be treated with respect and left alone. The booth became his, as if he had a small piece of ownership in it.

Years later the old man passed. Cools attended the funeral out of respect and continued honoring him by never being a cop at The Shelter. And although he has never been asked to pay, he has always left a healthy tip on the table, a generous contribution to support the bar that he has been frequenting for the past eighteen years.

Tonight everything remains the same, the dim lighting, subdued conversation from its sparse number of customers, and nothing but time to slowly drown his thoughts. Above the bar sits a television that he barely notices until the ten o'clock news begins.

"You are watching The KUBE Channel 9. Top story tonight: a man murders his wife on a live radio broadcast earlier today in Seattle: was it a prank or the real deal? Also problems with local labor unions, and the latest in ecological concerns stemming from the disaster in the gulf.

"Good evening, I'm Tabatha Sterns, and to our top story: KUBE Channel 9's exclusive interview with Joshua Siconolfi." His *GQ* picture flashes in the corner of the screen, as Tabatha goes on about the details of the story, getting most of it correct—basically all true with a touch of ratings enhancement. Cools pours another shot, lights another cigarette. Tabatha eagerly fills in the details as a picture of Kimberly flashes on the screen, displaying a very pretty girl. Until that moment Cools had not thought about what a prime-time event this really is. Joshua, a good-looking playboy type, and his pretty young wife wrapped up in a sick and twisted story. The picture of Kimberly fades away, and a very photogenic Joshua comes onto the screen, standing casually in his well-lit yard, where he's giving an interview to Tabatha.

Whatever happened to retiring within the sanctuary of his dwelling…relishing in his endeavors? Cools sits up in the booth; the leather squeaks as he positions himself closer to hear.

Tabatha is just rounding off a three-part question when Joshua says to the camera, "I would like to answer with a poem."

"Sounds interesting," Tabatha replies animatedly. Joshua smiles and holds out his hand, asking for the microphone. Then, with those piercing green eyes, he stares intently into the camera and recites,

"There is One,

Who was the Soul of fire,
Now He is many,
Cause of Angels' desires,
They beg for His darkness, His secrets of old…
They feast from His table, where torments are sold…
And sometimes, He whispers to Me!"

With that he politely hands the microphone back to the now speechless news reporter and strolls back into the privacy of his home, ignoring any pleas for more. The video clip ends, and Tabatha pops back onto the screen, in the studio. "Now that's what I call shock factor! And although we have no comment on what was meant by the poem, you can hear it again by going to KUBEchannel9.com. Click on the link and decide for yourselves."

Cools plays the poem over and over in his mind from memory, trying to solve it like some sort of puzzle. A buzz begins around the bar; he can hear others discussing it. He looks inside the bottle where he can see the words—*And sometimes, He whispers to Me*—floating on the shining brown liquid, but no answers. From his jacket pocket, he takes out a pad of paper and pen. He makes a few circles in the top corner to get the ink flowing and writes down what he can remember. Most of it doesn't matter a great deal; from the first couple of lines, it is seemingly clear that he is making some reference to a demon or maybe even the devil himself. But the last line, the one he writes down, is of interest. *And sometimes, He whispers to Me!* He reads it repeatedly, considering its implications. It tells him two things: one is that Joshua is probably more disturbed than previously considered, and two, the media is going to squeeze from this story its last drop of nectar. He gulps another tall drink to ease his rattled anxieties as his attention again turns to Tabatha.

It's now 10:06, and she's still going on and on, milking it from every angle. She brings in a couple panelists, expert psychologists of some sort. Cools isn't interested in listening. He has too much going on inside his head. Doesn't really matter; they're all the same, always inventing some disorder that the person is or was suffering from, basically excusing any and all behaviors; assigning blame to his childhood or the fact that he didn't grow up on the prairie in a little house. Why does it matter anyway why a freak is a freak? If a wild animal is found lurking in our midst, especially one who makes claims of the devil speaking to him, we do not make excuses defending them. Or if a bear comes out of the woods and kills a small child, no one would try to defend the bear because of his mental illness or the fact that he was an only cub or some other bullshit. An animal is an animal, even if it is human; if it preys on and kills smaller, weaker victims, then we hunt it down and fucking kill it!

He pours more drinks, keeping up the pace until things begin to blur, the room becomes a haze. An unsettling sense surrounds him, and his last remembered thoughts are uncertain.

Should I kill him? Do I have the courage?

Chapter Six

Six days later, she drives recklessly down a rainy-morning freeway toward Seattle, still twitching from last night's cocaine consumption. Tears drench her face, smearing pink eye-shadow, as worry and immense dread dominate her thoughts. Amberly Carlson has only two things on her mind: her missing friend and the fact that she has most likely just made the biggest mistake of her misguided life. She doesn't know what she should do, only that she must do something.

An irritating horn shrieks from another highway traveler demanding she slow down. And out of natural reflex, she flips the finger, holding back the tears long enough to yell, "Fuck off, asshole!" Amberly is a tough, streetwise girl, but today is one of those days where she misses the daddy she never knew. Her bleached hair is matted with sweat, and untamed curls beg for a wash; the thigh-high boots she wears, made of blue snakeskin, are sticking to her as she fights to work the car's peddles. It's a recently borrowed—or stolen, depending on how one would look at it—Lexus, which she loaned herself this morning from one of her many boyfriends. And although it is a quality vehicle, it is a stick shift that she barely knows how to operate. So the gears grind, the pink eye shadow runs, and anxiety clouds the troubled mind of the young girl as she speeds through congested traffic.

Miles later, after many near misses, a lot of cursing, and nineteen abrupt lane changes, she finds her exit. All the while the lack of drugs in her body screams for her to turn back. But she journeys forward, following the signs that lead her to the Seattle police station. She parks in a conveniently open handicap spot and leaves the car running, so she can freshen up her appearance. With a few strokes of eyeliner and a tease of her hair, she manages to transform her look from a two-hundred-dollar whore to a five-hundred-dollar one in a matter of seconds. In the mirror she gives herself a pep talk. "You have to go in there and tell them the truth. You didn't know you did anything wrong. You're not going to be in trouble, and even if you are in trouble, you still have to do it. You just need to find Detective Cools and explain what you did. You have to, so go now!" Then, powered by pure impulse, she exits the car with a chirp-chirp, activating the high-dollar theft detection system that apparently doesn't protect against desperate girlfriends.

She crosses the busy street, tugging her bag, along with a business folder found in the car held over her hair. In the wind her short dress dances near a full show as she shuffles up the steps to the large entrance door. It's heavy, but she uses her hips to push it open, entering into a large room packed with more cops than she's ever seen in her life. As usual she immediately catches the attention of the men, as she shakes her way quickly to the station's service counter. There she waits intolerantly until someone is ready to talk to her. "Hi, I'm Amberly. Amberly Carlson. Is Detective Cools here? I need to speak to Detective Cools."

"No, not at this time. Is there anything I can help you with?" the officer asks, blatantly looking her up and down.

"Yes, well, I need to report a missing person. And I need to see Detective Cools; is he here?" she asks, peering behind the counter, searching for him, even though she doesn't know what he looks like.

"Okay, missing persons...Take a seat, and I will have someone help you shortly."

"No, I need to talk to Detective Cools!" she blurts out like a spoiled child.

"Ma'am, I have your name, and you need to have a seat," the officer states, raising his voice.

Amberly stands her ground in protest for a second, until the officer's finger directs her to a row of empty chairs. She lets out a frustrated groan to show her disapproval of his hospitality, then turns sharply, swinging her bag, and stomps her boots to a seat, where she flops down hard. And there she waits, clutching her bag for thirty-five minutes, paying no attention to her onlookers, and praying to God she gets out of this without having to go to prison.

"Hi, are you the Amberly Carlson that wants to report a missing person?" asks a heavyset policeman.

"Yes, yes, I am," she replies, with a rush of anxiety.

"I'm Officer Renny; follow me." He then turns without even taking so much as a glance at her and waddles back through the station to a small cubicle. Amberly, rarely getting such a reaction from men, follows closely. A curious look reveals a wedding band. His desk is decorated with vacation pictures of his family surrounded by knickknacks only a wife would buy. Well, at least he's not gay.

He offers her a chair, and after taking a seat, she crosses ignored legs. She watches him quietly, attempting to hide her nervousness, but soon she's going to have to tell what she's done. Lengthy seconds turn into minutes before he pulls up the missing persons screen and begins asking the basics. "What is your full name? Where do you live? Where do you work? Your phone number? And who do you want to report missing?"

Suddenly she clams up. This is it; once I answer this question, there's no turning back. A voice tells her to run. Just get up and run out of the building as fast as you can.

Officer Renny, with his portly fingers on the keyboard and unwary eyes glued to the screen, repeats the questions.

"Give me a minute!" she blurts out.

He gives her an odd, fleeting look, only to return to the photos surrounding his space, apparently oblivious to her fidgeting, long, painted nails. Left alone she studies him. He is a rare man in her torn world, a loving and faithful family man, the kind that won't even look at her. She scrutinizes him, sitting in his chair peacefully, looking as if he only does this job to put food on the family table and take them to Disney World in the summers. Images of him dressed as Santa Claus entertaining the little ones on Christmas and cutting their turkey on Thanksgiving strengthens her determination. I bet he never raises his hand in anger. I bet he tells bedtime stories to his children and kisses them good night. I bet he makes love to his wife, instead of fucking her. She steadies herself, preparing to tell who is missing. Officer Renny, sensing she is about to give him something to type, raises his round fingers back to the keyboard. Then she releases, allowing the words that have been bottled up in her all night to fly from her lips. "Kimberly...Kimberly Siconolfi is missing!"

Amberly tenses in preparation for what is next, though nothing happens; all the protective armor she's built appears to have been unnecessary. It doesn't seem to get even the slightest reaction out of Officer Renny, who simply types in the name and asks, "And how long has she been missing?"

His unassuming response eases her reservations, and she begins to let it all out. "Well, she hasn't been to work. She doesn't answer her phone, and I just heard last night that there was a situation with her husband killing her on the radio. Her husband is a freak, you know. He abuses her and makes her do things—weird things! And I *know* he's done something to her!"

Officer Renny, now aware of whom Kimberly is, looks to her to confirm. "Is her husband Joshua—the guy on the news?"

She shakes her head yes, almost shamefully, and then begins to cry. "She's missing, and it's my fault. I mean, it's her husband: Joshua's done something to her. And there's something I can only talk to Detective Cools about. I think I may have done something wrong, and I don't want to be in any trouble, but I did come in on my own. I just need to talk to Detective Cools. I can only talk to him!" She begins to cry harder.

Renny quickens at her adamant plea for Detective Cools. Pushing down on the arms of his chair, he scoots his round body back to a more upright position to yell across to the adjacent cubicle. "Hey, Lonnell, do you have Detective Cools's number?"

"Just a second," an unseen voice returns. Then a few moments later, Officer Lonnell yells back a seven-digit number over the thin partition separating the two spaces. Officer Renny writes it down on a piece of paper and dials.

It rings five times before an exhausted voice comes across the line. "Hello."

"Detective Brad Cools?"

"Yes, who's this?"

"Detective Cools this is Officer Renny, down here at the station. I met you before at the—"

"Yeah, yeah, I know who you are." Cools cuts him off in a tone that says get to the point since he's just gotten out of the shower and is dripping wet.

"Detective, I have sitting in front of me a young lady named Amberly Carlson. She's here filling out a missing persons report on a coworker, Mrs. Kimberly Siconolfi."

"The same?"

"Yes."

Instantly Cools abandons all plans of sharing a passionate morning with the woman lying in his bed and replies, "Keep her there…And keep a tight lid on this, Renny. I'll be there in…in fifteen minutes." Click. There's no time for boxers, so he snatches his black slacks lying on the bedroom floor and hits speed dial, letting the phone ring while buttoning a shirt over his wet, muscular frame. "Michelle!"

"What's going on, Brad?"

"Michelle, listen, a coworker from the strip club is, right now, down at the station filling out a missing persons report on Kimberly Siconolfi. I need you to meet me at the station; we are going to interview her together. Something's going on; I can feel it."

"Slow down. It could be nothing, Brad," she replies, wondering how in the hell he got his name, thinking it should be Detective Brad High-Strung-Impatient-Angry-Drama-Queen. Anything but Cools.

"Michelle, I'm right about this. Something's going on. He may have killed his wife for real this time, and we're going to get to the bottom of it. I need you to meet me at the station in twenty minutes. So put your shoes on, girl. We got work to do."

A submissive sigh comes from Michelle before agreeing to his demands. "I'll be there, hon."

Cools snaps his phone shut, ending the conversation, when another hurdle presents itself.

"And where do you think you're going?" asks the pretty woman lying in wait.

He almost answers her before deciding not to. Then he mumbles, "Nowhere," while searching the floor for a pair of dress socks.

She sits up and grabs her eyeglasses—the naughty-librarian kind that she wears so well—from the lampstand to gain a better idea of what is going on. "Where are you going? It's our day off."

Cools has been in this situation before and knows his best play is to say very little, get out as quickly as possible, and then explain everything to her later. It isn't because he doesn't value her or care for her; he's actually very much in love with her. Still he knows that as soon as he starts answering, it'll only lead to more questions, ultimately escalating to a senseless argument, and that would only slow him down. So evading all eye contact, he continues dressing, throwing a few vague utterances her way. "It's a police emergency…I can't talk now. I have to go. Okay, baby?"

Chelsea, an attractive woman even in the early hours, is a thirty-two-year-old bank manager with a good head on her shoulders. Her only fault is that she has a weakness for the jackass now leaving her alone in his cluttered apartment. And knowing the game all too well herself, she does nothing more than curses a short, "Goddammit," and pull the covers back over her head. It isn't long before she hears car keys being lifted from a kitchen table and the door slamming shut.

A short time later, Cools enters the station, finding Amberly with Officer Renny and straightaway noticing her look. Her eyes are puffy like she has been crying, and she doesn't look well; he automatically suspects she's a party girl. Officer Renny introduces them. "Detective Cools, this is the young lady I was telling you about."

"Amberly is it?" Cools asks, using a warm, kindhearted tone. Experience has taught him that a caring first impression is the best way to cozy up and earn their trust prior to a progressively tough interrogation.

"Yes, that's my name. And I asked to speak with you, and you only," she replies, with a mixed expression of guilt and apology.

"I understand you believe Kimberly Siconolfi is missing?"

"Yes. She is. And I think her husband has done something to her."

"And you're a coworker and friend of Kimberly, is that correct?"

"Yes, uh-huh."

Cools feels confident he is going to tear her apart. Soon he will be shredding through her bullshit, gaining all that she knows. "Okay, Amberly, give me a second, and we'll be right back. Do you need anything...anything at all...a drink...or cigarette maybe?"

"Well, I could use a cigarette," she replies with a gentle smile, instantly feeling a little more at ease. She likes the way he looks at her, the way most men do, the way that comforts her.

"Sounds good to me too," he says. He then moves in closer, whispering, "We have a private office in here that no one is supposed to know about that we can smoke in." He finishes his statement with a wink, reeling her in. "I'll be back in a minute, okay, Amberly?"

"Yeah, all right then."

Cools leads Officer Renny out into the hallway. "What do we got here?"

"Well, not a lot. She claims she works with Kimberly at the Kitty Club, and according to her, they're good friends. They have a routine they do together."

Cools pauses a second, adult-visioning, as Renny goes on, "And her story is basically that she hasn't shown for work in days or answered any of Ms. Carlson's many attempts to contact her via cell, Facebook, text—nothing. So she doesn't worry about it too much until a friend tells her last night about the incident last week—Joshua's radio show. And for some reason, she's very firm about not knowing about that till last night. My first impression is that she's an addict."

"Yeah, I got that too. Is that all?"

"No, there's something else. She says she didn't know what she was doing at the time, but that she has done something—something she could be in trouble for—and she's made it very clear she will only talk to you about it."

"Okay, can you set her up in the smoking room, Renny?"

"Not a problem."

"Good, and can I trust you to keep tight-lipped on this one?" he asks, searching his eyes for the truth.

"You got it."

"Okay, I'm going to find my partner. And thanks again, Renny." With that he turns and disappears down the hall, assessing the situation. What does she know? Why has she requested to only talk to me? Whatever it is, I need to do whatever necessary to tie it all to Joshua, and this time I'll make sure it sticks!

Chapter Seven

"Chuck Sheumer, please."

"And who's calling?"

"Tell him it's Rainman. He'll know who it is."

"Okay, hold."

Seconds later a voice shouts back over the line, "Fucking Rainman, is that really you?"

"Yeah, it's me."

"Man, it's good to hear your voice. How long's it been?"

"Uh...about three years I guess."

"So how's the married life?"

"Oh, you know, it's good; we're buying a house, and things are good...yeah."

"All right then, let's go for beers tonight, on me...deal?"

"No, that's not what I was thinking." He lowers his voice. "Um, I want to talk to you...but not on the phone. Can you meet me at Charlie's Restaurant on 140th—ASAP?"

"Sounds serious," Chuck replies curiously.

"Well, I think you are going to like it, but time is a factor."

"You have some inside scoop?"

Rainman answers with another question. "How soon could you be at Charlie's?"

"For you, old buddy, I can be there in fifteen or twenty minutes."

"Okay, sit next to me at the bar but pretend to be just another customer."

"I can do that."

"See you there," Rainman says, ending the call. He sets the receiver back onto the base and stares at it; his heart is beating fast, his palms are sweating, and he questions if he's making a quick and easy buck or the worst decision of his life.

"I'm going to get something to eat. Anybody need anything?" Officer Lonnell shouts over his cubicle. After a few of the other officers decline, he snatches his coat and marches directly out of the Seattle police station. His stride is awkward with trepidation and excitement as he begins an eight-block jaunt to the restaurant. What he is about to do is not only highly unethical, he could lose his job.

Seventeen minutes later Chuck Sheumer steps keenly into the bar. He promptly scans the room for his friend. His attention is caught by a skinny boy of a man sitting at the far end, facing the entrance—Rainman, dressed in blue.

He could never get used to the uniform, thought it made him look somehow hypocritical due to all their youthful mischief. They'd met in grade school, where Rainman earned his name due to the fact his mother would never let him play in the rain. They remained best friends through high school then lived together for a while in a kind of a bachelor, after-hours-party pad. All the crazy things they'd done were monumental, and somehow, the fact that they never got into any real trouble made them seem even more so. And no one would have ever suspected Pete Lonnell would have ended up becoming a cop.

Chuck walks over and sits in the stool next to him and orders a beer. They both stare forward. Under his breath Chuck says, "You look good, man. Well… except for the uniform."

"Yeah, and it looks like you've put on a few pounds, huh?"

They both share a short laugh. Then Chuck asks, "So what brings about this sudden and unexpected meeting?"

"Well, I don't want to come off like a greedy bastard, but I do remember you telling me your newspaper pays for information, and I'm having some financial problems with the new house and all."

"Yeah, well, we do. It works just like anything else: big info equals big money; small info, not so much. What do you got for me, old buddy?"

Rainman leans in, lowering his voice, and says, "Joshua Siconolfi." Chucks eyes widen. "His wife, Kimberly, is being reported as a missing person by a close friend, a coworker."

"No shit!" Chuck spits out, attracting the attention of other patrons in the lounge. He coughs and drops his volume, stating, "We've been running his story all week."

"Yeah, I know," Rainman replies with a smirk.

"What else can you tell me?" Chuck asks, while digging a pen and paper out of his shirt pocket.

"That's all I have for now, but there is more to come. The girl said she has something very important but would only talk to Detective Cools—you know, the one who shot the hole in Siconolfi's driveway. And I get the feeling, whatever it is…it's big."

"And do you think you can get this information?" Chuck asks, hungry for more.

"I think so. I mean, yes…yes, I can."

"This is going to make my week. I should have no problem getting a front page spot."

Chapter Eight

"I'm here, Brad. I'm just pulling in, trying to find a place to park," Michelle says, before snapping her phone shut. Only thirty minutes earlier, she was getting ready to have a major discussion with her fifteen-year-old daughter, Lindsey, regarding the empty baggy that still had an odor of pot she'd found in the laundry. She'd had it all planned out: what she was going to say, the questions Lindsey might ask, arguments that might arise. Not to mention all the rebuttals she'd rehearsed in the morning mirror. All of it cut short over some coked-up pole dancer trying to enter the limelight of a fast-fading story. Michelle pictures her sitting in the interrogation room, stroking her partner's cock, pouting, "You believe me, don't you, baby?"

A few minutes later, she visits the interrogation window to spy on the lusty girl smoking alone in the bare room—looking like today's stripper and tomorrow's crack whore. Michelle adjusts her focus, catching her reflection in the glass to admire her thick, brown hair with new blond highlights that cost ninety-five dollars. Once satisfied it was money well spent, she moves farther down the hall in search of her partner. She takes a quick peek inside the video room. There she finds him all alone watching Amberly on one of the monitors, trying to learn all he can before he starts asking questions.

"Oh, I'm sorry; do you need to be alone?" she asks with a cheeky grin.

"Why would I do it this way? I have fifty dollars," Cools replies without a seconds hesitation.

While definitely amused, Michelle isn't laughing. "That's clever, partner. So what exactly do we have here?"

"Well, like I told you earlier, all we know is she says she works with Kimberly, that they're good friends, and no one has seen or heard from her in days. And that's not all. She told Officer Renny she's involved somehow, but will only talk to me."

"Why you? And involved in what exactly?"

"Well, that's what we're going to find out. I'm thinking maybe Joshua did the radio call to set up a sort of alibi in advance; so then if he kills his wife, he can say, 'Why would I pretend to kill my wife and then just days later actually do it?'"

"Yeah, maybe."

"Okay, I'm ready," Cools says. "I'm going in. Let's see what I can get out of her."

"Most likely herpes," Michelle retorts.

"Ha-ha. Okay, then, unless you have something else cute to say, I'm going in to get us some answers."

"All right, Brad, I'll settle down," she replies, bowing her head, feeling immature. He comforts her by patting her on the shoulder as he slips out into the hallway. From the monitor she watches him step into the interrogation room. In black and white, she can clearly see Amberly's reaction to him as he enters. Her expression is frail and genuine. Upon further examination Michelle comes to consider that maybe she's just a scared little girl. No longer does she see a dirty whore; rather she is a witness to a vulnerable and frightened human being squirming in her chair. How did she get mixed up with Joshua? What does she know?

Amberly peers up at Cools, attempting to say something, but before she can speak a word, he holds up his finger, shushing her. He sits down opposite her at the cold, steel table and stares into her eyes, saying nothing. He learned long ago that silence is a much more effective strategy than yelling and screaming. He patiently examines her, waiting for her to begin, but when she opens her mouth, he quickly shushes her, as if he's watching an important part of a movie and doesn't want to miss anything. And he is not only gazing into her soul, he is also taking in any and all facial tics and body movements. Silently she tells him much. He looks her up and down, taking her in, judging her skimpy outfit and her pasty, drugged-out skin. It all makes her so nervous; she forgets his rules and again tries to speak, only to be swiftly shushed once more. Then after he knows he's inside her head, he diverts his sight to the corner of the ceiling. Amberly's eyes follow his until she sees the camera pointing directly at her, warning her that all is being recorded, that anything she says can and will be used against her.

"And now...," Michelle says, pointing to the screen the very moment he begins his spiel.

"Listen carefully, Amberly. I'm a very serious man, and I want you to think long and hard about what you might say or not say here today." He then reaches an empty hand into his pocket and pulls out a pack of Marlboros and, without taking his eyes off her, lights up one for himself and offers her a fresh one. She accepts with a stuttered thank you and leans forward to the extended flame. Her trembling doesn't go unnoticed, which Cools utilizes to his advantage. "You seem uneasy to me. Are you nervous?" he asks in an insinuating tone.

"No...I mean, yes...I don't know...Do I seem nervous to you?"

Cools squints his eyes, nonchalantly nodding his head yes. And now that she's fully rattled he initiates his assault. "Okay, let's make one thing crystal clear, Amberly Carlson. If you plan to tell me anything but the absolute truth, you will find yourself in big, big trouble, young lady. Do you understand?"

"Yes, but—"

"Do not play with me. I can throw your young, sweet ass inside our jail, and I'm sure there are some hungry dikes that would *love* to see you. Are you absolutely sure that you understand what I am telling you?"

"Yes...I do, I mean...I mean, I will."

"Why did you ask for me?"

"Because, you know, because I talked to you the other day...and you seemed to be good person, so I thought...I mean, I think I should trust you."

Cools searches his memory and flashes an odd glance to Michelle behind the camera. "I've never spoken with you, Amberly, not until today."

"Yes, you did...a week ago...you know, when you called the club."

"No, I spoke with Candy."

"Yes, that's my club name...I'm Candy."

"Okay..."This comes as a shock to him, a connection he hadn't put together. After assimilating the information, he continues, "Officer Renny says you have something important to tell me."

"Yes...I do...but I don't want to be in any trouble. I'm a good girl, Detective...I never wanted anyone to get hurt."

Cools blows out his smoke, speculating for a second on the kind of tawdry comment Michelle is making to herself over the "I'm a good girl" comment.

Then he begins the big push and asks, "Amberly, did you drive here from Everett this morning?"

"Yes."

"And you did tell Officer Renny to call me in on my day off—the only day I can visit my daughter—to come down here to the station because you have a problem so sensitive that only *I* can handle it. Is that right?"

"No...I mean, yes," she replies, even more flustered than before.

Cools, childless, considers it his responsibility to persuade people to think twice about coming in here and fabricating stories to get even with coworkers or unfaithful lovers, or to exploit another person's misfortune. But with Amberly he is getting a good vibe: although she does too many drugs, she is a reliable source of truthful information. So he gives her a hand gesture that offers her permission to speak and says, "Let's hear what you have to say."

"Well...I didn't say that I wanted you to miss your daughter...not exactly. I just...I just wanted to—"

"But I did come down here on my visitation day, did I not?" he asks sharply.

"Yes, but—"

"So whatever you have to tell me, tell me now!"

"Okay, it's like this. I was...I mean, I was only doing a favor for a friend. And then when I heard the story of Joshua calling the radio station last night...I think...I think maybe I made a mistake, but I did what she asked me to do. We do it all the time; it's no big deal really...I guess, or not...I don't know."

Cools begins to breathe more quickly and shallowly—partly because he wants to know what she does, but mostly due to his lack of patience for female psychobabble.

"You do *what* all the time, Amberly?" he asks, pressing her.

"You know, make sure no one gets hurt or into trouble with boyfriends, and then last night I heard the news...then I called my friend, Justin, and...and he sent me a clip with the radio recording of the thing that Joshua did...and then I knew I was in trouble, real trouble."

She starts crying, but he unsentimentally pushes her further. "Why do you think you would be in trouble, Amberly?"

"Because...you see, Kimberly...she wasn't there when you called. I...I was just covering for her. Kimberly had this other guy she sees, and you know, I didn't know you were really a cop; the boyfriends get creative sometimes to find out things. So I told you she was there, but she wasn't there. And that was the day Joshua did his thing on the radio...and now I think he did something, because the guy, you know...the guy she was seeing—he came into the bar later that same night, and he was looking for her, and nobody's seen her since."

"Oh shit!" Michelle screams so loud it can be heard in the interrogation room, where Cools is now out of his chair, pacing back and forth, mumbling to himself.

"How could I be so fucking stupid!" he spits out.

"Am I in trouble...I didn't...you know, I didn't want to...I mean, I'm sorry. I'm so sorry. You have to believe me...I just—"

That is all Cools hears before escaping into the hallway, where Michelle meets him, so shocked she's speechless. He grabs her by the arm and makes his way straight for the stairway, so they can talk privately, incoherently cursing under his breath along the way. "How could...I took the word of a stripper named Candy—fucking Candy? I must have lost my fucking mind!"

Once they're on the cold staircase, securely away from any cameras or eavesdroppers, Michelle says, "So now I'm interested." Cools looks to her for anything, hoping she can piece something together that makes sense. Instead, she berates him. "What the hell does this mean, Brad? Did that little prick kill his wife on radio and make fools of us? And then we gave him close to a week to get rid of the evidence? How is that possible? How?"

"I don't know Michelle, but we better talk to Captain," he says, sensing a wicked storm of no mercy falling his way for the mother of all fuck-ups." He leads a straight course to Captain Jackson's office, foreseeing future headlines: Top Cop Lets Psycho Killer Go! Detective Cools Fooled by Local Stripper! Was Kimberly Still Alive?

Thirty seconds later they burst into Captain Jackson's office. Sitting across his desk is Detective Fredo, also known as JFK (Jack Fredo, the Kiss Ass).

"Hey! Hey! Hey!" their captain shouts.

Cools holds up his hands, saying, "Captain, we're here on about a nine and a half on the Richter scale." Then he points to JFK and asks, "And this is?"

Captain Jackson restrains his annoyance at the bombardment and replies cynically, "It's about a two."

"Out! Get the fuck out—now!" Cools orders JFK, who scurries out of the room. After the door shuts, he frantically lays it all down while pacing back and forth in front of Michelle, who is ignoring the display considering the implications.

Captain Jackson sits stock-still, digesting his detective's tirade, almost more concerned for his friend than the dilemma itself, as Cools flails his arms about rapidly, answering most of his own questions, until the captain can't take it anymore. "All right! All right—enough. Sit down, Cools, and be cool. Jesus, fuck, you get wound up, man!" Cools shuts up and moves to the chair his captain is pointing to. "Robertson," Captain Jackson snaps his fingers, breaking her trance. "Robertson!"

"What?"

"Sit down next to your partner."

They both comply without protest. Then Captain Jackson breathes vigorously through his nose, enjoying the first moment of silence since they'd busted into his office. The two of them look to him for orders, guidance. And both are equally caught off guard by his response.

"Listen up, the both of you; I'm not all that impressed with the story from your stripper. But I'm deeply troubled about what's going on in here. Cools, you're a cop. It's a job. Let me say that again: it's a fucking job! But you get so worked up I think you're gonna have a fucking heart attack right here in front of me. Do you think I wanna see you have a fucking heart attack here in my office?" Cools says nothing. Then Captain Jackson bellows so loud Michelle's body jerks in her chair. "Do you think I wanna see you have a fucking heart attack here in my goddamned office?"

"Okay, I get it, but I—"

"Are you sure?"

"Yes, but I think we should bring him in!"

Captain Jackson pounds a heavy fist on his desk and then holds up his large hand, shaking his head to and fro, emphasizing the fact that he should say no more. Cools knows not to press any further. Michelle wouldn't dare.

A few moments pass in palpable tension and complete silence. Then, Captain Jackson, the real cool one, begins to chart a course forward. "All right then. We're gonna start being professional cops up in here. We're gonna get a *grip* and begin to *slip* our way out of this shit. Do you hear me?" Both Cools and Michelle answer in humble unity.

"All right. Robertson, I want this Amberly to fill out a complete statement. I want her drug tested, and I want a lid on this shit—closed and sealed." Michelle nods, so he moves his attention back to Cools. "And then…maybe we consider bringing him in for questioning. But I want total control; he's already filing suit against you for the crater in his driveway, you know." Cools sits up, positioning himself for more arguing. Captain Jackson, sensing his challenge, commences to talk louder, "It's gonna go down like this: Joshua will say his beloved wife has run off with some other guy. And according to your witness, there *is* another guy, right?"

"Yes, but—"

"No buts, Cools. We'll bring him in for questioning if that's what you want, but you should know as well as I do he won't say a damn thing. He's gonna call his father and be riding home in time for lunch, leaving us with nothing more than we got now. And what exactly do you plan on asking him anyway?"

"I'll get something. I'll break him. You know I can."

"Cools, think it through. This isn't some street punk coming off a drug high that you can manipulate; he's been through the system; his father's a veteran attorney. You think he's gonna just let our DA push through a search warrant on a missing persons? Plus, from what I remember, he never made even the slightest of mistakes, did he?"

"No, he was lucky, Captain."

"Uh-uh," he retorts, waving his finger in the air. "He didn't get lucky, and you should know better. He played the system from arrest to early release with the efficiency of a skilled politician. He's a slick trick, that one, and you know it!" Cools doesn't respond, which gives Captain Jackson a second to gather his thoughts. He relaxes his large body back into his chair and sets the game plan in motion. "So we're gonna get all we can from the stripper; we'll put twenty-four-hour surveillance on our boy, and then we dig, we watch, and we wait, and we do what cops do. And most importantly we're gonna keep this out of the fucking media; they'll have a field day with this if this ever gets out! They've already been playing him and his creepy poem most every night." He pauses for a second then addresses a more important matter. "Now, one more thing... Cools, listen up, sport; you're one of my best detectives, and I need to know that I can count on you. So do not ever—ever!—give me unconfirmed information again. Is that understood?"

Cools lowers his eyes to the floor, replying, "Yes, Captain."

"He's right," Michelle says, finally adding something. "We really don't have anything except for a missing persons reported by a drugged-out stripper. And this way no one has to know that you, or we, screwed up."

"Exactly, finally someone's making some sense," Captain Jackson says, tossing a smile to Michelle. "Now we need to get more on him. So contact Kimberly's family members, talk to the boyfriend, dig through the garbage, follow him if you have to. And you really need to start listening to your partner, Cools. From what I get from her as well as some of the other guys around here, you have some anger issues, my friend; you need to slow down."

"Ah, fucking hell," he grumbles, as he springs from his seat; he turns his back on them and glares out the plate glass window.

Then, after a few uncomfortable seconds, Michelle takes a chance and recites in a girly voice, "I'm a good little girl...and I don't want to be...you know... in any trouble or anything." Captain Jackson looks at her, confused. She begins again, using the same voice. "I just...you know...cover the girls who have...you know, boyfriends and husbands...but I'm a good little girl, Detective."

Cools, still with his back turned, tries ignoring her.

Now getting the joke, Captain Jackson asks, "Is that how she talks?"

"Yes," Michelle snickers.

They share a laugh together until Cools responds by admitting he could hardly contain himself in the interrogation room, and all at once the three of them start laughing hysterically.

"I gotta get a look at this one," Captain Jackson says.

"Oh, you're going to like her, Captain," Michelle laughs out in a tone that tells him she's a hottie.

He looks to Cools, who, with his expression, verifies Michelle isn't kidding. He can also see the energy is now running in the right direction and decides to add to the joviality, asking, "Did you see JFK scuttle his butt outta here?" This sends the trio over the edge, and they laugh like they haven't in years, each of them adding witty comments on the spectacle until they're exhausted.

Finally Captain Jackson brings their meeting to a close. "All right," he says, clapping his hands together, "sounds like I'm gonna do an extended interview with Little Miss Innocent, while you two are gonna hustle up the dirt on our boy Joshua. This creep isn't gonna make fools out of us, not on my watch—you better believe it. Now, I think you should start with the boyfriend: find out who he is, where he is, and interview him right away."

"Okay, boss," Cools replies.

Likewise Michelle agrees and gives the captain an assuring smile to let him know she'll be taking good care of her partner. They all inhale a refreshing breath of air to reorganize their minds before Cools and Michelle are off in search of Kimberly's lover. The laughter served its purpose, to soothe their demons for the moment. Still, for Cools there is, just below the surface, an underlying sense that life-altering events are soon to take place—an uneasiness that makes you feel like you need to run, that you won't make it through the day, that today, for some unknown reason, you should be extra careful while crossing the street.

Chapter Nine

The deputy mayor of Tacoma sits alone in his master bedroom, uncertain as to what will come next in his existence. His skin is pale, with dark circles below his eyes. There is an eerie stillness that shrouds his thoughts as he makes a call.

His call is answered.

"My name is Trace Friesen. I have a beautiful, caring wife. I live in a beautiful home with my children, and I have a promising career. I've been preparing my run for governor, and yet today, I am here with a loaded gun in my hand."

The listener on the other end is Maggie, a student at Washington State University. There she studies psychology and volunteers in her off time as a suicide lifeline operator—this is her day off.

"Sir, what you're doing right now is the best thing you can do for yourself: reaching out. And I will help you through this; we *will* get through this together."

"I'm not asking for your help, Maggie," he says in a monotone voice. "I only call to clarify my reasons to someone. I already wrote a letter to my friends and family, saying that I am truly sorry to have let them down. But I just feel the need to talk to a person first—my notion of a confessional."

"Okay, I will do that for you, but first I ask you to do something for me: tell me why you are sorry. Why do you think you have let them down?"

He tries clearing his mind in preparation to tell the short and sweet answer. "I am a married man in love with a dancer—a stripper, to be more correct—and

I believe her to be dead. She was murdered by her insane husband. And I have been torn in days past, watching it unfold on the news, hearing others mention it continually, knowing it would catch up to me sooner or later."

"Are you talking about that creepy guy—Joshua something?" Maggie asks.

"Yes," he replies, disgusted that everyone everywhere knows him.

Then Maggie hears a change in his tenor from anguish to pent-up anger. "I've entertained thoughts of killing him, praying deadly misfortune his way... He used to beat her...And I did nothing! Anyway it's all over; I just received a call from a detective from the Seattle police department. At this very moment, he and his partner are en route to come question me. I have just lost everything—my profession, my beautiful family, my dreams of running for office, and the woman I love!"

Maggie tries to speak, but her persistence enrages him further.

Trace holds the phone out a few inches from his mouth and yells into the receiver. "That god-awful psychopath killed her. I know it from some of the things she has told me of him; I know he killed her...And I had to hear her die!" He then breaks down and begins to let out tears of misery.

Maggie, talking through her headset, says, "That's okay; just let it out; you sound like a nice man that presently has some problems. But we can work through it together. We can and will get you all the help you need."

Trace forces his revulsion back deep inside himself, returning to his monotone voice. "Maggie, I want you to tell my wife how sorry I am and that I always loved her. I want you to tell my children that I love them, but I cannot live with this anymore. I want them to hear it from a person, even if it's a stranger. I just cannot live with myself, being filled with the rage to kill a man, without the balls to do it! I couldn't protect her; I am a weak excuse for a man! And I am having very bad thoughts!"

Now sensing she's losing him, she begins some tough love. "Trace, think about the scene your wife or kids will see when they come home and see your brains all over the wall, think about how that will affect them for the rest of their lives!"

Her tactic doesn't work. He simply replies, "I left the door open for the detective, and I am waiting for him."

But Maggie isn't ready to give up. She retreats to her soft-toned voice, saying, "I know you've been through tough times before, Trace, and you sound like the kind of man who can get through this. And what do you mean that you're *waiting* for the detective?"

He ignores her statement and asks, "What is your name?"

"My name is Maggie—Maggie Aversen. Trace, please, please let me help you."

"Maggie, do you believe in God?"

"Yes, yes I do, and God can help."

Then for the second time, he begins to break down. His words crack with desperation as he strains to hold back the fear and frustration that have built up inside him. "Maggie, will you pray for God to help me?"

"Yes, I will, and we can pray—"

Next all she hears is what sounds like a choked-up thank you as the line goes silent.

Chapter Ten

A quick glance down the hall to make certain the coast is clear gives Officer Lonnell the green light. He sneaks into the video room and taps the space bar on the keyboard, activating the computer screen. Then, after a quick search, he finds what he's looking for—a file for Amberly Carlson. He plays the clip and, in a short time, learns all that he doesn't need to know.

Twenty-seven blocks away, at The Seattle Times, Chuck Sheumer and his editor are discussing whether to sell their new information to the television networks or just hope they're the first to break the story in tomorrow's paper. Little do they know but their decision will be made in a matter of seconds.

Chucks phone chimes, indicating a new text message.

Rainman: Kimberly was missing before Joshua did the deed—friend from kitty club says she lied for her—Kimberly was not at work when the police raided his home

Chuck: confirmed?

Rainman: Yes

Chuck: this is good—very good

Rainman: I want to be careful—erase these texts—meet me @ Charlie's 9:30

Chuck: done—see you then

Chapter Eleven

Cools stands knocking at the deputy mayor's residence. "Hello, is anyone home? This is Detective Cools from the Seattle Police Department," he announces through the open front door. "Hello, Detective Cools here; is anyone home?" Just an hour before, Amberly told them about Friesen. Then Cools made the call and spoke with him on the phone, so it seems odd, to both he and Michelle, that the door has been left partly open and no one is answering. They enter into the foyer. "Hello, Trace... Trace Friesen, are you here?" But still there's no response.

Then Michelle yells out into the lavish home, calling for him, her sweet voice resonating off the high ceilings—but no reply. She looks around; everything is clean, seamless, and ear-piercingly quiet.

Cools continues calling as they walk through the living room area, his loafers clicking on the hardwood floors. He and Michelle exchange looks of bewilderment. She thinks maybe it's just because they are standing in another man's home that the voiceless residence seems to have an unnatural presence. And Cools, after spying a few indoor security cameras, gets the strange feeling they're being watched. Even if they are, it should be very clear to anyone that they are the police. He is wearing a black suit, a thin black tie, and hanging from his belt is a detective's badge—the normal look for any detective, except Cools doesn't wear a bulletproof vest; he thinks of them as bulky and bothersome. Michelle also has her badge hanging from her dark gray pantsuit. Their host could very well be distracted by the upper part of her outfit, which is revealing a sizable amount of cleavage.

Michelle wanders into the Friesens' restaurant-style kitchen, wondering why a man in his position would be banging a stripper. Could he be responsible for her death? Then, she yells twice more, out through sliding glass doors into a well-manicured backyard, complete with swimming pool, fire pit, and volleyball net. "Must be nice," she says to herself.

Upstairs Cools searches methodically room by room until he reaches the master bedroom. A whisper inside his head warns him to move cautiously, as a cold breeze brushes past. He pulls his weapon from its holster. Again he calls through a partly open door, "Trace...Trace Friesen, are you in here?" Still no answer, so warily he nudges it open, and there he finds the man he'd just spoken to forty-five minutes earlier, holding a gun in his lap. The deputy mayor is slumped back over a red chair against a backdrop of bloody material. Cools's first thought is Michelle; he can hear her downstairs, still calling for the man, and knows they should no longer be seperated. Subsequently he heads back down the stairs, past framed pictures hung on the wall, the survivors of the deceased, as well as a large crucifix pronouncing the faith of his home. He rounds the corner near the bottom of the staircase and catches her eye. "Found him," he says, in a defeated tone.

"He's not...?"

"Yeah, partner he is. And it looks like he did it himself."

"You've got to be freaking kidding me."

"I wish I was."

Once more, with Michelle close behind, Cools enters the cold room, this time spotting Trace's phone near his bare feet. He pulls a set of clean latex gloves out of his jacket pocket. He puts them on and carefully picks up the phone, pressing redial.

"Suicide crises and prevention."

"Did you just receive a call from this number?"

"Sorry, sir, we do not have caller ID; it's to keep everything anonymous."

"Well, I am a detective from the Seattle Police Department; a call was made from this number at 11:51, just ten minutes ago, and—"

"Oh my God," the girl cries, "did he do it?"

"Are you the person he spoke with?" Cools asks, ignoring her question.

"No...no, it was Maggie; she's in the back, freaking out."

"I need you to put her on the line right now," he demands.

"Ah…all right then…Hold on. I'll see if I can get her."

Then, as he waits for the hotline girl, he watches his partner suspiciously investigating the scene, and remembers just how resilient she is.

"This is Maggie." Her sobbing voice comes over the air.

In an effort to deflect from the emotional state of affairs, he speaks candidly with her. "Maggie, are you the person who spoke with Mr. Trace Friesen?"

"Yes," she replies, holding back the tears.

"What did he say to you, Maggie?"

She pulls it together, answering, "He was making comments about Joshua, the crazy radio caller, killing his wife. He said he was in love with her."

"Maggie, are the phone calls recorded?"

"Yes."

"Listen up, Maggie. I cannot go into everything right now, but I need to interview you ASAP. I'm going to send a cruiser out to pick you up, and it is very important that you do not talk about this to anyone, okay?"

"I don't think I can…," she replies reluctantly. "Not now, I—"

"Maggie, yes you can, and you will. And make sure you have the tape." With that he hangs up and lowers his tone to attend to Michelle. "Have you found anything?"

"Not much. It seems pretty clear what's happened here," she replies, from a crouched position, searching the floor around the body.

"Are you all right, Michelle?" he inquires, like a protective older brother.

"Yes, I'm all right, Brad," she replies defensively. Then she stands glaring at him, folds her salon-styled hair behind her ears, and validates herself further. "I'm fine. I'm a grown woman, and I can handle this. You just do what you need to do!" There's a brief standoff between the two that subsides only when Michelle asks, "How's the suicide hotline girl going to help us?"

"Trace made comments that he knew Joshua murdered Kimberly."

"Then why wouldn't he report it to the authorities?"

"Not sure…But don't you think it's a good idea we find out?" She hesitates, but he knows her answer is yes. "Okay then, I need you to get a cruiser over to this suicide hotline place to pick up a girl named Maggie." Then, from Trace's phone, he makes a call of his own.

"Hello?"

"Milo, this is Detective Cools. I need you to get on your computer and get me the voicemail pin number assigned to this number."

"Uh…only…that is illegal."

"That's the easy part; the only part you need to worry about is calling me back with what I need, or I'm going to inform the task force about the secret garden you have hidden in your basement." Click.

Ninety seconds later Trace's phone rings. It's Milo. "Last four digits of his social: five-nine-zero-seven," Milo says proudly. "Now, are you going to tell me what this is all—"

After hanging up on Milo, Cools prompts Trace's phone to hear his old messages. He skips through, until one says it's from Kimberly—from eight days ago. "Michelle." He waves her over, so they can listen together. Standing close they listen intently. It's the first time either has heard her voice. She sounds upset. "Trace, I'm glad you didn't answer…'cause I don't think I could say this to you in person." There's a pause, with only her sniffling. "I just got back from the doctor's office; they did some tests." After another short pause, she cries out, "I have HIV. I am so sorry."

"We have to call Captain," Michelle says, flipping her phone open. She steps out into the hallway where Cools can hear her speaking breathlessly. He listens to her full reporting and then hears Captain's initial expletive as he screams through the speaker.

"Fuck! This is turning into a goddamned nightmare. Have you seen the news?"

"No, but hold on." Michelle steps back into the master bedroom. She quickly finds the remote for the television on the nightstand and turns it on.

"What're you doing?" Cools asks.

"Hold on." It doesn't take her long to find a twelve o'clock news program discussing their case.

"Sources say Kimberly Siconolfi was reported earlier today as a missing person by a coworker—name not known at this time. What's more—she's been missing for a week now. Meaning, as strange as it sounds, she was missing prior to the infamous radio call made by her husband, Joshua Siconolfi. We've tried contacting the Seattle police for comment, but they haven't returned our calls."

"Do you see what's happening?" Captain Jackson says derisively.

"Yeah, this is getting big, and we don't exactly know what we're dealing with yet," Michelle replies, feeling nauseated.

"All right," Captain demands, "I need you, Cools, Maggie, the fucking tape, and a full report in here yesterday; I'm gonna assemble a task force. This one's going prime-time, and we're not gonna look like slouches. Not to mention the fact that we've got a rat in the house! I bet it's that Officer Renny; I've never liked him anyway—that fat piece of shit. He's just too much a Goody Two-shoes!"

"Did you get anything more from Amberly?" Michelle asks.

"No, I haven't had a chance, Robertson! I've been dodging reporters since you two left. Now, call in the death of the deputy mayor and wait for homicide to arrive, then lead your partner to the car and get your ass in here!"

Chapter Twelve

A short time later, while traveling back to the station, Michelle rides shotgun with her hair blowing slightly in the wind from the cracked window that provides her some fresh air—a preferred alternative to the cigarette smells of Cools. The tight-fitting seatbelt she wears snuggles around her breasts as she mulls over the day's investigations and the coming headlines, speculating where this case is headed, how everyone really ties in, and whether or not her partner is ready to apologize.

After they called in the homicide unit, nothing of too much importance was found, except for a receipt pertaining to the weapon Trace had used—a Beretta PX4 purchased just three days prior, meaning it couldn't have been used in connection with Kimberly's disappearance. But Michelle, on a haunch, suggested that they also search for evidence linking Trace with any foul play concerning Joshua's wife or her death. As to this, Cools exclaimed his condemnation, accusing her of chasing phantoms, going off on a crazy goose chase. Her then sharp responses led to an equal exchange, quid pro quo, of professional insults, all in the presence of their colleagues—suggesting that the stress is beginning to wear on both of them.

Now, although the breeze cools her head, she's fuming inside. He's the one that's going on a hunch; Brad is the one thinking single-mindedly. I'm keeping all thoughts of reason open. I'm the one thinking like a real detective; he's just a dickhead! Then, noticing that he's trying to ignore her, she moves obnoxiously in her seat, with a grunt, reminding him that she is still frustrated over their previous exchange. Her adolescent actions are noticed.

"It's Joshua, Michelle. *He* killed Kimberly, and that's all there is to it!"

"Whatever, Brad. I agree that you're probably right, but still it is our responsibility to cover all the angles," she says, her tone jaded. "For all we know, she could have killed herself or just run off. Or maybe—just maybe—she was murdered by her secret lover who she gave AIDS to. It happens, you know!"

"Now you sound like his defense attorney," he replies mockingly, attempting to match her tenacity.

"Screw you, Brad. No, really, screw you!" she yells, extinguishing any responses he may have had. Her comment rides along with them as a third passenger for the next few turns until Cools realizes he's pressed her too far. She never speaks to him like this, so he rethinks his dispute, considers his personal responsibilities, and carefully chooses his words.

"Okay, okay, I was wrong." He looks to her with sincerity.

"Say it again, Brad."

"Okay, I was wrong about the way I treated your open-mindedness in front of the other detectives. I should have backed you all the way, and I fell short. I am an asshole." Michelle doesn't respond, so he then rolls his window down and hollers to the world traveling past, "My name is Brad Cools, and I am an asshole! I am a stupid fucking asshole! I need to show respect to those who deserve it! Did I mention that I'm an asshole?"

Finally Michelle lets out a little smile. She's never really understood why, but she has always found it difficult to stay mad at him for very long. He has a way about him, always seemingly in total control but still in need of someone to look after him—a duty she feels the calling to attend too. With her fingers she combs the sides of his hair back, saying, "Yes, you are; you are an asshole, but you're my asshole." They share a restorative silence, with only the sound of the car's motor winding down the road.

She remembers the first day they met. She was standing alone in the line at Starbucks, when out of the corner of her eye she saw him in the reflection of the glass, walking up behind her. There was something about him that caught her married eye. He stood close, and just before she was up to order, she turned ever so briefly. Their eyes met long enough for a flashing friendly smile. She ordered, and then he ordered, and left in a hurry. She gave it little more thought, since today was her big day. It was going to be her first day as a police officer on the Seattle Police force.

Two hours later, dressed in blue, she saw him again. He walked in, as sure of himself as the sun itself, he looked directly toward her, walked over grinning, and asking with the point of his finger, "carmal latte right?"

She blushed yes, and felt the security of making a new friend, a friend of chararcter and clout in her new job. They soon became close, enough so that the rumors began around the water-cooler, even more so when she was promoted to detective, and they became partners. But she doesn't care, she always feels safe with him, not only from the criminals they have to contend with, but also safe enough to really be herself, which is sometimes childish, and needing of attention.

"Have I told you that you look really nice today? And that I have not only noticed, but greatly approve of your new nail color."

"Uh, ha-ha, now you're just sucking up."

"Yeah, maybe some," he agrees with a smirk. "So how's your chubby husband?" he asks playfully.

"He's not chubby…just thick."

"Oh…He's thick, huh?"

Michelle responds with nothing but smiles.

"Okay, then, did you have your talk with Lindsey about the pot?"

"No, I didn't have a chance, Brad; remember, you called me first thing this morning demanding that I meet you immediately!" He doesn't react, knowing she has more to say. "She's such a pretty and smart young girl, and I just don't know what to do. All the kids today are moving so fast; it's hard to keep up, you know. I only want the best for her, but I feel like I'm losing all control." Michelle stares out the window, following the rolling scenery, her mind meandering to a familiar place of feminine fussing where empathy and worry rules queen. And not solely for her daughter Lindsey, but also for Kimberly, maybe even Amberly.

"She's going to turn out fine; you and your chubby hubby are doing great," Cools says, breaking her thought.

"Okay, enough about me; what about you, Brad? How're you doing? Still drinking your sorrows away at that Russian mafia bar?"

"Something like that. I do what works." Michelle flings him a piteous glance. "It's the only place that feels like home to me," he says, somewhat defending himself. "And I have a history there; it's where I belong." Cools perceives her unchanged expression and gives up. He knows that there is nothing he can say to sell her on the idea that drinking alone in a gangster bar is sound judgment. Maybe someday I'll share with her the story of Rueben the Jewish child molester, who I allowed to be excommunicated from earth so that a young boy named Nico could grow up normally and an old man named Sergey could find some justice and closure.

"Well, anyway, I was thinking we have a lot of weak characters tied into this case. Amberly, for one..." He holds out his hand, displaying one finger. "You know if she's hiding anything, we're going to get it. Two: there's Trace Friesen, and I'm positive the investigation into him is going to open some doors. And three is you and me baby—we're going to figure this out, just like you are going to maintain a solid grip on Lindsey and guide her to all the best things in life."

"Yeah," she hums with a smile, "you're probably right."

Michelle rides the rest of the trip in utter amazement at how he can sometimes make such good sense, even if he is scared to talk about himself. And she values his efforts to hold their unique friendship together. Also she is confident they'll root out the bad guys in this game; she even has the sense that they're close to being on the right track. But what she doesn't know is that given the information they have at this time it would be impossible to predict the twisted truth that lies ahead.

Chapter Thirteen

Captain Jackson is just finishing up a phone call with the chief of Tacoma, who is informing him of his intentions: he plans to give a press conference later today disclosing the fact that the death of Trace Friesen is tied into the Joshua Siconolfi case, including that there will be a joint effort between the Tacoma and Seattle Police Departments concerning any ongoing investigations. He's basically telling Jackson that they are going to work this case together—like it or not. Captain Jackson hangs up the phone. "That son of a bitch," he mutters to himself, while digging through his desk drawer for some pain relief medication. There he finds a half bottle of Vicodin; he takes out a couple and downs them with some bourbon. The bottle doesn't exactly have his name on it, and even though not exactly having your name on the bottle makes up for about 15 percent of the population in his jail, he doesn't feel one bit ashamed. Today he can break a few rules.

Suddenly he is startled by his intercom. The sweet voice coming through is that of Misty Lakewoods, his secretary. She's alerting him that Detective Fredo (JFK) is requesting to update his progress.

"Yeah, all right, send him in."

Detective Fredo comes in and says, "I have everyone ready, just like you ordered; we're just waiting for Cools and Michelle, but they are on their way and should be here shortly."

Captain Jackson grabs his jacket and scoots out of his chair, replying, "All right, let's go." Fredo holds the door for him. Even Captain Jackson thinks he's a kiss ass, but has always carried the attitude of "What the hell—it's kinda nice having a bitch boy close by your side." Together they move down the hall toward the meeting room—the war room.

Captain Jackson, realizing he has a few minutes to squander, tells JFK to go on in and wait. Then he slips down the hall and sneaks a peak through the two-way mirror. No one needs to enlighten him to the fact that the girl behind the glass is Amberly—the stripper. Or that she is on drugs, for that matter. She looks nervous and annoyed, most likely from being confined inside the small, claustrophobic space and not knowing her fate. If she knew the truth, she would have jetted out of the building hours ago. But earlier Cools bent a couple of rules and told her she couldn't leave until he could clear her of any wrongdoing. And now Captain Jackson is all alone with her. He takes a good long gaze, with the kind of eyeball he wouldn't dare if she could see back through the glass. I might just check out the Kitty Club some night.

Then across the hall and through another two-way mirror, he spies Maggie—the suicide hotline girl—and the officer who has just brought her in. She's kind of homely, with knotted hair, and way too skinny for his taste. He speculates: if one were to put the two together in the same room long enough, what would emerge—two strippers or two psychology students?

A commotion catches his attention, followed by the distinct sound of Michelle Robertson's voice, always trying to slow her partner down. A smooth step around the corner and he's hidden from view. He wouldn't wish for Robertson to catch him peeking. Captain Jackson thinks the world of her, and although he would never admit it, Michelle (who he always refers to as Robertson) could get away with anything as far as he is concerned. To him, she is probably the most perfect package of a women inside and out to ever cross his path. Standing motionless at the corner, he watches her, bouncing along after her hot-headed partner as they march into the war room. Then a voice inside his head says, "All right, Captain Jackson, it's time for you to get your big, bad, black ass in there and tell all those white boys what the fuck to do!"

Twenty seconds later he enters and sizes up his makeshift task force. It all feels surreal, having such a high-profile case land in his lap, right at the height of his career. He can taste the power of control, mixed with the fear of knowing that cases like these have all the potential of going bad, and often do. This he has learned from seeing his counterparts in other counties and states go into battle against a proficient counsel on one side, William Siconolfi, and the unforgiving media on the other. A wet and slippery road lies ahead, and he will never know what to expect, just that he needs to keep it as visibly clean as possible and always watch his back. Still, the distinctive circumstance does offer some prospective opportunity—like the advancement to chief of police, police commissioner, or maybe even a run for mayor. All he needs to do is win: first, by identifying the bad guy; followed with an arrest and then a successful prosecution; and last but not least, do it with observable integrity and well-dressed efficiency.

Do it with style.

Inside the war room sits a hefty rectangular meeting table bordered by his team. In front of them are laptops, notepads, digital recorders, plus a large multifunction conference phone waiting in the middle. The walls are draped in maps and dry-erase boards. They silence themselves and prepare for orders as Captain Jackson, at the head of the table, begins constructing the tone of the operation like a coach setting forth on the first day of ball camp. "All right, I hope everyone knows everyone," he begins, pointing around the room. "This is prosecutor Andrew Milkowski; Detective Michelle Robertson and her partner in crime, Detective Brad Cools; Detective Jack Fredo; Janice Dryer is our psychologist; and at the far end are Officers Jakew and Smithe. We also have two other officers in the field doing surveillance. I have another working data. And sweating away in our interrogation rooms, we are holding Amberly Carlson, the coworker, and Maggie, the suicide hotline girl. Now, is everyone familiar with each other?"

Everyone utters a soft affirmatives—all except JFK, who interjects with his tally of their consensus, then reports his findings as if Captain Jackson were blind. "Looks like we are all acquainted, boss." Michelle lets out a satirical sigh as things move ahead.

"All right, now, listen up. This is gonna be considered a homicide case. And we're gonna work as a team. Now, if there's anyone on this team you don't like, they're now your new BFF. Is that clear?"

Most steal a quick look at JFK before nodding in accordance.

"This is a highly sensitive case, as you well know, and I will not tolerate any mistakes. And if I find that any one of you even talks in your fucking sleep, uttering just one word to the media, I will personally destroy your careers and reputation! Do I make myself clear?"

Everyone nods.

"All right, let's start with Detective Robertson."

Michelle coughs nervously, then brings everyone up to speed, adding only the trivial information, just recently learned, that Kimberly seems to have no surviving family except for an aunt in Minnesota.

"Okay, I have a few things to add," Cools says, jumping in. "First of all I'd like to point out the fact Joshua has not reported his missing wife—as missing. And there's this: Trace Friesen stated on tape that he knew Joshua killed her."

They all look to Milkowski who holds up his hands, letting them know it's only empty speculation, and replies, "The testimony of a suicide is nothing, and as far as we know, anyone could have killed her."

"Are you the prosecutor or his defense attorney?" Michelle asks, then glances at her partner, realizing where she got the idea.

"All right, everyone calm down. Now, Robertson, like I told you before, we really don't have anything, not enough for an arrest, not yet." The captain then turns to Milkowski and asks, "What do we need to get a search warrant? Because I have to do something and soon. This is going into the spotlight as we speak, and the public will demand I do something. And I'm not gonna look the fool!"

Milkowski, this time, holds his palms out and answers them directly. "Here's the deal: this being a high profile case, you won't find a judge to sign a search warrant, not without something substantial. And I don't think you're bold enough for any shenanigans, not with everyone watching."

With that an uneasy Captain Jackson looks at Cools and slightly shakes his head, letting him know before his wheels begin to turn, that isn't the path he intends to take.

"I have an idea," says Janice Dryer, the psychologist. Everyone sighs before turning their attention to her. She wears the ideal attire for her profession—the skirt-and-blouse combo that's 70 percent classy innocence and 30 percent take me now. Her hair is pulled back into a bun, leaving a few strands dangling beside her cheeks. Although everyone would concede she is nice to look at, no one wants to hear anything she has to say. Janice knows this, and in spite of their judgment, she confidently explains her proposal with poise. In a soft voice, she says to them, "I think maybe he will just come in on his own."

Cools's eyes start to roll. Others curse under their breath in frustration.

Janice, noticing their reactions, begins defending her statement. "No, think about it: this guy calls a live radio broadcast with millions of listeners. So I ask you: why did he do that?"

"Because he is a psychopath," Michelle chirps out.

"Well, maybe…But there is more to it than that. I compiled a full psychological report on him. He drives a Lotus; his wife is a stripper; and have you seen his picture? Flashy hair, jewelry, tight abs, very metro-sexual—he's a playboy, a classic narcissist. And I believe he will welcome the limelight with open arms. I believe there's the very real possibility that, subconsciously, he wants to come in to parade in front of the cameras, just like his father. Have you ever seen him?"

Silence cascades over the room as all of them grant some consideration to her idea.

"That actually somehow makes sense," Michelle says, while others begin to gesture the same.

Cools surveys them all for a second before spouting out, "Are you guys losing your fucking minds? What are we supposed to do—just sit around here and wait for him to knock on the goddamned door?"

"Just be quiet, Brad. Let's hear what Janice has to say," Michelle says, with a gentle pat on his leg. Everyone returns their attention to Janice, some making note of the affection between the two detectives.

"So, do you have any suggestions as to how we're gonna get him in here?" Captain Jackson asks.

"Well, I do," Janice answers, feeling empowered. She scoots gracefully forward in her seat. "I want you all to consider this: egomaniacs are extremely overconfident, and if he's done something to Kimberly, he not only wants you to know about it, he's certain he will escape punishment for his crimes, especially given the fact that he's now had close to a week to cover his tracks." A few glance at Cools; others try not to as Janice rolls on. "I believe he wants to answer your questions more than you want to ask them. Think about it: he supposes himself as superior to you. And he not only wishes for you to know it, he wants the whole world to know it. If for no other reason than to boast, to be documented, acknowledged. So to answer your question more directly: he wouldn't be able to refuse control; he knows sooner or later he will have to answer some questions; all we have to do is plant the seed that he should do it on his own terms."

"So how do we use all that to get him to stroll in here with his hands in the air?" Cools asks.

"Maybe we could simply contact him and offer him the opportunity to present a statement, so we could state to the media that he is freely cooperating and not hiding behind his attorney, emphasizing the 'hiding behind his attorney' part."

"I think it's worth a shot," Captain Jackson announces, just as his secretary pops in.

"Excuse me, Captain, there's a call coming in from the two officers you have in the field."

"Send it in."

Then quietly brainstorming, no one says a word, waiting for the phone to ring.

After a moment, the call is connected. "Hello?"

"Captain Jackson, this is Officer Poulet; he's on the move."

"Is he alone?"

"Yes, it appears so."

"All right, keep us updated; I wanna know what he's having for lunch—got it?"

"Got it, Captain."

"All right, let's get this going. Milkowski, which judge offers the best chance to get what we need?"

"Judge Cooper maybe," he replies unconfidently.

"All right, I want you to start with her."

"She's not going to—"

"I said to *start* with her—get the ball rolling," Captain Jackson replies sharply. Then, letting Milkowski know their conversation is over, he turns to Cools. "You and Robertson, I want you to see what more you can get out of Amberly." He shifts his attention to JFK. "Detective Fredo."

"Yes, Captain Jackson."

"I want you on Maggie, the suicide hotline girl. Get me something."

"Yes, sir, I would be happy to."

"Officer Smithe, you're going to Tacoma. I've already talked to a Detective Shoemaker there, and he agrees to let you ride along in his investigation of Trace Friesen. This is a big shot for you; don't screw it up.

"Officer Jakew, you get the best assignment here—the Kitty Club. So go make some new friends." Next he speaks to the entire team. "Any and all new information is to be—and I don't care how little you think it is—needs to be given to me immediately! Is that understood?" Everyone agrees and begins rising to their feet. "Janice, you're gonna prepare a phone call to Mr. Siconolfi. We'll see whether you know what you're talking about. Does anyone have any questions?" There's a pause before JFK raises his hand.

"What is it, Fredo?"

"I think we should discuss the leak."

"Oh yeah, how could I forget that? Someone's talked to the press, and they're gonna pay for it when I catch them, and I will catch them." Then his eyes alter, drawing the group's full consideration. "If anyone leaks information, I will personally destroy you. I'm an old man with not much to lose, and—come hell or come heaven—I would have no problem going out with a vengeance."

No one utters a sound.

Again the phone rings, startling everyone. "Captain, Officer Poulet here."

"What's new?"

"He's made us, and he's running; we're half mile behind him on NE Sand Point, and he's moving fast—real fast!"

"Don't lose him!" Captain Jackson yells. Then he starts clapping his hands together, saying, "All right, everyone, let's get a move on—let's go. We meet back here at six o'clock. Fredo, get me a chopper in the air—now!"

With that everyone except Janice Dryer begins parting.

Chapter Fourteen

"Oh shit! Fuck!" yells Officer Poulet's partner, (Donovan), as their tires screech around a corner, the sounds quickly replaced by the revving engine. The transmission kicks down into a lower gear, launching them to 85 mph on a 35 mph road—all lights flashing, sirens blaring.

"Hold on," Poulet warns, stepping hard on the brakes and veering three feet over the yellow line, going into an S-turn. He's taking great risks for both him and his partner, just to keep up. Still the two young, adrenaline-driven cops are losing ground with every turn. The red Lotus they're pursuing doesn't just look faster—it is faster, lighter, with more horsepower and racing suspension. And the only asset they have is that they'd rather crash and burn than lose this arrest.

Up ahead, on a short straightaway, the highly tuned sports car passes up the middle between a camper van and a motorcycle in the oncoming lane. "This guy is fucking crazy!" Poulet yells, knowing he'll have to match the same level of peril if he ever stands a chance. He redlines the engine but gets caught behind the old camper van before the next set of turns.

"Fuck, fuck, fuck—get the hell out of the way!"

"We're losing him!"

Poulet turns back and forth wildly, within inches of the van's bumper, while Officer Donovan screams through the windshield. "Move it! Get the fuck out of the way!" He takes a chance and pulls into his version of the center lane, as they head into a corner, and punches the accelerator. The squad car lurches forward, past the rear bumper, rear tires, and almost to the driver's side door, when an oncoming GMC truck flashes at them like a bullet train.

"We're not going to make it! God!"

No longer seeing a middle lane, only a full head-on collision, Poulet hits the brakes and cranks the wheel, rubbing into the van. The large truck swerves but clips the cruisers front bumper and scrapes down the side, shaving off paint and the driver's side mirror.

Inside the van an old, burned-out Vietnam vet, realizing the situation, shouts out through his smoked-stained beard, "Not today, you yuppie bastard!" Then he yanks the wheel purposefully, crashing his vehicle over a ditch and into a grassy field. His van comes to a violent halt just as he sees the police cruiser fly through the debris cloud. "Go get 'em, copper!"

After a few more treacherous turns, Poulet finds a patch of open road and lets the cruiser loose.

"There—there he is!" Donovan yells, pointing to a red dot a mile ahead. "We can still get him! Let's go, let's go!" Poulet pushes the cruiser up to 95 mph. Their car begins to shake in the front axle. "Listen to me, Poulet. I've been your partner for two and half years now; I completely trust your skills, so don't hold back because of me. Let's show this asshole how to drive!"

"You got it, and if we make it…oh, am I going to beat the shit out of this fucking dirt bag!"

"Yeah, well you gotta catch him first!"

Poulet pushes it up to nearly 110 mph, and the shaking is getting worse with every measure of speed.

Captain Jackson and Janice are listening to the entire episode on speakerphone. She is speechless, and he remains silent, only waiting for a moment in which he can be of assistance, as the call gets louder and louder by the second. The squad car sounds to be rattling to pieces; even the volume of their voices is increasing as they speak over the noise.

The cruiser nears 120 mph, and Poulet implores, "Hold on baby; hold on for just a little bit longer!"

Out on the open, straight stretch, the cruiser has the advantage. And they are gaining a bit of ground, but the shaking has turned into more of a hammering: 120…122…124 mph.

"Ah, I see brake lights! He's turning south onto Lake Washington Boulevard!" 125…126…127 mph. "Ah fuck, you're coming in awfully fast!" Poulet steps on the brakes and shifts the automatic transmission down to third…second…

first—barely making the corner onto another twisting road. The Lotus now has the advantage, and at every turn it pulls a little farther away. "Goddammit! Can we get a chopper on him? I can't keep up!" Poulet screams over the receiver.

"We're working on that as we speak," Captain Jackson replies. "Just don't lose him." He then makes a quick call to the helicopter crew, but is told it could take four or five more minutes—not fast enough.

Janice, following them on the map on the war room wall, states, "Looks like you guys still have another two or three miles of curves."

The odds are not on their side.

Then Poulet almost loses the cruiser on a tight bend. The back end begins to slide at 79 mph, and he's forced to turn out earlier than he wants to. The tires straddle the ditch, churning gravel. They squeak through only to see the next obstacle. The road ahead is an incline with a long, sweeping corner at the top. "Ah, I'm thinking about not slowing down for this one, partner! Ah, I'm thinking we can hit it at top speed—and ride the guardrail!"

"That's insane!" Captain Jackson yells. But it sounds like his advice is being ignored.

"I'm with you, partner!"

"Fucking here goes!"

Next all Captain Jackson and Janice can hear is the constant speeding of the engine and then horrid sounds of twisting metal on metal. The controlled crash shatters the side and back windows, blows all the airbags, and buckles the hood; however, it works. They exit out of the corner at 74 mph, leaving a shower of sparks in their wake, and gain some ground. The Lotus is up about a mile. They see him turn again. Just two seconds slower, and they would have had no idea which way he went.

Donovan yells, "He's just turned westbound onto Madison!"

Forty-five seconds later they make the same turn onto Madison, where they find themselves in almost no traffic. And Madison, being straighter than Lake Washington, gives them a better chance. Soon Poulet reaches 125 mph, and although they're closing in little by little, the car is literally falling apart. A piece of the grill breaks away and crashes into the windshield, sounding like a bomb as it hits them and spiderwebs the glass.

"Ah, it looks like we're going to I-5!" This represents a scenario they definitely don't want: high-speed mayhem on the interstate will be a disaster in waiting. Then the brake lights on the Lotus shine bright as it banks hard, exiting the thoroughfare and once again vanishing out of view. "We're going to lose him."

The cruiser holds at 129 mph until the last viable second as Poulet prepares to make the same g-force turn. The cruiser makes noises never heard before, the tires nearly bursting into flames, and a moment later they realize where they are: a shopping center with a busy parking lot. Immediately he has to choose left or right. "Which way?" Poulet screams. "Which goddamn way?"

"There! There he is!" Donovan answers, pointing to the left.

Poulet sees him. He's already parked and is casually getting out. Though speed is no longer required, the blood is still pumping through Poulet's veins like a race horse, and he pulls in fast, locking the brakes. The cruiser skids to a stop, carrying with it two extremely anxious, armed, and pissed-off policemen. They unholster their weapons; Poulet jumps out, crouching behind his door. Donovans' door won't open, so he aims out the window. "Get down!"

"Get down on the ground—now!"

Joshua doesn't comply. He just leans over his car, adjusts his sunglasses, and stares at them, as if victorious. Just then, a deafening and low-flying helicopter emerges over the top of the mall, ruffling his blond hair.

"What's going on?" Captain Jackson asks impatiently.

"I don't know, Captain," Poulet screeches over the noise of the helicopter. "We're parked behind him…uh…We're at a mall!"

"All right, and what the hell is he doing?"

"Well…uh…he's just staring at us."

"This guy is fucking with us!" Captain Jackson shouts, slamming his fist into the table. Then he says, "All right, everyone, settle." Next he closes his eyes and pinches the bridge of his nose.

"What do want us to do, Captain?"

"I want you to shoot him! Shoot him right in the middle of his fucked-up head! But not now," he adds, changing his command before one of them actually does it.

"He's moving…he's walking into a computer store, Captain. What do you want us to do?"

Captain Jackson thinks for a moment then instructs Poulet to get a pen and a business card. "All right, now write this down on the back: Detective Janice Dryer. Then under her name, write my private office number—the line we're on now. Got it?"

"Got it, Captain."

"Now, I want you to walk into the computer store, politely hand him the card, say something to the effect that you applaud his driving skills, then ask him to call Detective Dryer, and then simply walk away. Do you understand? Nothing more, nothing less!"

"Uh...what?"

"You heard me—just do it!"

"Yes, Captain," Poulet replies, confused.

"Then go back to your car and follow him wherever he goes and keep us updated."

"Uh, Captain, I'll do it just like you said, but I probably couldn't follow an old lady across the bingo hall in this car. You're going to have to send us a new one."

"Done. And good work—that's to the both of you."

Officer Poulet doesn't even attempt to explain the conversation to his partner; he simply follows Captain Jackson's orders. After completing the task as requested, he adds his own personal touch, releasing about half of the pressure in all four of Joshua's tires.

Chapter Fifteen

Misty Lakewoods, Captain Jackson's secretary, resumes her position behind her desk, disheartened. She's just missed another opportunity to ask for a raise, a monetary promotion that she not only deserves, but which is long overdue. She has worked for him for two years now and is probably the most professional secretary he's ever had—efficient, never late, and not pretty enough to be a distraction. Rumor has it that previous secretaries were. It's something she's wondered about from time to time—whether her undesirability got her the job in the first place.

Anyway, she never had a chance. He jetted into his office with Janice Dryer so fast she wouldn't of had time to ask him for a piece of gum. Their only communication was that of him giving her very simple orders that if Joshua Siconolfi calls, to patch him straight through.

Inside his office he gives Janice orders, saying, "If he calls, number one, do not tell him you're a psychologist—today you are Detective Dryer."

"But—"

"No buts. Now, number two, do not let him onto any information we have. And number three, if you can't get him to talk, at least find out what the fuck that crazy devil poem means—it's been driving me nuts."

"Okay...well, sounds easy enough. I plan to play into his need for recognition. You understand he feeds off of control and dominance over others. A lot of it stems from early childhood; his father was most likely abusive or absent in his early years or was never—"

"All right, all right—enough! I believe in you Janice, and who knows, maybe this just might work." He then pulls a bottle of bourbon from his desk and pours himself a glass. "Would you like a drink?"

"No, I don't drink."

"Ah, don't tell me you're a recovering alcoholic?"

"No, I drink, just rarely," she replies, with a kind of nerdy charm.

He smiles to himself and swallows a mouthful, then sits back and closes his eyes, enjoying the warmth of the alcohol. Janice also takes a rest, mindlessly looking about his office. And in the passing minutes, they settle themselves. The room is quiet, so quiet in fact they can hear the phone ring at Misty's desk. They both listen closely.

"Captain Jackson's office." There's a pause. "I'll put you straight through."

"No shit. Are you ready?" he asks, looking to her, somewhat in disbelief.

"Yes," she replies, with a nervous smile and a hesitant voice.

Misty's voice comes across the intercom. "Joshua Siconolfi is on line one."

Janice takes a purifying breath in preparation, while Captain Jackson slurps another drink. Then he types a five-digit code into his desktop phone, activating its internal recording device, plugs in a headset, and hands the receiver to Janice. He says to her, as composed as possible, "All right, do your thing," and presses the flashing button.

"Hi, Joshua, this is Detective Janice Dryer. How are you doing today?" she asks politely.

"I'm doing great, lady. What do you want?" His tone is sharp and juvenile, but not what she'd expected; somehow she had anticipated the evil-sounding madman from the radio show.

"Well, I'm sure you can appreciate the fact that many of us down here at the station see a stark connection between your wife being reported as a missing person and the radio call you made last week. And some of my coworkers have even suggested the wild notion of arresting you for something and interrogating you. I said that I didn't think of you as the kind of man who would shy away from any questioning or *hide* behind an attorney. I told them you are an intelligent man who knows he will have to answer these questions sooner or later, and that you'd prefer to do it on your terms." Then Janice alters to a flirtatious tone. "Basically, what I'm saying is that I would like to meet…I mean, interview you."

"What's in it for me?" Joshua replies smartly.

"Well, this way you can say that you're cooperating—that you're not afraid of anything."

"Hmmm…What are you wearing, lady?"

"What?"

"I asked you what you are wearing. What color are your panties?" he says, his voice more demanding than inquiring.

"That is none of your business," she replies, genuinely offended.

"Well, doesn't quite sound like a great offer, Janice. Tabatha Sterns offered me an interview to set the record straight, and she would've come to my house and made me dinner if I so requested," he replies smugly. "And by the way, hers are black silk."

"Well, that's real nice, Joshua…But listen: I believe you need to answer some questions. And I'm sure you would agree it would be in your best interest if you just came in of your own accord. To go on the record, rather than the newspapers printing some distorted facts from an arresting officer. Remember Detective Cools?"

"How could I forget?"

"Well, how would you like the media running with his version of the events?" There's a pause. Then Janice strikes again. "We should give them *your* version—that is, unless you're fearful of something. But you don't seem to be the timid type."

There's another long pause. She can hear him breathing, the same malevolent panting she heard on the news. Then in a more sinister voice, his real voice, he asks, "Do you know Detective Cools?"

"Yeah…I know Detective Cools."

"Good. I would like to hear you say, 'Detective Cools missed his chance.'"

The statement stuns her. Her mind runs wild considering what he means. Is he saying Kimberly was there? Was her dead body in the house?

"Say it, Janice!" he demands.

"And if I do?"

"Then we both get what we ask for."

She wastes no time and replies verbatim, "Detective Cools missed his chance."

Joshua lets out an eerie laugh and says, "Does seven o'clock work for you?"

"Yes, yes it does."

Still chuckling, he says, "There's just one more thing."

"What? You name it."

"I think I did it!"

Her heart flutters; she feels faint, dizzy; she is not even sure she wants to ask the next question. "You did what, Joshua?"

"I will enlighten you later, as you will enlighten me regarding the color I asked for!" He hangs up.

Janice trembles in her seat. She holds the phone out to Captain Jackson, saying, "I think I will take that drink now."

"Yeah, all right, anything for you. That was the most amazing thing I ever heard. You did good, Janice—real good." He pours her a drink and watches her gulp it down. "Ha-ha. Are you sure you're not an alcoholic?"

"No," she replies. "That creep makes me so nervous. I am just so glad it's over. And correct me if I'm wrong, but did he just say, 'I think I did it'?"

"That's what he said."

"I thought I was going to drop the phone. But he couldn't possibly be arrogant enough to believe he can admit to it outright. He's up to something. I'm just not sure as to what."

"Oh, he's up to something all right, but it won't work. Let me tell you how this all plays out: the more they say, the more information we get, the more we can use against them. We just simply have to keep 'em talking."

"Okay, then I guess I'm a real crime cracker."

"Yes, you are," he says, and smiles at her. He can see that she's still shaken.

"I'm going to go home now and get into a soothing bubble bath—maybe even stop and get some more alcohol," she says, hoping with everything she has that this is all finished for her.

Captain Jackson blows out a hearty breath and tells her, "Janice, I'm not gonna lie to you: you're gonna do the interview."

"No, I cannot! You can use Michelle; voices sound different over the phone, and.... and she can listen to the recording, so she knows what was said."

Captain Jackson pauses, sees the worry in her eyes, and tries to console her. "You know you have to." She doesn't resist any further, just slumps back, dismayed, staring at the wall. He gives her a halfhearted pep talk, trying to instill courage. But deep down, they both know his words are disingenuous at best. The real truth be told, Joshua Siconolfi even scares the shit out of him.

Chapter Sixteen

"Well, the news begins anew. I'm Sheppard Smith in studio B, and the news starts now.

"You're not going to believe this: new discoveries in a story we played last week. Remember Joshua Siconolfi—sure you do—the guy who called a live local radio station and did, well, what sounded like murdering his wife. You may also remember, though, how the whole thing was put to bed, due to the fact that his wife—his stripper wife, might I add—was as safe as a stripper can be inside a stripper bar. Now it turns out, the coworker lied when she confirmed her whereabouts.

"So let's break it down. Joshua Siconolfi was excused for his exploits—pranks, as it seems—because his exotic-dancing wife was all safe and sound well after the fact. But now, new reports say she was missing *before* the incident. And this changes everything, not to mention raises a few questions.

"So the cops look into it and find out the wife—by the way, her name is Kimberly—also had a boyfriend. And not just any boyfriend: he was the deputy mayor of Tacoma. I say *was*, because—and check this out—when police went to his home to ask him some questions, he apparently had committed suicide. Do I have your attention now? You can't make this stuff up. And why does Scott Peterson come to mind? So we go now to our correspondent, live in Seattle."

"Hi, Shep; Anthony Westlake here. I'm standing outside the Siconolfi residence. We have not seen him yet, but earlier today, from one of our sister stations, Tabatha Sterns reported he was involved in some kind of high-speed chase with police. And we've also learned from neighbors that the Siconolfi's had a rocky relationship, telling us that authorities have been called to this home on many occasions for domestic violence and out-of-control parties. Also, Shep, we're being told that Joshua did time for third degree vehicular assault on a former girlfriend."

Sheppard recaps, "So we have strippers, lies, felonies, high-speed car chases, suicide, and maybe even murder...wow!" A picture pops up. "And you're looking now at one Joshua Siconolfi on the screen. Good-looking guy isn't he? And I'm sure we'll be hearing more on this. I wish I could spend more time, but as it turns out, there's other news.

"Remember the bailout package for Chrysler and GM? You know; we were told that Congress was going to—"

Captain Jackson clicks off the television. Looking anxiously around the war room, he asks, "All right, is everyone here?" After another quick glance around and a few acknowledgments, he holds a hand out, presenting Janice, who grudgingly smiles from ear to ear. He begins, "All right, here's the deal. Joshua's coming in. Janice's plan worked, and she's gonna interview him. He will know her as 'Detective' Janice Dryer." He looks at his watch. "He should be here at seven o'clock." Every face in the room expresses surprise. "Now, I have to give a press conference no later than eight. So give me something guys. Cools, Robertson, what do you got?"

"Not much, Captain," Michelle begins, "except for a few sordid facts about Kimberly. Turns out she was kinda weird; she followed some kind of ancient Egyptian religion: Ra. Also she talked of violence a lot. And I don't know what this means, but she left a message on Trace's phone stating that she tested positive for HIV eight days ago."

"Yes, we already heard this."

"I know," Michelle continues, "but she and Amberly were tested on the same day at Washington Medical Center. And they were both negative." She holds a piece of paper in her hand. "This is Kimberly's test result, left behind in the floorboard of Amberly's car."

"So why would she lie?" asks Officer Smithe.

"I don't know; I really haven't any idea," she replies, appearing perplexed. Officer Smithe makes a notation and leaves it at that.

Then Cools jumps in, adding, "I remember hearing something about the god Ra in preparation to Joshua's assault trial, from a statement made by—oh what was her name?" He clicks his thumb and finger together, trying to snap her name from midair. "I just read it—oh, Sherry—Sherry Hill. She told of his religious practices. And I know this is going to sound gross, but one of the rituals he performs is where he ejaculates into a golden urn and places it into a fire, where it is burned as an offering."

This at once appalls everyone in the room; mouths drop wide open; even Captain Jackson, who thought he'd heard it all, nervously scratches his scalp. Michelle stares down at her feet, shaking her head, while Janice loses color and appears to almost get sick. She holds her hand over her mouth and coughs, losing confidence, worrying even more about what she's gotten herself into.

"That is so wrong," Detective Fredo says, trying to fit in.

"All right, Detective Fredo, what did you get out of Maggie?" Captain Jackson asks abruptly, wanting to move along, at the same time catching Janice's dispirited aura. Her apparent weakness conflicts him greatly, to the point that, even at this late state in the game, he rethinks using her. To him she seems scholastically gifted but lacking the street smarts she'll surely need. He also senses he is not the only one who shares his sentiment.

JFK says, "Yes, Captain Jackson, we have the tape of Trace's call to the suicide hotline stating he knew Joshua killed Kimberly. But other than that, it doesn't tie in anywhere to Joshua, except for the fact Trace was involved with his wife. So I got all her information and sent her home, boss, leaving my schedule open for any further assistance."

Captain Jackson gestures his approval, saying, "I think I might have something in mind." He then looks to Officer Smithe, who speaks up directly, stating, "I too have nothing so far on Trace Friesen, other than what we already know. But that being said," he carries on with confidence, "I do believe it is vital that I continue further in this part of the investigation as I am getting the sense this may be political—that there's much more to all this than simply Joshua or his dead wife."

"You think maybe Kimberly found out something?" asks Cools.

Officer Smithe shakes his head, before answering, "Well, it's too early to speculate, but I do believe it's important for me to continue."

"And I think you're right, Smithe, and that's exactly where I intend to keep you. You're gonna stay on the big, big case all right." Officer Smithe receives his words like a gift. And his obvious expression of gratefulness does not go unobserved by anyone. At once Captain Jackson realizes something of greater importance—the compassion extended to him from everyone in the room, a man they barely know. His team is coming together, which is the age-old key for any successful investigation. A quick smirk then crosses his face as he turns his attention to Officer Jakew. "All right, did you get anything from the Kitty Club?"

"Well, I did talk to some of the girls and—"

"Yeah, I bet you did," Michelle pipes in. "I bet you did."

Officer Jakew blushes a bit, then ignoring Michelle's comment, reports, "I just got some of the same stuff Detective Robertson was talking about. It sounds like she was a very odd, maybe even violent woman. She would make sick and twisted remarks from time to time. Most of the other girls were terrified of her. And unlike the other girls, she didn't have any real schedule. This seems to have caused some jealousies; from what I get, Kimberly received a lot of special treatment, although no one knows why."

Next Captain Jackson turns to Milkowski. "What does this all add up to?"

"Maybe a novel by Steven King. But none of this will get you an arrest warrant. Although…"—he holds up a finger—"I do have some good news. I have talked with Judge Cooper, and I think I can get a warrant for Joshua and Kimberly's records: phone, credit cards, financial statements, properties, and so on."

"Well, that's something," Captain Jackson replies. "So, now here's the deal, everyone. Joshua should be here shortly; Janice here is gonna interview him." He pats her on the shoulder. "We'll be watching and then go from there. Now, Detective Fredo?"

"Yes, Captain Jackson."

"Get me a full report on the Ra religion. I want to get inside this guy's head."

"Yes, I can do that."

"All right, then unless anyone else has more to add, we should get going."

"Um…" Officer Jakew asks, "What do you want me to do now?"

"Go back to the Kitty Club. You're gonna become a VIP there. Someone there knows something, and I need you to keep digging. Stop on your way out and talk to Sheila, in finance; she has a credit card waiting for you with a modest expense account. And try not have too much fun, all right?"

Officer Jakew responds with just a short and sweet okay. But everyone can see the excitement burning in his eyes.

The meeting is dispersed.

Captain Jackson and Janice are seen leaving together, heading back to his office, while Michelle and Cools disappear in the other direction. He, as usual, is in the lead. They move swiftly down a long corridor back to the main lobby. On a hunch, they plan to set a trap.

They find Officer Renny inside his cubicle eating a sub sandwich, the crumbs of which cover his belly. Michelle asks a couple of known questions concerning his earlier interview. Then Cools, appearing to make gossipy small talk, offers the latest of details.

"I want you to know that your help was crucial to our investigation. And we're going to get him *this* time around."

"What do you mean, 'this time'?" Renny asks, taking the bait.

"Well, we've learned that years ago Joshua was one of the prime suspects in the disappearance of his high school sweetheart."

"Really?"

Michelle takes a rushed glance at her watch then declares, "We better get going, Brad."

The snare is set. Both Cools and Michelle believe the person leaking information to the media will soon be found out.

Chapter Seventeen

Officer Lonnell, crouching in the corner of his cubicle, opens his phone. Some more fortune has just landed his way.

Rainman: Joshua was prime suspect in murder of his high school sweetheart

Chuck: Are you sure?—where is your information coming from

Rainman: Detective Cools—is that good enough

Chuck: Works for me. Fucking love you man

Lonnell, wanting to swiftly leave the scene of the crime–his cubicle–heads for the break

room. Along the way sees a couple of his co-workers watching something of great interest inside

the booking seargents office. He lingers just outside and hears the announcer's voice..."Breaking

news here on CNN concerning Joshua Siconolfi, the Seattle resident who allegedly murdered his

wife on a radio broadcast earlier this week. We go live to Andy Warn."

Andy Warn, an energetic young journalist with spiky hair, reports, "Just minutes ago Joshua was seen leaving his home, driving a red Lotus Elise. He was followed to where we are now—the Seattle Police Department's downtown precinct. And it appears he has just, seemingly of his own accord, walked inside. Maybe to turn himself in; we don't know. But what we can report is that Joshua is, as we speak, inside the station, talking with investigators. And a press conference with Captain Jerome Jackson is scheduled for eight o'clock."

Chapter Eighteen

Inside the interrogation room, Janice waits, nervously fidgeting with her skirt. It's bad enough she has to interview a psychopath, but she has to do it in front of a full audience—with all of her skeptical coworkers watching, judging from the opposite side of the two-way mirror.

"Relax, Janice; you're going to do fine," Cools announces over the speaker. "Just do what we've agreed to: let him control the interview; you just keep him talking."

She adjusts herself, finding a more comfortable position in the plastic chair, replying, "I'm okay; is he here?"

"Yes, he's coming in now; just stick to the plan," Cools says again over the speaker, before turning it off and asking the captain, "Are you sure she can do this?"

"Somewhat late for that now, don't you think?"

Then the door opens, and Joshua strolls in with a pleasant demeanor. Escorting him is an officer, who quickly vanishes, leaving the two all alone. Janice notices he's dressed casually in designer shorts and a silk dress shirt, as she offers a handshake. It's a greeting he arrogantly ignores.

Wearing a teasing smile, he takes a seat opposite the metal table from her, lays his keys and cell phone down, and flirtatiously asks, "Well?"

Although she was hoping it wasn't going to come up again, she knows exactly what he wants. Reluctantly she answers, "Red."

It's as though her answer pleases him. He leans over the table, repulsively admiring her shape. Janice finds it incongruous that such a good-looking man could give her such a chill. Pretending it doesn't faze her, she takes a quick breath and starts in. "You said, 'I think I did it.' You think you did what exactly?"

"What do you think I meant, Janice?" he replies impetuously.

"I don't know. That is why I am asking you, Joshua."

"You're telling me that you gave no thought at all as to what *it* meant?" he asks, his voice getting louder.

"Well, some, but—"

"Because *it* could mean many things, Janice—good or bad. *It* could mean 'I fathered a child,' or *it* could mean 'I got the job,' or *it* could mean 'I sliced my neighbors' dog's fucking throat because it barked all time'!" As he says this, he mimics the deed, fracturing any steadiness she may have had into shards of absolute panic. And her distress is not so much as to what he's said, rather more from the speed of his transformation, the instantaneous altering from relatively polite and cordial to pure savagery, his eyes even changing color, from sea-green to pure evil.

She doesn't respond, not sure of what is coming next. Neither of them moves a muscle. Their eyes remain locked as Janice secretly prays for the moment to end. Cools stands on alert behind the mirror. Then Joshua breaks the sharp silence and, in a more formal tone, states, "Or maybe *it* is how I wish for death."

Janice, not even sure that makes any sense, clears her throat and asks, "Do you...do you have a death wish?"

He carelessly examines his fingernails. "I am concerned more with *how* I die, rather than *when*. Can I ask you a question?"

"Sure," she replies, now with a wish of her own—that she could answer no.

"Well, hypothetically speaking, what if your situation is that you have to die, but you can choose the manner in which you do. What would you choose?"

Janice considers his query for a second, then replies, "I would like to go peacefully in my sleep."

He stares into her, his eyes once again evolving. They both know what is next; he will convey to her all his ill desires. He will enjoy the telling, and she will be sickened. Cools, Michelle, Captain Jackson, and the others stand behind the glass, powerless. Then it arrives. "I wish to slowly burn alive...somewhat painlessly though. I would love to watch the flames lick around my body, an orange blaze dancing and consuming me as I return as smoke to Ra, relieving my soul from the thing inside that hates me—being baptized in fire!"

"That's real nice, Joshua," she replies curtly, becoming increasingly impatient with his foolish madness. "Now what did you mean when you said, 'I think I did it'?" He doesn't answer, just gives her a long tainted smile, perversely searching her up and down. "Okay, if you cannot answer the question, maybe we can try another one. What was behind your motivation for calling the radio station last week?"

"Ha-ha. I was bored. And it was quite amusing, don't you think?"

"No, no, it wasn't, Joshua," she says, trying to let him know just how unamusing she believed it to be. Her apparent disapproval doesn't seem to affect him in the slightest.

Then teasingly he begins to school her on her interrogation tactics. "You are not supposed to oppose me Janice; remember what they taught you in cop class? The first part of any interrogation is to establish trust and form a bond between you and your interrogatee." Again his mood begins to swing into hostility as if every word he utters enrages him more. "You are to be in control of the situation while giving a false sense to the subject that they are in command."

"Maybe that is what I am doing."

But he disagrees; he evenly and abruptly rises to his feet, leaning over the table, over her and cries out, "No, I do not think so! I am in control!"

Everything freezes; Janice is imprisoned in her chair while Joshua stands, hovering, showing what is within him, drifting closer. Cools, behind the glass, has his gun drawn, envisioning a 9 mm round piercing the mirror, shattering the glass, penetrating Joshua's forehead, bringing an end to him. Touch her; I dare you! But no one moves. Cools's trigger finger tenses rigidly. And a long frightening calm before an apparent storm holds steadfastly as Joshua fearlessly clenches in his stance, everything hinging on what he does next.

Control is his.

Janice fights the tight grip paralyzing her and springs into an attack. "Okay, that's about it! Let's quit playing games; I want to know where Kimberly is."

Cools lowers his gun, saying, "It's about fucking time."

Joshua lets out a muffled laugh and sits back down, savoring his actions.

"Tell me where she is! What have you done with her?"

"Okay, Janice, we can play, but I can only enlighten you as to where she told me she was off to, which doesn't mean much; she was a lying whore, you know. She told me she was going to take the trip we've been planning for months now, but that she was going it alone."

"Trip to where?"

"To the mountains of Peru; the local priests there practice a ritual using an ancient brew, ayahuasca, that…well, when ingested, you can see and talk with Ra."

"A hallucinogen?" she asks, finally steadying her nerves.

"Yes."

"And who is Ra?"

"Ra is God!" he answers, without elaboration.

"So tell me, when was the last time you saw her then?"

"She left the day after I called the radio station."

"Are you certain it was the day after?" she asks, taking notes.

"Yes, Janice, and now I am all alone." He blatantly looks at her breasts.

Janice moves forward to hide herself behind the table. "Have you had any contact with her since she left?"

"No, I have not. And now I would like to ask you some questions. I only think it is fair, don't you?"

Janice doesn't want to begin playing his games again but hasn't any real choice. Her face shows hesitant agreement, and Joshua wastes no time.

"Do you have something inside that hates you? Kimberly did."

Michelle looks at Cools and says, "Here we freaking go again. Sick bastard!"

Janice feels her stomach acids begin to rise in her throat and suddenly decides she's done fooling around. "Actually, now that I think it over, I believe that *I* will be the only one asking questions from here on out!"

"Yeah, that's my girl," Michelle says.

"Now, Joshua, will you provide some proof to corroborate your story, like showing us the purchase order of your plane tickets to Peru?" Defiant of her newfound authority, he simply glares at her, mouthing the words *fuck you*. Janice loses her sensibilities and attacks, "Okay, maybe you *are* a coward. And how long has your wife Kimberly been having sex with Trace Friesen?"

"I'm fucking done here!" He then stands, smiling at her, and offers a final deal. "Janice, if you look into the mirror behind you and say exactly what I asked you to say on the phone, I will give *it* to you."

She hesitates for a moment then, out of desperation, fulfills her part of the deal. She turns, faces straight into the mirror, and says, "Detective Cools missed his chance." Joshua, standing behind her, also starring into the mirror, erupts into nasty laughter. Cools loses it and punches the glass, leaving no doubt he is there.

"Now it's your turn," she says.

He grins like a dirty boy, moves in close, and sits on the table in front of her. Then he holds out his phone and says, "Read this text message I sent to a friend as we were talking earlier." The screen displays the time and date showing that the message was sent at 2:37 p.m. today, the exact same time they were talking on the phone. It reads:

Red—her panties are red.

Joshua leaves the police station without any further comments. He strolls out into the cold dusk of winter, where he's bombarded by camera flashes and a slew of questions coming from the packed lower stairs.

"Do you know the whereabouts of Kimberly?"

"What did you tell the authorities?"

"Have you done something with Kimberly?"

Without answering, he merely turns, points accusingly back at the station, and yells, "Lies, lies, and more lies! They are all lost in a wilderness of lies and twisted truths!" The journalists ignore his allegations and continue their barrage.

"Where is Kimberly?"

"Do you know where Kimberly is?"

"Where's your wife?"

Repeated shouts and queries from the crowd agitate his mind. He attempts to escape, but there's nowhere to go.

"Where is Kimberly?"

"Where is your wife?"

"Did you kill her?"

He shouts, "I have nothing more to say!" He turns his back on them, considering retreating back inside the station.

"Where's Kimberly?"

"What have you done?"

"Is she alive?"

The senseless repetition enrages him. He abandons all plans of maintaining silence. He faces them, holding his hands high, then seethes into a maniacal rant, transforming into a depraved preacher. "Do you not see the world machine? It controls all! It controls you! You believe you are calculating its measures, but you are not. Everyone presumes someone else is steering, but you are all only along for the ride. You only imagine to be pulling the strings through your politics, the courts, corporations, sciences, religions, even your military, but you are no longer in command. The world machine is running the whole lot, and every judge's gavel is hollow, empty, and worthless. Its heavy shadow is cast upon you;

the machine is the *great beast*!" With that he swiftly descends the stairs and fights his way through the mob, disappearing into the night.

Inside the station Janice gets a bottle of water and convenes with everyone back in the war room. She looks exhausted but appears to be wearing an odd smirk on her face.

"We got nothing from that skinny prick!" Cools yells, tossing his phone onto the table.

"No, no, we did get something," Janice replies. "It was something he said." Everyone looks to her. "He said Kimberly *did* when he spoke of having something inside that hates. Also he said she *was* a whore, referring to her in the past tense, as if she were dead! Meaning psychologically, he believes her to be deceased."

Everyone's eyes move to Milkowski. "That's perceptive, and it'll play well in a courtroom—the entire interrogation will—but it will not get us a search or arrest warrant. He's smart; he knows full well what he's doing. He is playing with you, and I get the sense he's far from done."

His words deflate what little was left of the room's energy. The war room is emotionally drained. Captain Jackson sees as much and ends the day. "All right, I have a press conference to do, and it has been a long one. So go home or to your favorite watering hole—I don't care which. Just get some R & R, and we meet back here tomorrow morning."

Everyone leaves.

Chapter Nineteen

The day may have changed much but not everything: Cools, practicing habits of old, lounges at his table near the back of The Shelter in the company of a bottle of Jameson. There he sits, meditating on the alcohol swimming through the bottle and keeping a keen ear attuned to the nine o'clock news. He's just witnessed his captain for the first time giving a high-priority press conference. According to Cools's assessment, he did pretty well—dodging most questions, answering only the safe ones, using the typical routine rhetoric that leaves all the backdoors wide open. The waitress pops by for a split second to change his ashtray. She says nothing to him, just the way he likes it. Once she is gone, he lights another cigarette and watches the smoke climb from the tip, wondering again about the press conference, wondering if all the news is bullshit.

The next story expands upon Joshua's diatribe from the top of the police station's stairs, sounding like a prophetic lunatic. Cools pours another shot and settles deeper into his environment. Everything around him is in motion, yet comforting: cigarette smoke flirting with the air, the ceiling fan casting musical shadows, the brown liquid rippling in the bottle. All are set to drown away the day's events still playing in his mind. If Joshua killed his wife, why is he being so arrogant? Most guys in that position don't try to attract attention, even assholes like him. And why would Kimberly lie and tell her lover she has AIDS? How does their religion tie into it all? Maybe...maybe Joshua and Kimberly were blackmailing

Trace Friesen? But for what? Maybe Joshua is attempting to set up an insanity plea in case he's trapped? Maybe he killed her as some sacrifice to his cultic religion? No! Fuck! The only thing that makes sense is that he's a jealous husband who was screwed to tightly together to begin with. He discovers his wife's affair with Trace, falls over the edge of sanity, where he's been teetering most his life anyway, and kills his wife. But like a bad acid trip, he's permaspun, never to return to reality. Then in my stupidity, I afford him almost an entire week to cover his tracks, as if the sneaky bastard left any to begin with. And now I have to deal with this crazy fuck and somehow put him away, or even make him pay myself; and I will do it if I have to; I might do it because I want to. Because maybe the pathway for evil to rise is left open solely by good men who stand by and do nothing!

His phone rings disrupting his mental tirade. It's Michelle. "Hey, Brad, how're you?"

"I'm okay, and you?"

"I just can't get this guy out of my head," she says in a slurred voice.

"Yeah, I know; me, too," Cools replies, picturing her wet eyes.

There's a long silence. "Where are you, Brad?"

"The Shelter."

"Just wastin' away in that dirty old bar…Why?"

Somewhat offended, he doesn't reply. Then, in a more concerned voice, she says, "And I'm worried lately about you too, Brad; you've been a little off." There's a pause. "How's your love life going, Brad?"

"Ah…wouldn't you like to know?"

"Ha-ha…your knowing I do."

Cools laughs a little, thinking how she always cheers him up. They've been partners now for some years and have been attracted to each other from the very beginning. But they also share a kind of brother-sister bond, and so far the sibling side of their relationship has ruled king.

"Chelsea—is that her name—yer flavor of the…month?"

"No, it's not like that; I really truly care for her. She's my one and only baby-girl," he replies, defending her insinuation that he's some sort of philanderer.

"So…is she treating you good, Brad?" she asks, with a hint of envy.

"Well, not as good as you would," he replies, teasing. "But we're doing all right. Actually—you know what—I think I'll give her a call right now. She always gets me out of my head."

There's another awkward pause. "Okay, partner, but don't stay up too late. We have a freak to get off…offa the streets tomorrow."

"Yeah, no kidding. I'll see you in the morning. Get some sleep, okay."

"Okay…okay, I mean, take care of yourself, and your little self," she says, and giggles before hanging up.

Swallowing another drink Cools dials Chelsea, visualizing her inside the clear part of his cloud as the phone rings—a gorgeous Italian with auburn hair, dark olive skin, and brown jewels for eyes. The sexiest eyes he's ever gazed into. When they are close, her smell is that of wildflowers, although Cools considers her greatest feature to be her naturally full lips. Sometimes it pains him to admit it, but her lips are also full of wisdom and good, common sensibilities. She is a rare true spirit and a constant optimist, who loves life and always bestows her refreshing purity upon those around her. Chelsea Simmons is not just the best thing to ever happen to him, she is the best thing that could ever happen to any man.

She answers in a deep husky voice, "Hello." He immediately gets the joke and asks for Chelsea anyway. Again, using the same voice, she replies, "Not now, she's resting. I guess she has some jerk for a boyfriend, some cop who doesn't pay enough attention to her, so she needed me to come over to keep her company. I'm her very good-looking, twenty-year-old coworker."

"Okay, baby, I'm sorry, and I miss you much. And you're right, so how about you let me make it up to you. I can pick up some Chinese, and we can have a late dinner at your place," he pleads.

"Ah, does that work with the other girls?"

"No other girls, baby, only you."

"Okay, but I'm locking my door at ten," she says and hangs up.

At 9:56 Cools catches his breath at the top of the stairs and knocks on her door. Chelsea answers, wearing only sassy panties and an expensive dress shirt—the one he left there on their first real date. The way it cuddles her breasts, he's never asked for it back. She steps back, giving him room to enter, with fire in her eyes. It is clear she has been dying for their rendezvous.

Ms. Simmons has only been with a handful of guys in her life, a few in high school, and then she married. Her husband was a gentle lover, which was good, though she'd longed to be taken passionately the way she'd seen in movies and read of in books. But she was always too insecure to divulge those secrets. It wasn't until she'd divorced and met Cools that true pleasure and sexual ecstasy entered her life. Never did anything have to be said, since he was somewhat of a ravisher from the very beginning—all that built-up aggression, she assumes. And tonight Cools displays the aggression of a bull.

He pulls her hard into his barreled chest, squeezing, touching. She wiggles playfully, attempting to break his grasp. He loosens, allowing her to break free, only to chase galloping naked legs down the hall. Soon he is recapturing and spinning her around in the hallway, diving lips-first into her sweet skin. She tears at his slacks, whimpering, "You can do anything you want." Wasting no time, and with little gentleness, he turns her away, forcing her quivering body up against the wall. "Oh, Detective," she groans, rubbing her round ass against him. His hand slips inside the back of black panties. She arches. The sounds of stitches ripping excite her more. Daringly his bulky fingers enter the awaiting wetness. She circles her hips riding his fingers, gingerly at first. Oh, I am going to fuck you! he says. With his free hand, he grabs a fistful of thick hair, reeling her head back to him, thrusting his fingers deeper. She turns, murmuring naughtiness, kissing feverishly, licking his tongue the way she now wants to lick him elsewhere. She spins, rips her shirt open, flashing bare breasts, now throwing her slave against the wall, taking control. Writhing all over, kissing, panting, and groping, she begs, "I want you to make me do it!" It doesn't take long to get what she wants. With both hands he pushes her down. "God, I love you," she moans, massaging him with her full lips, accepting him fully, purring. She is pleased to do it. She begins touching herself. He presses harder, and the more unrestrainedly he shoves, the faster she excites herself, inserting her fingers. Again he grabs a handful of thick hair, drawing her up, controlling her; they meet tongue to tongue.

"You're going to get it so hard!"

"Oh yeah! I don't think you can," she replies, with a silly laugh, somewhat embarrassed by her own words.

With that, he again pushes her into the wall and slides deep into her from behind, thrusting vigorously and further with each stroke, smashing her hardened nipples against the wall, holding out laboriously as long as possible until her body begins to shudder; her sounds become deafening, more salacious, oozing her love all over him. "I'm going to come," he announces, then wildly loses himself inside her. Together they hold tight, remaining locked, throbbing intensely, catching their breath.

Then Chelsea grabs his hand, leading her lover through the bedroom door, to her bed. There she takes care of him further, draining completely. The night is spent embracing, caressing each other romantically, and nourishing all of their erotic and sexual desires.

For Cools it is the greatest love-making night in memory, and immensely needed. The beautiful woman who sleeps contented in his arms holds the power to draw him out of himself and the ugly world in which he lives. She is his promise, his hope, his trust—Chelsea is his love.

Chapter Twenty

On the other side of the rainy city, Joshua lounges alone on his couch, enjoying an evening of laughter and drinking inside his dimly lit home, the only luminescence coming from the television and stereo equipment cascading shades of color onto the darkness. A bottle of scotch and ice stands tall on a glass coffee table positioned in front of him, and the liquor has already taken an effect on him, leaving his body warm and comforted.

He smiles into the shadowy room with pride glimmering through his eyes, enough so to almost to give an extra glow to the room. In his hands he clutches a blued-steel M4 assault rifle that's equipped with a fully loaded magazine, flash suppressor, night vision scope, and nine-inch silencer. Somewhat excessive for normal, everyday home protection, it feels common in his hands, making sense in his altered state.

He aims the weapon toward the flat-screen, pretending to fire upon the commentators who criticize him. Cursing, disputing, he yells, "To hell's fire with you, you fat piece of shit! Fuck you, you whore; you know nothing of my means!"

Every word uttered against him exasperates him further. Still he watches intently, fixated on their deficient analysis and sometimes demonizing criticisms. If they only knew the truth! Then, turning down the sound, he lies back to reflect on his day, cherishing the occasion at the police station, believing he's made no mistakes. His mind revisits the jewel of his evening: the image of Janice looking into the mirror, reciting her lines to Detective Cools. To the night, he smirks, savoring the moment that has been absolute since its very beginning. A contrived, seamless plot of deception that he's confident he will not suffer for. Clearly, Your Honor, my client is insane. He requires intense rehabilitation and professional therapy. Ha-ha, if I even get caught. They'll never prove a thing. Confidence encompasses him. He has given an adept performance, which is surely leading them astray. And with much more impending, he will gain all that is warranted.

A chill sets through him that he accredits to the cold steel of his weapon. He sets it aside, transferring his gaze toward the far wall. There, above his collection of guitars, his eyes fall on a portrait of Kimberly, or Kimmy, as he calls her. I forgive you, my love, for all you have done. He stares into her, remembering the morning the photo was taken.

She'd abruptly awakened him as a result of a telemarketing call from a compelling salesman, peddling glamour shots. Animated and eager to participate, she enlisted him, exercising her little voice of innocence, stating, "I've been in the mirror for seventeen minutes; my skin is radiating. I'm absolutely beautiful. My essence is balanced in every way." After, she promised many sexual favors, tokens of her forthcoming appreciation. Though they were manipulation tactics needlessly offered, since Joshua would've given her anything she'd asked for.

Lying on his bed, he caressed her, attempting to calm her excitement. He loved her more than existence itself. And adding to her contentment was the reason for his being, truly his life's pleasure. "Then we should go immediately," he exclaimed, granting her wish. She fluttered with exhilaration, kissed him thank you on the forehead, then sprang to her feet and began dancing down the hallway like a dove. Joshua presumed he would be with her forever, laughing, loving, and resting, in the absence of deceit and lies, throughout all afterlife.

Even in life Joshua had only lied to her once. The secret he withheld from her was that their marriage could only be in union with their god, and not with the state of Washington, because of his belief that an official marriage was taboo due to its origins in Judaic law. So he'd performed somewhat of a magician's trick. Upon his decision, they'd filed for their marriage licenses online. Then he romanticized the idea of having a private ceremony in their home, with no witnesses except for their god, Ra—a secret wedding with a real ring, a real wedding dress, and true love, all performed under the veil of fake papers and a paid actor playing the role of the pagan priest. Kimberly never had a fleeting notion of the truth.

An incoming e-mail chimes, breaking his trance. He retrieves a wireless keyboard from under the table and types in a few keys, pulling it up on his television screen. He doesn't recognize the one just coming in but opens it curiously. It doesn't take long to discover it's from a motivated reporter who's obtained his private e-mail address to grovel for an interview. Joshua clicks reply, snickering to himself as he types in, "One Million Dollars—non-negotiable, one-time offer," and clicks send. Then he notices an unread piece of mail from his psychiatrist. There's no need to open it since he already knows its contents; it's a final plea to restart his medications, which he quit taking three weeks ago. Joshua values his doctor's opinion, except for his contradicting analysis that his illness is an asset, a reward. Again he rests back into the cushions, this time closing his eyes, contemplating last night's dream.

All his life he's privately suffered from an affliction, or has benefited from a gift, depending on how one looks at it—something he surmises as *sequential dreaming*. It's a rare disorder that he alone seems to have—one that has been with him from as early as he can remember, one that serves as another reminder of his uniqueness. But it has come at a cost—he's never been able to reveal his condition to anyone, not even Kimberly. His lifelong psychiatrist only learned of it while administering hypnosis therapy to Joshua as an adolescent when he'd discovered that although his patient quite often experienced normal dreaming, like the rest of society, he mostly dreamed in chronological order. Each night is a direct continuation of the previous—full and complete narratives, some lasting for years.

As of late his mind has created a fresh new beginning, one that has a character with whom he senses a connection. He transcends into a state of neither sleep nor consciousness, the realm of previsioning. There he begins.

It is a tale of a cute little boy named Frankie Johnson. The scenes are filled with cars, clothes, and buildings that appears to be from somewhere around the nineteen sixties—even the language seems to be of that time. Little Frankie is a nine-year-old only child with long, blond hair and bright, hazel eyes. Somehow, the dream implies that little Frankie only has his mother. Her name is Betty, a pretty young woman who works as a waitress at Chuck's Diner & Bar. It's the local watering hole in a small town outside Birmingham, Alabama—the only place to be on a Saturday night, where they drink heavily, dance, and play country music till dawn.

Now, Betty loves her son and looks forward to time spent with him. But her current life is crowded by the constant struggle from day to day getting little Frankie off to school, making it to work on time, and keeping a healthy supply of men, cigarettes, and booze around. Never does she consider her parenting skills as compromised; she simply travels along the only way she knows how. And little Frankie never complains. He enjoys the excitement from the frequent parties, his many daddies, sometimes even sipping from ignored and forgotten bottles.

They live together in a small house, jam-packed with second-hand furniture, surrounded by pictures of movie stars and rock legends on dark brown, paneled walls. In little Frankie's mind, it is a perfectly normal life. He finds nothing whatsoever wrong with the excessive drinking, the smoking of the imported cigarettes with the strange smell, or his mother's explicit flirtations with men. Essentially, he doesn't know any other life. And his mother, although sometimes stressed and overwhelmed, is also seemingly content within the lifestyle she has created. Together they take pleasure in the latest Beatles *albums and the new color televisions, frequently using phrases like "that's cool, man," "groovy," and "far out."*

Frankie has gotten his blond hair from Betty, except hers is long and, this week, dyed light brown. She has dark blue eyes not far above bouncy breasts she commonly flaunts in shirts two sizes too small. The rest of her wardrobe consists of many tight shorts, fishnet stockings, and tall boots. She receives much attention from the daddies, including motorcycle rides, jewelry, toys for little Frankie, and even sometimes one of them will turn the electricity back on.

One Saturday while entertaining in the backyard with a keg of beer and a game of volleyball, in her pink two-piece, Betty is called to the phone. She shakes her way inside to learn her manager from Chuck's Diner is on the other end. She is asked about her current availability in a way that says "come into work and cover this shift or pick up your check at the end of the week." So, reluctantly, she complies, giving up a long night of sex and drugs. She says her good-byes by giving all the men long hugs and leaves her newest guy, Robert, who goes by the nickname Panama-Red, in charge of little Frankie. Then off she goes in such a hurry she forgets to kiss little Frankie. He's too young to know if he's disappointed or if it's understandable. At the moment, that is of little concern compared to his worry about being alone with Panama-Red. He doesn't trust him. And he, being more alert than his mother most of the time, realizes her attraction to him has much to do with his new, black 1963 Corvette. Because of the sporty car, she's overlooked some of his strangeness. Little Frankie is too young to know what the word "leery" means, but if he did, this is how he would describe his feelings toward Panama-Red.

This is as much of the dream story that has been given to Joshua. But he wants more; he needs more. So lying on the couch, he drifts into awaited slumber, glimpsing his last flashes of awareness, hoping little Frankie gets to see his mother again, hoping they don't find out where he put Kimberly.

Chapter Twenty-One

The cell phone alarm goes off with a muffled jingle. Cools awakens abruptly, but refreshed. Although procuring little sleep, he has slept well, rejuvenating his body and spirit. And wanting to be respectful, he slips gently out of Chelsea's silk sheets without stirring her. His feet glide across the hardwood floors to a patch of sunlight that shines through a curtained window. He prefers waking here, as her bedroom is wholesome—dressed in colors of whites and pinks, all adding to one's ease of mind. A vanity table and stool rest in a corner, arranged with lotions and scented oils that, in various combinations, comprise her smell. He smiles as he pictures his baby-girl sitting there pampering her skin. Carefully he cracks open the window; a fresh breeze softly ripples its light curtains, and in a rare moment, he leisurely inhales the crisp morning air. It all brings him serenity and purpose as he quietly watches over her, protecting her peaceful slumber.

After a time he wipes the crud from his eyes, then silently makes his way to the bathroom, reminiscing over the night before. All of it was miraculous: the hallway, their late dinner, making love deep into the night, then falling asleep intertwined around each other. The remembrance of the easy, accepting romance leaves him wanting of more; however, since nothing could reach the pinnacle of the preceding hours of darkness, he considers it best not to spoil the memory.

In the quaint mirror, he finds an undeniable youth in his eyes, and he cannot remember feeling better. He washes up and flashes himself a satisfied grin before softly stepping back to Chelsea's bedside. There he watches her rest. She is lying on her side, breathing steadily, with the covers only partially covering her legs. Cools gently brushes aside a few strands of her reddish-brown hair, exposing her natural beauty. She is such an Italian treasure. Why am I willing to leave this, only to step back into a sick, twisted world? He leans closer, stealing one more soft kiss.

She responds with "Mmm…" She squeezes her pillow but doesn't wake.

Suddenly he has an epiphany, and he knows why he has to return to his unforgiving world. It is to protect angels like her. The world is in need of men like him—real men that can get things done, who bring balance to good and evil, no matter the costs, and then willingly accept its price, only to remedy themselves later, first by acquiring a sanctuary to repair their wounds, a place to mend the mind's justifications by way of drowning inside a lover's arms. Cools leaves, sensing his importance, presuming that, with his cunning, motivated courage, and refuge for escape, he can do just about anything.

Nothing is beyond my reach.

Not long after, Cools, on the freeway, traveling to the station, makes a call to Officer Poulet. "Good morning, racecar driver."

"Yeah, you heard about that, did you?" Poulet laughs.

"Of course, I know most things. And I heard it's not the size of the car, but the skill of the driver that makes 'em come." He chuckles.

"Something like that," Poulet replies, prior to updating him on what's new. "I guess you want to know what's going on. Well, all I can tell you is that things are somewhat slower today, except that I'm no longer sitting alone outside Joshua's residence; I'm in a field of goddamned news vans."

"Any movement last night?"

"No, nothing…nothing at all," he replies, sounding disappointed.

"Okay, I have to go. But first, listen up. If he comes out to check the mail, I want to know about it, okay?"

"Gotcha covered, Detective."

Cools glances away from the morning commute, pushes end, scrolls to Milkowski, and pushes send while moving to the beat of a Bob Seger song playing on his CD. Today his body is teeming with energy as he carries with him a level of confidence typically only found in motivational speakers.

"Milkowski, Cools here; are we moving anything yet?"

"Yes, I think we may have something." His answer catches Cools off guard; given that he's been so used to getting nothing from him in this case, a simple yes wasn't anticipated. Milkowski goes on. "I'm getting a warrant for all data records—financial, Internet usage, communications, the whole lot—signed by Judge Cooper this morning."

"How'd you do that?"

"Well," Milkowski replies proudly, "I found a statute related to Homeland Security that gives us the right to monitor any suspected terrorist or—and get this—any possible threats to the welfare of citizens through unorthodox religious practices. The worshippers of Ra believe in sacrifice of life, and with a few distorted truths about Joshua's faith, I was able to convince Judge Cooper that he is an imminent threat to the community."

"Get the fuck out!" Cools yells, impressed. Milkowski, not knowing how to respond, remains silent. "Okay, good news! It's always great to start the day out like this."

Milkowski, surprised by the detective's cheerfulness, adds, "Statistically we are sure to unearth some level of dirt from the records that will advance investigations into other areas; we may even get a full search warrant for any and all properties or possibly an arrest."

"Great fucking news, Milkowski; we're on our way! Can you feel it?"

Milkowski, not really wishing to be chummy, answers with a short yes.

"Okay, I'll be there in twenty minutes." He snaps his phone shut to the beat of the music, then turns it up and rolls down the window, letting in an icy wind. The cold air stings his face, and the music vibrates his senses further. The stereo now plays "Last Kiss" by Pearl Jam, one of Chelsea's favorites, as he buzzes through traffic, drumming the steering wheel. He waits until the song ends then calls Captain Jackson. "Good morning, Captain."

It doesn't take long to figure out Captain Jackson doesn't share his effervescent frame of mind. "Cools, did you catch the fucking news?" he yells.

"No...no, not yet."

"All the networks are reporting that sources have leaked possible evidence that Joshua was at the Friesen residence the morning of the apparent suicide!"

Cools pulls into the right-hand lane, reducing his speed. "Is there any evidence to that?"

"None whatsoever! As far as I'm told, from Detective Shoemaker in Tacoma, there's no reason at all to believe it's not a suicide."

"Fucking lying ass reporters! If they don't have it, they make it up," he shouts, back to his usual self. "Anything else?"

"All right and there's this: it's also being reported that we've been investigating Joshua as the *only* possible suspect in the mysterious vanishing of his high school sweetheart." The captain continues, louder, "The fucking news media is making us look like assholes!"

"It's Renny, Captain. I set him up with that yesterday, looking for our leak. It's that fat piece of shit, Renny!"

There's a pause. Cools can hear him thinking. Then he detects a seldom heard sense of urgency in Jackson's voice. "All right, I'll take care of Renny. And I want you to think about this, old buddy: just between you and me, maybe we need to start stretching some truths ourselves. I'm really under the microscope here, and it doesn't play well that I basically said nothing in last night's press conference. I need to have something, anything—anything at all—I can arrest him for. I need him off the streets and away from these fucking reporters!"

"Okay, Captain, tell you what…I'll get something on him, and if I can't, then *I'll get something* on him," he replies, comforting his friend.

"Just play it safe, old buddy. But seriously, think about what I need. I'm getting another call; we'll catch up later."

Cools steers off of the interstate and parks on the shoulder. There he begins scheming Joshua's demise. He lights a cigarette, running through possible scenarios. And soon the cruiser is burning back into traffic.

Later that morning, he receives his second call from Michelle. He ignored the first one, and now he answers sounding annoyed. "Talk to me, partner."

"We just got the warrants; the geeks are taking over," she exclaims.

"Good, that's real good."

"Where are you?" she asks, hearing rustling in the background.

He hesitates. "Uh…I'm going over the Amberly video, trying to see what else I can get out of it. Can I call you back?"

"Sure, but first I want to—"

Click.

He feels bad about lying to his partner, but he cannot involve her in what he is about to do. He digs through some more boxes until he finds what he's looking for, one that reads, 'WA State vs. Santorini, Lucrezia—Evidence.' Applying a razor blade, he carefully cuts the 'Restricted—Do Not Open' tape and opens the box. He stares inside for a second and then looks around, making doubly sure he's alone—and alone he is, with twenty kilos of pure cocaine beside some other evidence. He reaches into his pocket and pulls out a pair of rubber gloves, then retrieves one of the packages and a cell phone still holding a faint charge.

It all fits nicely under his arm, and with his jacket covering the package, he files the box back to its original place and sneaks out of the evidence locker. Only three men have a clue of his whereabouts: himself, Captain Jackson, and Officer Malone, the evidence room officer, who received a strange call earlier from Captain Jackson instructing him to grant full access to Cools. All in all it has been a good morning for Officer Malone: not only did he get to smash that surveillance camera always watching his every move, but he is now four hundred dollars richer.

Chapter Twenty-Two

Just after noon, Captain Jackson lights up the phones. Forty minutes later most of his team has convened in the war room. Michelle sits next to Cools. She gets the sense that her partner is up to something. For the last half hour or so, he's been avoiding any real eye contact and seems to be completely absorbed in thought. She stares at him through her big, blue eyes, trying to figure him out, but he doesn't even seem to notice she's there. He's staring off into space, with a little blood vessel pulsing on his forehead, the one she sees quite often when he is about to explode. He's going to die young, she concludes, while fussing around in her chair, vying for his attention.

Suddenly he adjusts, jerks a notepad and pen out of his pocket, and begins scribbling. Michelle tries to peep, but Captain Jackson deflects her attention, posing a question.

"Robertson, did you see Officer Renny this morning?"

"No, I didn't, but I heard about it," she replies absentmindedly.

"Yeah, well after I confronted him, then suspended his fat-ass, he left here screaming. 'I've done nothing wrong! I've done absolutely nothing; I swear to God, I didn't do it!' And on and on."

"That's what I heard," she replies, trying to cut their chat short and sneak a peek at her partner's notes. But it is too late; he's already secured the notepad back into his suit pocket.

"What's that?" she asks, with obvious interest.

"Nothing." She squints her eyes. "Oh, I mean, it's nothing…uh…I'll talk to you about it later." Again he looks away.

She doesn't press any further, deciding to leave it alone for the time being.

Just then Milkowski walks in. Captain Jackson stands, presenting an air of hopefulness, and waves his hand to the department's computer analyst. "All right, let's hear what you got."

He's a young, skinny man—the one they call Ghost—all junked-up on energy drinks. "Well, we have a few things here," he nervously replies, thumbing through his papers. Ghost gets his nickname from his pale white skin, pale due to the fact he hasn't left his computer to venture outside since he was fifteen. But if you asked him, he would claim it originated from his uncanny ability to retrieve information from the Internet. In jittery diction, he continues, "Okay, let's start with his finances. He had some money left to him by his grandfather, Earle Siconolfi, a Freemason, who made a fortune after World War Two selling vacuum cleaners. Earle Siconolfi was a pioneer, operating one of the first full-scale door-to-door businesses." Everyone quickly grabs for their pens; he speaks so fast they can barely keep up. "And in the seventies, he was one of the largest distributors of vacuum cleaners in the US. He died in 2004, leaving a substantial amount of money to his only grandson—Joshua."

"How much?" asks Michelle.

"Nearly four million, but it looks like he's already burned through most of it—all but about a hundred and sixty thousand. And for some reason, he's been withdrawing ten thousand a week in cash for the last ten weeks. And get this—he took out an eight-million-dollar life insurance policy on Kimberly just eleven months ago, with a special clause: if she is murdered, it pays double."

"That doesn't make any sense," Cools yells out. "He would never get it if he kills her himself."

Ghost shakes his head. "Yeah, I don't know; it doesn't really fit. But anyway there's a lot more I think you can use. I cannot find any tickets purchased for Kimberly Siconolfi—or Kimberly Sharons, her maiden name—bound for Peru or for anywhere for that matter, and if there was one, I would have found it," he announces arrogantly.

Michelle rolls eyes at Captain Jackson. The captain just grins and motions her attention back to Ghost's apparent genius.

"Now for the real goods: his credit card purchases on the twenty-sixth, just three days prior to Kimberly going missing." Everyone takes notes. "Sixty-eight hundred was charged to the Seattle Yacht Mariner for a one week's rental of a '41

Riviera FB. Eleven hundred for gas purchased the same day. Then an odd purchase from Danny's Boat World: a steel cage crab trap. I say 'odd,' because crab season does not open for two more months. I researched it on the Washington State Fish and Wildlife website." He briefly glances to them for admiration and then moves ahead. "Also the same day, a purchase from Wal-Mart: one thousand feet of half-inch nylon rope, one hundred feet of quarter-inch rope, a complete set of gym weights, and a Pepsi—diet."

Cools interjects, "That son of a bitch took her out, killed her, put her in the fucking crab cage, weighted in down with the weights, and dumped it into the Puget Sound." Everyone nods in unison before turning to Milkowski.

He exhales slowly, ignoring them all, staring at the pen he's twirling in his hand. "I can take this to Judge Cooper, and I already know what she will say: put a team of forensics on the boat, a team in the water, and then get back to me."

Cools turns back to Ghost and says, "Seattle Yacht Mariner?"

"Yes," he replies, proudly nodding like he's just single-handedly solved the case.

Cools ignores the young man's expectation of being venerated and looks to Michelle, saying, "Sounds like we have a boat to take apart."

Thirty minutes away (and twenty-four minutes later), Cools and Michelle pull into the parking lot of the Seattle Yacht Mariner. Michelle, in between phone calls and holding on for her life, found some time to ask her partner a few questions, but to no avail. They park close to the entrance, and since Michelle has already called ahead, D. J. Adders, the manager, is waiting for them, as he said he would be. He's a heavy but good-looking guy sporting short sandy hair and a goatee. They exit the car and introduce themselves promptly. "Good afternoon, I'm Detective Robertson, the one you talked to on the phone, and this is my partner, Detective Brad Cools."

"Very nice to meet the both of you," D. J. replies in a warm and friendly approach, shaking their hands. The three of them all wear sunglasses given that it's an unusually sunshiny winter day.

"Can we see the boat?" Cools asks impatiently.

"Yes, follow me, if you will; and allow me to inquire: did he do it?"

"Uh…I cannot comment on that at this time," he answers, exercising restraint.

"Well, I have followed this saga quite closely in the news and am hoping to be of assistance," D.J. says, appearing somewhat offended by Cools's response.

"Also there's something you should know; he has done a fair amount of damage to the railing of the Riviera."

Cools's ears perk up. "What kind of damage?"

For a brief moment, D. J. grows a bit standoffish as they round the outside corner of the showroom where the marina comes into view. "Well, let me show you," he replies, pointing toward the ramp that leads down into a sea of luxurious yachts, all of which are parked side by side a hundred yards into the sound, extending a mile up its curved coast.

Michelle is immediately impressed. "Wow, now this is amazing! I guess I wasn't expecting all this."

Her admiration pleases D. J., and he informs her further, "This is home to over seven billion dollars of nautical craftsmanship, owned by the likes of Paul Allen, Elton John, Ichiro, and actress Salma Hayek."

"Wow" is the only response she can muster, as he swipes his security card and types in a code on a keypad. The gate buzzes.

Then Cools, not as nearly impressed, asks bluntly, "Did you meet with him to arrange the rental?"

"Yes, I did indeed," D. J. replies spiritedly and somewhat proud to have shared the presence of someone so infamous.

"What was his demeanor?" asks Michelle.

"He was quite pleasant. I was certainly astounded to hear of his exploits later."

"Did he mention what he intended to use the boat for?"

Suddenly D. J. stops cold in his tracks, looks her keenly in the eye, and replies, "Joshua divulged his intent was to—and I quote—'return his wife to the sea.' When he said this, of course I didn't intrude further into the matter; I merely ascertained his wife had somehow succumbed to her death, leaving him a widower, and he was arranging to scatter her ashes to the deep. It is not that uncommon, so I did not surmise a great deal more of until...well, until a few days later when I heard his name again on the news."

Michelle echoes his statement. "He said he was returning his wife to the sea?"

"Yes, those were his words, precisely."

There's a short silence, and then they continue as they near the end of the dock. Cools makes a note while following alongside and asks, "Did you ever see him with anyone else?"

"No, and I never saw him again after that day we signed the papers. We gave him the keys to enter the marina, and our records reveal that he sailed out late that night and returned in the early morning."

"Do you have video surveillance of the marina?"

"Absolutely, and every time a code key is used, it activates our lighting systems. And here she is," D. J. says, presenting the Riviera. Michelle and Cools give it a good look. It is pearl white with a tinted window flybridge dressed in stainless steel lock downs, mounted lights, and railings. And from their position, they can also see the interior of the cabin; it's complete with a stereo system and a wood-trimmed liquor cabinet. Immediately thoughts of taking it out for a sail with her husband and select group of friends enter Michelle's daydreaming mind. She is the first to board the craft, with a little help from D. J., with Cools following close behind. Once aboard she leads them straight to the bow of the vessel to assess the damaged railing. D. J. steps between them and demonstrates his claim by jostling the rail back and forth. It's obviously loose and broken.

"And you're positive this damage was not done before?" Cools asks.

"Yes, I am quite certain of it; every one of our yachts is thoroughly inspected on a routine bases."

Michelle pulls out a camera and begins taking pictures while D. J. begins his assessment of what he believes to have happened. "You can clearly see the base is wrecked here," he says, pointing to the main structure of the yacht that supports the rail posts. "This is where a fairly cumbersome article was thrown overboard."

"How're you so sure it wasn't broken from something being pulled in?" Cools asks.

"Do I detect some questionable skepticism, Detective?" D. J. replies playfully. He smiles then mounts a demonstration by pressing outward on the rail. Cools follows him, observing the cracks made in the fiberglass. The fractures on the inside of the rail are only a few elongated lines, while the cracks around the outer rail are crushed like puzzle pieces. "This is exactly what we discover when damage occurs by throwing an object overboard, Detective."

"Maybe someone simply fell into it?"

"Then explain this to me," D. J. replies, waving him nearer. All three of them lean in for a closer inspection. He is now pointing to the top of the railing, where they can clearly distinguish two heavily scraped areas approximately three or four feet apart.

Michelle then takes a more accurate measurement of the distance between the two markings, by using her arm as a guide, judging the expanse to be approximately three and a half feet. Immediately she gets on the phone and calls Ghost. "What were the dimensions of the crab trap purchased?"

At first she only hears the clicking of his keyboard; then he replies, "Two by three and a half by three and a half."

"Thank you."

Excitedly D. J. blurts out, "Have you established he used our Riviera to dispose of the body?"

Cools sharply states, "We're just investigating any and all leads, and that is all we need from you for now. I would like you to leave my partner and me alone, and thank you for your cooperation."

D. J. replies, disappointed, "Well, then I must be on my way."

Once he's out of earshot, Michelle reiterates, "These abrasions here are three and a half feet apart, same as the crab pot."

"Yeah, I heard, and look at this." He pushes the railing out again, this time further allowing the bright sunlight to shine inside.

Michelle observes it more closely. "Looks like blood!"

"Now we're getting somewhere," Cools says victoriously. "Okay, I need you to call in forensics; they should be able to get us some answers by this evening. And if it's whose blood we think it is, then we got him—we fucking got him!"

Chapter Twenty-Three

After making the call and being informed it will take the better part of an hour for a forensics team to arrive, Cools and Michelle speak additionally with D. J. Thanks in part to his unrelenting desire to be involved, they quickly retrieve the videotape showing Joshua sailing out alone, carrying a crab trap and two large bags filled with what could be anybody's guess, only to return hours later empty-handed.

It seems to be case closed, but it feels like something else.

Cools and Michelle order some takeout and travel to a spot overlooking Puget Sound—a place Cools visited as a child while spending part of a summer vacationing at his aunt's house. It's a rare jewel of a little park that sits atop a knoll alongside the glistening bay in a hard-to-find location. It is a journey just to get there, through a labyrinth of twisting turns along a scenic route. But upon arrival Michelle sees that bad access is the spot's only burden. At first sight she falls in love with rolling green lawns surrounded by old Madrone trees, which grip the rocky outcrops, and dry bluffs that open to a view of sailboats in the pristine waters below—all nestled within sight of the majestic snow-packed peaks of MT. Rainier.

Cools secures a prized bench at the headmost perimeter by simply waving his badge at the two young lovers occupying it. They slip away without incident, leaving the detectives alone, providing them some peace and an opportunity for Michelle to meddle. She sits on her side of a wooden picnic table, eating and appreciating the beauty, while he divulges the park's secrets. He tells how he and his cousins played soldiers and threw rocks over the bank, waiting, listening for them to splash into the water, and daring each other to stand closer to its edge.

Michelle listens until she cannot take it anymore. "Brad," she says, gaining his attention, "what ideas do you have bouncing around in that big head of yours?" He doesn't move, but in his eyes she can see his thoughts traverse, leaving his boyhood remembrances as more serious lines appear in his face. She presses further. "I know you have some theories that you're keeping to yourself about what's going on, and I want to hear them. Talk to me, Brad."

"Okay, okay, I'll tell you, but don't interrupt me; just let me speak."

"When do I ever interrupt you, Brad?"

He sighs, ignoring her question. "I'm thinking maybe Joshua and Amberly have more of a thing than meets the eye." Michelle begins to respond, but he holds up his silencing finger. "Think about it for a second. What do we have? We have a missing wife, which was only brought to our attention by Joshua's radio call and a surprising visit from Amberly. What if Joshua is playing her, taking advantage of a naive drug-addict? He's definitely craftier than her, and maybe—just maybe—he's planned to rid himself of a cheating wife and collect the much-needed insurance money by seducing little Amberly and framing her for Kimberly's death."

"But everything points to him."

"Yeah, it does *now*, but explain to me the nagging feeling that this is far from over, a sense that I know you share—that we're closer to the beginning of this than the end."

She remains silent; a silence he swiftly takes advantage of. "Consider this: maybe Amberly was sent because we missed something at first. Something we weren't supposed to miss."

"Missed what, Brad? What could we have missed?"

"I don't know, but something. For all we know, Amberly could've killed her, and Joshua was only hiding the evidence."

"But he cannot collect the insurance money if she's never found."

"Maybe he intends for us to find her. It's all a little convenient, don't you think—that he made all those purchases using his *personal* credit card. Seriously who's stupid enough to rent a boat and buy rope and weights and crab traps? Think about it. It's almost as obvious as a shovel and duct tape."

Adding to his line of thought, she says, "Maybe he called the radio station in a scheming attempt to put the spotlight on himself for the moment, knowing that we would investigate a path leading to Amberly."

"That's exactly what I'm saying. And I suggest we spend some more time with Little Miss Innocence—there's more she knows."

Michelle agrees, and in less than forty minutes, they're parked outside the Terra Villa Apartments in Everett—Amberly's residence. Cools unlatches the gate and enters the complex, holding the small notebook that shows her address—ending in Apt. 9. Moving along they can hear a small dog barking in the distance and see a woman standing on her balcony smoking a cigarette. Soon they find their way around the back to a partially open door with a number nine above the trim. As they step closer, they hear the distinct sounds of a vacuum cleaner. He pushes the door wide, and he and Michelle walk into an apartment devoid of all furnishings.

"Hey! Hey!" he yells to the older Hispanic woman doing the cleaning. She turns off the machine, but soon they learn she doesn't speak any English. Then they quickly locate the manager, who tells them that Amberly packed up in a rush and moved out earlier this morning. Next Michelle calls the Kitty Club, only to be informed that she has picked up her things, along with her final paycheck, three hours ago. They call her phone, but it's been disconnected. They now realize how little they know about her and fear she's gone, perhaps indefinitely.

Back inside the car, heading again toward the Seattle Yacht Mariner, Michelle puts out a call to Officer Jakew—the young officer conducting investigations at the Kitty Club. He reports back that he'd seen her earlier, but she was in such a hurry she blew him off when he attempted to talk to her, and it's the first he's heard of her quitting. Michelle ends the call and screams, "Goddammit, why didn't we have her under surveillance!"

"Okay, okay, let's think this through. She's a drug-addicted stripper; we can find her," he replies confidently. "We'll get someone to call every strip club in the Seattle-Tacoma area; we'll tell them that rumors have it they're using underaged girls—that a girl who goes by the name Amberly Carlson is only seventeen, and we're looking for her, and if she applies for a gig, they need to call us immediately."

"That's…eh…that's pretty slick, Brad; I'm impressed."

"Yeah, I have my moments."

Next Michelle calls the station and asks the sergeant if he has any go-getter rookies looking for some overtime. He says he does, and soon Amberly has a man hot on her tail, hunting her through open fields of tits and ass.

They return to the Marina, where the forensics team hasn't found anything definitive except that the red substance inside the cracked fiberglass tested positive for blood. So it's back to the station to listen to JFK's full report on the god Ra.

He stands to give his report. "Ra is the sun god of ancient Egypt, the all-father of creation whom all other gods worship. He is a divine but aging god, who has become too tired to deal with all of his children (humankind) any longer, except for those—the purity—who hold the truth and wisdom of before time. It is believed that Ra will spend eternity watching over the heavens, while Horus, his apprentice, is master of the earth and the underworld. Zealots of this ancient religion deem that they're the chosen sons and daughters of god and believe that they will become under-gods themselves. According to myth, Ra is the creator of all living things, which he spoke into existence by uttering their secret names, and the architect of all humankind, which was conceived from his sweat (his labors) and tears (his sorrows). Sacrifice is a common practice for adherents of this religion; some believers even performed human sacrifice. But the victim has to be truly evil for Ra to be awakened, to consume."

"Jeez," Michelle says, "this freak is a walking, talking, believing nightmare!"

"It just means that he has a strange religion. Keep in mind, a lot of other religions advance similar notions," Milkowski adds.

"Okay, but there's more. With all due respect, prosecutor, I would like to point out that most other religions do not practice human sacrifice. And there's this: I did some further research and found that *alm tahat hep*—what scholars often translate as 'truly evil'—literally means 'adulterous wife.'"

Everyone remains utterly silent, with the words *adulterous wife* seeming to echo around the room, as JFK quietly hands out copies of his report.

Then Captain Jackson speaks up. "All right, we're gonna wait for forensics to come up with something. I already spoke to them, and they're telling me they won't have anything till tomorrow." His tone sounds weary and beaten. There's a short, exhausted pause. "So let's call it a day, unless anything else comes up. We'll meet back here in the morning."

The meeting begins to disperse, when he adds, "And I want everyone to be assured we're gonna get this creep, if it's the last thing we do."

Cools and Michelle leave, keeping their theories to themselves. Alone in the hallway, he asks her, "You want to get some drinks and smoke some cigarettes with me?"

"I would love to, Brad, but I haven't seen my husband in a while, and tonight is our date night," she says with a silly grin.

"Okay, partner, I'll see you first thing in the morning."

Later Cools walks into his apartment and runs through his mostly usual routine, kicking his shoes off next to the door, throwing his keys and wallet onto the coffee table, putting one kilogram of cocaine in the icebox, getting a cold one out of the fridge, and turning on the television. The local evening news won't be on for a few minutes, so he flips through the channels, contemplating what should become of the drugs. If I don't use it to frame Joshua, what do I do with it? It would really be dumb to get caught taking it back. I could sell it, I guess, or maybe throw one helluva party. Fuck it; it's safe for now; I'll figure out something tomorrow.

He cracks open a beer and relaxes back into his recliner. Once settled he goes over the scribbles in his notepad. Connecting the dots, he presumes he's on the right track.

Then, from his notes, he dials a number into a cell phone.

Chapter Twenty-Four

Joshua pulls the blinds aside, unveiling the line of news vans parked outside his home. He smirks as he witnesses Tom and Louise Something-or-other, his nosy neighbors, talking to reporters. In his mind he can hear what they are disclosing. We always knew he was no good. We fear for our lives just sharing the same block as him.

Imprisoned within his home, he's becoming ever more suspicious, paranoid. His phone rings. Caller ID reads "Santorini Lucrezia." Presuming it's a journalist, he answers smugly, "What in the hell do you want, Mr. Santorini?"

The person on the other end spits out a few quick statements. "I am not Santorini. I am the guy who is onto your schemes—the guy that is going to take you down. You're going to rot in prison, you sick, demented fucking piece of shit!" The caller immediately hangs up.

Missing any chance to reply, Joshua's head begins to spin, like it does sometimes. Briefly his thoughts visit his dreams, and little Frankie, the nine-year-old boy who was left alone with his mother's new boyfriend. And although he knows exactly who the caller was, he's completely unaware of what's to come.

Chapter Twenty-Five

The ten o'clock news comes on, with Tabatha Sterns documenting the latest. Tonight her satiny, blond hair is pinned back, and smile curling her lips says she has much to report. Cools views the show from his easy chair, drink in hand, exhaling cigarette smoke. His menacing thoughts are becoming numb. But the alcohol already in him is soliciting for more.

Michelle watches, fitfully lying on her bed, dressed in a slutty garter belt, waiting for her husband to step out of the shower.

Tabatha comes on in an animated style intended to woo her listeners. She opens, "Good evening, I'm Tabatha Sterns. Brace yourself for our top story tonight; we have a new twist in the fast-paced Joshua Siconolfi story. So let's take a quick look at an interview I finished just three hours ago." Next she appears in the top left corner of the screen, standing out of doors somewhere with a heavyset man.

Cools abruptly scoots to the edge of his seat, yelling at the screen, "Ah fuck! You gotta be kidding me."

Michelle just shakes her head and accepts it, realizing it was only a matter of time.

As the interview begins, the small box fills in the whole screen. "I'm standing here outside the Seattle Yacht Mariner beside D. J. Adders, the association's acting manager, who says he rented a large, seagoing vessel to Joshua just days prior to the infamous radio call. Also, as you can see behind me, the Seattle crime lab is here investigating." The camera zooms in on a boat swarming with police. Tabatha motions toward the scene, asking, "Is this the very same yacht your company rented to Joshua?"

"Indeed it is," D. J. replies enthusiastically.

"And would you repeat to the cameras what you told me you overheard investigators saying?"

D. J. peers into the lens. "I distinctly heard one inform the other that use of the craft fit the timetable."

Cools again yells to the television, "You nosy prick!"

Michelle only hears the shower turn off.

Tabatha flashes a quick grin before pressing forward. "And what did Joshua say his intentions were?"

"He confided in me his intent was to dispense of his late wife's ashes into the sea."

"So you were under the impression Kimberly was already deceased at this time?"

"Yes, but I merely supposed him to be a widower; I never considered anything nefarious in nature."

"And, D. J., is this yacht thought to be in connection with the abrupt disappearance or murder of Kimberly?"

"I believe this to be so."

Again the camera zooms in on the site surrounded in yellow police tape, with a full forensics team working busily and talking privately in small groups—all shouldering a plethora of equipment. Their movements suggest they may have found something important—something incriminating. They begin setting up a tarp to conceal their activities.

Then Tabatha asks D. J., "Did you find anything strange in your dealings with Joshua?"

"No, nothing whatsoever. As I told the detectives, I found him quite pleasant actually. But now that I've had time to reflect, I do recall a few things to have been out of the ordinary."

"Like what?" she asks curiously.

"Well, his main concern was whether or not he could sail the Riviera out at night; in addition he rented the Riviera for a full week, but employed it for the one night only."

"Did he have anyone with him?"

"No, it appears not. Earlier when I went to unearth the surveillance tape for Detectives Cools and Robertson, I viewed it first. And although he carried many articles onboard, he sailed out alone."

"Articles? What sorts of articles?"

"Well, one was very distinctive—a crab trap. We see many of those. But then there was a robust cooler of sorts and also quite a few large bags. And upon returning he carried virtually nothing but a small gym bag."

"Very interesting," she says, looking into the camera.

The broadcast cuts back to Tabatha in the studio, beside Joshua's *GQ* picture, as she recaps.

Click.

Michelle's husband enters their bedroom wearing only a loosely fit towel and the irresistible cologne she bought him for his birthday. She turns on some music.

Cools listens additionally until Tabatha finishes. "Well, that's all for now. A more detailed interview with D. J. Adders here at eleven thirty, and you don't want to miss it." In disgust he drinks the last of his beer and heads out for the night. Soon he's at The Shelter, fast-sipping his whiskey until Tabatha's eleven-thirty, "and you don't want to miss it" show plays on the television above the bar. It isn't long before he is greatly disappointed, seeing as she had nothing new to add except for more of D. J.'s self-gratifying elaborations. He then makes his way to a familiar door and after a little pleading is let in.

Chapter Twenty-Six

Deep into the night, Cools sleeps warm and sound, snuggled next to Chelsea. She's curled in a fetal position, with his arms wrapped around her. Completely bare-skinned they melt into each other, dreaming in tranquility. Over them, eternalness looms promising. Suddenly a sound awakens him; it's his cell phone, and the clock reads 3:47 a.m. He answers, half asleep and disturbed.

"Hello!"

"Cools, are you awake?"

"I am now!"

"All right, here's the real deal," Captain Jackson says. "Luminal testing shows a large amount of blood was recently cleaned from the boat's deck."

Cools, seeing that Chelsea is still fast asleep, moves to the bathroom to listen further, mumbling, "Uh-huh."

"And listen up, the blood we got in the damaged fiberglass has DNA; it'll take a few days to get an exact match to Kimberly, but here's what we know: it's not our boy Joshua's blood type; it *is* Kimberly's. And that's not all. Her blood type is AB Rh negative, the rarest of its kind."

"So you're saying it is hers or not?" he asks, rubbing his face, waking himself.

"Close enough. Also the yacht he rented has a GPS unit that Ghost is playing with. He's in here now and tells me that he can configure the memory chip, and it'll show the exact route he took; we'll know exactly where he went. So

I'm giving you what you've asked for: we're gonna take him downtown, Charlie Brown. We're hitting him at quarter to five; that gives you about an hour to get your ass in here. Do you feel me now?"

"I'll be there within the hour." The call ends, but Cools still answers his captain's question to the bathroom mirror, "Yeah, I feel ya. I definitely feel ya." Subsequently he calls Michelle, and fifty-five minutes later they're both at headquarters, coffee in hand, ready to go.

Captain Jackson directly introduces them to Sergeant Wielder, a retired military man who now leads the Seattle Task Force. Cools, somewhat intimidated, shifts his coffee to his left hand to shake with his right. Not many men have this effect on him, but at six feet five and nearly three hundred pounds, a modest caution is always wise. Sergeant Wielder greets his handshake with a low, guttural, "Good morning," the voice of a hard and determined man. His tone coincides with his far-from-deceptive appearance, as even his softer features resemble that of a pit bull. His specialty is the expedient extraction and apprehension of the most dangerous individuals. And he even has a sexual appeal that becomes apparent as he's introduced to Michelle. She reddens and slightly wiggles when shaking his large, rugged hand.

The room around them is bustling as more and more of Sergeant Wielder's team are entering and arranging their gear. They're all dressed in black, so when an officer in blue comes rushing in, it seems out of place. The papers in his hand are quickly delivered to Captain Jackson, who grumbles a bit at the torn corner near the bottom where Judge Cooper obviously signed in a fit. But it doesn't matter, he has what he needs—full search warrants for the properties of Joshua Siconolfi. Captain Jackson nods to Sergeant Wielder.

"Listen up, everyone!" he demands, taking complete control. The words leave his lips, and a pin could be heard dropping on the floor. Cools and Michelle follow along as he makes brief introductions and lays down the plan—not much different than the time before, except it will be executed even harder and faster.

A storm is coming to Joshua.

Then, once he's assured his team is on track, he turns to Cools and Michelle for final guarantees and instructions. "Do you understand the plan?"

They both answer yes.

"You will hold back; you will do *nothing* more and *nothing* less than I say. For the next hour or so, I am your commander. You will not question or have a single thought of your own. If I say abort this mission, you will do so without hesitation! Do I make myself clear?"

"Yes."

"And for the love of God, do not shoot any holes in his driveway!"

"Yes," Cools replies, with his head humbly tilted. Feeling at first a sense of embarrassment, he then determines the level of influence Sergeant Wielder holds over his team. In most groups the comment would have produced outright laughter or at least a few chuckles, but his present company stands firm without even so much as a flutter.

Next he turns to his team, shouting, "This will be textbook. The entire world is watching, so no mistakes—no mistakes!" There's a short pause before everything is set into motion.

"Let's go! Let's go!"

At 4:52 a.m. the media vans are pulled back, and Joshua's house is surrounded by a team of five entry soldiers near the front, three around the back, and two atop the roof on each side, all in full combat gear awaiting orders under the cover of darkness. They carry AR-15s, ventilated face masks, tear gas, and flash grenades. Also in full gear are the news reporters, down half a block with cameras rolling. Sergeant Wielder makes a final check that everyone is ready, wipes the rain from his mask, and makes the call, which obviously awakens Joshua. He answers, "Hello?"

"This is Sergeant Wielder outside your home with the Seattle Special Units Task Force. You are completely surrounded; you need to immediately walk out the front door, with your hands in the air!"

There's a pause, followed by Joshua's response. "No, come back at nine thirty." He hangs up.

Sergeant Wielder is not impressed or amused. Without hesitation he points a finger, and the noose begins to tighten. Two officers quickly position themselves at the front with a battering ram. Another holding a tear gas gun crawls to a post lying across the lawn and locks on. Cools and Michelle, as previously instructed, crouch behind the cruiser. And the two on the roof hang over the edge, gripping tight to a secured line. Then one of them at the front door drops his hand, and all hell breaks loose.

Bang, bang, and shattering glass as the smoke grenades go in. Bang, bang: blasting more glass and the flash grenades go in. Boom, boom, boom-boom, bursts of lightning go off inside the home. The men on the roof swing down in a controlled crash through side windows. Simultaneously a loud thud and the distinct sound of wood splintering: the door flies open followed by voices, muffled by their face masks, "Go, go, go!" They swiftly penetrate the smoke-filled house from every side. Cools and Michelle listen to fifteen to twenty seconds of more intense yelling and crashing sounds, then mostly silence.

Cools's phone rings. Sergeant Wielder says, "You may now enter."

The two detectives dart in, wanting to take full advantage of Joshua's shock to ask a few key questions. Through the disintegrated door, they cross into the smoky room still full of activity, officers with guns drawn searching every nook and cranny. Across the space they see Joshua deflated and cuffed on the couch. Cools wastes no time. He runs directly to him. "Where's Kimberly?"

"Fuck you, top cop!" Joshua replies, tussling in his restraints.

Cools leans in close, violating his space, and asks again. This time he only responds by turning his attention to Michelle, seizing a long look; his smiling, evil eye gazes up and down.

Then Michelle screams, "Where's Kimberly, asshole?"

Cools adds, "And where is Amberly?"

Without moving a muscle, Joshua's eyes shift their focus from peering at her to peering through her. Michelle, at that instant, knows they're not going to get anything out of him. She diverts her attention to the room, the shattered windows and curtains strewn throughout, lying across his audio system—it seems odd to her that it's turned on.

Cools continues, demanding, "What have you done to Kimberly? Where's Amberly?" He remains highly agitated even as the rest of the men around them begin to settle down. "Tell me where the fuck your wife is."

Joshua angles his stare back to him, stating, "You've made a big mistake, top cop!"

"And how's that?"

At first Joshua doesn't answer, he just nuzzles his head back into the couch cushions and, seemingly very comfortable and sure of himself, whispers, "The devil comes, the devil does, and the devil goes; and I bet you think the blood on the yacht is Kimberly's."

Stunned and exasperated, Cools grabs him and yells, "Listen here, you freak. I'm tired of hearing your bullshit. I don't need her blood. I will find her body. And now that I have you, I have your DNA. And I don't care how careful you think you are, asshole; I will plant your hair, your blood, even your semen if I have too."

"She's my fucking dead wife; why wouldn't my blood, hair, or semen be on her, top cop?"

Instantly Cools realizes what a stupid comment it was and looks around hoping few had heard it.

"Brad, settle down," Michelle warns, pulling him back. Then she motions for the remaining officers to take Joshua away.

They spring back into action, pluck him from the couch, and seconds later emerge from the house. "Move, move, move!" they shout, with Joshua cuffed, his feet bouncing along as they half run, half drag him to an open side door of a van. They throw him in and slam the door shut as the engine roars to life. One of them bangs on the side, the tires squeal, and they're gone.

Then forensics moves in, snapping pictures of everything. They find a room converted into a shrine for Kimberly. Her picture, the same picture, haphazardly pasted to every square inch of the walls. Standing in the room, Michelle asks, "How did he know about the blood?"

"I don't know; something isn't right."

"Did you see his smirk? I'm starting to think everything we find is…is what he wants us to find."

"No, we're going to get him!" Cools yells before he recognizes how upset she is.

"Brad, he frightens me."

Cools places his arm around her and holds her. "Yeah, I know; he scares me, too."

They embrace for a time, letting the agitation subside. Michelle needs him more than she lets on, but he knows. He tells her how sweet her hair smells, calming her enough to regroup her thoughts. And it isn't long before she begins to analyze the incident.

"Did you get *anything* from him when you asked about Amberly?"

"Not even a twitch."

"I feel like he's playing us, like he's going to get out of this somehow."

"No, he won't; he'll leave something unchecked. They always do. We just have to keep searching." He scans the house for a place to start. Then, remembering Joshua's financial troubles, he walks over to a filing cabinet in what would be a dining room that's been converted into an open office. The cabinet looks to be just the kind of where someone would stash a kilo of cocaine. Then, not knowing whether it's locked, he yanks on the top drawer. Unexpectedly the whole front comes off. The entire drawer is missing; he pulls at the second one, getting the same result. Soon he realizes it's been hollowed out. He rips the remaining doors off, exposing a vacant expanse. "Look at this!"

Michelle comes over and shines her flashlight inside. It's smeared with a gooey substance. "Is that blood?"

Cools yells out, "I need a luminal light in here!"

Right away a woman from the forensics team appears and waves a beam of light into the empty cabinet.

The distinctive glows of splattered blood come alive like a laser light show.

Chapter Twenty-Seven

Cools and Michelle leave Joshua's home and return to the station. At first there's some confusion as to where he's been taken. Michelle calls Captain Jackson, but he doesn't divulge any information, only tells them to go to his office and wait. After two and a half hours, they are found by Misty Lakewoods, in the cafeteria. She says, "come with me," and leads them to the task force headquarters, located in the third level of the basement. Neither of them has ever been down to this part of the building, but Misty seems quite familiar with the place as she delivers them to a waiting armed guard—one of Sergeant Wielder's team.

"Here you go, and I would like to say congratulations on getting Joshua into custody," she says, before leaving them alone with the guard. He escorts them through the command center, which is nothing more than a long soundless hallway with closed doors along each side and a large metal door at its end.

"Why are we down here?" Michelle asks, as they reach the end of the hall. The guard doesn't answer her; he just punches in a security code, and with a mechanical clank, the door opens into a small space. Cools and Michelle are speechless. They enter, finding Captain Jackson quietly standing in front of a large plate glass window and next to Sergeant Wielder, who is talking into his phone. On the other side, Joshua sits strapped to a chair. And in an instant, they begin to understand where they are: it's some kind of private interrogation room. The door locks behind them.

"What's he doing down here?" Cools asks, looking with interest about the room.

"Shush!" Captain Jackson spits out, without taking his eyes off of Joshua.

Although anxious and curious, the two detectives abide by his order and simply study the animal before them. Soon enough interrogations will begin, an occasion that will haunt them all.

They quickly survey the secreted room. At first glance it is like any other, except it has an enormous three-feet-thick two-way mirror. On the viewing side are four fixed seats and a lot of electronic touch pads on the wall. The mirrored side, where Joshua sits, has a table, a couple of chairs, and a lighting system, in addition to stadium-sized speakers.

"What is this place?" Michelle asks.

"All right, now, listen up," Captain Jackson replies, speaking to them through his reflection in the glass. "This guy is not gonna fuck with us anymore. The blood in the crack is Kimberly's; I'm sure of it. How he knows about it, I don't care—it doesn't matter. He's in our house now, and he will tell us all we want to know. We're gonna do whatever is necessary to get a statement from this maniac and seal the deal. He's *my* puppet now, and *I* will pull the strings!"

Michelle hears the sinister tone in his voice and asks, dreadfully concerned, "What exactly do you mean by 'whatever is necessary,' Captain?"

He turns and stares directly into her, giving her the feeling of being at a crossroads. Then he asks solemnly, "Do you want to know why he's winning?" Michelle doesn't know how to answer. "It's because he thrives on all this. He's becoming a rock-star killer right before our very eyes. The media worships him; they hang on his every word, and he feeds them one freaky statement after another. And he is far from done." She and Cools start to get the sense that their captain knows more than they do. He speaks as if he is not himself. He doesn't exert his usual body language, and his voice is ominous.

"Is there something we should know?"

"Yes, there is Michelle. I got a call from forensics. The blood in the filing cabinet is not Kimberly's; it's B-positive—the same as Amberly's! And they found more," he says, looking distraught. "They found a leather-bound book of ancient religious practices tied with a silk scarf. In it, scribbled atop almost every page, are the names of missing girls going back nine years."

"Oh my God!" Michelle feels bile rising in her stomach.

"What are you planning here?" Cools asks.

"We...the four of us"—he twirls his finger—"are gonna get him to confess, so there will be no plea bargains, so he will get nothing short of a dose of lethal injection!" Then he continues conveying information to them they never could have imagined. He asks, "Do you see his complementary cup of coffee?"

They both reply, "Yeah."

"Well, then I will let Sergeant Wielder take it from here."

Sergeant Wielder, no longer talking on the phone, clears his throat before he begins. "In it is an experimental drug, Dimeophoximien, that we used primarily in Operation Desert Storm to retrieve vital information from suspected terrorists. It should be coursing through his veins in approximately ten minutes. It alters cognitive functions and perceptions by overloading his brainwaves and simultaneously firing all receptors of both the left and right hemispheres of the frontal lobes. It will bring the deep recesses of his mind to the surface. He will involuntarily do and say things he doesn't intend to, attempting to react one way, only to do the opposite. For example, he may try to scream from the pain but start singing a song he cannot stand. Or attempt to spit on you, only to piss his pants. And best of all, he will try to answer questions in one manner but admit to things inadvertently—things that will help us get a conviction."

Captain Jackson explains further. "Also you should know that I released a statement from my office stating that Joshua is currently being held in Tacoma, where a few obstacles are in place, but they'll figure it out within a couple of hours. That means time is short."

Cools and Michelle are utterly stunned by his words. But Michelle finds the strength to express her thoughts. "This is illegal; we could go to jail."

"Well it *is* a grey area," Sergeant Wielder answers, "but dark enough that we aim to keep it under wraps. Think of it this way: it is only intensified coercion, albeit of a type that the public is not ready for." Michelle gives him a gaze suggesting she is unconvinced. He asserts, "We cannot operate with our hands tied!"

"Have you two done this before?" They both linger implicitly, giving her the answer. "You've got to be kidding me. My God!"

Cools starts to say something, but Sergeant Wielder holds his hand, signaling he needs to communicate more. "What I am about to tell you must remain entirely off the record." He gives them a look displaying his resolve. "I am technically still employed with an elite unit within our military. I have full authority to execute these actions. And if anything ever came of it, I can argue that he is a religious terrorist, relieving you at least from any prosecution."

"Prosecution! I can't get freaking prosecuted. I'm married; I have a child."

Captain Jackson grabs her shoulders, shaking her. "Listen, Robertson, we're not gonna give this savage any chance to live out his days in a cell filled with commissary and fan mail. He has to die, and this is the only way—the only way for us to protect our community, to get justice! Think of all those young girls dying horrible deaths at his hand. He's not gonna go unpunished!"

Michelle looks to Cools, only to see he is already silently onboard. She breaks Captain Jackson's grip and turns to the window, staring at Joshua, absorbed in thought. At first she feels like crying, until the vengeance that's in the air sets in. She takes a long look at him then pivots back to the three men in the room. Immediately she can see the difference; the men in front of her are strong, principled, noble.

They are her protectors.

Then she remembers her childhood and her father, and the way he had always said to her mother, "Men know best." It was a statement she thought of as funny and playful, until her college years when the adage morphed into a hated phrase—an egotistical, discriminating, and oppressive comment that at that time in her life she advocated against in support of the women's movement. But deep down, in places she would never outwardly admit, she felt it to have some level of truth and prudence. She looks to Sergeant Wielder, seeing a man sure of his doings. He postures, showing her the security she is looking for. Then Detective Michelle Robertson turns the corner, asking, "Are you *positive* you can protect us from any prosecution?"

"Michelle, we will do everything possible to keep this under the radar, but if it ever comes out in any form, I can make it go away," he replies, assuring her.

She hesitates, pressing her captain to close the deal. He recites to her a motto he learned from his former captain. "We punish wrongdoers. We kill evil. He has to die Michelle, and this is the way."

She closes her eyes for a moment, saying a short prayer. Then she opens them, with a new mind. "Okay, okay then, let's do it. Let's break this disgusting freak!"

Sergeant Wielder springs into action, explaining the inner workings of his enhanced interrogation room. "I want to prepare you for what you are about to see. The room is outfitted with some devices that will augment the effect of the drugs. Creating nightmarish flashes of lights, the temperature will fluctuate rapidly between one hundred thirty and ten degrees Fahrenheit. Speakers will pound reverberating bass, more like shock waves actually, with the deafening, high-pitched sounds of a disturbed woman. Her voice will be acute, wailing orders to comply, to obey, as well as attacking him personally. But the primary mechanism is the air pressurized chamber he now sits in." He breathlessly explains as Michelle's and Cools's eyes widen. "We call it IEC, for 'intelligence extraction chamber.' And how it works is simple: The room is completely air tight and can hold up to five hundred pounds per square inch of pressure. Three of the four walls are stationary, while the wall to his left actuates in and out, generating very high pressures. It is painful and extremely disorientating; it can even rupture his internal organs. The stresses will also bow the two-way mirror, distorting his reflection. Now, I want you to know that what you are about to witness is extremely effective and will surely amaze the both of you." Then, without allowing any discussion, he begins pushing controls on the keypad. Cools and Michelle hold hands, appropriately unsettled, while Captain Jackson stands expressionless.

On the other side of the glass, Joshua starts to feel a dizzying sensation, the embers of nausea. The wall left of him closes in, and the mirror twists, deforming his image. He encounters a pulsing force as his sickness steadily increases. Next neon lights begin to flicker. On and off, off and on, sporadically, while others strobe in an array of colors. The force subsides momentarily and then drives harder, pushing on him from every angle, crushing him. The drugs are coming on strong, and his bending image frightens him. The lights strobe faster, more off than on; the room heats up, and sweat runs down his face. Bass speakers roar to life, rumbling through him, enhancing the pressure as other amplifiers are piercing his ears, screeching. "Obey! You will obey! You are nothing!" The demands are followed by sounds of a woman taunting and cursing. "Ahhh! Ahhh! Ahhh! You are trifle! Void! Disgraced!" Her screams curdle him as panic shudders through his body. "You can only obey! Ahhh! Ahhh! You coward!" The temperature falls; his core shivers. His sweat chills him, and the woman's shrieking grows louder, coming from the left of him and then the right. His mind is sealed with paralyzing fear, his bones are being constrained, his brain is twitching, and confusion surrounds his consciousness. "Ahhh! Ahhhh! Ahhhhhh! Die! Depart from life!" Her voice is menacing, and inside his strobe-lit lips begin to beg, to abandon all and plea for their mercies.

Then it stops.

He exhales relief, whimpering. Much-needed oxygen and white blood cells rush to aid his body. Only the bottomless ringing in his ears and trembling pain remains. Then it comes on again, even more intense than before. Shocking his inner being, his throat begins to swell under the heaviness, suffocating. Terror sets in, and the woman continues shrilling, "Ahhh! Ahhhh! You are disorder! Obey me!" Rhythmic stresses seize his functions; he wets himself. But he's not sure that he didn't do it on purpose. His internal organs coil like the image seen in the carnival mirror, a masquerade of visual echoes. Complete and utter horror surges inside…It stops.

He has a brief moment of reprieve with isolated thoughts of where am I, why am I? Again it comes alive, faster, with more weight, more chaotic sparks of light, an inescapable hallucination of morbid realities. "Ahhh! Ahhhh! Ahhhh!" The heat rises, almost burning his skin. He tries to stand, but instead his arms flail about; he tries to close his eyes but cannot; he tries to speak, but his mind won't let him. Thoughts of suicide flood his psyche; he thinks of Kimberly, Ra, and little Frankie—anything to make it stop. But the woman won't quit fucking screaming. "You are a genius! A madman! You are hell! Ahhh! Ahhhh!" He drools on himself; he wants to tear at his skin. It stops, yet he knows it will soon return, an inevitable nightmare of doom and condemnation. He attempts to cry but instead launches into uncontrollable laughter.

"Ahhhh! Ahhhhh! You are worthless!" The temperature drops, stealing his breath. His eyes bulge from the strain; his face appears to have aged.

Michelle and the men observe as it starts again. The room resembles a lightning storm, and the movement bends the viewing window. It hisses as compressed air escapes on their side.

"Oh my God, that's intense!" Michelle yells.

"Yeah, it is!" Cools agrees, with a dry mouth, watching Joshua thrash about, his veins bulging out of his bruised skin with every pulse.

"How long do we do this for?"

"We leave him in there for another ten minutes, suffering, until he pleads to tell us all we want to know."

"It seems extreme," Cools says, somewhat pitying the man he despises.

Sergeant Wielder replies, "I will not lie to you; some men never recover even after five minutes, but I guarantee its results. He will tell us what we want."

They can see it halt and can hear Joshua pleading incoherently. "Make it stop! Please, make it stop! I want to tell you nothing…No, I will give you anything. Please!"

Sergeant Wielder turns it up a level, and the psychotic chamber roars to life for another session.

Inside Joshua struggles against it, enduring her horrendous screams, "Obey me! Dismiss your beliefs! Ahhh! Ahhhhh! You are mine!" He vomits all over himself and grinds his teeth, breaking off the tips of two of them. The mirror compresses, collapsing his form so that he hates himself, followed by more constricting as the flashes and the woman work in unison, beating him into submission. "You are a fraud! You are not worthy! You will only obey! Ahhhhhhh! Help me!" Within himself he desperately searches for truth, for an escape as the scorching heat comes. Everything escalates the intense pressure; the lights are pulsing faster with each of her excoriations, two times for each word, then two and a half, then six. "You will obey! You are soulless! Your labors will not be rewarded! Ahhhhhh! Ahhhhhh!"

It stops, and he has a fleeting glimpse of awareness, beginning to have an idea of where he is. But it starts again; it's killing him, and he has to find a way out. His inclination is to oppose the voice. "You will obey! Ahhhhh! Ahhhhh! Obey or pain!" Joshua plays messages over and over in his mind—something that he can control. First it is only a few: "I'm at the police station. I was arrested." Then he begins adding more. He practices his motor functions by squeezing his hands, rerouting, circumventing brain synapses to beat it, methods learned from many bad trips on hallucinogens.

"You are my scapegoat! Inconclusive! Obey or pain!"

"No...I am not!" Joshua chokes out.

"Ahhhhh! Ahhhhhh! Ahhhhhh! You are vile! Obey or pain!"

"No! I am...I am more...I don't have to...have you inside me!" He can feel the drugs losing their effectiveness; he's gaining influence.

"What is going on?" Cools yells.

"I'm not sure," Sergeant Wielder replies, turning the room to its strongest level, increasing the volume, making even the viewing room shake violently.

Still Joshua defies it power, wailing inhumanly loud, "I am in the police station! They arrested me! I was arrested!"

"You're going to kill him!" Michelle shouts out.

Sergeant Wielder orders Captain Jackson. "We need to go in now. He's beating it. I don't know how, but he is beating it. Our best chance is to go in now!"

"All right, Robertson, get in there now! You get first crack at him. And get us what we need!"

Inside the chamber of horrors, Joshua battles to the end, slumped over the table and asserting to himself, "I am at the police station! I was arrested!" Liquid runs out of his ears. Blood vessels have ruptured on most of his face, and the pressure has excreted all his bodily fluids. But it stops. It finally stops. He hopes.

Next he hears the air-locked door open, and Michelle bursts in, questioning, "Where is Kimberly? What did you do with her? Tell me where Amberly is.

Look at me!" Joshua welcomes her but ignores her still, only breathing, restoring, provisioning for the next wave of attacks. Except now the onslaught comes exclusively from her. "Talk to me! Tell me how Kimberly's blood got inside the railing. Are you involved romantically with Amberly?"

Slowly he can feel his strength replenishing, fueled by anger and the desire for retribution. He now knows what it can do and is confident he can contend with it, if need be. Awareness pours in, reminding him in greater detail where he is, who he is, and why he is here. They've drugged me, but it won't happen a second time. They've made their play, and the worst of everything is over. He spits out a bit of agonizing laughter and lifts his head.

Michelle gasps upon seeing the damage done. His face is a mess, bruised and drained of life. But what concerns her more is the grin, the hatred in his eyes. She knows he is far from broken. He's like a freaking weed you can't kill!

Joshua wastes no time inspecting himself in the mirror and seizing a creepy glimpse of Michelle, challenging her.

With composure she returns a look that says, "Not in a gazillion years, freak!"

Then he coughs, finding his voice. "I want my fucking…phone call, bitch!"

"Why don't we answer a few questions first," Michelle counters, narrowing her eyes. "Tell me where Kimberly is, or we *will* turn it back on!"

"Let's do it; let's fucking do it. I can handle it! I dare you to make my face worse. I am going to sue this entire fucking department!" He lunges for her, but the straps hold him just within reach. "Do you know…know who my father is?"

"Yes, I do, Joshua, and he will never know of this," Michelle snaps back, concealing her uncertainty.

"You can't keep me here forever! I want my fucking lawyer." He begins to cry, then asks, "What are you charging me with?"

Michelle can see the drugs are still having an effect on him; his eyes are floating, drifting. She answers him directly, "You're being charged for the first degree murder of your wife, Kimberly."

"Sounds like a good time not to answer…or answer any questions without my lawyer then," he replies smartly. "You march your sweet little ass out there and get me a phone, so I can call my father." He directs her with his finger.

Captain Jackson, behind the mirror, tells Cools to get in there. Michelle pulls her hair back and blurts out, "But that's not really living it to its fullest, now is it, Joshua?"

Just then Cools steps in. Joshua looks to Cools, asking, "What is she talking about?"

She starts to explain as Cools simply points his finger back toward her. Joshua, out of curiosity, reverses his attention to hear her say, "It's because you're smarter than us, Joshua. You can handle our little examination. You haven't made any real mistakes, and I think you would agree that we should play—that is, unless you can't handle a real woman without your daddy. And a detective here that—what did you say?—missed his chance."

"Ha…ha-ha…you're good," he replies, wiping blood from his mouth. Then he moves his attention to Cools, who isn't laughing, and says, "I don't believe I said such a thing; actually I remember it to be Janice, your 'partner in goodness,' that made that comment."

Cools storms back out, grumbling, "Oh fuck you, you little prick." He says this mostly in a pretense of anger, attempting to play into Michelle's little charade and permit him the first round.

"Okay, lady," Joshua says, smiling through the pain, "gimme all you got!"

"It's Detective Robertson," she answers sharply. Then, in a softer voice, she adds, "But you can call me Michelle."

He chuckles to himself. "Okay then, what would you like to ask me, *Michelle*?"

She stands over the table between them, with a pen and paper, and begins. "Where is your wife?"

"Peru—for all I know."

"When was the last time you had any communication with her?"

"The day she left—Sunday."

"Did you take her to the airport?"

"No, she said a friend was taking her."

"Who? What friend? Amberly?"

"I don't know; all she said was a friend!"

"Isn't it strange she hasn't tried to contact you for over a week now?"

"Not so much."

"Are you in love with her, Joshua?"

"She is my love, my destiny."

"Really! Then why…why did you rent the boat, Joshua?"

"I was going to take her fishing, but then she left."

"So did you go fishing by yourself?"

"Yes."

"Catch anything?"

"No."

"How did you do the damage to the boat?"

"I was drunk and fell into it."

"How did you know there was blood?"

"Who's ahead?"

"What?" she replies, not understanding the question.

"What's the score, Michelle?"

"So far zero to zero," she replies.

"Now let me ask *you* a question," he says, his head still spinning from the drugs. He then pauses dramatically and coughs up more blood before posing his question. "Michelle, how can one repent of a terrible thing without asking for forgiveness?"

"Have you done such a thing, Joshua?"

"I'm not sure. Is it a terrible thing if it is deserved?"

"Why don't you tell me what we are talking about," she says, growing steadily frustrated. Then she asks, "What if I told you we have found Kimberly's body?"

"I would ask you, is she still in it?"

Michelle lets out a short, cynical laugh. "Is she still in it? That's...well, that's... You know, you're a real funny guy, aren't you? You think you're just too freaking cool!"

"Get back in there, Cools; she's losing it!"

Cools races in just as she is in the middle of a tirade. "You repulse me! I would like to watch a real man beat you to a freaking pulp. Or maybe I should—"

"Okay, okay, Michelle, take a break; go get some coffee, okay?" Cools pats the small of her back. "Michelle, let me take it from here."

"So now it's your turn, huh, top cop?"

"Michelle, will you get me a cup of coffee?"

"Sure, Brad. Fine!"

She storms out, and Joshua beats Cools to the punch, asking, "I have a good idea. Why don't you repeat what you said to me in my living room?"

"I don't know what you're talking about," he retorts, matching Joshua's smirk.

"Sure you do, and you *will* repeat it again; believe me you will. Believe *me*, you fucking will!" He coughs up some of his stomach lining. "Now, I refuse to speak another word to you until I see my attorney." Then he seems to change his mind, and in a commanding tone like a man speaking to a dog, he orders Cools to leave the room. "You leave this second; you tell that painted whore to come back to me! You tell her to bring me two notepads, a pen, and some coffee. She has three minutes or I swear to Ra I will speak no more!"

Without hesitation and devoid of any other real options, Cools complies.

A couple of minutes later, Michelle enters, fumbling the notebooks and coffee in her hands. She places everything in front of him and sits down, trying to prepare herself. Joshua starts to write on one of the tablets and says, "I am going to give you something you want, and for this you will truthfully answer my questions." Michelle, thinking that he's writing a statement, agrees. "Who gave you the cross necklace?"

"My husband," she answers, knowing the questions are going to get more personal and maniacal.

"Are you a Christian?" he asks, in a tone that reveals his disgust for the religion.

"Yes."

"Do you love *Jesus*, Michelle?"

"Yes, I do."

"And your husband—is he a Christian like you?" She wavers for a second. "Is he?"

"No," she replies sorrowfully.

Joshua stops writing, looks up, and asks, "He is going to burn in hell for all eternity then?"

"Well, no, I don't think—"

"I said to answer truthfully, you stupid bitch! You say you're a Christian; that means you go to heaven and non-Christians go to hell, isn't that right?"

She pauses and then gives him what he wants. "Yes, that's true, but I will get him into church someday, someday before we die."

Joshua stares directly into her eyes, reading her, before stating, "I do not believe you believe that. I think he will burn!" Michelle takes it and doesn't say anything more, as Joshua places the first tablet face-down and writes for a short while on the other. Once he's done, he opens both and slides them across the table for her to read. As she is reading, he exhales slowly, "God, I would like to fuck you!" She is disgusted more at the words on the paper than his remark. Then, seeing that she is finished reading, he points to the first one and says, "If you do this and let me out of this fucking room..." He points to the second one. "I will sign this."

Michelle's eyes start to swell, and a tear falls from her cheek. She is about to do the unthinkable. She gets out of her chair and kneels in front of him. Joshua raises his hands out to his side, palms up, posturing. Then, with his head presented to the sky, he accepts her supplication.

"Oh God, Joshua, father of all creation, I pray to thee and ask for you to forgive me of my sins."

Moments afterward she emerges, trembling and weeping, from the interrogation room. She hands off the second notebook to Cools and runs for the bathroom to wash away her ugliness.

Cools reads the statement:

> "I Joshua Siconolfi did premeditate and murder my wife Kimberly Siconolfi!"

Chapter Twenty-Eight

Number 7519650 is swiftly taken to an undisclosed infirmary, where he's strapped to a bed. IVs are placed in both arms, feeding him vitamin and antibiotic therapies to heal his wounds. And although the drugs have subsided, her voice still rings in his head. "Obey or pain! Ahhh! Ahhh! You are despised!" He wishes her away and then remembers his mother—mostly from details generated by his father's stories of her. Joshua loved to hear him speak of her. He would watch his father gaze into the void as if seeing her right in front of him, giving count by count narratives of her mannerisms and silly doings. His father cherished her and spoke often of her beauty, although usually seeming somewhat irritated with her. At the age of six, two years after she'd run off, never to be seen again, Joshua felt from time to time as if she were with him, guiding his spirit through durations of boundless and constant worry. And when she wasn't, he missed her immensely. Sometimes he would sit alone for hours, staring at his bedroom door, waiting for her to appear. In his mind he would play it over and over: first hearing the latch turn, the door would swing open, and she would be standing there, glowing.

"Are you comfortable?" asks the nurse.

He smiles, enjoying the fact they have to pamper him during his healing process. And since there's no doubt his wounds will be almost entirely healed before he's allowed to appear in public, he has an agenda that calls for being gentle to the woman. He answers, "Yes, but I could use some more painkillers."

"They always help. I'll be right back, okay?" She leaves promptly.

Joshua, now fully aware of his surroundings, gains notice of his room—the clean white walls, the small television set bolted high in the corner, the assortment of electronic hospital equipment around his bedside. There, within the mundane, he reflects upon his maneuvers during the interrogation, repeating in his mind the gratifying memories of Detective Robertson's prayer to him. A proud grin forms on account of his performance, his masterpiece.

The nurse returns to his room, carrying a syringe filled with generosity. "Oh, you're going to like this," she says, pushing the plunger down. Instantly Joshua can feel it warming him, relaxing him. He snuggles deeper into the hospital bed as she caters to him, applying aloe and vitamin K lotions—natural ingredients that stimulate epithelial growth and speed healing times. Her hands are soothing. Nothing concerns him now, not being tortured or signing a statement of guilt; the outcome was still the same as intended.

Just outside his door, he recognizes Sergeant Wielder's voice conspiring with Captain Jackson, only he can't discern what they're saying. If he could, he would hear Captain Jackson stating, "All right, I'm gonna release a statement saying he went crazy, broke the camera inside the interrogation room, and we had to subdue him physically. That'll explain why we don't have any footage of his confession, or lacerations. Then we'll leak some video of our previous interview, showing his violent behaviors. So when he tells his stories of secret tortures, he'll be met with nothing but skepticism. Besides he already says all his crazy things; the public already views him as somewhat of an advocate for the dramatic; quite simply put, they won't believe him. I'm also gonna say he had a seizure and was shipped to Western State Hospital. And by the time they figure out he isn't there, we'll say he's returned but, due to another episode here, had to be sedated and cannot appear in court until Monday morning."

"You know the media is going to run wild with his accusations," murmurs Sergeant Wielder.

"All right, I got it. But in the end, he'll be discarded just like all the other scumbags who come through here. You should know that when it is all said and done, no one believes them. They are discredited by their crimes, their choices to use drugs, and their unwillingness to follow our suggested paths."

"Yeah, but this is different."

"No, it's the same, only on a larger scale. The job's already done; we just need to clean up the mess!"

Then Joshua can hear them moving down the hall and their muffled voices fading away. The nurse also departs; leaving him in isolation. It's a healthy break from a disordered life, and he thinks of Frankie Johnson, the boy who was left in the care of Panama-Red—his mother's new, risky boyfriend. The warm waves roll through him; his eyes begin to flicker, as he nods off and falls into a dream state, revisiting the 1960s and the uncertainties of little Frankie.

As soon as Betty leaves the party, Panama-Red takes over, and the mood changes steadily. Within an hour the stereo is playing full blast, with harder music, and the volleyball yard has altered into dancing and drunken mischief. Most of Betty's friends have left and been replaced by Panama-Red's rougher-looking and much louder compadres, who begin to frighten little Frankie. They blow the smoke from their funny-smelling cigarettes into his face and sniff white powder from the coffee table. A few of the thugs even take turns punching him in the arm to gauge his strength while voicing troubling comments about his mother.

Then suddenly a black man, one little Frankie has never seen before, bursts in the front door and yells, "Panama! Panama, we've got a fucking problem, man!"

Panama, clearly startled from his statement, recklessly shoves the coffee table out of his way, messing up the rows of white powder he's been working so hard on, and springs to his feet. "Be cool, man. What's going down?" The music is turned off, and the party comes to an immediate halt.

The black man surveys the room and its company, deciding something. "Not here, man. Where can I tell you about it?"

Panama squints and answers by motioning the black man to follow him into Betty's bedroom. They quickly make their way inside, slamming the door shut behind them. Little Frankie can hear a torrent of yelling from inside her room as everyone else pretends to ignore it, some even deciding it's a good time to leave. Confused, little Frankie stands unmoving, wishing his mother were still there. He watches the bedroom door, praying that it doesn't open.

Then after a long, rage-filled dispute, they come out, and immediately Panama begins yelling, "Everyone out, now!" But apparently people aren't moving fast enough, so he yells again, "Everyone get the fuck out now!" He begins picking up their jackets and throwing them at his less-than-happy friends, still shouting, "Go! Get the fuck out of here!" Then, as the last of them hurry out the front door, he puts on his jacket, retrieves a gun from under the couch cushion, and says, "Ah fuck! We have to take the kid."

Four hours later Joshua awakens back in present time. The pain medication has dissipated, and although he has a mountain of current troubles of his own, he can only think of little Frankie. He senses that undeniable connection with him, as he lies there, longing for the return of his own mother.

Chapter Twenty-Nine

Two days later at three thirty in the afternoon, and after a good deal of anticipation, Joshua is said to be appearing in court. Speculation has been rising regarding the suspicious mix-up over where he has been. And some believe they have been detoured though a spinning circle of misinformation. But those who wish to publish Joshua's story do not dare compromise their relationship with the police. They tread a fine line between gaining the facts and pissing off their sources. And now they wait restlessly in a courtroom filled to capacity inside the King County courthouse.

Cools and Michelle sit near the front, suitably out of the microphones' reach. They have just spent the last fifty-five hours hiding from and shunning journalists and columnists of every kind, all wanting interviews for their newspapers and sensationalist magazines. Joshua is fast and furiously becoming the story of the year, and anyone close to him is considered exceedingly valuable, especially the arresting detectives. They sit close, protecting each other, so close in fact that Michelle can smell the liquor on his breath. She worries about him and knows why he went to his car earlier. It wasn't, as he said, to get his notepad; it was to gulp a few drinks from the bottle he hides under the seat. But at least this way he's calmer, she concludes. He catches her staring at him and just pats her on the leg. It's not a time for conversation since both their minds are puzzling over the news declared to them this morning from Officer Smithe, investigating the suicide of Trace Friesen in Tacoma: the verified parallel that William Siconolfi and

Trace Friesen—two very powerful and ambitious men, who are tightly woven together in the midst of a stormy scandal—both hold seats in the private balcony of the same parish .

Michelle had Ghost crunch the data, using what he calls *coincidence of circumstance software*. He explained to her that, given the population of the greater Seattle-Tacoma region of approximately 3.4 million, the probabilities of two prominent men being tied to the same place of worship, a secret love affair, a murder, and a suicide gave a rating of "highly improbable." Ghost clarified that he ran the information as raw data, taking in consideration the unlikelihood of Trace and Kimberly ever having a chance encounter at the church. Everyone agreed that no evidence or even a remote possibility could be considered that either Joshua or Kimberly ever attended services at the parish. Ra is their god, an opposing religion to the church. Also there is no evidence supporting that Trace Friesen and William had any dealings together, financial, professional, or otherwise. And even in the event they did, would it make sense that William would introduce Trace Friesen, a well-known political figure and fellow parishioner, to his crazy son and stripper wife?

Captain Jackson enters and makes his way through the reporters while sidestepping only one question. "All I can tell you is I've been informed from the jail authorities that he was uncooperative and had to be moved for a short time to Western State Hospital for evaluations, and now he's back here in King County. All right, now, that is all." Then he strides to the front, where a spot is waiting for him next to Detective Fredo. He frowns, shaking his head in annoyance to Michelle and Cools before sitting in the adjacent section of seats.

Then the prosecution entourage arrives, dismissing the mob in an air of conceit. Milkowski, holding an armload of briefs, stops and whispers something to Captain Jackson before seizing his table directly in front of Cools and Michelle. The rest of his team fills most of the table with folders, and they all cozy in next to each other, lining up for war.

Sheriffs and bailiffs, doing their best to keep the excitement in the courtroom to a professional level, hold their posts, intimidated by the numerous cameras pointed toward the defendant's table. The logos read BBC, MSNBC, FOX News, CNN, and Associated Press—all surrounded in a sea of other journalists and magazine writers, every one of them readied to feed the ferocious tabloid hunger. They've discovered a bottomless reserve of fodder, in Joshua, and today the film is rolling to catch every bit of what may come.

Their handheld cameras begin flashing as William strolls in wearing a three-thousand-dollar suit. Everyone knows exactly who he is because his pictures have been circulating on the news over the last couple of days, the story being that he's been on a discreet assignment in Vatican City. Questions are blurted, attacking every angle.

"Will you be personally defending Joshua?"

"Will your son be pleading not guilty?"

"How does Archbishop Malea view the defense of your son?"

William raises his hands, quieting them in preparation for a statement. He looks regal and plays his part well. After a few moments, they settle.

"First and foremost I would like to state the fact that Joshua Siconolfi is one hundred percent innocent! And *yes*, I will be representing him. Also, to answer your question, I have spoken in private with Archbishop Malea, where he counseled me too follow my divine calling to be here. That is all I have at this time," he adds and then slices through the room to the defense table. Tracking close behind him are four of his male colleagues and a woman, who seems out of place. She scoots through them as the defense and the prosecution teams share proper acknowledgements, finding her station under the judge's bench. There she makes a short phone call.

"All rise for the Honorable Judge Cooper!"

Michelle grips Cools's hand, interlocking fingers as they stand. A small door opens behind the bench, and Judge Cooper steps in briskly with an air of preparedness. The cameras lock onto her. Through their lenses her image fits nicely, as she is a stern-looking, firm-statured woman in her fifties, wearing a simple head of graying hair—very judge-like. She takes her chair and, with a strict hand, waves everyone to be silent.

"You may be seated."

The clerk announces, "Next on the docket, we have number 7519650, Joshua P. Siconolfi." A door to the side of the courtroom opens, and the bailiff escorts him in, in handcuffs and shackles. William stands, and Joshua grins for the cameras. They love him; he's camera friendly, mysterious, utterly diabolical, and as of late, he *is* the news. And even though many in the courtroom do not see him as such a rock star, he prevails still. His light blond hair is wetted and messy. And the orange jumpsuit fits him nicely (under which most picture the thin, muscular physique previously seen in swim shots). He clangs over to the defense table, receiving a brief hug from his father, and stands before Judge Cooper, who doesn't afford him a second look since she's a no-nonsense arbiter who tries little to hide her emotions. On this day her countenance reads of utter contemp. Cools and Michelle share the same disdain as she, except they cannot take their eyes from him—for different reasons than most, as they are searching his face for signs of trauma, though he appears to be fully recovered.

The noise level slowly rises in the heat of it all. Judge Cooper bangs her gavel, addressing the crowd curtly before things get out of hand. "I can close these proceedings to the public in an instant! If anyone makes an outburst in my courtroom, I assure you that you will spend the night in my jail. Your being here is a privilege that I have granted, and one that *will* be respected. I want silence. And all cell phones will be turned off." She stares at the crowd for a moment then turns to Joshua. "Is your full, complete name Joshua Paul Siconolfi?"

He compliantly answers, "Yes, Your Honor," then smiles for his attention givers.

Judge Cooper ignores his antics, stating frankly, "You are being charged by the state of Washington with murder in the first degree, which is a capital offense and can be punishable by death. How do you plea?"

William, standing next to his son, speaks softly into his ear. Everyone holds their breath, willing him to say something outrageous or maybe even recite another one of his poems.

"I plead not guilty, Your Honor."

"Duly noted; the defendant pleaded not guilty. So now I will consider granting bail." She looks to the prosecution table.

Milkowski rises as some of the cameras pan. "Your Honor, we have sufficient evidence, including a signed confession, to convict Mr. Siconolfi with this crime." All reporters look back and forth to each other, seemingly perplexed; in all of their eyes burns the same question: did he just say they have a signed confession? Milkowski moves along. "And also, I would like to add, he is currently under investigation for thirty-four—yes, *thirty-four*—other missing persons, all young women. He has an extensive history of violence and has not been cooperative while in custody, so we would like to request the court not to grant bail."

The judge makes some notations on an unseen tablet then looks straight to William, purposely disregarding Joshua, and says, "At this time I will grant you a few minutes to surmise as to why I should not follow the petition of the prosecution."

William shines a welcoming smile. "Your Honor, with all due respect to the prosecution in this case, there simply is not enough evidence to prove *any* crime has been committed, let alone that the defendant is responsible. And it is my understanding that any ongoing investigations concerning missing persons are based solely on a list of names written in a book. There is not any evidence that this is his book or that he's the one who wrote the names in it. So I would ask that you realize the gravity of the situation—that is, these unsubstantiated claims are the telltale signs of a desperate prosecutor who is motivated by the spotlight." Milkowski shakes his head. William carries on. "Now, my client has had some issues in the past, most due in part to alcoholism. And he has paid his debt to society." William continues his narrative, speaking amid well-practiced hand gestures. "And I am pleased to inform the court that he no longer uses alcohol and attends Alcoholics Anonymous regularly." Judge Cooper rolls her eyes, recalling the report she'd read detailing the cocktail Joshua was holding when police were dispatched to his home. She glances at him, seeing he is wearing his innocent-little-boy face as William adjusts, recatching her view. "Also, Your Honor, my client is a homeowner here in the great city of Seattle. And if need be, he could, with any reasonable conditions, be remanded into my personal care, where I would assume full responsibility for him while awaiting the dismissal of these charges." Judge Cooper again rolls her eyes, this time blatantly. William, noticing her impatience, closes. "So, Your Honor, my client is in no way any threat to the community, and I am pleading with the court for bail to be set and to be set within reason. Thank you."

All interest shifts to Judge Cooper. She scans over her notes, looks directly at Joshua, and replies, "I have already read statements from both the prosecution and your attorney concerning bail, and I set your bail at fifty million dollars."

Rumblings begin to mount. Michelle mutters, "Thank God."

Judge Cooper raps her gavel and, in a sharp tone, says, "Moving forward!" Then she spends a minute reviewing her paperwork and advances procedurally. "I am going to set a trial date for June 17."

Joshua yells out unexpectedly, "I demand my right to a speedy trial!" Everyone listens intently, hoping for more, since his statement feels like only the fuse has been lit.

"I clearly instructed you to be quiet!" She waves her gavel, staring at him, signifying her control over his future. Then she adds in inflexible terms, "You will be silent, or I will have the bailiff gag you and strap you to a chair if I need too." These are her only words, but other threats are made with her staunch expression. William also scolds him inaudibly as she waits for him to comply.

There is a tense moment of resistance before Joshua responds with a simple, "Yes, Your Honor."

The room relaxes as she returns to her notes. "Fine, I will grant you your request and set trial for February 19—that's six weeks from today. That is all," she says sharply, before banging her gavel and excusing herself promptly.

Joshua is quickly escorted away as his father assures him he will be visiting him soon.

The reporters, disappointed he didn't make a scene or utter some evil verse, scurry out of the courtroom to transmit the details to their awaiting stations. William joins them outside the court. And even in the early beginnings of his tirade, his skills and strategy are apparent. The drumbeat is scored, repeating over and over again of Joshua's innocence while defending his right to practice the religion of his choice, making claims that this is a modern-day witch hunt. Then, unlike his son, he doesn't let them down; he gives them what any one of them would literally kill for to have exclusively. He holds his hands high and says, "I have an extremely important admission to include." All attention is on him. "I was not a good father, and I..." He bows his head with a hint of shame; his eyes moisten. The cameras are captivated, sensing something nuclear. William becomes visibly and uncharacteristically fragile and is obviously struggling to press forward. "Joshua...Joshua, my one and only son, is and always has been eccentric, to say the least; he suffers from numerous afflictions, including paranoia and schizophrenia. I know you think he's a monster, but I assure you he is not." William fights himself to keep it together, and his battle is heartfelt; compassion is extended to him by everyone in the hallway as he tells all. "My Joshua is a very confused young man...and Kimberly...his wife...is a figment of his imagination. She has never really existed!"

At first everyone is speechless, until one of them argues, "But we have her photo."

William holds his hand over his forehead, giving his reply, "And if you visit his home, you will find the same portrait hanging in his living room. But I assure you: it was most likely stolen from the photography studio he worked at during college. Kimberly is simply not a real person! That's why they will never find a body. She is made up—his supposed lover. She is not missing or dead; she's merely his delusion!"

Thirty seconds later newscasters from around the world interrupt their broadcasts with various declarations.

"News alert."

"Breaking news."

"This just in..."

Chapter Thirty

"Oh my God, are you freaking kidding me! We have to prove that Kimberly is real! A woman who has no family except for... what...an aunt somewhere in the Midwest, and her best—maybe only—friend, Amberly, is missing; her boyfriend has committed suicide, and her husband is a freaking psychopath." Michelle finds it difficult to mention a woman's boyfriend and husband in the same sentence, but right now that is the least of her worries. She wants to pull her hair out, and Captain Jackson, her partner, and Ghost are not saying a goddamned thing. "Are you getting anything?" she demands from Ghost.

"I'm working on it," he replies, without taking his sight from the computer screen.

"So what do we do now? We have to run around...and what?"

"Settle down," Cools says, trying to quiet her so he can think. "All we have to do is get the marriage certificate, find a couple of strippers who'll say that they knew her, and use the GPS tracking system from the yacht and locate her body. She's out there—I know it!"

"No!" Captain Jackson jumps in. "It's not gonna be that easy. I just spoke with Milkowski, and he tells me that this is unusually problematic; it's a real tricky-sticky situation. And although he assures me it can be done—that is, convicting someone of murder without a body—it cannot be done if her very existence is in question. And have either of you even considered the fact that maybe she isn't real? What if he's messed-up in ways we cannot even imagine? No, our hands are tied. We have to prove Kimberly was an actual person, that she was in fact Joshua's wife. And that is exactly what we're gonna do. So, first things first."

"Oh, I'm really beginning to hate this asshole—and his father! He's a clever son of a bitch; you gotta give him that. This is going to be a gigantic waste of our time and resources." Michelle's statement of the obvious hangs in the air as Captain Jackson and Cools look at her the way she and Captain Jackson typically look upon her partner.

"I think I have something!" Ghost blurts out. "I mean...I'm getting nothing on...Look!"

"What?"

He peels his eyes away from the monitor long enough to explain. "You're not going to like this, but I cannot find an actual marriage certificate for Joshua and Kimberly. I've searched every state, municipality, and every country they've been to. I double- and triple-checked before saying something."

"You're telling us they're not legally married?" Cools asks, a bit staggered.

Ghost proceeds with caution. "No, I...I mean, yes, they are not legally married. And it looks like the fact that our computers said they were ever married in the first place originates from an arrest of Joshua two years ago for disorderly conduct. The arresting officer simply typed it in his notes from what Joshua had told him. But I promise you they are not and never have been married. And it gets worse. I'm coming up empty with her maiden name: Sharons. It is starting to look like it was an assumed identity."

"So how do we prove who she is?" Cools asks.

"Well...uh..." Ghost coughs nervously. "It's like this: when people assume fake identities and take steps to hide their true selves, it becomes extremely difficult to prove who they are. This is how it's done in our international spy networks and with undercover DEA agents. About the only way is fingerprinting or DNA analysis."

"No body, no DNA, no damn fingerprints. Great!" Michelle adds negatively, throwing her arms in the air.

"Yeah, but we do have her DNA; we have her DNA in her blood found on the yacht."

Ghost responds carefully to Cools's summation, "Well...yeah, in part you are correct; you have blood that has a DNA signature, but it doesn't do you much good without anything to compare it too."

Then Captain Jackson corrects them both by stating, "But we do have her DNA; it's at the clinic where she and Amberly took their HIV tests." He doesn't even wait for their reply; he pulls out his phone and makes a call. "Fredo, I want you to get over to the clinic where Kimberly and Amberly took their HIV tests and get us what's left of her blood sample. Better yet, get both of them."

"Yes, Captain, I'm on it now."

"Piece of cake," Cools says, "we'll get the blood samples, match the DNA, and problem solved."

There's a moment of silence as everyone thinks it through. Then Michelle changes the subject. "I wanna know why nothing is being said about, you know, when he the signed confession."

"I'm not sure. It doesn't seem to make much sense that he would say nothing or that William wouldn't have at least mentioned it," Captain Jackson replies, in a tone suggesting that is all he cares to speak of it. Cools's demeanor tells her the same.

"He didn't mention…he didn't what?" Ghost asks, now looking at them nosily.

No one answers as he shifts his suspicious eyes to each of them.

Captain Jackson clears his throat. "It's nothing for you to worry about Andrew Levingston…Ghost…whatever they call you! And it is nothing for you to speak of, if you get my meaning. After he signed the confession, we placed him in a cell, where he began screaming and banging his head into the concrete walls; he then made claims that we somehow beat him to talk. So let's get something perfectly fucking clear: we never did anything to him. But just the accusation could make us look bad."

Cools and Michelle wait motionless for him to respond. The tension is cut short with the chiming of his laptop. Ghost shifts his gaze back to his computer, where his expression pales even whiter. "Oh shit," he squeaks out.

"What is it?" Cools and Michelle ask at the same time.

"It's a reply to an e-mail I sent an hour ago to Natalie Hunsaker, Kimberly's aunt in Minnesota, and only known relative." He turns his laptop slowly, so they can all read the message. The monitor displays the same picture they have of Kimberly. And the text beneath reads, "This is not my niece. Who is this? How did you get my e-mail?"

In disbelief everyone reads the message over and over until another surprise rushes into the room.

JFK, catching his breath, rapidly says, "Captain, the number for the clinic was disconnected, so I Googled it, and a newspaper article came up from ten days ago: it burned to the ground, destroying everything."

Michelle spins, flinging her hands in the air. "For the love of God!"

Cools begins to say something, but Captain Jackson cuts him off. "All right, that's it; we're gonna do some groundwork—starting right now! Cools, I want you and Robertson to go to the Kitty Club and get anyone—I don't care if they're coked-up hookers. You just get us some corroborating witnesses, anyone who can verify that Kimberly worked there and that she's identified to be the wife of Joshua. Fredo!"

"Yes, Captain?"

"I want you to interview all of Joshua's neighbors, getting the same! And Ghost, you better start getting me some goddamned answers, or the next time I see you, you'll be delivering my pizza!"

The officers exit in a hurry, leaving their captain staring warnings into the young computer analyst. Cools leads Michelle to their cruiser in the parking garage. He moves fast, and before she can get in, he has lit a cigarette and removed the bottle from its hiding spot. He takes a straight drink. She knows better than to say anything since it will only start an argument. So instead she complains, saying, "Fine, that's the way you want to be. At least roll down the window; I cannot stand your smoke!" He doesn't respond; he just lowers the window and heads for the interstate.

Soon they're cruising down the freeway at 15 mph in almost complete gridlock. Michelle reads out loud from her laptop. "05/20/2012: first degree arson, St. Luke's parish: dismissed due to lack of evidence." She ascribes more under her breath while changing screens. "Here it is. Ten days ago fire stations 35 and 51 were called to a multialarm fire at 2240 SW Challine Street in the business district of South Seattle. Firefighters couldn't control the blaze and had to let the entire building burn itself out—a total loss. The two-story structure supported three businesses in the area: Martin's Furniture, Computers Inc., and Challine Street Medical Clinic. Arson is expected to be the cause, and damage is set at over twenty-nine million dollars. What do you think about that, Brad? He burned down the damn building to destroy her DNA!"

"Yeah, I'm sure he did, but that's a whole other case. Right now we just need to focus on what we can get today." Just then the traffic begins to move, and thirty minutes later they're pulling into the Kitty Club entryway that funnels them to its back parking lot, a ways off from the main thoroughfare.

Being a guy, and somewhat of a car buff, Cools appreciates a few of the luxury automobiles stabled outside the club walls: a Porsche Carrera GT, Lexus LFA, Cadillac CTS-V, Acura NSX, and more. He wonders for a second if this is some kind of sports car club as well. Michelle seems not to notice, so he decides not to mention it. Besides, all she is mindful of, for the moment, is what is on the inside, because she's never been in a strip club before and is looking forward to the experience. Cools pays the forty-dollar cover charge, and they enter into a dark hallway and, brandishing their badges, pass by two serious bouncers. The inviting music grows louder, and excitement mounts as they pass black curtains into an unexpected atmosphere. It is nothing like the seedy brothel she'd pictured. It is lavish and clean. Three round stages with shining silver posts form a triangle. Leather chairs and spacious tables surround them. The patrons are well-groomed and finely dressed men, wearing Rolexes and expensive suits. And the girls are beautiful, flawless, supermodels. Michelle studies them for the slightest of imperfections. The one on the center stage whips her glittering pink and blond hair, flashing naughty grins while seductively dancing to the music and lights, with red lipsticked lips pressed on her ass. Her large, round breasts, shapely legs, and flat belly are all accentuated by tight, mouthwatering skin. Michelle instantly feels sexual. Oh God, she thinks, if I were a man, I would want to play with her!

Cools captures a quick look, moving to the bar. Welcoming them is a young stud bartender lording in front of glistening display cases of exotic liquors. Cools places his badge and orders a glass of Jameson.

Michelle checks him out as he searches the wall behind him for the bottle. Then back to the girls. "This...uh...is a lot nicer than I thought," she yells over the music.

"Yeah, not too bad," he grins.

The bartender, sporting a tight-fitted shirt, sets the drink on a coaster and says cordially, "I'm Aaron. Can I get you anything else detective?"

Cools swallows the liquor in one gulp and motions him to lean in closer. He pulls Kimberly's picture out of his pocket and shouts out, "I came here to get every last bit of information there is on her. And I promise you, if I leave here today not knowing all you know, I will return and shoot you in your pretty face."

Aaron looks to Michelle for help. He finds none. Then he nervously replies over the noise, "You want to talk to Tommy, the manager!"

"Where is he?"

"I'll...uh...get him for you," he says and begins to back away.

"We'll come with you," Cools says and tracks him to the far side of the stage area. Michelle steals a couple more quick glances at the girls before they enter another dark hallway. The music sounds more distant as they round each corner and travel through a maze to the rear of the building, taking note of the names on the doors: Lovers Lace, Ecstasy, Ablaze, Lady Demure, and so forth.

Aaron opens a door and begins to say, "There are two police—"

Cools pushes past, followed by Michelle, who slows with a warm smile in front of the bartender.

"Hey, what the fuck is this?" Tommy yells.

"You know exactly why we're here. Now I want some answers. Tell me everything you know concerning Kimberly."

Tommy lets out a sigh, waves his bartender away, and offers them a seat.

Michelle inspects him and his office. He's a tall, fit, bronze-skinned man in his midforties who would be very good-looking if it weren't for the pock marks covering his face. His small, square office is cluttered, and glass-enclosed frames cover every available surface on the walls. Inside are numerous girly magazines: *Penthouse*, *Hustler*, *Playboy*, *Maxim*, and *Club*. Michelle presumes the featured girls make up the weekend lineup on the stages.

As they sit Tommy sets the rules like a shrewd businessman. "Fifty million dollars bail shelters my thoughts for the time being, but let me ask you this: is there any chance of him getting out?"

Cools, immediately understanding his concern, answers confidently, "No, he's not going anywhere. And even in the event he does, he'll be under twenty-four-hour surveillance. Also I want you to know anything you say here today will be between you, me, and my partner, Detective Robertson." He presents her.

She smiles while Tommy muses over the circumstances for a spell, then replies, "There's a lot you need to know, and some of it will be hard to believe."

Chapter Thirty-One

The cold, pallid cement walls, where Joshua sits, are paint chipped and adorned with graffiti, gang symbols and obscenities: "Blue-dog is a Rat," "Fuck the police." An electric deadbolt actuates screeching steel, and a door opens. William, trying not to touch anything, walks past mothers, girlfriends, and gangster buddies until he sees *his* problem waiting behind the glass. Joshua wears an unusual grin and is sitting tall.

William takes his seat on the round, stainless steel stool. He picks up the phone, ordering, "Listen to me, Josh. Do not utter a word until I have finished saying all that I need to say."

"No, you listen to me. I—"

William slams the phone back into its cradle.

Joshua protests for a spell then relents; his muted appeals are barely heard through the thick screened-glass barrier. William holds out until he's sure he will get the chance to speak first. He is a prudent man who has just spent the last hour procuring a judgment to have the recording system turned off while conversing with his son. Still he does not trust them and doesn't intend to permit an opportunity for Joshua to say anything incriminating. Also he has an obligation to keep this scandal as far away from the archdiocese as possible. It is a delicate dance, as none of this rests well with the church—his prized client, which he's represented as chief legal advisor for more than a decade and aims to protect at any cost. The wealth gained in service to them has guaranteed his devotion and has become a large part of his professional and personal life. For better or worse, it is who he is, even if it is all a sham. Attorney William Siconolfi is forever putting on a show, practicing the art of spin and deception, not just in the courtroom but in the public light as well. The greatest decision he ever made for his career was the blueprinting of his public Christian persona, projecting himself as a follower of the faith:

a hypocrite for hire.

Again he picks up the receiver. "I need you to say nothing; this conversation could be monitored, and anything you say can be used against you. Sometimes cases can be won or lost due to the slightest bits of information given up by the defendant. Now, I already know you are innocent, so you need not try to convince me otherwise." Then he attempts some small talk to ease things over. "How're you doing in there? You look horrible."

Joshua, pressed to behave, starts in an even tone. "Dad, I know I say some crazy shit sometimes, but listen to me carefully. They really did torture me; they have this room with chaotic lights; they drugged me and kept me in some kind of pressurized cell, and I want it told to the press. I want the world to know. I want them to pay for what they did to me!"

"That's' not important right now." William shakes his head, finding the fortitude to tell it to him straight. "Josh, I'm not…we're not going to attack this with accusations of police brutality. We all know it happens, but in the end, it's not a good defense strategy, basically because no one cares. Half of the public won't believe it; the other half silently condones it."

"I don't care; I need you to tell the press about my forced confession!"

"Fine. If that's what you want, I'll make a statement. Now answer my question: how're you holding up?"

He laughs sarcastically. "I'm doing just fine. Is that what you want to hear?"

"Do not speak to me in that tone, son; I think you should show some respect and appreciation that I'm even here."

There's a pause and then Joshua asks, "What're they saying about me in the news?"

"They're saying all kinds of things, but none of that's important. Now listen to me. We're in a lot of trouble here, and the fact that you seem more interested in your media coverage makes me question your very sanity even more so. They want to execute you, son!"

"I don't care; they can try if they want. And who gives a shit anyway?"

"I give a shit! Yeah...you know, you may be my wayward son; you screw off all your money, and I put up with all your nonsense, your religion, your fantasy world you live in with your stripper wife, your...your drugs! And still I care."

Not wanting to get roped into another discussion of drugs, Joshua changes his approach. "What do you mean *we're* in a lot of trouble. I'm the one in here, remember?"

"Oh yeah, it's all about you, isn't it? Well, let me tell you something. I've lost ten pounds since you started all this mayhem. And I'm walking a fine line trying to save you and my practice. I'm hesitant to show my face in public because of you, and I have the nagging notion to walk away and wash my hands of all this completely!"

Joshua changes and pushes his face to the glass. There's a boiling anger in his eyes, looking as if he could smash through with hatred alone, but he says nothing, since it is nothing new—this talk from his father and his position in the community he's heard all his life. William can see his son drifting to wherever he goes when he's this way; he attempts to pull him out of it, saying, "I told them Kimberly isn't real—that she's only in your imagination."

"Sure, that's just fucking like you! Let's quit playing games, or maybe we could talk about your church. Why don't we talk about the fact that—"

William hangs up again, motions for the guard, then watches his son being escorted away without looking back. A parental guilt rises in him. Maybe I could've been a better father; maybe things would've been better if he still had his mother. I have to do anything and everything possible to get him free. But more importantly I have to shield the archdiocese; I have to protect myself.

Joshua is taken back to isolated confinement. The guards call ahead, clearing the hallways before moving him. They have to stay vigilant and keep him safe because of the many other criminals who may attempt to make a name for themselves.

Chapter Thirty-Two

Tommy replies, "There is a lot you need to know, and some of it will be hard to believe!"

His visitors listen ardently, taking notes.

"She came to me a year ago, begging for a job, but said she couldn't reveal her real name. My first thought was she was under age. So I put her on the stage, hoping she'd fail miserably, that I could get rid of her right away. But it was just the opposite; she was a natural, and desirable; she took to it like I'd never seen before. Her moves were naturally sensual. She said she'd never danced before, but we didn't believe her. And after some of us took a good look at her and concluded she was of age, I hired her on the spot. I told her to come back later that evening at nine, but she never showed. I tried to call, but she didn't answer. Then two nights later, on a Saturday night, the place was packed; she strolled through the front door dressed as some sort of queen vampire. She wore a black see-through cape with a red choker. Then she stole the center stage. All eyes were on her as she interrupted the other girl, simply staring at her, saying nothing, with a glare telling her to leave. She was powerful, and needless to say, she had our full attention. The other girl—can't remember her name—bounced away in a fit. And Jeremy, our DJ, played into the theme. He lowered the lights and beamed a bluish, glowing spotlight on her and a slow pulsing strobe; the set held a trickle of decadence and sin. Then she began to dance in ways never seen, bending her silken curves, teasing, inviting all of us to feast our eyes, and we did. But after she was done, she fled the club without saying a word. I thought she was going to get away, but I chased her down in the parking lot and, after a lot of pleading, persuaded her into doing a regular show."

"The one with Amberly?" Cools asks.

"Yes, yes, it was a dual act she and Amberly performed; they were our most asked for. I had men *begging* me for Kimberly; one even offered one hundred thousand dollars for her."

"What do you mean, *for her?*" Michelle asks cynically.

"Uh…maybe I'm stepping out of bounds here trying to help you? If my information isn't helpful then maybe—"

"No, that's okay," Cools quickly clarifies, then looks to Michelle and says, "We're not here to investigate anything that has to do with the operations at the Kitty Club." Michelle rolls her eyes without reply. Again Cools turns back to Tommy. "There's nothing you tell us here today that will incriminate you." Tommy returns a skeptical look. Cools holds a finger, pulls out his cell phone, and calls Captain Jackson. While it rings he asks for Tommy's last name.

"Cools what do you got?"

"Well, not much yet, Captain. But in order to take this where we want it to go, I need to get credit for Mr. Tommy Latson and the Kitty Club."

"Your timing couldn't be more perfect. Sit tight; I'm gonna call you right back in his office."

"Okay."

"What is that—a credit?" he asks.

"Exactly what it sounds like. If you or your business ever find yourself in any legal troubles, you now have credit. And Captain Jackson said he's calling us right back."

Michelle sighs in frustration; she cannot condone extending a free pass to men who take advantage of lost girls. Inside her mind a fitting catchphrase materializes: "Pimps with Connections."

Just then his desk phone rings—Jerome Jackson. Tommy pushes a button, answering it with the speakerphone. "Hello?"

Captain Jackson's voice comes through, "I presume I'm speaking with *only* Mr. Tommy Latson, Detective Cools, and Robertson, is that correct?"

All three answer at once.

Then a moment later, there's another voice, one neither Cools nor Michelle have ever heard before, though Tommy seems to immediately know who it is. The voice says, "Tommy, I am going to ask you to fully comply with any questions these detectives may have, absent any names of course. And feel free to inform them as to what it is we do, so they get the full understanding of what they are dealing with."

"Are you sure about this? There are going to be some that won't agree."

"Anything they want!"

The call ends.

"Who was that?" Michelle demands.

"Uh...I'm *very* certain I'm not going to answer that."

She looks insulted and presses further, "What do you mean you're not—"

"Michelle, leave it be! Let's just get what we came for. Tommy, you were saying?"

He takes a long stare at Michelle, his eyes becoming more serious. He sits forward. "OK, we all know what goes on here, so let's not kid ourselves. But the Kitty Club operates on a much higher level—all the escorts from Vegas would kill to work here. And we have a special club within a club. No doubt you've noticed a few of the exotic cars in our parking lot?"

Images of the expensive automobiles spotted earlier flash in Cools's mind. "Yeah, I was going to ask you about that."

"Well"—he grins pretentiously—"on prearranged nights, the Kitty Club is not open to the public; it is invitation only. We have a car club, and we race at night. You ever have to detour past sections of freeways or thoroughfares at night because they're blocked off for construction, but when you drive by the next day it doesn't seem like anything's been done?"

"Okay, go on."

"That's because we have them shut down and detour traffic onto side roads, opening them up to race on. Then we meet back here and have another kind of party."

"You mean an orgy?" Michelle states, growing increasingly disgusted.

Tommy, like a politician, answers, "Meaning... We all have a good time, and no one has to do anything they don't want to."

"And was Kimberly part of these *parties*?"

"Yes."

"And what about Joshua—is he a part of it too?"

"I cannot answer that directly. I am bound by solemn oath never to utter the names of the clubs members. Most of them I couldn't tell you their names if I had too, because I simply do not know. Nearly all of our members wear full masks and only use their fraternal names. Although I will answer you this way:

I have reason to believe that *a person of your interest* is an extremely dangerous man as well as a grave risk taker behind the wheel—like no other. Let's say this allows *him* to win more than *his* fair share and that *he* is hated within most circles. Rumor has it that he is protected by his god and cannot die. Anyways I don't know how any of this can help you. I believe the main concern of yours is this. I heard the news where it was said Kimberly wasn't a real person. But I assure you she was; even so, you will find no one here to confirm that...other than maybe a few of the girls. And is that what you want to do—parade a bunch of strippers into court? And that's not to mention the fact that our stables are not filled with permanent positions. The majority of our employees do not work here much longer than a week or so, since we like to keep a steady flow of new and interesting entertainment."

"So you're saying you cannot help us, so you can protect your little orgies and car races?" Michelle yells, standing up.

"Detective Robertson, I am protecting powerful men. I'm sure you can find other avenues to prove she is a real person; this is *nothing* but a hornets' nest to you. Now I have told you all that I can." Tommy stands, suggesting that the meeting is over.

"I might need to ask more questions," Cools states. "Give me a good number I can reach you at any time."

"Fine." Tommy spells out his number as he walks them out of his office and down another dark hallway—this one leading past other security guards to the side parking lot. It is now dark as night has come upon them rapidly. "I'm sorry I couldn't be of more help; if I dig up any information that I think you could use, I will call you. And at the same time, it is my hope that we all get through this and conclude by punishing *only* the one who deserves it." Then he slips back inside, locking them out.

There they take a closer look at the cars in the lot, make a few notes, then head back toward the station. In the cruiser Cools, on a hunch, makes a call to Officer Smithe, working on the Trace Friesen case. "Officer Smithe, Cools here. Let me ask you: did Trace have a sports car?"

"Yes, yes, he did as a matter of fact, and a very expensive one at that. We found a storage facility in his name, and when we went to check it out, we found a Ford GT-50."

"Was anything in it?"

"Yeah...and it's odd that you would ask. We found a mask...some sort of devil zombie, and it's not your typical forty-five-dollar Halloween mask—this thing is handmade, more like a movie set mask. Why are you asking; do you know something about it?"

"No. Well, maybe. Listen, there's a couple of things you should know, so I'd like you to call Michelle; she'll fill you in, okay?" He snaps his phone shut.

"God, you're an asshole. I'm not your damned secretary, Brad; quit acting as if I am!"

"Calm down, Michelle. I'm not supposed to talk and drive at the same time," he replies playfully, in an attempt to smooth things over. It's somewhat contradictory though since he dials out again. Then her phone rings, with Officer Smithe on the line, as JFK answers Cools's call. "What did you get from the neighbors, Fredo?"

"Well, I've procured statements from the Swansons, an elderly couple who've had many friendly conversations with Kimberly and knew her to be the wife of Joshua. How did you and Robertson fair at the strip club?"

"Not so good…uh…good work, Fredo." Click. "Man, I really hate that guy, but it sounds like he's got some neighbors that can confirm Kimberly lived there."

Michelle doesn't respond because she's busy explaining everything to Officer Smithe, after which there are a few miles of concerted silence before a probing discussion ensues, in the car, concerning the secreted club, the mystery man who spoke to the strip club manager from the captain's office, and how Trace Friesen, Kimberly, and Joshua are really tied together.

Soon, in Captain Jackson's office, Michelle speaks first, expecting to get some answers, "Who was the man on the phone?"

He snaps back in a way that she isn't accustomed to. "All right, listen to me carefully: who he is, isn't important. The identities of any of the car club members are not important. Do you hear me?" He doesn't wait for a response. "Now, go talk to Ghost; he has a few things. I don't think we're gonna have any problems proving Kimberly existed; that sneaky William cost us a day, but that's gonna be the end of it."

Michelle throws a small fit and storms out, leaving the two men alone. Cools searches his captain's eyes and says, "Okay, well, I guess we'll see you tomorrow," wondering why his old friend is acting so strange.

"Yeah, tomorrow…we'll see you tomorrow." Then he guides him to the door.

Cools leaves, unsure of his friend. He then catches up to his partner, now sitting with Ghost, whose demeanor tells him he's dug up some dirt. He asks sharply, "What do you have for us?"

"Well, it's like this. I found her; she was an orphan who bounced around from home to home. Her real name is Wallingsford, and Sharons was the last of her group home families. I spoke with them, and they informed me that the last they'd heard was that she'd died of a drug overdose years ago and said that they couldn't be positive that the picture of her was really her or not. So I'm not sure you want to open this can of worms; maybe I should bury this, so they can't use it to further their allegation that she was never real."

"Yeah, let's do that…for now anyway," Cools says.

"But why wouldn't she just go by her real name?" Michelle poses.

"I thought the very same; her driver's license and social security are under Wallingsford with fake addresses. She has no arrest record for either name, and I cannot outline why she'd pretend to be someone else."

Cools looks at Michelle, appearing as if he's just figured something out. He excuses the both of them from Ghost's office and again pesters her to go out for a few drinks with him, somewhere away from the station.

"I can't tonight, Brad. But…let me see…tomorrow's Tuesday…I'll find a way to get free tomorrow night, sometime after nine, okay?"

He agrees, and their date is set.

Chapter Thirty-Three

Inside his ice-cold cell, Joshua, confident he will be punished by the guards for what he's about to do, works diligently with a found piece of broken glass, scraping obscure messages on the walls. He's certain they will be told to the outside world.

This can only hold me for a time…I have sent you a

>poetic verse< …Can you not even find what IS existent!

The writing tires him. He crawls into his bunk and drifts off to a place of comfort, locating deep inside his mind the nineteen sixties and his compassion for the continuing tale of little Frankie. The last he'd seen was the nameless black man who'd brought to Panama-Red rumors of betrayal, which now sends the three of them driving into the unknown.

Synapses release, sparking neurotransmitters within Joshua's unconscious mind.

Outlines of shapes and colors come together forming the picture of a black Corvette Stingray, amid sounds of squealing tires and an enraged Panama-Red at the wheel, cursing to the night. His friend, wearing a large afro, sits nervously in the passenger's seat with the terrified boy in his lap. Little Frankie is missing his mother as the car speeds through the backwoods hills faster and more dangerously than he's ever gone before. Worry and uncertainty take hold of him; Panama-Red appears to be totally out of control. The car is jerking back and forth over the white lines, and he's swearing so vehemently spit is flying out of his mouth, carrying on and on about some guy who didn't pay some money.

"Turn here . . . turn in here, man!" the black man yells.

Little Frankie tightens. They turn off the road onto a long dirt driveway that leads to an old, broken-down farmhouse, where seconds later the Corvette skids, stirring a cloud of dust. It comes to an abrupt stop just a few feet short of the porch. Panama points his finger at little Frankie and yells, "You stay here! Wait in the car!" Then he pulls the slide back on his gun, chambering a bullet, and orders the black man to cover him. Petrified little Frankie does as he is told. He only watches out the window, not moving a muscle, hoping it all ends soon.

Panama moves as fast as his anger. He leaps up the steps, screaming, threatening, and in one motion violently yanks the screen door off its hinges. There he finds a locked front door which only maddens him further. He begins pounding and kicking it, with his partner in crime sneaking cautiously up the creaking steps.

Boom! Boom!

A thunderous noise explodes through the door, blasting it into pieces. Little Frankie starts shaking when he sees the splinters of wood and bits of Panama as they hit the windshield. The black man turns and begins running across a field. At the same moment, a beast of a man, dressed in tattered blue coveralls, comes through the broken doorway. Boom! He shoots again into Panama's dead body. Chilling screams of a woman echo from inside the farmhouse. Then, moving to the edge of the porch, the big man raises his sawed-off shotgun once more.

Boom! Boom! Boom!

A blaze of fire roars through the dark air, nearly hitting the black man jumping over a barbed wire fence. Everything rings before going dead silent. And these are the last sounds little Frankie will hear for quite some time, even though later in life he will be told that there was never any physical damage done to his hearing.

Midnight rounds are being made at the jailhouse when Joshua, or at least the little boy inside him, loses control of the narrative. He then dreams of meeting Kimberly in death, pleased at the thought of being joined with her once again.

Chapter Thirty-Four

The following day a YouTube featured video—"The Spirit of Heaven"—receives 1,644,512 views.

Another of Joshua's mesmerizing poems bids for the spotlight. It was sent, the day before his arrest, to a professor at the School of the Art Institute of Chicago, who now explains the work in detail on the video. As intrigued followers type in "Joshua Siconolfi" in the website's search box, "The Spirit of Heaven" pops up, and then the video starts with rolling text.

The Spirit of Heaven
Is to,
"Live on Forever of no evil"
An everlasting sign,
In Palindromic chime,
"Live on Forever of no evil"
To Me His words He sends,
The Beginning and the End.
"Live on Forever of no evil"
GOD'S simple Truth in verse,
Can be read <u>Forwards</u>,
or <u>Reversed</u>.

Next the professor comes onto half of the screen; the other rendering the poem in full. He wears a tweed jacket over a tightly fitted sweater, looking every bit the elitist. "My name is Professor James F. Whitley," he says, from underneath a long and eccentric graying mustache. "And this masterful work of art was mailed to me personally from Joshua Siconolfi—the one and the same—who obviously knew that I would be proficient in explaining to you the complexities of this poem. To me the core verse, 'Live on Forever, of no evil,' is intended to assert that 'Heaven' is to live eternally, absent of any evil. However, it is more than that. What we are witnessing here is a rare form of art known as a palindrome. A phrase arranged in sequence to read equally in either direction. I implore of you to take a closer look at the core verse, 'Live on Forever, of no evil.' And see that it reads the same, forward or reversed. Furthermore, I believe…"

This is basically the spot where most have tuned out Professor James F. Whitley to take another look at the poem itself, to search it for clues and attempt to decipher its hidden connotations. Millions are fascinated; it quickly becomes the topic of the day.

Chapter Thirty-Five

Tuesday night, at quarter past ten, Michelle Robertson, the wife, called her hubby and told a little white lie. She asked if he would mind if she went out for drinks with her girlfriends tonight—the story being that Sheila, one of her college friends, fears that her boyfriend may be messing up, and is in need of a little girl-to-girl counseling. Mr. Robertson agreed, thinking to himself that his wife could use the chance to blow off some steam. And now Michelle Robertson, the detective, sits across from Cools in a bar on the outskirts of the city.

The place is mostly empty, with rustic decor. Photographs taken in the distant past hang on the walls in black and white: a stagecoach drawn by brawny horses, homesteads from the late-nineteenth century, and muddy, commerce avenues crowded with turn-of-the-century automobiles. The ceiling is open and has large wooden rafters and fans circulating the air. They sit opposite each other in a booth, mutually enjoying a moment of quietness. She is speculating about him, noticing that he's been calmer lately and is now only drinking beer. He has a couple of insights about her as well. She appears to be quite comfortable lying to her husband and venturing out alone in his company. While at the same time, a profound frustration presides within her. As of late she has been more outspoken, more cynical, and he contrives that she's becoming hardened.

Their older waitress scoots across the hardwood floors, bringing Cools a fresh cold one and Michelle another White Russian. "Here you go, you two," she says politely, then makes change using the money left on the table's edge and leaves them in seclusion.

Michelle, over the light sounds of a couple playing billiards in the back, asks, "How are things going for you lately, Brad? Are you doing something different? You seem less strained…less agitated." He starts to answer, then takes another swig. "Brad, answer me!"

"Uh…okay. I went to the doctor, and I started taking some medications to slow me down. But that's just between you and me, okay?"

"Sure, Brad. What did they put you on?"

"It's an experimental psychotropic, but there's no charge."

"What!" she cries outs in disbelief.

"I'm kidding; settle down. I'm taking Lexapro, and I think it's helping. I was wondering when you were going to get around to saying something about it, or at least I was hoping you would notice."

"Well, I've definitely seen an improvement, Brad," she replies favorably. Cools responds with a gratified smile, watching her drinking from her straw. She quickly reaches the bottom and waves the waitress over for a third.

"Drinking a little fast, aren't we?" he teases.

"Yeah, but I deserve it. And I…" She pauses for an instant. He understands she has more to say. "This whole case is so stressful, even though we have him. I just feel that he's still controlling things…or maybe someone else is controlling it. I don't know. Did you read his latest poem, his palindrome or whatever, on YouTube?"

Cools holds up his iPhone. "Got it right here. It's definitely out of the ordinary, maybe even—and I hate to say it, but…witty?"

"Yeah, that's my point exactly. He *is* clever Brad, even if he is insane. And he's surrounded by powerful figures, and I'm just…I'm afraid that somehow he's going to get out of this. Everything is moving so fast! They're treating him like some notorious rock star in the news. We didn't find anything today—nothing of any interest anyway. And I'm getting calls at my home—my home, Brad! And what's the deal with Captain and his secret friends?"

"Okay, there it is. I was waiting for you to bring it up. I have a couple ideas concerning all this; I think you should listen, but bear with me, what I'm about to say might alarm you."

She opens her hand, stopping him before he speaks, as the waitress returns with a new drink for her. "Is there anything else I can get for you two?"

"Yeah, I'll take another beer, and"—Cools reaches in his jacket pocket, pulling out his badge—"what would I have to do to get an ashtray around here?"

The waitress chuckles and then, in a husky smoker's voice, says, "Honey, you might just be onto something." She looks around, assessing the damage it may cause, as he flashes her a flirtatious smile, egging her on. "You know, ain't nobody else coming in here tonight; besides all our regulars have gone." She checks her watch and winks, saying, "I'll be right back."

"Wow," Michelle exclaims. "I am impressed. You sure do have a way with the ladies, don't you?"

"Well, you know," he replies with a grin.

Less than a minute later, the waitress returns carrying a beer and an ashtray. She pulls out a cigarette of her own, asking, "Do you need a light, honey?" She lights his cigarette first and then her own. Michelle laughs to herself, examining the two of them, looking like teenagers getting away with something. "Now, you two enjoy yourselves, you hear," she says and leaves, happily smoking.

Michelle lets him enjoy a few drags before inquiring a second time, "So what're your ideas about what's going on, Brad?"

He takes one more quick puff, gathering his thoughts. "I think we both feel something much bigger here; the real question is: what do we do about it? I have no doubt that the car club may very well be a hornets' nest, maybe even more like a shark tank full of fearless thrill seekers with a lot to lose. And although it's possible they could be nothing more than innocent men who like to drive fast, this thing could be something very different, seriously different—it could be more menacing than we could ever imagine. What if they're mixed up in Joshua's religion, or maybe even responsible for not just Kimberly and Amberly, but all the other missing girls? How many were there, thirty-four?"

"Yes, thirty-four," she replies in disgust.

"And if that's even partially true, how far might they go to protect themselves? What happens if we become a foreseeable threat?" Michelle doesn't answer, but there's a look on her face that says she's entertained similar ideas. "Wait a second; I just thought of something," he adds, and makes a phone call.

Michelle's head begins to whirl. She's not sure she wants to continue with this conversation. I think I feel a panic attack coming on; I should drink more.

"Come on, answer the phone."

"Hello."

"Ghost, Cools here. I need you to look up something for me. William—does *he* own a sports car?"

"Do you think?" Michelle chirps out.

A few clicks of the keyboard, and Ghost responds back loudly over the phone, "Yes, yes, he does; he owns a 2011 Mercedes-Benz SLS AMG, and it looks like it's the real deal—lists at $183,000, and that's just the base price."

"Thanks, Ghost."

"Oh my God, Brad, do you think? That connects William to Trace; they're both members of this racecar club! They go out, race their cars, maybe perform religious ceremonial acts, and have orgies on Saturday night, then meet up at the church with their wives and children on Sunday morning. How creepy is that?"

"We don't know they're involved in Joshua's religion," he states, correcting her, then swallows the last of his beer. "But that being said, I'm concerned about what *we* do, because there may be a point of no return if we keep digging... Maybe we should leave it all alone. Think about what we could gain if we uncover some scandal. Think about what we could lose if we uncover some scandal. I don't know that we're prepared for this; we don't even know what we're dealing with."

"Now you're scaring me, Brad." She shivers at the chilling thought of finding herself on the wrong side of an influential sect of religious disciples, especially those that lust for ultimate stimulation.

"My thoughts exactly! I'm scared myself. We're not talking about taking down some drug dealer or proving a woman poisoned her husband for the insurance money. No, we're dealing with"—Cools starts again with his fingers—"one, William Siconolfi a dominant and crafty attorney; two, Trace Friesen, who was immersed deep in politics; three, the fucking Roman Catholic archdiocese; and four, the fact that these guys are mixed up in illegal car races, prostitutes, orgies, and maybe even secret religions. This is not something for us to delve into; these are powerful men who can only be taken down by other powerful men, not a couple of cops!" Michelle nods in agreement. "Now, I've been thinking about it a great deal, and we have our guy. He's not going to get out of this. He'll be convicted and sent away, plain and simple. We..."—Cools waves his hand back and forth—"we need to consider ourselves...your family." He lets it sink in for a second. "For all our troubles, we actually have pretty good lives. I have Chelsea, and you have your husband and Lindsey. Why would we risk all that? Why should we?"

The waitress has approached unnoticed. "Is everyone doing okay? Can I get you some more drinks?"

Michelle looks away, staring at one of the pictures on the wall.

Cools answers, "Yeah, one more quick round. Thank you."

The waitress walks away.

"And if they are guilty, we just let them bury it?"

"Maybe better *it* than *us*."

"You know, I've never seen you run from anything, Brad. Is there something you're not telling me?"

"No, I'm not running! It's only that I...I have this idea of what these men are like, and it frightens the hell out of me...thoughts of ritualistic pleasure killings by wealthy untouchable men, men who can hide behind their clout and influence, eliminating anything or anyone in their way." He lights another cigarette. "Just listen, I'm not trying to talk you into anything. I'm not even sure...I'm not sure I've made up own mind. It's just that sometimes it's best to look the other way; I don't want to be in a position to *have* to let them bury something—maybe it's best to just not know some things in the first place."

"I don't know, Brad," she sighs, obviously exhausted, "maybe you're right."

They finish their drinks without discussing much more and, after a short, comforting hug outside, part ways. Their conversation has induced uncertainty and paranoia. Cools envisions situations of being suddenly approached.

And Michelle, who hardly ever drinks and drives, does so cautiously. The liquor is having quite an effect, and her wits are altered. Just eight more blocks, just concentrate on what's in front of you. She makes it to her home without incident, but there's a nagging troublesome feeling that someone has followed her.

Chapter Thirty-Six

Another couple of days slip by and things slow down, without any new evidence emerging. It is a fact that being a police officer is sometimes like prison or war, 99 percent pure boredom and dead ends, followed by intense hours of utter chaos. But the calm that has as of late surrounded them is poised to give way to an evil head rising once again.

Michelle is awakened by someone pounding at her front door. She looks at the clock; it reads 9:37 a.m. She has slept in, and her husband and daughter are already gone.

Bang, bang, bang!

The knocks are so hard they shake the house and stagger her thinking; she grabs her service revolver, checks that it is loaded, and treads lightly out into the hallway to listen.

Bang, bang, bang-bang!

She isn't expecting any company, and normal people don't knock nearly as hard. Cautiously she tiptoes down the stairs in her pajamas, gun at her side, until the front door is in view.

Bang! Bang! Bang!

Each thump startles her more; she can now see a shadowy figure through the tinted glass bordering the entryway. The shape is moving abruptly, trying to see inside. Her body tenses as she creeps to the door and peers through the peephole. There, a man she's never seen before stands in a uniform, holding flowers. He has quit shifting around, and she knows that he knows she's behind the door. She cocks her weapon, conceals it at her back, and unbolts the lock. Then she opens the door, hiding her fear behind a gaze of contempt for the man's gross behavior.

"Are you"—he looks to the card—"Detective Robertson?" he asks, absent of any emotion, presenting a bouquet of black and white roses.

"Yes, I am," she answers, stealing glances around him at the outside. None of her neighbors are out, and even though she's at her front door and in the open, she feels cornered. I'm getting roses; I should be delighted. Why does this feel so wrong?

"Here you go. These are for you," he declares, handing over the gift. She grabs them silently, using her free hand as the man adds an indifferent explanation, "I apologize to you, ma'am, for knocking so hard." He then begins to walk backward down the steps. "I was just told that you'd be home and that you'd certainly want to have these."

She thanks him in a weary tone, returns inside, locks up tightly, then watches the man march out of sight and disappear down the sidewalk. This is very strange; he was strange. Who would send me black and white roses? Why isn't he parked out front? She opens the card and immediately drops it to the floor alongside the flowers, realizing now that she's in grave danger. The detective in her grips the gun firmly, instantly becoming acutely aware of her surroundings, searching again through the windows. Nothing is moving. The man is out of sight, but where he went she doesn't know. So immediately she runs throughout her home, locking all the doors, checking that the windows are secure, all the while considering the card from memory.

"Be forewarned, You and your Partner should be very Cautious! ...You should adhere to the worries of your conversations!"

She flies back up the staircase, barricading herself inside the master bedroom, and finds her cell phone. But it is barely holding a charge. Please make a call out. With shaking hands, she calls Cools. "Brad! Brad!" she shrieks. "I need you to come here right now!"

Cools sits in traffic. Right away he can hear the urgency in her voice. "Here? Where?"

"At my home, Brad, they sent me a threatening message—a man was here! And I'm freaking out!"

"I'm on my way."

She hears his engine rev before the line goes dead. Hurry, Brad, please hurry! She sits on the bed, holding a pillow and her gun, just staring at the door.

All the talk from the past couple of days comes to mind: the car club, ritualistic thrill killings, sex parties, thirty-four missing girls…Could they be responsible? How far would they go to protect themselves? Who is their leader? Her senses are heightened; she can hear the slightest of noises: the hum of the heat pump in the backyard, her cat pacing outside the bedroom door, the downstairs living room fan spinning. Adrenaline pulses in milliseconds with erratic jolts preparing her to fight or flight. A checklist for noises of concern enters her psyche—door locks being tampered with, footsteps, breaking glass—as she tries to remember every detail of the flower delivery man: tall, thin, fit, midthirties, no name tag. How have they heard our conversations? Dark eyes, untanned skin, short, dark brown hair. Listen for door locks. Expressionless, scary eyes. Tires squealing. Car door slamming…

Bang, bang, bang!

She clenches her gun tighter, almost squeezing the trigger, then freezes up.

Bang, bang, bang!

"Michelle, are you in there? Open up!"

It's Brad; get yourself up. Move!

She runs downstairs and checks to make sure before opening the door and pulling him inside. She clamps onto him so firmly he can barely breathe. He can feel her body quivering, her sweat mixing with his.

"Where is he? Where is he? Where did he go?"

"He left…I think he left. He gave me this!" She picks up the card. He reads it, noticing the flowers strewn across the floor. "Oh God, Brad, I was so scared. I…I…I was up most the night thinking about them, and when someone started banging on the door—oh God, I was so scared. And then I read the note." Suddenly her tone changes from jittery to pissed off. "I don't want to go any further with this Brad. I want out. I'm going to tell Captain. I want off this freaking case!"

"Okay, calm down. We're going to figure this out."

"No, Brad, I'm done. I'll quit if I have to. I don't care! You can go after these guys on your own. How do they know about our conversations? Somehow they're listening. They're listening to us, Brad. Whatever—it doesn't matter. I am done!"

Cools reads the warning again, then moves around the room, searching out the windows. "What did he look like?"

"He was tall, thin—it doesn't matter. I want to get out of here right now. Come on. Let's go!" She grabs him again by the arm and tries to pull him outside.

"You gonna go in that," he says, referring to her pajamas.

"Oh shit, wait here. Wait right here!" Then she bounds back up the stairs, vanishing away onto the second floor. From there she continues to yell, "Don't go anywhere, Brad. You better not go anywhere!" Normally he would be laughing at her, but he realizes the threat is real. And he can't help but feel like they're being watched even at this very moment. She comes running down the stairs. "Okay, I'm ready. Let's go!"

They leave together in Cools's car. On the way their conversation covers much ground, all coming to one final conclusion: the flowers and their warning came from the racecar order. He drives, looking more behind him than in front of him. By the time they reach the station, they've come to the consensus that they're done investigating anyone or anything that has any connection to the car club.

At the station Misty Lakewoods says, "Good morning," and waves them in.

Captain Jackson has been waiting patiently inside his office in preparation to hear them out, to abide by their demands, to grant their liberation. Like a skilled performer, he will sympathize with their cause and act stunned by their new information, though he already knows all that they're going to tell him. Michelle enters first and begins frantically explaining every detail.

When she is exhausted, he asks them both a simple question. "All right, do the both of you fully understand that once I take you off this case, for no reason will I put you back on it? Once you're done, you're done."

"Yes, Captain, I understand fully."

"And you, Cools?"

"Well, where are we at exactly in terms of securing a conviction? Can Milkowski get it done?"

"All right, here's the deal. We can prove she was real. Nice try, William. And that she was thought of by many to be the wife of our boy. The circumstantial evidence is enough to persuade a jury that he alone murdered her. Simply put, we'll get a conviction. Although it seems quite apparent his antics will continue, with no foreseeable end in sight." He holds the bridge of his nose. "On this morning's news, they were saying we beat a confession out of him. One reporter was asking, 'What's this country come to when we arrest the deranged, who not only believe they have a wife but have imaginarily killed her?' Now, it all plays well in the media, but the end will be the same: he will be convicted and sent away. I promise you. Oh, and he still paces all day naked in his cell."

"Yeah, he's a real freak," Cools says. Michelle remains quiet.

Captain Jackson chuckles forcibly. "Yeah, he's one interesting white boy—that's for sure. But soon he'll only be a memory. Now, I'll give another press conference telling them you and Robertson are being taken off the case due to the fact we've secured sufficient evidence to go to trial. And any further investigations into the matter will be conducted by Fredo."

"I like that idea. I want the whole world to be guaranteed of that. I need to protect myself and my family."

"Exactly. All right, then, consider it done, Robertson. Now, if that's all, I do have other matters to consider. But first I would like to talk with you Cools." They both look to Michelle, evidently the third wheel. "Wait in the war room, Robertson, and I'll be in shortly to debrief you, okay?"

"Yes, Captain," she says and leaves his office.

Once the men are alone, Captain Jackson says to Cools, "Have a smoke if you want."

"Yeah, okay, what is it you want to talk to me about?"

"All right, a couple of things…first, what're your plans with the coke?"

"Well, I can't risk getting caught taking it back. I guess I will just get rid of it."

Captain Jackson studies his face, hesitant to accept his assertion. "All right, good enough, but you better do it; I don't want to hear of any of it hitting the streets. Where are you hiding it?"

The question surprises him. He delays his answer, somewhat confused. At no other time has he ever felt a reason to withhold anything from his captain, his friend. But a sense inside him advises to be evasive. "I hid it where no one will ever suspect to look; it's safe enough."

"But where…where is it?"

He feels pressured; paranoia sets in, so he lies. "I stashed it under the kitchen sink in Chelsea's apartment."Then he senses the weight of his captain's stare but holds his demeanor.

"You said there were a *couple* of things you wanted to talk to me about?"

"All right, there are. And I'm gonna give it to you straight.You look like shit, Cools, and I want you to take a vacation. Take your girl somewhere, get laid, get drunk, get all this nonsense out of your mind, and get prepared for trial."

Cools wasn't expecting as much, and actually believes things to be the contrary. He hasn't felt this good in years; he's been more relaxed and getting better sleep, although he does grant the thought an inkling of consideration. "Well, if that's what you think I should do, I guess…yeah, I could use some R and R."

"I do; I really do." There's a moment of silence, with Captain Jackson looking into him, studying him. Then the captain stands, grabs his jacket, and orders, "Stay, have a couple drinks, smoke a few cigarettes, think about it. I'll be back in twenty minutes; we can talk some more." He gives an encouraging nod and continues, "I'm gonna have a little talk with Robertson…get her under control."

He exits the room.

Cools finds a bottle of Jameson, pours a healthy glass, and flows into a daze, thinking only of tropical islands. And before Captain Jackson returns, he's made up his mind and left a note on his desk.

The note reads, "I think I'll start packing my bags this afternoon."

Chapter Thirty-Seven

Believing Cools is secured inside his office, Captain Jackson attends to Michelle in the war room. He walks in, finding her all alone. "Need a cup of coffee?"

"Yeah, okay," she replies, then silently watches him fill two Styrofoam cups. He dispenses a healthy portion of sugar and creamer into hers—the way he knows her to drink it—before joining her at the table.

"All right, Robertson," he says in a comforting voice, "there are some things you need to understand. First of all, you know I have great respect for you. I really like you, Robertson. I think you're a class act; you hold my heart." Michelle smiles. "And you're making the right decision to leave these stones unturned, which do not concern you." He reaches across the table holding her hands in his. "You're cold."

"Yeah, I…I'm still a little shaken up over this morning," she answers, wondering where all this is going.

"I can appreciate that," he says, trying to ease her mind for what he's about to say. "I have to tell you some things, Robertson. There are men—powerful men—who sometimes have to compromise by committing various evils for the greater good. This you must trust. And these men require the absolute need to privacy." Michelle's thoughts lead briefly to the mystery man on the phone call from his office. "This you can relate to, I'm sure. There're times when we have to bend a rule here or there to get real justice."

Michelle realizes this is one of those situations in life where one should respond fittingly. "I do understand, Captain. I really do. I have a good life, and even though they may be racing their cars around and sleeping with prostitutes, I...I believe we have Kimberly's killer behind bars, and that's the end of it for me. That is all that I care about now."

He grins; he knows she is holding her tongue, yet he discerns, in time, she will learn to hold fast to her own words. "All right, then I want you to spend the day with Fredo. I know he can be a bit challenging to work with, but I need you to fill him in on everything you know or that you think you know. Tell him any and all ideas you and Cools may have, and then we'll get you reassigned to something else tomorrow, okay?"

"Thank you, Captain; thank you so much." She squeezes his big hands.

"All right, wait here; Fredo will be in shortly. I have to give a press conference. If you need anything, do not hesitate to call—for anything, anytime." He gets up to leave.

"I will, and thanks again; thank you."

He takes one last look at her, gives her a wink, and exits the room. Then he walks to the bathroom, contemplating how to handle Cools. Three minutes later the urinal is finishing its flush, and he's washing his hands, looking at himself in the mirror. My part is almost complete, he thinks.

Soon he leaves his reflection and returns to his office waiting area, where Misty Lakewoods says she wishes to speak to him. He ignores her request and orders, "I need you to call the media and schedule a press conference ASAP. The subject will be addressing the allegations of abuse and the reassignment of the investigating officers."

"Yes, Captain, I can set that up in about an hour; sound good for you?"

"Yes, that'll work, thank you."

"Oh, and I renewed your subscription for *Car and Driver*."

"All right, thanks."

He then turns to enter his office, but she begs nervously for a moment of his time. "Captain, I would like to talk with you about possibly getting a raise. I feel that it is due and that I deserve one...I'm sure you would agree that I am a special asset and that I am worth it. You know that I know everything that goes on here."

"All right, why don't you schedule some time tomorrow, so we can go over the details."

"Will do, then; and thank you, Captain," she says, grinning ear to ear. "Oh, and I should tell you that Detective Cools had to leave."

"He what? I told him to stay here!"

"Oh, I didn't know…he just came out in a rush and said he had to go. That's all I can tell you."

Captain Jackson opens the door and glares at the empty chair where Cools should be sitting. Then he finds the note notifying him that he's heeded his advice. This soothes his nerves

Chapter Thirty-Eight

Inside his personal cell, Joshua spends his days watching them talk about him on the news, writing in a journal he has started, and reading the little notes that get slipped under his door. After a small charitable donation of thirty-five hundred dollars was made to Sergeant Willis's, his day guard, vacation fund, he is now privy to all that goes on concerning the inner workings of his case. He knows that Kimberly hasn't been found. He knows that his two favorite detectives are being reassigned; he knows that the smile he wears is warranted. His one and only burden is his visions of little Frankie. He fears for the boy who's been lost to a world of drugs, murder, and disarray.

Chapter Thirty-Nine

Two days later, a security guard stationed at the metal detector at Puget Sound Bank and Trust spies another customer approaching: a tall, well-shaped man with natural good looks. Somewhat oddly, though, the man motions him aside for a private question. "Hi, I'm Detective Cools from the Seattle Police Department," he says, as he opens his sport jacket, displaying a gold-covered badge and a Beretta 9 mm. The security guard sizes him up until he's satisfied that everything is kosher, then pushes a button and tells him to go on in.

He walks in, admiring the enormity of the building. The ceilings are three stories high. Twin marble staircases lead upward toward open offices. He uses the stairway to his left, hopping every other step till he crests the third floor. Normally he would be out of breath, but today his energy level is high. Even his spirit is elevated, since lately he's been thinking a good deal about his life: who he is compared to whom he aspires to be; what the important things are in life. He has come to conclude that he's not one man whose sole purpose on earth is to singlehandedly save it. Rather, he's here to enjoy the gifts of the world and to share them through others. He's becoming a changed man. And today an epiphany has revealed itself to him—Detective Bradley Cools is crazy in love.

The third floor is bustling with action, men in suits and women in skirts moving around carrying folders and checking their text messages. He catches a hurried young woman and asks, "Where's Chelsea Simmons's office? I know it's up here somewhere...I just don't know where."

She points to a chiseled relief hanging above large black doors that reads Executive Offices. "Go in there; her office is down the hall."

"Thank you," he says as he turns, pressing forward. His heart races, and he feels that his new life cannot begin until all that is contained within him is fully disclosed. Through the executive doors, the hallway turns to the right. It is absent of any windows, only doors every thirty feet. He searches the nameplates. I have to tell her I love her; I have to convince her to run away with me. Near the end he locates her title written on a black plaque: Chelsea Simmons, Executive Account Manager. Under the inscription an intercom displays a blue-lit call button. He pushes it and asks, "Chelsea Simmons, please?"

Chelsea, sitting at her desk, clicks her mouse, opening the perimeter security camera; she cannot believe who she sees. The intercom instantly speaks back, "Brad? What are you doing here?"

"Well, uh...open up and let me in. I need to talk to you." The door buzzes open. He steps in as she stands behind her desk. She is radiant, wearing a form-fitting black skirt buttoned tight over a silky auburn blouse. Her hair is pinned up. And the entire far wall of windows not only offers a sunlit city view, but shines an orange glow upon her.

"What are you doing here?" she asks, smiling heartily.

He moves to her, gently captures her hands in his, and sits her down in one of the guest chairs; she is even more beautiful viewed from above.

"Brad...what's going on?" she giggles.

"Chelsea Simmons?"

"Yes," she replies, losing her breath, imagining him proposing to her.

"Chelsea, I love you...and I need you to go away with me." He then reaches inside his jacket pocket and pulls out two plane tickets, destination—Aruba. As she peeks at them, he remembers her longing to vacation there. A few months back, on a lazy day, she'd thoroughly explored the island Eden on the Internet, sharing all of its secrets as they lay in bed pillow-talking, daydreaming of its glistening, sun-drenched beaches.

"Aruba! You got tickets to Aruba?" she yells ecstatically. Subsequently she snatches them from his hand, inspecting them carefully. "When are they for?" she asks as she finds the date. "Today! Today...and four hours from now...Are you serious? How can...I can't...What were you thinking, Bradley?"

"Hold on now; just listen to me; we can do this." He then begins selling his plan with palms held out. "You can tell your boss something, anything...I don't care; we can leave now, pack our suitcases, and escape for a week. You deserve it; *we* deserve it!"

She leaps from her seat, begins pacing around aimlessly. "I can't just tell my boss something...tell him what exactly?" Cools steps back, saying nothing, allowing her the time to work it out. He knows she won't be able to decline his invitation. "How could I...how could we pull this off? Maybe I can tell him I have an emergency...a family emergency...No, no, I don't have to lie...I can...I do deserve some time off...Things are running very smoothly here—did I tell you about our numbers?"

"No, you haven't mentioned them," he replies with a grin.

"Well, they're good—great actually." She begins to squirm within the room, roaming faster. "I did just buy that new summer dress; I was going to show it off to you this weekend. Oh Brad..." She bounces over and climbs into his lap. "You're going to take me away...and make love to me on white sandy beaches in Aruba? You really, really love me, don't you?"

Cools laughs to himself, enjoying her inner little girl. He kisses her fervently, grabbing a handful of her. She scoots more into him, opening her mouth wider. I want to fuck you right here in your office—a thought he quickly abandons as he looks to his watch. He fights his mouth away from hers, explaining, "Baby, we have to go. If we don't get this party started, we're going to miss our flight."

Shortly thereafter she explained to her boss that "her man," maybe soon to be fiancé, had forced this upon her at the last moment, and to refuse the offer would foster regret. The enthusiasm and passion she possessed—how could he have told her no? As a result they worked out the details, and it isn't long before their plane has taxied down the runway and is flying high above the earth's surface.

Onboard they snuggle close, intertwining each other's hands, as they talk for hours regarding their future; Chelsea, advocating a cute little home with children, and Cools, envisioning a summer party boat where they can entertain friends on searing swim-suited days. Then, in a loving compromise, both dreams are intermingled into a fantasy of them on a pleasure boat, one little boy and one baby girl dressed in lifejackets with Cools at the helm forging through crisp blue waters while Chelsea applies sunscreen and hands out picnic sandwiches. And although it's never mentioned, the proposition of marriage rests on their horizon. Soon Chelsea falls fast asleep to finish out the twelve-hour flight to an equatorial paradise, where tomorrow's endless beginnings will be waiting for them when they land.

Cools stays awake, thinking all the right decisions have been made. The second and easiest of which was to fly far away with his love. And the first, the one he'd made earlier, was to forget. It was an easy decision for him actually when he'd found the bouquet of black and white roses resting on his doorstep and the card reading, "Plata O Plomo—You should go far away and forget what was behind you!"

Then he detected a brown-wrapped package underneath the flowers containing fifty thousand dollars. He understood the message well: *Plata O Plomo*, a Spanish term meaning "silver or lead." The message couldn't be clearer—take the money and look the other way, or end up with holes made by metal.

In the early morning hours, he wakes up in the midst of sleeping passengers. It takes a second to remember where he is. Chelsea is sound asleep, so he tucks a blanket around her and checks his watch, 4:35 a.m.—four more hours before landing. I sure could use a cigarette...Maybe I can read myself back to sleep? He spies a couple of pamphlets. Inside the first one, he finds a printed sheet of paper; he sets it aside and begins thumbing through the scenic pictures and tourism information. He reads through every brochure, and he still can't sleep. Then, becoming annoyed with insomnia, he picks up the printed sheet of paper found in the first leaflet. He holds it in his lap and slips a pillow under Chelsea. Even as she sleeps, she is such a treat to his eyes. He opens the paper.

"Joran Van Der Sloot is the Aruban national who is thought to be in direct connection with the disappearance of Natalee Holloway." Oh yeah, I remember this story; he killed her, but they could never find her body. How odd of a coincidence... Wasn't she also thought to have been buried her at sea? "Van Der Sloot is currently serving a twenty-eight-year sentence in the famed Peruvian Castro-Castro maximum security prison, for the first degree murder of Stephany Tatiana Flores Ramírez. Exactly five years, to the day, after Natalee Holloway went missing, Van Der Sloot was apprehended in Chile and then deported to Peru, where he allegedly confessed. It was a confession he later challenged—faulting the torturous interrogation tactics of the national police of Peru for his forced admission. But a Peruvian judge ruled his confession was valid." Just like Joshua's statement will also prove to be valid. Just like he will be convicted...I wonder what sort of interrogation rooms they have?

He folds the paper and sticks it in his pocket. Usually reading helps him doze off, but now he's even more cognizant than before. He stares at Chelsea, watching her sleep, admiring her exquisiteness, and envisioning growing old with her, maybe even giving her the children she longs for. After a time he nestles closer, shutting his eyes. Her warmth comforts and organizes his ill-at-ease mind as her beautiful image transfers with him into unconsciousness; he drifts away, playing, flirting, embracing atop ocean sands.

"Ladies and gentlemen, this is your captain speaking; we are preparing to make our final approach into Queen Beatrix International Airport. Please fasten your seatbelts and prepare yourselves for the glistening pearl beaches of Aruba."

Cools and Chelsea awake into the blinding sunlight that shines through the windows. They smile to each other through squinting eyes.

"Good morning, baby," he says, flashing a sly grin. The reason for his wily expression is that his first waking thoughts of her were erotic in nature.

"And good morning to you," she replies, returning a smile. They kiss. Then she pulls in a steady breath of fresh air and comes alive. "Oh, where's my bag? I must look a mess." He helps dig through the blankets for her purse and, as she is freshening up, diverts his attention out the window, monitoring their descent. The plane touches down, and soon they are wide awake, bursting with life, and geared up for an invigorating day of ocean breezes and chance adventures. They exit the plane and stroll, arm in arm, through the terminal so as even a blind man can see they are in love.

Koenraad Ludger, an Aruban native, stands in the airport with a sign in his hand when, out of the corner of his eye, he catches a glimpse of a striking woman: a tall auburn-brunette with a shape that saunters gracefully. Koenraad receives much pleasure from seeing the many attractive women who visit his island. But this woman in particular is extraordinary. Then, for no apparent reason, she begins laughing and wistfully twirls to the man beside her, giving generous hugs and kisses. Then, the man accompanying her looks directly at him and flashes him a thumbs-up. Not knowing all that is happening, Koenraad decides that they must be Mr. and Mrs. Bradley Cools, as the marker he is holding displays.

Chelsea introduces herself as Mrs. Cools to Koenraad, who escorts them out into bright skies to their pending cab. It's an open-top Suzuki Samurai, white, equipped with roll bars, readied for fun. Cools climbs into the back, granting the front seat to Chelsea. She gleams a loving smile at the gesture, and they all jump in. Koenraad hands them a cache of sunglasses to choose from. "Compliments of the hotel," he says, then pulls out into traffic, driving excitedly past the famed white sands of Paardenbaai Bay. Cools and Chelsea ride in awed silence, filling their eyes with the turquoise oceans and windy palms, as Koenraad, in broken

English, points out places of significance, all the while explaining why he is the best guide they could have ever wished for. Chelsea instantly adores him and finds his accent refreshingly spirited. "This is our capital city, Oranjestad. There is much for you to be doing here. And this is our Manchebo Beach—lots of lovely ladies to see." He presents each destination with an extended arm. "Also you can always find yourself a good times here at the Aruban Resort Casino. And to the left, our very own Bubali bird sanctuary." Koenraad shakes his head. "Although not so much to do there." Cools smiles at Chelsea; they're both enjoying his charming energy. "And now we are arrived here at the Occidental Grand Aruba; your hotel awaits."

As they step out of their taxi, Cools adds a few known details of the hotel. "Baby, this place has six restaurants and five bars, water sports, and a free-form pool...and I don't even know what that is." He laughs. "There are gift shops, a casino, massage parlors...We're going to have a lot of fun here—a lot of fun!"

"Oh, it is so gorgeous," is all she can say, still unbelieving of where she is. They enter the magnificent vestibule decorated in potted palms, where an enormous, blue-lit marquee built of polished marble displays the hotel name. Instantly the sounds of the large indoor water fountain are heard, bringing a bit of tranquility to their excitement. They follow Koenraad through the lobby, exploring the grandeur of the many open bars, lounging areas, and high vaulted ceilings which adorn countless skylights, beaming in the island sun. Chelsea is speechless. She firmly clutches Cools's hand as Koenraad ushers the contented twosome to the elevators, presses the eleventh floor, then delivers them to their suite. "Oh, this is absolutely amazing," she cries out. "I love it!"

"Yeah, this is nice," Cools agrees, studying her. He's gratified to see his girl smile, and at this very moment, she is beaming. He then gives Koenraad forty dollars, American, and says "Thank you," nodding him toward the door.

"If you need anything, I'm your—"

Again Cools gestures him to the door. He courteously submits and exits the room, leaving them alone for the first time in several hours.

Chelsea grabs his hand. Then pulling him along throughout the room, she excitedly praises every piece of modish furniture, the wide-open view of Palm Beach, and the ocean that unlocks the brilliance of the deep. She loves it all so much she tosses away any concern of how he's paying for everything. Right now she simply doesn't care. The only thing she is mindful of is leading him out onto the balcony, far above the sands, and showing her appreciation. There they embrace. And softly she whispers, "This is the most beautiful place I have ever seen. It's elegant and peaceful; it is so much more than I deserve. Kiss me."

They kiss long, building heat until she is steaming. Then he pulls away, teasing, "What would you like to do first on this island, baby-girl?"

"Oh, you know what I want to do. I want to fuck you like you've never had it before, then eat a gigantic plate of food, then go play on the beach!" Cools beams his approval, but she has more. "After that we will take a short restorative nap, then you will make love to me till you hate me so much...till you beg for me to stop!"

"Is that all?" he replies playfully.

She fires back by pulling her dress up over her hips and attacking him, pushing him until they fall backward and land onto the colossal-sized bed. There she descends upon him with her burning tongue in his mouth, moaning her hot breath, taking control, and stripping him until he's inside her. She pushes down. "I want you to watch me come," she moans. He poises himself, attending to this ravenous woman working herself into a frenzy, quenching her fire, panting, grinding, pinching her nipples. She licks her lips as she begins her rising cry. Then lastly they release together. It's takes a minute or so before she catches her normal rhythm and says, "I love you, Bradley. Tell me you love me."

"Completely! And at this very moment, more than you could ever imagine." She buries herself into him. And there they recoup for a time.

Then suddenly she jumps up and out of bed. "Get up! Come on, get up, and let's get going; we have so much to do, and I am starving. I wasn't kidding you about the gigantic plate of food!"

Cools puts up no resistance to her demands. They venture to one of the hotel's eateries, where she herself eats three plates of Caribbean seafood, foreign cheeses, and island fruit. Her energies are revived, and by midday they're exploring the many beaches in a rented Jeep. They laugh and play, fully adoring one another until evening, when it's decided to catch a two-hour nap before drinks in the sunset. Two hours turns into four as they barely make the outdoor lounge prior to the sun surrendering its heat over the distant waters. There he tells her of his immediate agenda. "I want to take you by the hand, lead you to the ocean waves, and kiss you under the stars."

"Who are you lately?" she asks. But he can't answer; he's not sure himself. "Oh, I don't even care; you can take wherever you please, Bradley Cools."

They buy a bottle of Vermeer Dutch Chocolate Liqueur and ascend onto the beach, where, under the moonlit heavens, they build a small fire and soak their feet in the warm sands.

The morning after, back in the hotel, a sound invades the room: *tchew-wew, tchew-wew*. Cools wakes suddenly. At first he hopes he was hearing things, but it comes again: *tchew-wew, tchew-wew.* He envisions a gun with a long, black silencer. He jumps out of bed. *Tchew-wew*. Swiftly he moves to the sliding glass door of the balcony and peaks out the corner, surveying the landscape below. Then he sees him. It's a male purple martin, the largest North American swallow, which he read about in one of the brochures. He catches his breath and checks that Chelsea is still sleeping soundly. He then steps out onto the balcony and lights the morning cigarette, laughing to himself and searching the pristine landscape for the answers to his troubling questions. Some second-guessing has invaded his thoughts—primarily the decision to leave the case. Somehow the idea to cease his pursuit of them held more merit when it was his. But instead, it was ultimately made by Captain Jackson, an anonymous threat, and fifty grand. What if Kimberly and Amberly learned something they weren't supposed to—who the men of the car club are, or maybe even some sinister political plot? Maybe they killed them, framing Joshua to take the fall. How close is Captain Jackson to them? And what about the money—will that be the end of it?

He then sends a text to Michelle.

Cools: Just thinking of you? Anything new?

Michelle: They found the crab trap, but it busted open on impact due to the weights inside...nothing was found except small traces of blood.

"I'll bet you're staring at the sea, dreaming of me, aren't you?" Chelsea asks, sneaking up on him.

He turns and kisses her. "You read me like a book, baby." Then he turns his phone off.

"What are we doing today?"

"I was thinking about...uh...going scuba diving. And then maybe getting a bird gun."

"A bird gun?"

"Never mind."

Chelsea gives him a funny look. "Maybe we better get you some breakfast there, cranky-pants. I'm jumping in the shower. If you order any food, I would like some scrambled eggs and a bowl of fruit, okay?"

"All right, I'll call room service."

It's not long before both of them have showered and begun their day, diving around the coast, where they witness a fabulous array of corals and see how sting-rays hover above the seabed. The afternoon is set aside for shopping—Cools's idea—for imported merchandise from the island's motherland, Holland. For Chelsea, he purchases perfumes, sexy underwear, and an elegant eighteen-karat white gold bracelet; and a new watch—a TAG Heuer Monaco—for himself, the sticker price topping fifty-five hundred dollars. Then he treats her to an expensive dinner before gallivanting her around to all the known hot spots of clubs and casinos for a night of dancing and gambling. The main events of the night are the slow dance they share at the Carlos 'n' Charlie's and the fight Cools almost gets into at the Crystal Casino. It seems he may have had too much to drink.

After sleeping it off until 10:48 a.m., Chelsea shakes him awake, panicking, "Brad...Brad...Wake up, wake up! I need you to go get me my breakfast from the lobby!"

"What?"

"My hair is all wet, honey, and I need you to go down and get my eggs. I'm starving! And I want to get an early start today."

His head pounds as he tries to understand. She shoves slippers on his feet. "Uh...are you kidding me?"

"No, it's almost eleven; it's time for you to get up, and room service is backed up. And the only way for me to get my eggs is you have to go downstairs and get them. And I'm really, really hungry."

He tries to argue but to no avail, since she's now practically pushing him out the door. "We could get breakfast in the restaurant..."

"No, they've already made my order, so please just go; it'll make me really, really happy," she says, using her most sensual voice, guiding him into the hallway.

"Hurry," is the last he hears before the door shuts behind him, and he finds himself standing alone in the hallway, half asleep, still half drunk, in his pajamas, and the clock is ticking.

Then he notices he's not wearing his slippers, but her pink fuzzies. "Oh well," he mutters, moving swiftly to the elevator, wanting to finish the task as soon as possible. Along the way he passes a chuckling couple enjoying some joke. And then in the lobby, everyone—even the hotel's personnel—seems to be a little extra giddy. The hostess girl, who gets his order, asks him if he's all right, and in short manner, he appears to be the spectacle of the morning; even some of his fellow vacationers are rudely gaping, giggling and chatting among themselves. Cools, not one to often feel insecure, struggles to ignore them. However, a level of paranoia has already set in. Seriously? How can pink slippers be so damned funny? He examines his footwear more closely, which only escalates the matter as two teenage boys start outright laughing and 360 degrees of eyes are upon him. What's the big fucking deal? He grabs the eggs from the hostess and makes it back as fast as he can, past a blushing maid and a mother who holds her daughter tight as he passes. He storms into his room. "Fuck, thanks a lot, Chelsea! That was a bunch of bullshit!" He shoves the to-go box at her.

"Why...what happened?"

"What happened is you threw me out in the hall wearing your lady slippers. What do you think happened? Everyone was staring and making fun of me. Fuck!"

Chelsea holds back a giggle of her own, suggesting that he splash some cold water on his face. He turns for the bathroom, missing her muted laughter as she hides behind a pillow.

Then there's a moment of silence, followed by, "Oh, you sneaky little brat! What the fuck is this?"

Chelsea bursts into uncontrollable laughter. And Cools steps out, wearing a face completely painted with makeup, with his girlfriend reciting a comedic line from a movie they'd seen. "Gotcha good, sucka!"

Later, after Cools *cools* off, they have another grand day hiking along sandy trails and sharing the sights, sharing each other. And although he secretly plans on getting even, by late afternoon he has all but forgiven her. They drive to an area just north of Hooiberg, where the Casibari Boulders present somewhat of an enigma due to their size and unusual patterns. Chelsea snaps pictures, inspecting them in wonderment. He, needing a cigarette, walks back to the Jeep, leaving her to examine the curious rocks further. From there he watches her move. There is no denying they are a true match.

Inside his pocket he thumbs a little black box containing a 1.15-karat diamond solitaire set in platinum. He pulls it out and examines it for a moment, rehearsing his lines. As visualized, he holds it out to her, saying, "Chelsea, you are the love of my life, and I wish to spend the rest of my years with you close to my side."

Then he sees her returning. She is smiling and very much in love. The moment is perfect. They lock eyes as she reaches the car. She suspects something and asks, "What are you doing?"

He freezes. "Nothing! I'm not doing anything!" He drops the ring back into his pocket. "Are you ready?"

She gives him an odd look, replying, "Yeah, let's get going. I want to get some dinner."

"Sounds good to me, baby-girl," he says and starts the motor. They drive away in silence on a highway bordering the sea. Cools searches the steady waves for reason. I'm very much in love with her. She's definitely the right woman for me, and I know she feels the same. We will be great together. We are great together. Everything is perfect...But it isn't; something is unsettled, unfinished.

Chapter Forty

Alone to his devices, Joshua scrutinizes his fan mail from countless news agencies and tabloid magazine writers who beg for interviews to religious old ladies who plead with him to give his soul to Jesus. A few of them he finds humorous, like the nutty woman who wants to marry him and the bodybuilder who asks whether he is gay. He decides to ignore them all and map out the rest of his course. Soon he will be appearing in court, presumably to expound upon his allegations of police brutality, but he has other plans. The events of today will not only produce the headlines he desires, but pave the way for his journey home.

Once everything in his mind is in place, he eagerly closes his eyes and submits to his affliction of sequential dreaming, projecting the specter of little Frankie. As of late the emotional connection he feels is so strong and the pictures so vivid that Joshua believes the boy exists. Or at least he existed. What's more, Joshua can now view from within him as well as without. In his thoughts he summarizes what he's previously seen: the 1960s, Alabama, Betty running off to work, Panama-Red, the black man, the farmhouse, shotgun flashes, Panama being killed, the large man in blue coveralls, and the fact that the incident is so chilling and sordid the young boy has temporarily lost his hearing. Soon he is returned behind little Frankie's eyes, feeling a motionless and soundless form that peers through a blood-spattered window of a black Corvette.

Unheard but seen is a distraught woman, who exits the farmhouse and stares in disbelief at Panama's dead body, now lying cold on the unlit porch. Right away little Frankie realizes that the woman, now jumping up and down frantically, is as angry and scared as he is. And it isn't long before she loses control and begins hitting the man with the shotgun, screaming silently.

After tolerating a bit of well-deserved abuse, the man grabs her, and they disappear inside the house. Little Frankie stares at the open door until he sees the two of them emerge hurriedly carrying suitcases and keepsakes out to an old, beat-up Ford truck. Back and forth they go until it is filled. Then the woman, while on her way back, stops dead in her tracks, and for the first time notices little Frankie sitting all alone in the car. Once more she breaks out in hysterics. "Oh my God…oh my good God!" She runs for the car as the man drops a bag and leaps off the porch. She opens the door of the Corvette, and they both gaze in shock at an emotionally frozen child.

"I cannot believe that asshole brought his kid with him!" the woman yells, looking dumbfounded at the man. Little Frankie says nothing; he doesn't even cry; he only thinks to himself that the man is bigger than he thought and that the woman's red hair is pretty.

"What in the hell're we gonna do with this here boy?" the man asks.

Nothing is said for a moment; then the woman turns to the man and replies indisputably, "We're taking him with us to Idaho."

The cell door unlocks. An incoming guard echoes his commands inside the room. "Siconolfi, it's time for court. Let's go!" Three minutes later Joshua is handcuffed, shackled, and tramping down the hall.

Outside the courthouse a whole host of reporters are lingering for another high-ratings press conference. William Siconolfi is attempting to have Joshua's confession thrown out due to police brutality—the debate of the week. A podium is assembled, and cameras dialed in.

William watches with his colleagues from a hidden vantage point, observing all the commotion. Then he prepares himself and says, "Let's do this thing," and strides out into the open and up to the podium, wearing a million-dollar smile, his talking points rehearsed. "Good afternoon. As you know my name is William Siconolfi, and I, along with my team, will be defending Joshua Siconolfi. Now, my client has been a victim of police brutality. He was tortured with physical as well as psychological violence. These are the methods they used to secure the so-called statement of guilt. And conveniently, or perhaps suspiciously, they have not been able to produce any audio or video recording of the event. Because my client signing a statement of guilt absent from being beaten to do so does not exist—just the same as Kimberly does not exist! Joshua has committed no wrongdoing, as we will prove to the state of Washington. He is absolutely, undeniably, one hundred percent innocent!" He lets his words hang in the air before stating he will take a few questions. Then he designates a questioner.

"Mr. Siconolfi, what proof do you have that Joshua was tortured?"

"We have a recently released King County inmate, who will remain nameless at this time, who witnessed Joshua being carried to the infirmary just two hours after his arrest."

"Did you ever know Kimberly?"

"Ha-ha. Is that your feeble attempt at a trick question?" He pauses, deciding something, before adding, "I will answer you this way. Yes, I do feel as if I know Kimberly since my son spoke of her often. Now that is all."

Its shot, recorded, and live fed to a waiting audience.

Fifteen minutes later in the courtroom, the clerk announces, "On the docket today, we are scheduled for a suppression hearing concerning Joshua Siconolfi, number 7519650."

Two guards escort Joshua in, wearing the same orange jumpsuit and ankle jewelry. Again the room is packed. William, fully prepared to give a fiery sermon contesting the validity of the signed confession, is standing up front, opposite prosecutor Milkowski. William pats his son on the back. Joshua flares a confident smile toward the cameras.

The legal jargon begins. And as proceedings are under way, the court is interrupted. "Your Honor," Joshua yells, obviously displeased, "I would like to address the court!" William attempts to silence him, without success. Judge Cooper is clearly perturbed. She bangs her gavel, but Joshua speaks over her. "Your Honor, I will be from this juncture forward be representing myself!"

At first he's disregarded as an unruly defendant. "You will not disrupt my courtroom!" Judge Cooper bellows.

Joshua doesn't flinch. He just stares at her with adamant eyes, stating over and over again, "I wish to represent myself. I will be from here forward acting as my own counsel," until she acknowledges his request.

"Are you serious, or is this just another of your games?"

"No, Your Honor, I wish to represent myself in this case." Then he stands still, grinning ear to ear, as the rest of the room explodes.

William throws his papers in the air, pronouncing, "You're on your own, son!"

The reporters go crazy, running in every direction. The top story of the week has been simply laid out with a few, greatly unexpected words.

Chapter Forty-One

Sci-Poll, an independent scientific media company that publishes and distributes information based on public opinion polling, has released its latest findings, subsequent to 858,600 persons surveyed.

Do you believe Joshua Siconolfi to be guilty of murder?

Yes—59 %

No—26 %

Not Sure—15 %

Sci-Poll denotes a sampling error of plus or minus 3.5 percentage points. In addition, after crunching the data, the analysts from Sci-Poll articulate their final analysis: game on.

Chapter Forty-Two

Nearing the end of paradise, Cools and Chelsea unwind in silence during their final hours in Aruba. Twice more he's attempted to propose, both ending in the abandonment of what would've been a treasured moment in an unforgettable place. He eventually concludes that first he must get through the trial, clean up his act before inviting her to share his messy life, seeing that she is worthy of so much more than he currently has to offer. This decision awards him with a sense of accountability and maturity while at the same time an impression of opportunity lost.

Inside their hotel room, soft beams of morning sunlight and sea breezes flow through the open balcony, puffing gentle gusts of wind that dance around the curtains. Cools lays peacefully across her lap as they listen to the waves, reminiscing about their vacation. They muse over the morning they rode WaveRunners off the sun-kissed shores and then in unison chose to skip the parasail for fear of its height, deciding instead to spend the afternoon combing the beach for sand dollars and splashing in the surf. They laugh again at the day he thought he'd caught a shark while deep-sea fishing, but it turned out only to be an eight-pound Atlantic bonito. They revisit the excitement they felt when he won sixty-five hundred dollars in one of the island casinos and the grief when he lost it all and more the following evening, the sadness of which was forgotten by wasting the rest of the night away in their hotel room, smoking some of the island's *Nederweed*—the high-potency marijuana grown in The Netherlands, which he scored from a bartender at one of the local beach bars. Like two teenagers they giggled themselves silly and fooled around, experiencing new insights as to how best solve the world's quandaries and speaking much of their personal viewpoints, as well as agreeing closely concerning religion and politics, as they melded together in perfect harmony.

Cools asks, "Hey, what are we going to do with the rest of the pot? We can't risk taking it with us."

She thinks for a second before snickering, "Maybe we should give it to Koenraad?"

"Yeah, I bet he would like that; he could go to the beach and watch all the lovely ladies."

"Let's do it; let's give it to him," she exclaims, proud of her idea. Then she pushes him. "Get up; get off me, you big lug. I want to go downstairs; my skin is getting dry, and I need to get some lotions." She springs from the bed as Cools lies back, making use of all the pillows, watching her prepare for her jaunt to the hotel's gift shop. "Do you need anything?" she asks.

"Only you," he replies with a contented smile. "Only you, baby-girl!"

She leaves, blowing him a kiss, and makes her way down to the lobby, ignoring all the attention she receives from other men. There, in a world away, she sees a familiar face. She walks over to one of the sitting tables in the hotel's foyer and picks up the local newspaper, *Aruba Today*. Its front page shows a picture of Joshua along with the story of him firing his attorney father. Her first thought is to deliver it directly to Brad, but quickly she changes her mind, deciding that he needs a full and complete break from it all. Besides, we will be back tomorrow, she thinks. He will know soon enough. I wonder what it must be like to have to contend with these psychos. She then sits, crossing her legs, and dials a number borrowed earlier from his phone.

After the fourth ring, she hears, "Hello, Detective Robertson here."

"Michelle, this is Chelsea."

"Well then, how's the sunshine? I heard you and Brad flew off to the Caribbean somewhere...Aruba is it?"

Chelsea doesn't like her calling him Brad but overlooks her pet peeve to inquire of a few things. She asks directly, "Why were you and Brad taken off the Siconolfi case?"

Michelle sighs, "Didn't he tell you?"

"Tell me what? That's why I'm calling."

Michelle hesitates, considering the implications of what she might say, then replies, "If I tell you a few things, they're just between you and me. Is that agreed?"

"Yes, I'll keep it to myself until he comes out with it, although I think I should know what is going on," she quips back.

"All I can tell you is this..." Michelle takes a full breath. "The case came to a point where we were probing into areas we had no place being."

"What do you mean? That's your job, isn't it?"

"No, you don't understand Chelsea. They threatened us! And I don't want to talk any further about it."

"Okay, then answer me this: were you given any money?"

"No! Now, I should go, and you should also leave this alone." Michelle hangs up.

Chelsea reclines back into the chair cushions to pore over every word of their brief conversation. What did she mean, they threatened them? Who are *they*? And where did he get the money? Maybe he's protecting me. Maybe he's protecting us. I should trust in him; I will trust in him.

Soon she returns with her moisturizers and, close by his side, squanders the rest of the day sunbathing, making love in the afternoon shower, eating fresh calamari at the beachside restaurant, and drinking margaritas. They share one more tender moment, in the form of a cozy nap, before boarding the plane at 1:20 a.m. One thing she is sure of is that they are unmistakably in love, and they will find their way. She never asks him about the money or the spontaneous decision to leave, but still it burdens her thoughts. On the plane ride back, she stares out the window, reflecting on the past week, somewhat disappointed, somewhat confused. It doesn't make much sense to her; it was only a few days prior she'd heard him revealing his intentions in his sleep. Over and over, mumbling, "Will you be my wife? Will you marry me?" And then to spend a wonderful week in Aruba that provided many opportunities for him to pop the question? And then he just doesn't! Why? Did I do something wrong?

Cools, nestling next to her, reaches out to hold her hand. His eyes are closed, but his mind is visiting the very same concern. I didn't get cold feet; it's just not the right time. I feel there's something I have to finish, something significant—I just don't know what.

They land back in Seattle, home of the rain, oddly welcoming it. Not much is said, just kisses and a warm embrace of gratefulness before going their separate and largely dissimilar ways. Chelsea is returning to her perfect apartment and ordered life, while he evaporates into his former reality of wrong choices made for the right reasons. He attempts to cling to his week shared with Chelsea. But it is short-lived, as he then does the worst thing possible. With one little click of the remote, the news of Joshua and his latest shenanigans—the firing of his father, the best defense attorney in Seattle, only to represent himself—intrudes on his consciousness. What is he thinking? It's like he's trying to get convicted. Maybe he has a death wish. He wants to be martyred!

Chapter Forty-Three

Weeks go by without a great deal of theatrics since very little spills out of Joshua's twisted mind and into the limelight. He's been eerily silent, almost purposefully estranged from his followers. Cools has been spending his days laboring over old case files alongside Michelle in addition to late nights watching movies and eating home-cooked dinners with Chelsea. And apart from the media's day-to-day drum beat of the upcoming trial, things have been normal. But still a light anxiety mounts as Joshua's day in court draws closer, and everyone prepares for an anticipated hell storm.

Inside his office Captain Jackson sits, waiting for a meeting with prosecutor Milkowski.

Outside his office Misty Lakewoods beams of newfound enthusiasm and self-worth, for today is the day she'll receive the first check that will include her increased pay. She couldn't be happier. And now the clothing magazine, lying upon her desk, parades a few of the items she intends to spend the extra money on.

Then abruptly her fantasy shopping is interrupted as prosecutor Milkowski rushes in carrying an overflowing briefcase and shouldering his laptop. He fretfully looks at his watch, which reads 3:50 p.m. He's twenty minutes late. "Is he in there?"

"Yes, and he's waiting for you, so you should go right in." Her tone is slightly commanding, per her instructions from Captain Jackson. She's been coached to always make an effort at telling Milkowski what to do.

"Thank you," he mutters, and heads in.

"Sorry, I'm late," he says, noticeably keyed up. "I, as of a few minutes ago, had a run-in with a little birdie. This little birdie informs me that William has obtained all police reports and a list of my witnesses."

"All right, well, we had suspicions of this from the very beginning to make us believe Joshua was going to defend himself. Huh, they thought they'd catch us with our pants down. Now, tell me where we're at—what's the game plan?"

Milkowski draws in a great deal of oxygen, as his overweight body struggles. "Well, it's pretty straightforward actually. First, I'll be bringing in the neighbors and two of the girls from the Kitty Club to verify Kimberly was a real person—also generally thought of as his wife. Then we go into all the circumstantial evidence: the recording from the radio show, the taped interviews conducted by your office, showing all his madness, the blood found on the yacht, and the crab trap, not to mention the odd purchases of rope and weights. The love affair between Kimberly and Trace Friesen is ample motive. And I'm going to try to work in his occult manuscripts, found with all the names of missing girls, but it borders his religious freedoms; and Judge Cooper is reluctant to let in constitutionally protected liberties. Besides he could just say he read their names in the paper and was praying for them."

"Yeah right!" Captain Jackson barks, jerking his head in the air. "All right, then what about Cools and Robertson?"

"Don't worry," he answers, addressing the situation as if he has it all under control. "I plan on having a long discussion with Cools before we go in. The worst thing that can happen is for the defense to provoke him into one of his fits."

Captain Jackson nods in concurrence, adding, "I'll have a talk with him myself."

"Okay, good, I think that's a great idea."

Then there's a pause ahead of the big question hanging in Captain Jackson's mind. He asks directly, "And will you get a conviction?"

"Definitely. Even if his father represents him, I cannot foresee any way out for him."

"Sounds good, Milkowski; sounds real good. Now, listen up; there's something else I need to talk to you about."

"Okay, I'm listening," he replies, curious although somewhat reluctant.

Captain Jackson stares him down. "All right, here's the deal. At no time can there be any mention of this racecar club and/or Joshua's involvement in it. Is that understood?"

"Enough said. I can appreciate that this is a delicate situation."

Milkowski leaves the meeting, relieved that simply not mentioning the car club—something someone more influential insisted of him earlier—was all that Captain Jackson had asked of him. He presumed there would be more.

Chapter Forty-Four

Across town, while trapped in gridlock, Cools receives a couple of phone calls. The caller ID on the first one lights up with a well-recognized name—Tabatha Sterns. He answers with a friendly hello.

"And a hello to you, Detective Cools. How've you been?"

"Fine, except being stuck in traffic, and you?"

"I'm good. Listen, I'm hosting a special Friday night, and I'd like you to come on as one of my featured guests."

"What's the topic?" he replies playfully.

"Well," she begins haughtily, "tomorrow night my guest appearance is also *your* latest arrest!"

Cools's head whirls in amazement, being well aware of the courting done by every media outlet, including the major networks, to land this interview. "Wow, that's impressive, Tabatha. How'd you pull that off?"

"I have my ways. So what do you think of me now, Detective?"

"Congratulations, Tabatha, but unfortunately I'll have to decline your offer; my Captain would never go for it." Then he says something he's wanted to for a long time, "And you know what, I don't really like the way you people keep giving him the spotlight, so he can spew his lies to the world."

She doesn't react to his insolence and lets it dissipate with a moment of silence before replying, "Well, maybe we could go for drinks; you could give me a chance to entice you with my proposal?"

He thinks instantly of Chelsea and cuts the conversation short. "Listen, Tabatha, I'm grateful for the invite, but it just isn't going to happen. What time does it air?"

"Fine then! You can see what you are missing tomorrow at seven. My show is doing a full hour. And I think you should know that your name will certainly come up since you were the arresting officer. I was only extending you the opportunity to defend yourself. All the same, if you decide to change your mind, you have my number." Click.

"Whatever, you little tease!" he says. He shuts his phone, lays it in his lap, and drives along speculating about what Joshua might say. What kind of bullshit will he come up with this time? He'll talk about us torturing him—that's what. Or say we framed him. And most likely keep plugging the idea that Kimberly was never real, further poisoning the jury pool. What if he mentions his affiliation with the secret car club? Or my threats?

His cell phone rings again. It's Michelle. He answers, saying, "Hey, guess who I just got off the phone with? Tabatha Sterns—she's doing an interview with Joshua tomorrow night."

"Really? What did she want to talk to you about?"

"She wants me to be a guest on her panel."

"What did you say?"

"I told her Captain would have a coronary."

Michelle laughs. "Yeah, that's true. I never really liked that Tabatha Sterns anyway; she's nothing but a floozy with a microphone! And I don't know why she's calling you; she knows you can't do that. What's she thinking?" Cools doesn't respond. "Anyway, I have something for you; I want you to read an e-mail. I'm sending it to you right now; it was printed this morning in *Men's Fitness*."

He opens his laptop sitting in the passenger's seat and sees he has incoming mail. "Okay, I just got it." While keeping one eye on the traffic, he begins to read. "Vitalisep: Maximizing vitality and stamina for a better life."

"Michelle, I told you I'm taking Lexapro, and I'm happy with that."

"Brad, just read the advertisement," she demands impatiently.

"Okay, fine."

"Vitalisep acts quickly, increasing vitality and stamina without having to consume high-calorie energy drinks. It affords you the freedom to stay awake longer, be more alert, and get more done. But until you know how you will react to Vitalisep you should not drive or operate machinery. Call your healthcare professional if problems occur. In some cases side effects may cause restlessness, irritability, hallucinations, and depression, also an increased chance of suicide."

"What chance of suicide?"

"Just keep reading, Brad!"

"Do not take with alcohol as it can develop into engaging in activities you cannot remember. Other abnormal behaviors include aggressiveness, agitation, violent actions, and/or risk taking. Some have reported dizziness, difficulty in swallowing, night sweats, and/or shortness of breath. Severe allergic reactions such as swelling of the tongue and throat occur rarely, and may be fatal. And like most medicines, Vitalisep carries some risk of dependency. When taken over extended periods, you could experience severe paranoia, confusion, nightmares, and tooth decay, loss of jobs, friends, respect, and possible imprisonment. If such problems occur, stop taking Vitalisep and call your doctor right away.

"The makers of Vitalisep would also encourage you not to take this product as it is made entirely of methamphetamine and is not sold in stores. We recommend you to consult with your physician before considering taking illegal drugs. I am the wrongly accused Joshua Siconolfi, and I approved this message."

"What the fuck is this?"

"It's an ad taken out and paid for by you know who, which has sparked off a ton of controversy. Many are coming out against the publisher of the magazine, asking why they would give this creep a forum to disgorge his rhetoric. The publisher defends it, stating they felt the ad was creative, thought provoking, and an inspiring anti-drug campaign. Then in addition, there's a full page-and-a-half article on him talking about what a misunderstood person he is. But I think it's just an attempt to soften his image. Trial begins next week, and he's trying to sway potential jurors."

"Yeah, he's one resourceful son of a bitch, isn't he?"

Then she asks in a concerned tone, "Brad, are you thinking at all…about… you know?"

"No, and neither should you. We've chosen our path, and it's most likely the best decision we've ever made." His words reverberate across the airwaves, ending their conversation. They both respectfully say their good-byes. But neither of them has forgotten about it, nor fully resolved to leave it be.

Chapter Forty-Five

At 3:35 a.m. Joshua's cell door opens. He awakens in confusion as the guard yells, "Siconolfi, roll it up!"

"Huh...what?"

"Roll it up. You just made bail, so grab your stuff and come with me."

His mind rushes as he gathers his bed roll and documents. Fifty million dollars—who would've...who's paying to get me out? Could it be them?

The guard ushers him to the booking and release station, preparing him for discharge. He hands him a plastic box holding all his possessions—clothes, shoes, wallet, watch, sunglasses—and points to a holding cell. "Go in there and change out of your jumpsuit."

He hesitates, then asks, "Who's bailing me out?"

"We never know—just that your bond is secured and I'm to cut you loose. So get dressed 'cause I don't got all night."

It's less than three minutes before he comes out wearing shorts and a T-shirt. His clothes feel good on him. He checks his watch. It's dead, but that's the least of his concerns.

"Over here." The guard motions.

Joshua steps up to the window and signs his release papers. He reads, "Bad-Boy Bailbonds." My dad wouldn't have paid my bail. Who else could? Who else would? Who's out there waiting for me?

After a few quick signatures, the guard instructs, "Okay, go to door number four and wait for it to open. You look nervous; you all right?"

He coughs and nods with an offended look, then does as instructed. He waits, disorientated and with much expectancy, for it to open. What is going on? Should I leave? This isn't right.

The electronic bolt begins to grind, tension mounts, his heart rate flutters.

Then another guard yells, "Oh shit, wait a second! It's Joshua Sitelli that's made bail, not Siconolfi. Get him back in his cell where he belongs."

"No, fuck that!" he yells back, uncertain but defiant. "I already signed my papers; open the fucking door."

"Do as you're told," the guard demands, followed by promptly getting on his radio and calling, "Code five in booking! Code five! Code five!"

Without any place to go, he begins moving around pointlessly. Other guards start pouring into the small room; soon he's surrounded. "Get on the ground, Siconolfi! Get on the ground!" they command. But in his state of mind, he doesn't comply fast enough, and he's hit with a Taser.

Next he's immediately dragged back to his cell, and once again the door closes.

The guard returns to the booking room; he picks up the phone, laughing, "Ha-ha…yeah, you should've seen his face, Captain Jackson. It was fucking priceless, absolutely fucking priceless!"

Chapter Forty-Six

The news gets out of the approaching interview of Joshua from his jail cell, jump-starting a hurricane of dialogue as media trials are born inside every newsroom, showcasing under the banners of "The Siconolfi Riddle" and "Trial of the Twenty-First Century," someone even coining the slogan "Prison-Cell Diaries." All agree that his trial will rival that of O. J. Simpson or the Floridian party girl Casey Anthony, acquitted of killing her two-year-old daughter, Caylee. Panels are assembled, presenting well-groomed men and bleached-blond beauty queens offering in-depth coverage of Joshua's father and his ties to the Roman Catholic archdiocese, Detective Cools, the reckless arresting officer who blasted a hole in Joshua's driveway now accused of police brutality, and the adulterous affair between the late Kimberly Siconolfi and ex–political figure Trace Friesen. Programmers dedicate entire segments to the discussion of the Egyptian religious manuscript hiding the names of the missing girls. Several mention his poems, his unveiled talents that afford them a diagram of his sanity, or insanity, depending on who is commenting. First it's mostly the major networks, until everyone gets into the game, franchising them into minitrials complete with distorted facts, conjecture, and countless critics, attacking from thousands of viewpoints and arguing the lot, from largely damning circumstantial evidence to some of the most ridiculous excuses that wouldn't work on prepaid jurors. One asshole after another dreams up possible defense strategies, inspiring and teaching the world the fine art of lying and creative bullshit. Clever-talking wannabe lawyers, arguing, speaking over each other, and opposing all opinions except their own dominate most perspectives. Everyone is vying for time in front of the cameras and solely approving of one thing: that although Joshua is sick and deranged, he's a noteworthy and fascinating individual.

Cools channel surfs from one news broadcast to another, growing increasingly perturbed. Little by little he's getting caught up in it again. With every added crumb of attention given to Joshua, a piece of the detective's psyche turns darker, blacker. He ventures to The Shelter for harder liquor and guidance. There he makes a call to Captain Jackson, asking, "Can you stop this interview? I don't think it's a good idea to let him do this."

Captain Jackson thinks that Cools is right, but answers, "I don't really have a choice, Cools. I'm getting pressure from every fucking angle."

"What angles? Who?"

"Don't concern yourself with it," he snaps back, defensively. "I have to do what I have to do. He's going on, and that's all there is to it!"

The call ends on that note. Cools pours another full glass of Jameson and, for the first time, thinks about doing a little of the cocaine in his freezer.

Chapter Forty-Seven

"I can hear them coming. I have to go," Joshua speaks into the vent in his cell.

The keys crack the lock open and a guard orders, "Siconolfi, step out!"

Joshua walks out into the corridor, where he's met by three more guards and the lieutenant, all wanting to control the conditions. Wasting no time the lieutenant underlines his authority. "First, let's make one thing known, Siconolfi. I can terminate this interview at any moment—do you hear me?"

Joshua nods with a slight smirk.

"Here's my rules. You will say *nothing* that implies *any* mistreatment or personal concerns you may have with my jail. That means you will not mention the food, the temperature, water, health services, cleanliness, or the conduct of my staff. Is that absolutely clear?"

"Yes, I get it. And you listen to me; my aim is not to—"

"I don't give a fuck about your goddamned aims, Siconolfi. All I care about is the reputation of my detention center, and if you don't get that, I can put you back in your cell."

Joshua returns him a look of repugnance, replying, "I got it. Now, can we go?"

The lieutenant catches an impatient breath and narrows his eyes. "If you fuck with me, Siconolfi, I'll put you in Erubiel's cell. Do you know who Erubiel Cruz is?"

Joshua shakes his head, countering smart-alecky, " Why? Should I? Who the fuck is Erubiel Cruz?"

"Erubiel is a three-hundred-pound killer; he's a Mexican national, calling shots for the Sureno street gang. And he lives to hate the white boys!"

"Go ahead; put me in there. I'll have him doing my fucking laundry by day's end!"

Everyone chuckles, even the lieutenant some. "Okay, keep pushing me, and we just might find out!" He then turns, leading the way, adding, "Oh, and another thing, quit talking to Benson through the vents; we can hear you."

Nothing more is said as Joshua follows along toward the library, where a cameraman and a make-up girl wait with Tabatha Sterns. She wears a dark blue, casual pantsuit, which matches her eyes. First things being first, they have him sign several legal papers, most of which he is not interested in. His only concerns are the agreed-upon one hundred thousand dollars and that the interview, in its entirety, will be offered to all other news organizations.

Tabatha, somewhat preoccupied with a phone call, asks if he needs anything.

"No, I'm good to go," he replies confidently. He sits and right away the make-up girl steps over to him, introduces herself as Amy, and begins applying hair gel, even a few touch-ups. The cameraman pins a microphone just beneath his collar while the guards watch their every move through the windows.

Ending her phone conversation, Tabatha looks over and snaps at Amy, "Do it right! I want his hair messy, like the photo I chose." She then promptly transforms back to her mask of purity, saying to Joshua, "I want you to look your best." He can effortlessly read what Ms. Sterns is all about. The immediate impression she projects is that of warmth and the welcoming woman, but he can see past her facade. She reminds him of one of those phony, feed-the-children personalities wearing thousands of dollars of jewelry and over-the-rainbow expressions of compassion and kindness. They strive to impress upon you their sickening sweet intentions and charitable values—those who become apparently overjoyed and jubilant of your very presence, but only when they want something of you, as the same of this kind can strike at you with the efficiency of a poisonous snake in an instant. Their very presence is a lie; Tabatha Sterns is a lie.

Yet still, she was chosen long before the beginning.

Tabatha scoots over, as Amy finishes up, and pats him on the leg, saying, "Oh my, you really do look magnificent; you truly are a handsome young man. Now, with your permission of course, I think we should take a sneak preview at some of the questions I intend to ask before we begin recording."

"You can ask me anything; I have nothing to hide," he replies sharply and confidently.

"Well, my kind of man," she counters humorously, then swiftly alters to that of a skilled administrator. "But we do have a couple of rules. Number one, please keep any cursing to a minimum, as it doesn't fit well with our audience." He nods in compliance. "Number two, answer to *me*, not the camera—just pretend it isn't even there. Number three, address me as 'Tabatha.' And number four, take all the time you need to answer; I want to get the full perspective of your take on things, okay?"

"Yeah, I'm ready, Tabatha. Let's do it."

"Wow, you really are my kind of man," she replies, looking him up and down. Then the cameraman turns on the lighting, and Amy positions the chairs, as Tabatha double-checks her hair, as well as her cleavage, in a pocket mirror.

Joshua watches her. If she wasn't such a fake whore, I would definitely want to take it from her, smashed down, bent over, pulling that blond hair hard.

"Okay, are we ready?" Tabatha asks the cameraman.

He gives the thumbs-up and begins counting backward. "Five, four, three..."

"Good evening, I'm Tabatha Sterns, and you're watching our primetime exclusive interview here on KUBE channel 9. Tonight we are going to explore the mind of an incarcerated man accused of murdering his wife. His case is currently set for trial, and he vehemently denies the charge. No body has yet been found, and there's a great deal of uncertainty as to whether his wife ever existed in the first place. You know who I'm speaking of: Joshua Siconolfi. And he is sitting right in front of me here at the King County Corrections Center." The camera pans to him as she continues. "Joshua..." she asks in a concerned tone, "may I call you 'Joshua'?"

"Yes, please do."

"Good, now, Joshua, I would first like to start by asking about Kimberly. Tell us what your relationship was like."

His eyes brighten, and he stares into nowhere for a moment. Then he speaks adoringly of her, as his lost love. "Kimmy was... She was beautiful, more beautiful than any woman I've ever seen. And when we were together, we were everything we needed—nothing, not anyone else, mattered. I loved her deeply and miss her every single minute of every hour."

Tabatha, seeing that her cameraman is cutting in a quick shot of her, displays her understanding. "And when was the last time you were together?" she asks.

"The day before…you know…," he answers, seemingly remorseful.

Tabatha advances gently, "You mean the day before…the radio call?"

"Yes."

She makes a notation, then asks him directly, "Why did you make that call that day, Joshua? What was going on inside you?"

He looks to her for understanding. She extends her graceful eyes. And although nobody expects him to openly answer, he does. "I don't want to make excuses… But the conditions were that I had drank an entire bottle of absinthe, 'The Green Fairy,' an alcohol that was previously banned in America and most of Europe due to its hallucinogenic properties; it's said to bring forth the voices of madness."

"I've heard of this; it was popular among poets and artists in the nineteenth century, wasn't it? Didn't Vincent van Gogh cut off his ear while high on absinthe?"

"Yes, that is correct: van Gogh, Oscar Wilde, Manet, not to speak of Ernest Hemingway. In fact his masterpiece *For Whom the Bell Tolls* was written under the influence of it. So I was curious to try it, but gravely ignorant of its power…It absolutely made me crazy, and I cannot remember anything from that day."

"Don't you remember talking to me, reciting your poem?"

"No, not even after seeing it on television."

"Sounds like you had what we call a blackout. Have you ever had a blackout before?"

"Never! I never drink like that."

The camera zooms in for a close up as Tabatha moves quickly to another topic. Being a skilled reporter, she knows that when someone claims not to have any recollection, it's time to redirect and pull a sneak attack at a later time. Deflect and ambush—Tabatha's code. "Okay, let's talk about something else—something of a personal curiosity to me. Tell me, Joshua, of your religion. Convert me if you will."

"We do not convert anyone; you have to seek first the wisdom of Ra to gain acceptance; however, we believe in the balancing of one's soul. If something is lost, you must find. If something is taken, you must take. And if something is given, you must give. God has given us much, but how do we give to him? We do this through truly selfless acts."

"Sounds quite interesting," she replies, ever so slightly patronizing him. "And how does one accomplish this?"

He inhales and explains, "In our view a truly selfless act is when I, you, do something for someone else without ever receiving anything in return, not even the recognition for doing so. I believe this in itself to be the greatest gift I or you can offer to God. It can be anything, but it has to be done in absolute secrecy, without ever telling another soul of your good deed. Neither can anything be asked of God; rather, it is given as an endowment for all he has already done for us. I would like to give you an example of what I believe is a truly selfless act."

"Yes, I would like to hear that," she says, flashing a wide-eyed smile for the camera. Though she'd never admit it, she recognizes full well that her high ratings are in large part due to her sex appeal.

"I'm sure you've read the anonymous poem, 'Footprints in the sand.'"

"Yes, where God carries us in our time of need."

"It is an inspirational work of art, and I would surmise that its author had to have known of its greatness when he or she wrote it, also that he or she could've profited from it, and not just monetarily, but received immense recognition for the work. And I believe that this person simply and anonymously gave us this beautiful poem and kept it secret as a selfless act, as a gift to God. And if you do this, if you complete your life with the blessing of selfless acts, I promise you will find it enriching to your soul here on earth as well as in the hereafter."

"Oh, I see. That's very inspiring, Joshua," she responds in an encouraging tone. She holds her pose, for a moment, in view of the camera, then yells, "Cut, cut!" The cameraman flips the switch, and Tabatha goes to Amy for a touch-up. Joshua rests back, watching her; he knows she will never do a selfless act, as he can see that she is now conflicted with it.

The cameraman says to Joshua, "That's some pretty heavy shit. Are you some kind of—"

"Don't! You do not—" Tabatha wields a halting finger. "You do not ask the questions here. I do! Okay, I'm ready. Are you ready?" The cameraman signals he is. "And you?" She looks to Joshua.

"I'm always ready," he snaps back, composed, self-confident, enjoying seeing her frayed around the edges.

She sits and fusses in her chair. "Okay, let's roll."

"Five, four, three..."

"Now Joshua, your trial is set for six days from now. Will you be representing yourself?"

"No, I have spoken with my father, and he's going to represent me."

"Oh really? But I thought you'd fired him. What was that in regard to?"

"I cannot comment on that at this time. But I will say this: once this is all over, you will know the truth, and I will be vindicated. And to answer another question: I, with the full support of my father, will most definitely testify. I *will* be defending our good name on that stand!"

"That's interesting since it is usually considered unwise to do so."

"Clearing your name while making fools of your accusers is never unwise, Tabatha. I already told you: when something is taken, you must take."

His quick retort startles her, so she decides to startle him back. "So, using *your* logic, it would be fair to say that if someone took Kimberly from you, then it would be sound judgment to take Kimberly from them. Did you take Kimberly from Trace Friesen?"

Her tactic doesn't faze him; he answers back, as if rehearsed, "Kimberly was never harmed by my hand."

"Okay, then what about the missing girls written in your book?"

"Do you know that it is customary for some Christians to write the names of the deceased in their Bibles for protection?"

"Well played," she murmurs under her breath, knowing it can be edited later. She then looks to her notes and asks, "Is Kimberly a real person?"

Joshua gives her a puzzled look and answers, "If something is real to one, but not the other, does that mean it isn't?"

Unsure of how to respond or where to go next, she asks, "Are you guilty of murder?"

He then defies her rule number two and looks directly at the camera, answering, "No, I am innocent; I will prove that at trial as I defend my name from the stand."

"But didn't you sign a statement saying you did murder her?"

He turns back to her and replies, "Yes, I did." Then he stands out of his chair and shouts, "Why don't you ask me about more important issues—like police torture!"

"Cut, cut!"

His outburst brings an end to the interview. The guards rush in and haul him back to his cell. There he tells everything and then some to his neighbor, Benson, speaking through the vent. They both agree it will change people's perceptions of him. Then he lies on his bunk, mulling over every aspect of his performance, knowing he's saving the big show for his trial.

Chapter Forty-Eight

Day one of the trial arrives. Inside her car Michelle waits for Cools in front of the courthouse. She fidgets with her tightly fitted, dark blue dress and pantyhose as she watches the frenzied horde of reporters and police fighting for position—none of which comforts her. From earlier news reports, she knows that many of the people crowding the steps are the distressed family members of the missing girls written in Joshua's book, probably more distraught over the fact that none of it will be admissible in his trial. And sadly, they're surrounded in a sea of others, who seem to have come only because they have nothing better to do with their days but join in the madness. They hold signs that read "Death Penalty" and "We Want Justice," or "No Evidence—No Crime." Young women wear black-and-white T-shirts emblazoned with catchphrases like "Live on Forever of no evil" and "Selfless Acts." Michelle shakes her head in frustration. Why? What are they thinking?

She startles when Cools knocks on the passenger window. She smiles and presses the unlock button. He jumps in, wearing a pressed black suit and clean, pearl-white shirt; his hair is neatly combed back, and he's smelling of musk. "Good morning, sexy thing," he says, clearly excited and full of energy. "Guess what I just heard." He points to a girl clinging to a "Kimberly isn't Real" sign. "I was told these girls are paid protesters from Team Siconolfi."

"Really? Well, that makes better sense; I was starting to wonder if these silly girls had totally lost their freaking minds."

"Yeah, ha-ha...But it definitely tells us these guys are not going down without a fight. And don't think for a second that they don't have more tricks up their sleeves. Hey, there goes Captain." Michelle glances up to see her boss pushing through the crowd, only stopping briefly to answer a few questions. "We better get in there," Cools adds, and opens the door to light up his last cigarette. He smokes it fast and smashes it on the walkway before they approach the restless mob. Michelle sinks into his arm as they navigate past the reporters. And soon they make it inside, where they find their reserved waiting room, the place they'll be sitting for the next few days, passing the time until being called as witnesses.

He glances around at the small expanse with nothing other than a table, a couple of chairs, and a tiny kitchen counter. "Well, at least we get free coffee," he says, and pours her a cup.

"Brad, how're you and Chelsea doing? Have you been seeing her lately?"

"Yeah, I have been seeing 'Chelsea Lately,'" he quips back, referring to one of her favorite shows.

"Ha-ha," she smiles with churlish lips; then she tries again. "Seriously, Brad, how are you two?"

He looks at her hesitantly. She raises an inquiring eyebrow, pressing for his answer. "We're good; she's great," he begins generically, searching for the words, knowing his partner of many years isn't about to let him off the hook that easy. "We've been spending a lot of time together and—"

Suddenly someone knocks twice at the door, and two men burst in. The men are very thin, and both are wearing suits and carrying equipment of a type Michelle has never seen before. The taller of the two says, "Good morning, Cools. And you must be Detective Robertson." He extends his hand. "Hi, I'm Lee and this is Brian. We oversee security here at the courthouse, and we're going to conduct a routine sweep of the room and your persons for any electronic devices."

"What the hell? Brad, what's going on?"

"It's just procedure, Detective Robertson," Lee says, as his assistant Brian starts waving his equipment over the walls. "This is the way it's done now in all high-profile cases. Could you stand; I need to sweep you and your personal effects." She lets out a sigh and rises to her feet. Lee pulls out what looks like a handheld metal detector and commences guiding it over her voluptuous shape. Cools catches him sneaking a look but says nothing. Next he runs it over their personal belongings. Their gadget sounds a beep over both of their phones, and immediately Lee and Brian look to each other curiously.

"What's that?" Michelle asks.

He coughs, seeming to stall, "Ah...It's probably nothing...Many cell phones give off false readings. Just in case though, I need to take both of them, and I'll have all your personal information transferred to the exact same models; you'll never know the difference." Then he places them in his pocket.

"But that's my phone! When will I get it back?" she asks, obviously irritated.

"I can have them back to you in about an hour," he replies. "Brian, you getting anything?"

"No, the room's clean."

"Okay, looks like we're done here; sorry for the inconvenience. I'll be back in an hour or so with your new phones." Then without saying much more they leave, taking with them the only connection Cools and Michelle have to the outside world.

"What was that all about, Brad?" Michelle asks, disbelieving what she's just witnessed was routine.

"Listen, our phones were bugged. He had to play it off by saying it was procedure."

"What? Our phones are bugged? How? And how can you be sure, Brad? Lee said a lot of phones give off false readings."

Cools sits her down, holding her arms, "Michelle, listen to me. I called my friend Lee; he and Brian run a security firm, and I told him about how we were being listened to when we were out at the bar a few weeks back. And he told me that it's possible to put a bug in a cell phone remotely; they don't even have to touch 'em. That's why I was so rude with you the other day on the phone." She forces a smile. He continues, "So, I did some digging, and I found something."

"You're freaking me out, Brad!"

"Just listen. I cross-referenced the leaders of the archdiocese and some of their most powerful members with DMV records and found that many of them own exotic sports cars. And take a look at this." He presents the Kitty Club business card. "See the logo with the bright stars emerging from the darkened flames? I looked it up; it symbolizes destruction before rebirth; the dark is giving to the light. It was used in many obscure and ancient religious philosophies that advocate extremism. So I started doing some research on religious extremism. Their ambition is to achieve a heightened sense of awareness by tapping into their fears and pleasures, which they believe brings them closer to God." He lowers his voice. "Like, driving dangerously is risk-taking, secreted religions is sneaky and devious. Not to mention the fact that it's hypocritical...to pretend to be one religion but, covertly, practice another that promotes orgies, drugs, strippers, and maybe even murder or human sacrifice. They believe that they are brought closer to God in these finite moments. One website even suggested that there was no greater reward than to kill during sexual intercourse as others watch, worshiping the act itself!"

"Brad, now stop it! This is far too freaky for me. I can't do this anymore." She stands and paces, holding out a firm hand. "I don't want to talk about it. I don't want to hear anymore. All I care about is that sick freak in there. He killed his wife, and we're very close to sending him away for life for it. And like I said before, if rich weirdos want to do their things to get closer to their God, then I don't give a damn. They scare me, Brad; they really scare the hell out of me!" She starts to break down. He holds her, letting her cry as she sobs into his suit, soaking his jacket. "I can't even sleep anymore... We can't mess with these people... and I can't wait for this trial to be over. I want it to all be over as soon as possible."

In that moment Cools decides that she is right. She should stay far away from it. But her fears and tears are just fuel for him to do what has to be done. The price for seeing her in this terrified state and turning a blind eye regarding the missing girls written in Joshua's book costs a lot more than fifty thousand dollars.

Two hours and forty-five minutes later, the jury has been selected—seven women and five men from various racial and ethnic groups. All are recluses and antisocial types that somehow haven't heard much or anything concerning this case. Prosecutor Milkowski readies himself for his opening arguments, in front of attentive jurors. The cameras pan back and forth from Judge Cooper to Milkowski to the jury box to Joshua, who is clean cut and undisturbed, huddled next to his father and the rest of his defense team. It's apparent he's been awarded some kind of special treatment; he looks like he's just spent three days at the spa. His blond hair is freshly cut and styled, his skin is tanned, and he's even had his teeth whitened. He wears a tailored suit that matches the posh gold Rolex on his wrist. And he holds a couple of secrets that only he and his defense team know about: he is wearing some airbrushed makeup and contacts that brighten his naturally green eyes. And, along with his refinements, he displays sinister and amorous smiles, coming across like a blazing and risky boy toy from a daytime soap opera.

"Prosecutor Milkowski, are you ready?"

"Yes, Your Honor."

"Then you may proceed."

"Good morning, people of the jury. My name is Andrew Milkowski, and I will be prosecuting this case, *State of Washington v. Joshua Siconolfi*. The charge in this case is first degree premeditated murder of Kimberly Wallingsford. This is a circumstantial evidence case; even so, I intend to prove without any doubt that Kimberly Wallingsford was murdered in cold blood, placed inside a crab-fishing trap, and then discarded into the Puget Sound like yesterday's trash. And that this was all done solely by her jealous, vengeful boyfriend, whom you see sitting here today." He does a theatrical spin, pointing accusingly at Joshua, who appears to be genuinely unaffected. Then he presses further with both vigor and passion, in a preemptive attack against their defense strategy, slowly raising the tempo, resembling an evangelical minister making an altar call. "The state will show you timelines, financial motives, blood and DNA evidence, a signed statement from the defendant, and last but not least the actual audio recording of the murder itself. I want to repeat that you are going to *hear* her being murdered! And you are also going to hear the defendant clearly stating what his intentions are prior to brutally cutting her throat!" He pauses for a second, before continuing, "The defense plans on persuading you that the deceased was never a real person." Cameras cut to the confused look on the jurors faces as Milkowski holds up Kimberly's picture, asking, "Does *this* look like a person who wasn't real?" He then places her photo on an easel behind him and walks over to the prosecution table to check his notes. "Also you are going to see police-conducted interviews of the defendant behaving in very strange and violent ways—showing his true nature. Nevertheless what I want from you—what I need from you—is not to convict him due to his peculiar religion or the fact that (and I'm sure you will agree) he is an extremely disturbed person; I need you to deliver a verdict of guilty based on the facts. Those being that on December 29, Joshua Siconolfi"—he points to Kimberly's picture—"murdered this woman in the prime of her life, in a vicious and cold-blooded attack!"

He then caringly removes the photograph from its resting place and lowers his pitch. "I want you to take a good look at her. This is the life that was taken." He marches up and down the jury booth, wielding it until her image is burned into their minds. "I want you to see her on her wedding day." He pivots, pointing to the prosecution table, where his assistant holds up an empty frame. "And this is her when she is pregnant with her first child." Another empty frame is held up. "And here she is standing with her loving family in front of their first home." Another vacant frame. The juror's eyes begin to swell as their anger rises. Milkowski embraces the moment with them, his eyes also full of tears and wrath.

His voice shakes as he moves ahead, "I am a very passionate man, and I have a daughter myself close to this age. And this is one of those defining moments in each and every one of our lives. You have to help me enact justice for her; you have to deliver a verdict of guilty. That is all."

He nods and walks to his seat, outwardly saddened and appalled, though at the same time feeling impressed with his presentation.

"Next we will hear opening statements by the defense."

All cameras shift in unison. William pats his son on the back and stands, eager and confident. He saunters, deep in thought, past the prosecution table, approaching the jurors with palms out. Their expressions are telling of their distrust. Still he states to them through a bottomless voice, absent of any doubt. "My client is absolutely not guilty! My client has in no way committed a crime. But just the same, he is culpable and to blame. He's the reason we're all here!" The jurors are visibly perplexed as a result of his declaration, an emotion easier for him to work around than their loathing for his son.

"By the way my name is William Siconolfi, and my last name is no coincidence, for I am the defendant's father. But I will not be representing him as my son; I will be representing him as a wrongly accused citizen of our great United States of America. Now, when I say that he's culpable and to blame, my meaning is that he is *only* responsible for not providing the police an explanation of events, which is his right. Now here are the facts. William points to Joshua. "He, just like Mr. Milkowski, does not know where Kimberly Wallingsford or Kimberly Sharons or Kimberly Siconolfi is. They're not even clear as to whom she is, and frankly neither am I. And none of us can possibly know for certain if Kimberly—whatever her name—was ever even a real person."

He holds up his hand as he can see their wheels spinning. What exactly does he mean she wasn't a real person? He lets it seethe in their thoughts then says, "Although we'll get to that later."

"First I'd like you to understand that all of the so-called evidence will not only be straightforwardly explained, but it could've easily been explained at the time of his arrest. But put yourself, for a second, in his shoes." He gestures to Joshua, who smiles like the friendly neighbor boy trying to sell his lawn-mowing services, so he can take his girl to the dance. "What would you do if you were arrested for murder? You, like my client, would probably use your best judgment and not answer any of their questions. Deep down we all know how hell-bent and single-minded these cops can get. It's no secret how they work—fast and loose like a bunch of presumptuous inbred cowboys!" He receives a few grins from his jurors and pauses for a moment, letting out a little line.

"And we all know from television shows and past cultural experiences that when these police get the idea inside their heads that you've done something wrong, they will *only* adhere to evidence that supports it. They will only use the things you say that make you look accountable and ignore anything that would exonerate you. I bet just about every one of you has a brother or a cousin or a coworker who's told you accounts of how these guys operate. And we all know from historical news stories that when a woman goes missing, their first thought is it's the husband or the boyfriend. So now, if you are this husband or boyfriend and you yourself don't know where she is and cannot produce her, well then you must have murdered her. But this case presents an additional ambiguity: the fact that the prosecution cannot even prove this person"—he flashes a hand to the photograph—"ever existed as Kimberly Wallingsford or Sharons or Siconolfi in the first place! The prosecution cannot even prove that this lovely woman is even named Kimberly or that she ever lived in Washington state or that she isn't a model taken out of a magazine—only that Joshua had this picture blown-up, framed, and hanging in his home."

Milkowski tosses his pen in the air, exhaling loudly, exhibiting a show of irritation over William's absurd defense.

William immediately turns and levels a firm finger at the prosecution desk and begins an ardent tirade. "Do not give in to this childish role play! I'll bet he throws his pen at every trial. And don't be fooled by any of his innuendos, his exaggerated truths, conjectures, and inventiveness. For I tell you all, he is a crafty and seasoned professional in his form of occupation. He will not deny that he holds to his credit a solid 98.2 percent conviction rate. But do you believe that 98.2 percent of everyone accused of a crime committed that very crime? If you do, you would have to believe that police officers do their job with 98.2 percent accuracy. Let's put that another way. Do you assume that all state and county employees work with 98.2 percent efficiency? Ask yourself: have you ever known a police officer to be wrong or mistaken? Or what about your mailman? Have you ever found mail that doesn't belong to you in your mailbox? What about our politicians, our governors, our congressman, even our president—do they work with this level of effectiveness? I think that you would answer no. I think that you're reasonable people who realize that none of our officials fly at this high of an altitude. Rather, I would contend that they perform at a rate closer to that of a weatherman." The jurors share a few brief smiles, even a chuckle or two. "Yet, prosecutor Milkowski does. And the way he achieves this success is by playing on your sentiment, twisting the truth, and flat out misleading you! He tells you he's a passionate man, and I believe him, but his passion is *not* for the facts, it is for the winning and advancing his career! You will see this as we go along. You will hear, from this man, many circumstantial possibilities, but from us, all you will hear is straight talk. And here it is..." William goes to his prepared chalk board and rotates it so that it's facing the jurors as well as the cameras. On it is a short numbered list written in large chalk marks. He points to each one.

"First, my client suffers from paranoia and schizophrenia, which he is currently taking medications for. Secondly, this Kimberly is nothing more than a figment of his imagination. He tells people of her, myself included, because he believes her to be existent. Thirdly, there is not one single shred of evidence that a crime has even been committed here, much less that my client is somehow responsible for it." William moves back to the jury box, whispering to individual jurors, "She was never a real person in my client's life. I've never met this woman. She is imaginary, make-believe. She never was."

Then, after an intimate moment, he walks back to his table and stands behind Joshua, placing a caring hand on his shoulder. "Think about this...Have you ever been in a circumstance where it looked as if you'd done something wrong, but you didn't? Have you ever heard humorous anecdotes where someone else was caught in a situation where it appeared they'd done something wrong? Maybe you we're accused of gawking at another from your wife or husband...or maybe the smell in the room did not come from you. Maybe someone has accused you of saying something that you didn't say. Maybe you've experienced an incident where you were misinterpreted, taken out of context, or perhaps someone else simply got the wrong impression of who you are or what you're about."

William lets his examples of reasonable doubt roam free. Then, looking even deeper into their souls, he concludes, "My client is an innocent man, simple and true! And it will all come to pass when this is all said and done. But first you will hear embellished realities and unjustifiable speculations. And my money says at first you will be drawn in; remember, prosecutor Andrew Milkowski is legendary at persuasion. On the other hand, when he is done, I will *prove* to this court their disreputable nature and then, and only then, will you begin to comprehend why my client has chosen to tell his story to a jury instead of telling it to them. And when we are done here, you will know without a doubt, that you have made the right decision, by bringing back a verdict—the only reasonable verdict—of not guilty. So for now, I will essentially remain silent, awarding them an empty playground, so we can see how they play with others. Just keep one thought close to your hearts, and that is the fact that Joshua Siconolfi is not guilty of any crime—not because he is perfect, but because there is no crime! I would like to thank you for your time."

"Okay then," Judge Cooper says to an astounded, speechless courtroom, "I think this would be a good time to take lunch. Court is in recess until one thirty."

Bang. Bang.

Chapter Forty-Nine

Ten minutes before court is to resume, from the fifth-floor windows, Milkowski surveys the mob outside while stuffing his face with pastrami on rye. Even as a boy he was heavyset, earning him the nickname Fat-Cow-Ski. Presently, as then, he overindulges to curb his anxieties, finding comfort through his taste buds. With a Diet Coke he washes down the coveted flavors, musing over the attributes of his newfound nemesis. That fucking incessant prick!

While losing himself in another bite of thousand-island-smothered brisket, Captain Jackson sneaks up on him, catching him off guard. "How we doing, Andrew?" he asks in a tone demanding of an answer.

"Well, uh, fine... We're doing fine. However I did receive a bit of a wakeup call in there earlier. You know it's a whole different ballgame with a man like him." Captain Jackson shakes his head, listening. "All the same I do have a big production designed for this afternoon; it'll be 'shock and awe.' He wants to play dirty; well I can play dirty too."

"Uh-huh," Captain Jackson mumbles, moving closer toward the window to share the view below. "Would you look at this mess," he says, referring to the scattered multitude of journalists, picketers, and vendors selling screen-printed T-shirts featuring Kimberly's picture under the tagline "Avenge Me!" The captain shakes his head again. "Whatever happened to the good ole days, Andrew?"

"They are a distant past," he replies. Then there's a quiet minute as they watch the crowd. Milkowski takes one of his antianxiety pills, given that he always feels a tad jittery when in Jackson's presence. And he doesn't know which is worse, conversing with him or simply sharing the silence. He ponders on it for a moment before deciding he better say something. "Are we getting any closer in finding her body?"

"Maybe," Captain Jackson replies, dispirited. "We're starting to get the idea the crab trap was a decoy. Now we're looking into other areas." Then he raises the issue he came to inquire of. "All right, you're gonna carry this out in the way I asked you, right?"

Milkowski glances around, double-checking no one is within earshot, and says, "Some matters need not be raised."

"All right. Well, you should get back in there. Last thing you wanna do is have Judge Cooper waiting for you."

"Yeah, no kidding," he agrees, then waddles away leaving Captain Jackson assured that everything related to the car club is well and fine.

Inside the court room, Milkowski is primed to live up to the credentials accredited to him by his rival. Judge Cooper gives him the green light, setting him in motion. "Good afternoon, people of the jury. I hope you had a nice lunch." His subtle consideration earns him warm smiles; they take to him right away, the way they always do. There's just something about a thickset man with olive skin and black wavy hair people fall for. Or possibly it's the fact that he's the variety of fat man who wears his pants buckled over his belly, which depicts him as friendly and unassuming. Still, his likability and discernible social skills are somewhat of a contradiction, being that he is an unconditional loner.

He begins gently, humanly. "I am dreadfully sorry to inform you that we are daring to start this afternoon off with a horrendous and heart-wrenching audio recording. I will be playing a clip from a radio show call the defendant made from his home the morning of December 29. Ladies and gentlemen, I must prepare you for what you are about to endure. It is beyond gruesome and frightening; so much so, I feel as if I cannot prepare you enough. I need you to fortify your minds for utterly lurid and ghastly sounds. This will absolutely be the most appalling recording you will ever stomach—truly the stuff nightmares are made of! But, according to the defendant's own words, what you will hear is to be considered nothing more than a prank, or a practical-joke. And I will never ask you if you interpret it as such—since you will not."

While continuing his verbal assault, two bailiffs role in a high-tech stereo system wired to home-theater-sized speakers, as he wants it heard in full 5.1

digital surround sound. "This is the crux of this case. You are about to listen to three minutes of viciousness, in addition to, the actual murder of Kimberly Wallingsford! None of you will have any doubt but that the defendant *is* killing her. And how does he choose to do it? He calls a live radio broadcast and murders Kimberly, for millions to suffer through. How do we know it's him? Because he admits to it. How do we know it's her? Because the defendant says so himself. How do we know she's being killed? Because he not only clearly states his intentions, you will be able to hear this young woman undergo his torments, and then you will hear her very last painful breaths." Milkowski can see the blood drain from their faces. "I told you this wouldn't be easy." He pauses, gathering his thoughts. "And lastly, how do we know he did what he said he was going to do? Well, because he lets us know when he's finished; he lets us know precisely when Kimberly's life was taken. You will also hear the defendant claim Kimberly merited having her throat slit. As he says: she deserved it!" Then without turning, merely continuing to stare into their eyes, he holds a remote over his shoulder and pushes play.

First there is curiosity on the expressions of the twelve, but it quickly fades to horror, which darkens further to nausea, as the sounds are seared into their unwelcoming ears.

"Okay, caller 'Unknown' from here in Seattle, what are your views?"

There is a long silence. The jurors lean closer.

"Caller, you're on the air, and we would like to hear your analysis concerning our huge national debt. What say you?"

Eveyone can hear Joshua breathing lightly.

"Caller, you are on—"

"I'm going to kill her."

"I am sorry, caller. I'm not sure what you mean."

"I am going to kill this bitch!" His malevolent tone trembles the very fabric of the jury's core.

"Who are you going to kill?"

Again, silence.

"Caller, are you still there?" the talk show host asks, her voice obviously cracking.

Then a calm and unnatural *yes* comes over the audio.

"Caller you're giving me very little info about who you are, who you wish to kill, and most importantly why you believe this person needs to die. I want to hear, in detail, all you have to say; leave nothing out.

The jurors can only hear Joshua breathing heavily.

"Caller," the radio show host says more forcefully, I presume you called this show because you have something to say, a message you would like the world to hear; is that the case?"

"Yes, I do want the world to hear. I want the world to hear her die!" Joshua blurts out furiously.

"Who?"

"My fucking filthy wife. She's playing me. She thinks she can get away with it. I have her tied up in a chair and a knife in my hand, and if you even *think* about taking me off the air, I promise I will torture her first. I have a drill and eight-inch wood screws I will bore into her legs."

Cameras's pan over the jury box, catching dropped jaws, widened eyes, and sickness.

"Okay, okay, let's settle down. I've listened to what you've said, but I want to know more and I want you to know that I know your pain; my ex-husband cheated on me constantly; I *know* how you feel."

"You have no idea how I feel, bitch! You are *all* the same. You think you can do whatever you want and then cry your way out of it. You make excuses for all that you do."

Everyone in the courtroom can sense an unadulterated evil mounting in his voice with every word.

"I've given her every chance to tell the truth. She cannot tell the truth. She is a lying, cheating whore, and she *is* going to die!"

The jurors, sitting on the edge of their seats, hear the audio change and realize Joshua has put the call on speakerphone. They all jerk when he begins screaming out his hatred in the background.

"You fucking fantasy! You think you can fuck my friends and get away with it! You believe I do not have the *power* to do something!"

Then for the first time, they can hear the woman in the room. "Mmm... mm...mm."

"I have the power! I have all the power from God to make you suffer!"

Between his screams all kinds of other noises fill the courtroom: like a chair being thrashed about and the strained sounds of struggling.

"Mmmrr...mmrrr...mrrraahh!"

More thrashing, and Joshua roaring, "Die, you fucking lying, disgraceful whore—die!"

"Mmmraghh! Mmmrr! Mmmrr!"

Then suddenly it all comes to a stop. Her cries suddenly cease, and there's complete stillness in the courtroom, only the heavy breathing from the defendant.

"Caller, talk to me. Caller!" the talk show host shouts, panicked and disarrayed.

Then they hear Joshua taking in a deep breath and exhaling the words, "She got what she deserved. They all did!"

After the hellish sounds, there's a moment of eerie silence. The few that can even look in Joshua's direction find him staring into the distance, deficient of any real emotion. Judge Cooper asks the jurors if they need to take a break. Her question is mostly answered by their body language. She calls for a recess, sending them to roam dejected toward awaiting lavatories to get sick, to rinse away the stain.

Thirty minutes later, still with the taste of a Snickers candy bar in his mouth, Milkowski sets up for round two. He embarks on a journey of circumstantial DNA evidence. And knowing the weakness of the connection between the blood found on the boat and Kimberly's rare blood type, he decides to put it up first. The idea is to exhibit the level of confidence he has for the discovery and interject it at a time when the jurors are still in a state of shock. He calls his first witness, Dr. Lutin, a DNA expert who plainly explains that the blood found on the boat is AB Rh negative, an uncommon blood type, which only 1 out of 167 people have. Then he is turned over to the defense.

William walks over to Dr. Lutin, leans on the witness stand, and says, "I heard your credentials—pretty impressive. I feel confident you'll be able to answer my questions. First, would the amount of blood found on the boat have been life threatening?"

"No, it was a very small amount in fact."

"Thank you," William says, as if he has just scored his first point. "Now, is it possible that her blood could have been placed into a container, then brought at a later time to the boat, and then spilled?"

Dr. Lutin shakes his head, doubtful of the idea. "Well, it would be highly unlikely but—"

"No. I did not ask for your opinion of its likelihood. I asked you"—his voice getting louder as he enunciates each word—"is…it…possible?"

Dr. Lutin, now clearly aggravated, replies, "Yes, it is possible."

"Thank you. I have no further questions for this witness."

Next Milkowski calls Nicole West (a.k.a. Destiny) and Brittany Jacobsen (a.k.a. Kiki), two young employees of the Kitty Club who testify to have worked with Kimberly but knew nothing of Joshua. William only asks them about their profession and past legal problems. Then Milkowski brings in the Swansons, the elderly neighbors, who testify to have known her. But, during the cross-examination of Mr. Swanson, it turns out that neither of them ever actually spoke with her and had only seen her driving in and out on a few occasions. Mr. Swanson departs from the court, leaving an impression of being old and confused.

They take another break, and the rest of the afternoon is spent going over the details of the boat rental, the video tapes showing Joshua leaving and returning, and witness testimony from D. J. Simpson, whom William declines to cross-examine. The day wraps up by five thirty. Judge Cooper and Milkowski are pleased with the speed at which the trial is moving, although they both wonder why William has made few objections or even tried to slow things down in the least.

Soon the trial will begin again, on cable, at six o'clock, with special editions at seven, and once more at ten and eleven. Monologues and discussions concerning father and son Siconolfi are being carried out on blogs and in chat rooms, earning *Siconolfi* the title of most-Googled name.

Chapter Fifty

Two hours later, after the sun has gone down, Cools, Milkowski, and Captain Jackson gather round a bottle of bourbon in the captain's office, mostly talking shop and relaxing while waiting for Michelle. Cools is already a little buzzed after a couple of drinks and the Vicodin Captain Jackson gave him earlier. And knowing he has his captain's attention, he pops off, "Hey, Milkowski, so I was traveling with my girlfriend down at the Multnomah Falls in Oregon last year, when she comments on the Lewis and Clark Trail. And since we'd been, just two days before, out on the coast where she'd seen a park in their name, and obviously not knowing much about them, she asks me, 'So now, how far did Lewis and Clark go?' And I said, 'I think they may have went all the way baby!' Ha-ha..." Cools slaps his leg, and Captain Jackson breaks out into old-man, long-and-winded laughter. Even Milkowski parts from his white-collar demeanor for a short chuckle.

Michelle walks in. "Sorry I'm late, guys," she says with a flirtatious smile, the same smile that has worked her entire life when behind schedule.

Wasting no time, Milkowski says, "Okay, I would like to discuss a few of my concerns. I'm putting both of you on the stand tomorrow, and I believe it's in our best interests to share the same frame of mind. First of all, do not let William rattle you. There's nothing worse than for him to present you as angry cops or to show that you hold personal feelings toward the defendant. Simply answer his questions directly—nothing more, nothing less." He speaks openly to Cools, leaving little doubt as to whom he is referring. "Also I want you to direct your answers squarely to the jurors, and warm up to them as much as possible."

"I gotcha, Milkowski; whatever you need to put this creep down," Cools replies, shaking his head low. Michelle agrees with her eyes.

"Oh, and he's definitely going down—downtown like Charlie Brown," Captain Jackson says, seeming to be also getting a little buzzed.

"Maybe going down like Lewis on Clark," Cools slips in.

They all start laughing, even more so than before. Michelle has to beg them to stop howling and playing around long enough to explain to her what's so funny.

Just then JFK and his rookie partner, Officer Bill Carter, walk in to deliver some papers to Captain Jackson. Fredo informs them that they've learned nothing new. They leave after only five minutes of small talk, presenting an opportunity for Cools. He uses the voice of a different character and says loudly, "Hey, I gots a joke for ya guys." Captain, Michelle, and Milkowski lend their undivided attention. Cools flips out a lighter and lights up a cigarette amid a silly grin. Then he says, "So Jack and Bill went up the hill…They both had a buck and a quarter. Jack came down with two-fifty…Fucking cocksucker!"

At once they all begin laughing hysterically. And over the next hour or so they enjoy a delivered pizza, and more stories and laughter, sharing in the victories of the day. It is a memorable time for each and every one them as the feeling in the room suggests that they are optimistic that tomorrow will bring forth the same fruits.

Chapter Fifty-One

A few blocks away, at the county jail, the source of the impending tumultuous events tells of his day to a hungry-eared Benson through the ventilation shaft. He celebrates the horror on the jurors' faces and lists with pride all of the news stations and major newspapers covering his story. Benson, from the other side of the vent, doesn't understand his elation, as Benson believes the end result for Joshua is going to be nothing less than growing old and dying in a cold prison. Still he allows him to talk until he runs out of steam, then asks, "Do you think they'll ever find Kimberly?"

Joshua chuckles and replies, "Hell no! They're so fucking stupid! They couldn't find her if I left them a trail of blood; they can't even see past the obvious."

"What does that mean—the obvious?"

"I shouldn't say anything more; they're probably listening." Then he changes the subject and asks Benson what all he has in his cell.

"Ah, I've got a few things…some store…a few books. Do you have any good books?"

Joshua thinks for a second and replies, "Yeah, I've been reading this one called *Little Frankie*. It's about a nine-year-old boy who lives with his mother, and it's set in the sixties. I'm only partway through it though. But the story goes: This little boy's mother was called into work, and she left him in the care of her new boyfriend, who ends up getting killed in a drug deal. Then the people—this hillbilly couple—think little Frankie is the son of the man they just shot to death, so they're now going on the run to Idaho, taking him with them."

"Then what happens?"

"That's as far as I've seen…or, I mean…that's as far as I've read. Maybe I should read some more, and I'll tell you about it tomorrow."

"Yeah, do what you got to do, man—anything to keep your mind off your trial."

Joshua steps away from the vent and lies down on his bunk. Soon he's forcing himself to sleep, knowing little Frankie is close.

In an old Ford truck, little Frankie rides in the middle of the bench seat, motionless and silent. They're traveling fast and urgently down a dark highway. To the dreamer's eye, it is sensed that the couple will now be his new mommy and daddy. The mommy, Sally, also sits quietly, simply watching the moonlit landscape go by, with her red hair blowing in the muggy summer wind. Devoid of any makeup, she's still a nice-looking girl, apart from being too thin and ratty. And little Frankie thinks she doesn't appear to be much older than the high school girls that live down his street.

At the wheel, wearing the same dirty, blue coveralls, is her husband, Abe, the man who just blasted Panama-Red to death on the front porch. He's outwardly agitated and restless, though seemingly more so with little Frankie, since he won't say anything, than he is over his own situation. Mile after mile goes by without getting a single word out of the young boy, but he isn't giving up; Abe figures he will just keep talking until little Frankie says something back. "Alls them boys back home—they calls me Big Abe. Dat's 'cause I'm so big an' all. Da you have a name, boy? Maybe weez could be friends?" He gets no response. So with communication lost, he attempts making funny faces, but only receives some strained laughter out of Sally. She shakes little Frankie gently, encouraging him to do the same. Yet he only stares out the windshield in utter silence, frozen, emotionally paralyzed. Then Abe, in a more serious tone, says, "I dint mean ta kill yer pa boy. I was jus' trying ta protect me an' my wife, an' dat's it."

"Let's just leave it be!" Sally yells. "He's been through enough, don't'cha think?" She holds little Frankie tight, like a real mother, and says, "Weez gonna take real good care a you, little fella. You don't have to worry 'bout a thing. Weez gonna take real good care and make sure you get to a good school an' all, and you don't need to be scared of Abe; he's always been real good to me, an' he's gonna treat you all the same. Ain't that right, Abe?"

"Dat's right, little fella. My sister—she lives in Idaho, an' she gots herself a real nice place dere, an' she has little ones too, 'bout yer age in fact. Yer gonna be jus' like brothers."

Little Frankie doesn't budge, bodily or mentally, although the talk seems to make Sally and Abe feel better; they just smile at each other and continue on down the road, meaning every word they say.

Joshua rouses awake, sweating in the midst of skepticism. He has the strong sense that Abe and Sally mean a lot of the things they say but feels that they're the dangerously unreliable types who invariably voice their forethoughts of good-will, but always seem to choose the wrong path.

Chapter Fifty-Two

On the second day of the trial, as the lawyers begin with a number of preliminary legalities, the jurors stare in confusion at Joshua, scrutinizing his every move, desperately trying to figure out what could be churning inside his soul. They all find it hard to believe that this well-dressed, handsome young man did and said the things they heard just yesterday. Some entertain ideas of split personality and toy with thoughts of demonic possession. Others consider him an attention freak, who may very well have killed his girlfriend solely for the spotlight. But one thing they sense of Joshua is that he carries within himself the potential fuel for a centuries-old storm.

Detective Michelle Robertson is called to the stand.

She gingerly makes her way to the witness box with a wriggle and a nervous smile. A great deal of energy has been put into her toning down her normally flashy look, and the results are incomparable. From her easy silver-blue dress that matches her eyes to her light makeup and limited jewelry, she is stunningly classy and promising for the cameras. Later, on the news, she'll be referred to as "The Lady Detective," as well as offered an interview on one of the major networks, which she will gracefully decline. And although this coming evening her sense of worth will be lifted, presently she is sitting in front of the world just trying to steady her breath.

She is sworn in, and Milkowski approaches, asking if she was one of the arresting officers.

"Yes, I along with Detective Cools and Sergeant Wielder's team arrested Joshua at his residence the morning of January 5. He refused orders to exit his home and surrender peacefully, requiring Sergeant Wielder's team to go in and forcibly extract him."

"Very good, Detective Robertson…or may I call you Michelle?"

"Yes, please do," she replies, loosening up some and adjusting the top of her dress. She does it modestly but with the confidence of a real woman.

"Okay then, Michelle, were you also part of the interrogation process?"

She directs her answer to the jurors as Milkowski had instructed and unknowingly drops a bombshell. "Yes, and he was somewhat of a nightmare."

"What do you mean when you say he was a *nightmare*?"

"Well, when we first brought him in, we left him alone without handcuffs; we do that sometimes: let them sit by themselves to think about what they've done. We simply study them through the two-way mirror, learning their nervous tics. Next thing we know is he gets up on top of the table and starts yanking out the video monitor and before we could get in there he…he had the whole thing torn out of the wall."

"You lying fucking whore!" Joshua bolts to his feet, clanking his restraints.

Judge Cooper slams her gavel. "Order! Order in the court!"

"You lying little bitch! You motherfuckers tortured me!"

"Order!" The judge shouts, still banging her gavel. "Order in my court!"

"Fuck you! Fuck you all!"

"Bailiffs, restrain him now!" Judge Cooper yells. Her command is slower than their reaction time, though, since two of them are already on top of him, holding him still with heavy knees on the back of his neck. Everyone else is in shock, deathly still. Judge Cooper looks as if she is about to apply capital punishment to him right then and there. She demands that he be stood, facing her. He's dragged to his feet. She then points her gavel at him, stating in the most composed voice she can muster. "I am ordering you to be gagged for the remainder of the day. No one says things like that in my court!" She wants to utter more but painstakingly holds her tongue. She slams the gavel twice more. "This court is in recess until the defendant is properly bound and gagged."

The reporters scramble to set up live streaming to their news affiliates, feeding the world the curses from Joshua.

Headlines read, "You Motherf——rs Tortured Me!"

William and Milkowski are called into Judge Cooper's chambers after the bailiffs haul Joshua away. Not a pebble of what they discuss is known, although a mountain of speculation stimulates numerous media theorists. They surmise everything from the most probable—that they're having a discussion regarding Joshua's outburst and how best to control him—to giving credit to his claims of being abused by the police.

Soon, everyone is returned to their positions, and Joshua is brought back in. But he doesn't wear the gag Judge Cooper ordered, mostly due to the reality that it would appear excessive as it played later on national news. But his ribs are now sore, and one of the bailiffs is standing three feet from him, wielding a Taser.

Michelle is called again; this time she appears more nervous than before. And Milkowski, wanting to get her through this as soon as possible, begins questioning her about what Joshua said during his interrogation. She slumps and becomes visibly weak; the jurors can see her revisiting a time of personal anguish. "He taunted me, saying that my husband was going to burn in hell because he doesn't go to church." She starts to weep. "And he leered at me, sharing his desire to have sex with me. But he didn't use those words. Then..." She fights her emotions. "Then he presented me with a proposition. He said if I did something...that he...he would confess and write a statement. And that's my job. To get them to confess," she adds, defending herself.

The jurors are puzzled, gripped.

"What did he ask you to do, Michelle?"

She begins to tremble as she pulls a folded sheet of paper from her purse. Then she looks at the cameras. She looks for Cools, but he isn't there. "I don't know if I can do this...I don't know if I..."

Milkowski holds her hand, reassuring her that everything will be all right.

Judge Cooper interjects, asking if she needs a break, but Milkowski answers on her behalf. "No, Your Honor, she can do this...This is what she is. Detective Michelle Robertson was created for this post, to not only search out the truth, but to bring her findings before the court."

Instantly she begins to weep out loud, though only for a second as she abruptly regains her composure and through newfound inspiration opens the folded paper and reads. "His request required of me to get down on my knees." She shakes the paper out of frustration, although it doesn't change the words written upon it. "And I said these things because it is my job to do so! I said, 'Oh God, Joshua, father of all creation, I pray to thee and ask for you to forgive me of my sins.'"

The crowd begins to murmur.

Joshua smirks contently.

Milkowski whispers, "You did well." They share a brief moment, even if it is short-lived, seeing that he now has to turn her over to the defense.

William stands, remaining at his table. And from across the room, he directs a long and peculiar gaze at her conspicuous cleavage. "Detective Robertson," he asks, "is that a cross necklace you're wearing?"

She clutches it in her hand, answering yes.

"And are you a Christian?"

"Objection: I do not see how the witness's religious preference is permissible in this court."

William counters. "Your Honor, the witness just testified to praying to my client. I think it's reasonable to ask if this is a common practice among her beliefs."

"Overruled: Detective Robertson, you're to answer the defense's question."

"Yes, yes, I am."

"Hmm…So enlighten me, Detective Robertson, is praying to a man an ordinary practice in your religion?"

"No, it is not!" Michelle retorts, feeling the room's judgment of her.

"Is it blasphemous?"

"I believe so…it is."

"So tell me, Detective Robertson, if you are willing to blaspheme your Lord and Christ, what *wouldn't* you do to get a statement? Wait. Wait a second, Detective Robertson. I don't want you to answer that question." Everyone looks to William, trying to understand. Then he adds, "I like you, and I don't want you to perjure yourself." And before Milkowski can object, William declares, "I have no further questions for this witness."

Judge Cooper subsequently jumps in and calls for a twenty-minute recess. Everyone disperses, excluding Milkowski, who remains seated and a bit concerned as he watches Michelle escaping through the back. All in all, she did well, he thinks, except he doesn't understand why she answered the question relating to the video camera differently than they had explained to him before.

When court resumes, Detective Bradley Cools is called.

He enters the courtroom, excited for the opportunity to drive one of the final nails into Joshua's coffin. Without missing a beat, he walks briskly past the defense table, purposely shunning Team Siconolfi, and in midstride nods to the jurors. They accept him right away. Milkowski waits for him to position himself in the witness stand before asking any questions. Next, they systematically go over every detail of his part in the investigation. Then he's turned over to the defense. Milkowski holds inner worries as he returns to the prosecution table. Please be levelheaded. Please don't fuck this up.

William springs out of his seat, marches aggressively toward the witness box, and, in a loud accusing tone, asks, "What exactly did you say privately to my client outside his home the morning of December 29?"

Cools smiles, amusingly at William's intimidation attempt, and replies freely, "I inquired of the defendant as to the whereabouts of his wife."

"I didn't ask you what you asked him. I asked you what you said to him."

"Maybe I don't get your meaning; I do not recall saying anything to him." He turns to the jurors. "I'm a detective. I only ask questions."

"Well, allow me to refresh your memory. I'm sure you remember threatening Mr. Siconolfi with your gun."

"Objection: Your Honor, this is argumentative."

"Sustained: That will be enough of that, William," Judge Cooper says firmly.

"Okay, Your Honor, I will rephrase the question. Detective, did you threaten Mr. Siconolfi with your gun?"

"Absolutely not," Cools answers straight to the jurors, most of who return warm sentiments, bolstering his confidence.

William mutters lightly under his breath, "Chelsea's a sweet little slut," then asks the courtroom, "Detective, did you at any time during your investigation threaten Mr. Siconolfi by means of planting his DNA?"

"No, I did not!" he answers, raising his voice.

Milkowski waves a hand, telling him to slow down, as Joshua looks across the jury box, shaking his head and mouthing, "Yes, he did. Yes, he did."

"Yeah, I thought you'd be less of a man without your gun."

"Objection: Your Honor, he is merely badgering the witness!"

"Sustained: Strike that from the record. William, I am not going to warn you again."

"I apologize to the court, Your Honor," he answers back, and continues questioning.

"Detective, were you first called to Mr. Siconolfi's home the morning of December 29?"

"Yes, I was."

"And you're a detective in the homicide division, is that correct?"

"Yes."

"Now does the homicide division usually respond to prank phone calls?"

"We did not believe it to be a prank call," he answers, upholding his decision.

William just stares, mockingly. Then he asks, "Now, could you describe for us what Mr. Siconolfi's demeanor was like when you arrived at his home?"

"He was uncooperative; he was drunk and smart-alecky."

"Drunk?" William goes to his table and thumbs through his papers. "Was he ever breath-tested?"

Cools hesitates. "No, but he was holding a drink in his hand and had a high odor of intoxicants."

"Okay, so you say he was drunk, how so then was he belligerent? Or was he a happy sort of drunk?"

"He seemed…amused."

"Amused? Would that mean Mr. Siconolfi, in your opinion, appeared not to appreciate the severity of the situation as you did?"

"Uh…"

"Let me ask you another way. Would you say that amused and smart-alecky are attributes closer to that of a prank phone caller or that of a man who, as you say, just minutes prior viciously slashed a woman's throat?"

"Objection: Your Honor, Detective Cools is not a psychologist; he cannot be asked to know the defendant's mindset."

"Overruled: I believe Detective Cools can establish as to how he perceived the defendant's state of mind. William, could you rephrase your question?"

He nods and then, believing the point to be made, begins another line of questioning. "Now, Detective, when you searched his home, did you find any signs of foul play?"

"No."

"Nothing?" Cools gives him a look, refusing to answer the question a second time. "OK, then after finding nothing out of place, what did you do?"

"We questioned the defendant and left."

"Detective?" William pauses, looking to the jurors through wounded eyes. "Detective Cools, did you torture my client into writing a false statement of guilt?"

"No, I did not," he answers resolutely. But the accusation and the denial divides some considerations.

William stares at him accusingly again, leans over the witness box, this time muttering, "We've watched you fuck her." Cools bites his tongue, picturing himself assassinating both Siconolfis. And next William asks, "Can you tell us what happened to the video camera in the interrogation room?" He doesn't know exactly what Cools's answer will be, only that there's a good chance it won't be the same as Detective Robertson's. He presumes this because just minutes prior to her coming in to testify, a text was sent to her phone, seemingly coming from Captain Jackson's, telling her to say that Joshua tore the camera out before the interview began.

Cools embarks upon his practiced rebuttal. "The defendant freaked out during the interview and jumped up onto the table. At first we didn't know what he was doing, so out of natural reflex, I, along with Detective Robertson, scooted as far back away from the table as we could, so he couldn't kick at us. Then he started yanking on the camera, and before we could stop him, he'd torn it down. We had to use force but finally got him under control, and then we stuck the camera back on its brace…believing it to still be functional."

"You say he got away from you *during* the interrogation?"

"Yes, just like I told you."

"Really!" William replies with lighted eyes. "And how far into the interview were you at this point?"

"Uh…I'm not sure."

"Well…approximately?"

Cools exaggeratedly searches the air for the answer, the way he and Captain Jackson had trained so many times. "I would say about an hour, give or take," he states directly to the jurors, who seem to be peering at him with indifference.

"And was Detective Robertson in the interrogation room with you at this time?"

"Yes."

"Hmm? Could it possibly be that this so-called incident happened *before* your interrogation? And you and your partner witnessed it from behind a two-way mirror?"

"No! It was like I told you!"

"Then you should be able to provide video for at least the first hour of this so-called interview. So where's the first hour, give or take?"

He replies as rehearsed, "When he yanked it down, some of the wires must have crossed, and it short-circuited the entire system; however, we didn't know this until after the interview was conducted." Cools reads their faces. Oh shit, they're not buying any of this! What's going on?

The jurors are unsure of his answer. William waits for all their eyes to land back on him. And when he sees their doubtfulness, he returns to his table, stating, "That is all I have for this witness at this time, but I may very well need to question him further at a later date."

Judge Cooper calls for a break, informing everyone to reconvene at quarter to two.

The noontime break is filled with news flashes explaining and exaggerating the inconsistent statements from the arresting detectives. And once more allegations of coerced interrogations highlight the theme.

Cools is pulled aside by Milkowski. "I think we need to talk," he says sternly, then leads him to his office, fending off reporters along the way. He slams the door and raises the issue. "What the fuck was that? Is there anything I should know?"

"No," Cools replies, defending himself, "everything was done by the book."

"Are you sure?" Milkowski asks, unconvinced.

"Fuck you, Andrew. You do your job, and I'll do mine! Everything he said in there is all bullshit. We never had any discussion with him about writing a statement, and we didn't torture it out of him! That prick writing a statement was the last thing in the world we thought we'd get."

"Then why do you and Michelle have two differing stories concerning the video camera?"

"What? Why...what did she say?"

"She clearly testified he'd torn the video camera out *prior* to the interview, adding that you and she viewed the entire event through the glass!"

Now things begin to click—the way the jurors were looking at him. Oh fuck, why would she say that? We discussed it in detail. What do I tell Milkowski? He's waiting for an answer.

"Listen...Andrew, what I'm going to tell you, you cannot repeat to anyone. We stumbled onto some shit we shouldn't have; they threatened me, and... and they must've gotten to her. Maybe they forced her to give a contradictory testimony."

"Fuck! His statement was the best piece of evidence I had," Milkowski yells, throwing his briefcase atop his desk. Neither of them says a word for a full minute; then Milkowski motions for him to sit down and does the same. He says in an even tone, "William is calling an expert witness, a signer."

"A what?" Cools replies, genuinely confused.

"A signer for the deaf. I can't figure out why or what he's up to. Does this mean anything to you—anything at all?" Cools thinks for a moment but is also stumped. "Well, I need you to mention it to Michelle; see if you can come up with any scenario that gives rationale for it. I'm going to spend the remainder of the day presenting the rest of the evidence and then give it over to William to start tomorrow. So tomorrow you need to be in here; he didn't excuse you as a witness, and I assume he is going to call you again. Be prepared!"

"Okay, I'll be here," he says, and excuses himself immediately.

Milkowski finds a bag of Fritos inside his desk; he eats a handful, and then another. He doesn't believe one word of what Cools told him. No one threatens someone without first trying to buy them off. And Cools just went to Aruba with his girlfriend. Michelle was telling the truth. He's fucking up this case. He's fucking up my jurors. And I won't let that happen!

Cools doesn't know it, but he's about to be hit from all sides.

Chapter Fifty-Three

Without remembering much of her way, Michelle makes it home after five strong mixed drinks. She shuts the door and leans back against it, breathing heavily. The house is silent and still, with only the steady drone of the heat pump. She staggers to the awaiting cushions of her living room sofa, curls her feet up, and turns on an easy listening CD. Her husband and daughter are gone and won't be home for two hours. And she needs all of it to find symmetry, peace. At rest, she contemplates the good judgment of her decisions—her courage to do what had to be done in the courtroom, her initiative to look the other way of the racecar club, as well as just now leaving her bothersome phone outside in the car.

Then the unexpected feeling that someone is with her brushes her thoughts. At once she becomes fully alert, shifting her gaze, seeing a sudden shadow.

Bang, bang, bang!

Instantly she jolts up. She reaches under the cushions. Maybe she'd left her phone in the car, but her gun hasn't left her side since the unidentified man banged on her door last time. She cocks the hammer, moving directly to the front entrance. Last time she was 90 percent scared and 10 percent pissed off; this time it's just the opposite. She controls herself, aims the weapon at the center of the door, applying weight against its trigger. "Who is it?" she demands.

"Open up! It's Cools!"

She lowers her gun and unlocks the door, yelling, "Brad, you asshole! Stop pounding on my freaking door!"

He ignores her distress and yells back, "What the fuck was that about? Why did you change the story?" She looks at him, confounded. "Tell me why you said he broke the camera before the interview. We went over this a million times!"

"What are you talking about? I got a text from Captain just before I went in saying it was changed."

"No, he didn't!" Cools snaps accusingly, suspecting she's up to something.

"Sit down. I'll show you then." She points to a chair and quickly slips away to the garage to get her phone. She returns, bringing up her last text.

Captain Jackson: Change of story - he destroyed the camera BEFORE the interview started.

Cools replies to the text: Captain call me.

They both stare at her phone until it updates: message failed.

"This didn't come from Captain!" he shouts.

"Well, what did you say in court?"

"What do you think I said? I said what we...that he broke it *during* the interview, that the wires crossed and fried the system!"

"Oh shit! Then that means...Hey, it was your guys who switched our phones, Brad!"

Cools begins to argue but stops, realizing she could be right. "I'm calling Captain." This time he uses his phone.

After four rings it's answered. "Cools, I'm glad you called. I'm sitting here with the mayor, but I need to talk to you and Robertson. It's important. Do you know where she is?"

"Yes, here...I'm at her house."

"Stay there; I'll call you back in a couple minutes."

He clicks his phone shut, searching his thoughts for answers. How did those sneaky bastards pull this off? And why does Captain always have to call us back? Then he notices that Michelle is about to break down. He grabs her and holds her, telling her over and over it isn't her fault, that there's no way she could've known, until their moment is broken by his ringtone.

He answers, with Michelle listening in, "Cools, they found a body with her throat slit in a wooded area in Everett. And check this out: it's only half a mile from the Kitty Club!"

Cools excitedly asks, "Is it Kimberly?"

"Too early to tell," he replies, "but you and Robertson should get out there now."

"What about Fredo? I thought this is his case."

"To hell with Fredo. I said I want you and Robertson on it! All right?"

Cools looks to Michelle, who pulls it together and nods. "Okay, Captain, we're on our way."

A short ride later, they are at the site, where the Everett police as well as news reporters have already infiltrated the scene, taking pictures, asking questions, hypothesizing. After only a short inspection, they can see the body is too decomposed to make a match, and outwardly there's little other evidence found except for tattered skimpy garments, dime-store jewelry, and a broken meth pipe.

Another dead end.

Cools drives Michelle home. They ride mostly listening to the radio since she's too tired, or maybe too distressed, for much conversation. Then, after dropping her off, he heads for the Shelter, where he washes down another one of Captain Jackson's Vicodin. And as he sits there drinking, he decides not to think about his day. Instead he seriously considers a different life—one with Chelsea, far from the city, and all the sanctuary of a simple existence. He sees a rural homegrown town, a small home with a large backyard, possibly even a German shepherd.

Bradley & Chelsea Cools Residence.

We could spend our weekends planning vacations and making babies. I could get a management job at a security firm working nine to five, and Chelsea could be waiting for me when I get home.

Suddenly he remembers a plaque he'd seen above the adjacent booth. He stands, leans over, and reads the passage.

"Better is it to be in a bar, thinking of home—than sitting there, wishing of here."

He doesn't agree. He leaves immediately for Chelsea's apartment.

Chapter Fifty-Four

Judge Cooper receives a phone call informing her that everything is set and ready to go. She double-checks her hair and marches like a soldier toward the front lines. Outside the rear of the courtroom, she situates herself at the judge's entrance. Adjacent to the door, there's a touch screen keypad. She types in her number, pushes confirm, and from inside the courtroom, she can hear the muffled voice of her court clerk saying, "All rise." Judge Cooper makes her entrance and finds everything just as she expected—William and Joshua are sitting pretty, wearing masks of innocence; the reporters are lined tightly against the back wall; and there's not a vacant seat in the house—all being equal of the previous two days, only with subtle differences. The jurors are dressed similarly but wearing different clothes; the reporters, the same, except now in differing positions; and the bailiff standing next to Joshua with his Taser is still eager to use it, but he himself is new. The only real difference is the mood. The unmistakable restlessness within the courtroom's atmosphere tells her, per her experience, that today will be momentous, remembered.

"You may be seated."

Milkowski lets out a dramatic cough then asks for a shortened, or even an excused, day due to his unexpected illness. In actuality it's to buy more time for the forensics team, so they can determine if the dead woman in the woods is his missing link. Next Judge Cooper listens to a concise argument from William reminding the court of his client's right to a speedy trial. Milkowski's request is denied. He has no choice but to state that he's presented his case and turn it over to the defense.

William rises to his feet, looking very prepared, and says, "Your Honor, I would like to submit into evidence a video surveillance disc in addition to an audio recording."

"Objection." Milkowski jumps up fretfully. "Your Honor, my office was not made aware of these recordings, and I ask that they are not allowed in due to discovery procedure."

"I would like both of you to approach the bench."

William quickly crowds a prized position in front of Judge Cooper and, in a quieted tone, states the facts—that he was fired then only rehired as of less than a week ago, and Milkowski has curiously missed some of his calls. Judge Cooper gives Milkowski a smart glance as William continues his reasoning. "Your Honor, these discs are a record of the first interaction my client had in this case with Detective Cools on the day of his arrest. And I believe that in the new light of the investigating detectives' conflicting statements yesterday concerning *when* the video surveillance monitor was broken, and the fact that there's an accusation of coerced interrogation, that these discs should be allowed in, so we can get to the bottom of it now instead of on appeal."

"What do you have to say, prosecutor?"

"Judge, this is ridiculous. I was not made aware of them, and need I mention that Detective Cools is not on trial here."

Judge Cooper turns back to William, asking, "Why weren't these discs turned in as discovery?"

"Your Honor, I myself did not know of them until late last night when I had my investigator go to my client's home, and this is what he found."

"And I assume your investigator is here today to testify to this?"

"Yes, Your Honor, he is."

"Okay, I'm going to allow it this one time—and one time only. Do I make myself clear?"

"Thank you, Your Honor," he says, followed by turning around and hurling a stern theatrical glare toward Captain Jackson and his entourage in blue and making sure the jurors see him challenging them.

Judge Cooper reports to the court that she'll be allowing the new evidence and hands them over to the bailiff. Everyone's eyes follow them like a UFO sighting on a clear night.

Then William amusingly calls his first witness. "I would like to call Professor Seth Johansen." All attention moves to a small man with long, dark hair and glasses as he makes his way to the front. He seats himself comfortably, and William stands in front of him and begins questioning. "Professor Johansen, would you tell the members of the jury where you are employed?"

"I'm a tenured Professor at Washington State University, where I teach signing."

"And what is *signing* exactly?"

"It is a language in which instead of using vocalized sound patterns, we use visually transmitted sign patterns to communicate."

"So you teach sign language for the deaf?"

"Yes."

"And do you teach any other classes?"

"Yes, I teach an advanced class that includes speechreading."

"Tell me about speechreading. Can anybody do it?"

"Well, yes, anyone can learn. It's better known as lipreading; it is the technique of learning speech by visually interpreting the movements of the tongue, facial muscles, posturing of the lips, and then simply converting the physical information into context, or language."

"Can you read everyone's lips?"

"Well, yes and no...It depends much on the person. Some I can read with one hundred percent accuracy, while there are a few people who pose more of a challenge." William nods for him to explain in more detail. The professor continues. "One example would be a man who has a bushy mustache; another would be what we call a *dead cell*—a person who speaks using little or no emotion."

With that William grins and faces the jurors, turning his back on the professor, and declares loudly to the courtroom, "I believe Professor Seth Johansen to be a liar and a fraud!" Everyone seems confused. The witness seems oblivious. Then he again places himself directly in the professor's sight and asks, "Professor Johansen, are you yourself deaf?"

"Yes, I am."

The crowd is impressed, and some commotion begins until William speaks over them. "And how well were you able to read the person on the disc I sent you?"

"Quite well. In fact, I—"

"Objection." Milkowski stands up fast, holding out a hand to halt the witnesses' testimony. "Your Honor, I thought these discs were found just late last night?"

"Overruled," Judge Cooper sighs, giving Milkowski a look that says "We all know William's full of shit, and we both know it's next to impossible to deny any evidence in a high-profile, circumstantial murder trial." Besides that, she herself is curious as to where all this is headed.

William presses forward, asking the question again. "Professor Johansen, are you able to read with one hundred percent accuracy the person on the disc?"

He looks to Judge Cooper, who says, "You are allowed to answer the question, professor."

"Yes," he declares proudly. "The person on the disc is quite easy to read. Actually, his speech is very timed and concise, and his delivery is full of emotion—anger, actually, the easiest of all emotions to read. When people are angry, they tend to use extremely precise facial expressions, not to mention the fact that I went over it many times to make certain of my testimony today."

Milkowski wears a mocking exterior for William and his witness; however, on the inside he's screaming. *What in God's good name did you do, Cools? What the fuck did you say?*

William smiles wide to the jurors, none of whom return the gesture. Then he very politely asks the bailiff to hold in the air the disc titled "Video," as he emphasizes, "This is exhibit A. It's a home surveillance recording that was taken the first morning Detective Cools came to my client's home. In it you will see the two of them engaging in a conversation in the driveway. And Professor Johansen will explain to you word for word what Detective Cools is saying." Then he asks the bailiff to play the disc.

Judge Cooper gives him a nod, and he leaves the courtroom, returning shortly with a television on a rolling stand. Next he hands over the remote to the witness.

Professor Johansen pivots toward the jury to set things up. "Ladies and gentlemen, I have speech-read the person on this video clip, and I can tell you every word he says. But don't just take my word for it; I'll show you. What I've done is written down all the words he used and put them to a musical scale, so I will be reciting what he says in synch with his movements; and you will see for yourself exactly what he is saying."

Then he adjusts his paper in front of him. He presses the play button and, when cued, begins to narrate. "I have to let you go for now, but first...I do not like you—you sick fuck!" Then the jury can clearly see Detective Cools eyeball his gun and flash it around. And again the professor recites, "These things accidentally go off some times, punk. It's rare, but it happens. Next time...next fucking time!"

The jurors gasp. Newspaper reporters turn off their recorders and rush out. Milkowski leaps from his seat, trying to argue but to no avail. People start whispering, even the jurors, and then begin talking less discretely. Joshua lifts his hands up and down, encouraging an uproar, and the courtroom becomes louder with every passing second. Judge Cooper slams her gavel down hard. "Order! Order in the court!" she bellows, motioning Milkowski to sit down, since they both know there's nothing he can say or do anyway. He returns to his seat as she addresses the jurors, in her now quieted courtroom, stating, "This is all evidence you will be taking into consideration at the proper time—that is, at the end of the trial—and not one moment sooner." The fear of her, in their eyes, tells her they understand. She then turns back to William, asking, "Are you done with this witness?"

"Yes, I am, Your Honor. And now I would like to recall Detective Cools to the stand."

"Very well," she replies, still eyeing each and every person in her court. "Bailiff, please bring in Detective Cools." Again the bailiff leaves as everyone waits with much anticipation, watching William and Joshua joke back and forth privately.

Cools walks in and right away knows something has happened. He senses them evaluating him. Joshua stares at him, smiling, and lets out a subdued laugh of victory. Cools returns a glare. The tension between them is clear to everyone.

William then adds to Cools's annoyance by flashing a wink and asking in a smartass tone, "Detective, do you now remember the conversation you had with Mr. Siconolfi in front of his house on the twenty-ninth of December?"

"No, I do not," he replies to the jury, realizing that they don't seem to believe him.

"Do you now remember when you threatened Mr. Siconolfi to make a statement?"

"No, I never did any such thing!"

"Then how about the threats you made the day of his arrest?"

"No! I read him his Miranda rights, and that is all."

William raises his eyebrow. "And is that all?"

Feeling the need to add more, he says, "I may have told him how much he disgusted me, and that I would prove he killed his wife, Kimberly."

"Anything else ring a bell, detective? And I would like to remind you that you are under oath."

Cools perceives he's missing something and is growing increasingly agitated. Milkowski waves a finger, catching his attention, swaying him to slow down, while attempting to lend the sense that everything is going to be fine. But

Milkowski, as well as everyone else in the room, can see that Detective Bradley Cools is going down in flames.

For an extended moment, he reflects on the morning in question and subsequently answers as calmly as he can, "No, I do not recall any other conversation."

William then spins nimbly on his heels, offering exhibit B and requesting the bailiff to play the compact disc. And while the bailiff is cueing it up, he explains to the jury that the night prior to Joshua's arrest, he'd accidentally left the audio recording system on in his living room music studio. Suddenly it begins to play over the very same speakers brought in two days before by the prosecutor, Milkowski. First they can hear Joshua.

"You've made a big mistake, top cop!"

"And how's that?"

William pauses the CD and asks Cools if this is his voice.

Immediately he remembers some of the things he said and contests it, stating, "It doesn't sound like my voice…and he could've dubbed it in with all his studio equipment."

"That's fine," William exclaims neatly. "I'll be bringing in a voice analysis expert who will confirm that indeed it is." Then he plays the CD again, turning up the volume.

The jury strains to hear a kind of whisper.

"The devil comes, the devil does, and the devil goes; and I bet you think the blood on the yacht is Kimberly's."

"Listen here, you freak. I'm tired of hearing your bullshit. I don't need her blood. I will find her body. And now that I have you, I have your DNA. And I don't care how careful you think you are, asshole; I will plant your hair, your blood, even your semen if I have too."

The rumbling in the courtroom starts up again; however, Judge Cooper is expedient with her gavel. "Quiet down! Quiet down now!"

And as she's dealing with an ever angrier crowd, William skips back and plays once more, even louder: "I don't care how careful you think you are, asshole; I will plant your hair, your blood, even your semen if I have too."

The excitement mounts as it plays a second time, burning the unforgiving words into their ears, burning vengeful passions into their hearts.

"Order in the court! And sit down William. Do not play that again!" He obeys, although most of the press ignores her as they discuss the implications. She slams her gavel repeatedly. "I said order in the court! I will have you removed…" They finally submit and begin to quiet down, and all eyes move back to Cools.

No one has any doubts that his career is over. Some suffer feelings of sympathy, while others hold utter contempt. Nonetheless, they all expect a reaction.

But the one they get does not come from him.

Joshua explodes within the sudden stillness. "Ha, ha, ha, top cop. I told you, you were fucking going down—you fucking dirty pig! You liar! You fucking—"

"Subdue him!" Judge Cooper screams. The bailiff hits him with fifty thousand volts. Joshua begins flailing around, out of his chair, onto the floor. Members of the courtroom step backward and position themselves to see Joshua, who is still uttering muffled curses between the shocks. The voltage is increased to the maximum amount allowed; he jerks harder. Everyone loses their breath, and then at last he surrenders.

William seizes the glowing moment. "Detective, now do you remember?"

Judge Cooper raises her gavel, intending to bang the holy hell out of her bench, but instead she turns to Cools for his answer. Everybody turns. His eyes are boiling, his muscles bulge under his shirt, and he looks like he's about to detonate.

"Answer the question. Answer the question, Detective!" William pushes.

Cools wrenches in his seat. The color in his eyes melts away like man prepared to die for vengeance. And no one is quite sure if he's going to stay in the witness box or spring from it in a violent rage. He says nothing, just holds a long, scorching, homicidal stare until Judge Cooper demands him to answer.

"I...I am going to plead the Fifth Amendment," he replies furiously, broken.

Then Joshua points his finger at him and spits out all he can muster. "You tell lies, and when they work no longer, you hide like a coward!"

"Fuck you, you fucking piece of shit!" Cools shrieks, pouncing out of the witness box.

The bailiffs intercept him. Judge Cooper pushes the red button, calling in reinforcements as they struggle around tables and chairs with Cools cursing, "Fuck you! Fuck you!"

Judge Cooper bangs her gavel. "I'm calling an emergency recess; I want Joshua taken immediately back to his cell!" The jurors are swiftly escorted out, and other security guards rush in to diffuse the situation. Judge Cooper continues shouting over the mayhem. "And I want all council in my fu—in my damned chambers right now!" Everyone starts moving in all different directions. "And you, too, Detective Cools. In my chambers!"

Ninety seconds later William and Milkowski stand in her chambers next to Cools, who's sitting in a chair with a bailiff above him. "This is a goddamned circus," she wails, glaring at all of them. Each one of them knows to be utterly silent, even William, despite the fact that he's reveling in his glory. She paces back and forth, gaining her bearings, trying to figure what course to take. She inhales a breath of air before talking it out. "Milkowski, I'm throwing out Joshua's statement, leaving you to win with what you have."

"Sounds good to me," William cracks. "And if it's all the same to you, I'd like to leave you all to your problems, so I can prepare for my next witnesses."

"You don't have any other witnesses on your list," Milkowski states, somewhat confused.

"I'm calling Detective Cools again. I never excused him, and I am not done with him yet. And then I'm putting Joshua on the stand."

Milkowski coughs nervously. "You are seriously going to put Joshua on the stand?"

"You would if you knew what I do," William beams arrogantly. "Now may I be excused?" Nobody says a word, and from the looks of them, no one is standing in his way to leave their sight. He walks out, engorged with pride.

The door shuts behind him, and Judge Cooper continues chastising them. "Cools, this is probably already on Fox News and CNN, so you're going on a leave of absence, effective immediately. And if I were you, I wouldn't say one word to anybody until you talk to your attorney."

"Judge, I'd like to just say—"

"Stop! I said do not say anything. I like you, Cools, and I am trying to help you. You're going to get back on the stand, plead the Fifth over and over again, and when you leave, you're going to say nothing to the press. Then go talk to an attorney, because you are in a lot of trouble, Detective. Now get out of my sight and be ready to be in my courtroom in two hours!"

Devastated and disillusioned he heeds her advice and walks out of her office toward the rear exit, where he can escape the building undetected.

Milkowski drops his face into his hands and listens in as Judge Cooper makes a call. "Captain, your boy just left my office. I want him shepherded for a while. I want to make sure he doesn't do anything stupider than he has already… Uh-huh…Oh really…Shit…Well, that's not going to help…Okay…Good-bye."

"Okay, Andrew, here's the deal. Word just came from the coroner's office stating that Jane Doe from Everett is twenty-seven-year-old Julie Something-or-other, known prostitute, died from a heroin overdose. Now, I'll grant you two hours,"—she checks her watch—"so you'll need to be ready to go at one. And when William puts Joshua on the stand, I want to see you break him. Use every trick you have; destroy this asshole! And bring this fucked up trial to an end!"

Chapter Fifty-Five

Cools—now a complete madman—squeals out of the courthouse parking lot in a police cruiser. One of Captain Jackson's men follows. Cools is so infuriated he doesn't notice his shadow, as he recklessly drives to the Shelter. He needs a drink, many drinks. He parks in the back alley behind the bar; Captain Jackson's man parks a half block away and watches him storm into the seedy establishment, and yet another man, who is also following, takes detailed pictures of both of them.

Chapter Fifty-Six

Inside his office Captain Jackson yells into the speakerphone, "Cools is a man with nothing much to lose; under no circumstances will you let him out of your sight. I want you inside that mobster bar, sitting in the booth right next to him. And if he tries to run, you're gonna arrest him and bring his ass to me!"

Milkowski storms in and stands impatiently in front of his desk. Next the captain says, "All right, I'm gonna put you on hold for a second." He pushes the hold button. "What do you want?"

"Between the deputy's, Hubbard or Martinez, which one can I trust most?"

"What's this all about, Milkowski?"

"You're better off not knowing; now tell me—which one?"

There's a pause of consideration before he replies assertively, "Martinez."

With that Milkowski leaves as fast as he came. And once back inside his office, he makes a call. "Hello, is this Martinez?"

"Yes, who's this?"

"This is prosecutor Milkowski, and I need you to do something for me, and then I will owe you one."

Martinez, knowing the value of prosecutor Milkowski owing him one, and the potential consequences of not complying, replies, "I'm listening."

Chapter Fifty-Seven

After viewing a television report claiming a loss of control over her courtroom, Judge Cooper has extended the recess until two thirty and has ordered some local contractors to build a temporary, soundproof, Plexiglass box for Joshua to sit in. Plus the builders are paid double if they disclose to the media that construction was scheduled for yesterday, giving Judge Cooper some retroactive clemency. They work expediently, but it's after three o'clock before she can organize everyone and get things rolling again. So now, with the gang all back in positions, Joshua fidgeting in his new surroundings and a half-drunk detective waiting in the hall, the trial resumes. She lends the court to the defense, expecting that William will be calling Cools, but he has a slight change of plans.

"Your Honor, I would like to petition the court, with prosecutor Milkowski's consent of course, to add one more thing into evidence."

Milkowski is thrown a bit and stammers, "Uh…"

William continues, "I'd like to add into evidence a taped client-attorney conversation that explains how my client is responsible for the blood being on the boat."

The jury's attention shifts back to Milkowski, who holds up a finger asking for a moment. It has to be some kind of a trick. He expects me to object. But why would I? The more Joshua says, the more ammunition I have when he takes the stand. Besides I really don't have a lot to lose at this point. He drops his finger and replies. "I have no objection, Your Honor."

Judge Cooper looks surprised at his unexpected accommodation and affirms, "Well, if the prosecution doesn't contest it, then I will allow it."

William glances at Milkowski with almost pity and moves to insert an audio CD into the sound system. Milkowski now reasons that he's made a grave error.

While holding the remote control, William sets it up. "Good afternoon, ladies and gentleman. This is a private conversation between not just client and attorney, but that of father and son. Some of the dialogue might strike you as bizarre, and I apologize in advance for any of my personal shortcomings, as this recording was never expected to be public record." He presses the remote, and Joshua's voice comes across unusually soft and genuine. All cameras zoom in on him sitting inside his strange-looking and confining glass cubicle.

"Yeah, I called the radio show and pretended to kill my wife…I was drunk, and I thought it was funny."

"But, Josh, you don't have a wife, and even if you did, it's not funny."

"Well, each to his own. But if you need to know, I don't think it's funny anymore, okay? I don't think any of this is funny, especially them trying to charge me with murder."

"Listen to me, Josh. They *are* charging you with murder, and in the first degree, and you have to answer some questions. Now, I need you to tell me why there's some woman's blood on a boat you rented."

"If I tell you, you're just going to diminish my religion, like you always do."

"No, I won't Josh. Now, I need to know, and I need to hear from you: why is there blood?"

"Okay, I'll tell you, but first you have to understand that my religion is real, Dad—not like Kimmy, but really real."

At the prosecution table, Milkowski closes his eyes and shakes his head, now understanding what he's gotten himself into. The jurors don't even notice because they're glued to Joshua inside his transparent partition, envisioning the meeting between father and son.

"I know it's hard for you to accept the fact that I have a differing belief than most. But it is *you* that does not understand. I pray to Ra, the true God. And I give sacrifice to Ra on the winter solstice, since it is required of me."

The word *sacrifice* buzzes in everyone's ears. And there's a sense that they may very well be listening to a confession with some sort of religious argument.

"Wait a goddamned minute, Josh. You're lying! Now, I've heard your talk of this winter solstice bullshit before, and I looked it up. The winter solstice is on the fucking twenty-second, not the twenty-sixth of December, when you took the boat out!"

"That's because *you* do not comprehend that the universe changes and that millennia have passed. Also that your religion was spawned from mine. I am remembering the true solstice, or *Sheiva ta*, from the Tablet of Origins, or its more familiar English translation, the Sabbath! It is *you* that denies your obedience to remembering the Sabbath!"

"Uh-huh, okay, well... So it was the solstice then. Still, what were you doing?"

"I was giving a sacrifice of many items, including letters of poetry, herbs, wheat, maize, pottery that I had labored hours over, and our blood. I took them out to sea at the appointed time, and I placed all the sacraments in a vessel; this time I used a crab pot to lower them to the sea floor. And in doing so, one of the urns holding our blood spilled onto the boat railing—this one obviously Kimmy's."

Milkowski, failing to remember what had happened the last time, tosses his pen in the air. He attempts to apologize but is at a loss for words since he has just listened to Team Siconolfi explain away everything.

"But, Josh, listen to me. Kimberly isn't real! Whose blood did you have?"

There's an extended silence. Everyone in the courtroom can hear the other breathe.

"Answer me, Josh! Whose blood did you have?"

"I got it from Amberly! But Amberly is Kimberly. She is *one* who lives within the dependent and the damaged—she lives within Amberly!"

"And this Amberly—she's the same woman who told the police that Kimberly was missing?"

"Yes."

Then, with a click of the remote, the room falls still. William stands with his head down somberly. Joshua appears to be innocently confused.

Clap... clap, clap-clap... Milkowski alone starts a slow, building, sarcastic applause. The smirk he wears is a medley of admiration for the performance and repugnance for the altered realities of truth. And he no longer cares about the media watching or even what may happen to his career. All he knows is that Joshua is up next and that the gloves are coming fucking off. But then William announces that the defense rests, and all the blood drains out of him. He now realizes he won't get his chance to cross-examine him and that he let them tell their story for free.

He's been played.

Judge Cooper recognizes this as well and calls for a recess.

Milkowski's exhausted eyes move to a report lying on his table—the one written and hand-delivered to him by a colleague, who didn't warrant either his trust or his confidence. He'll probably never know which.

At the top of the report, her name is written in delicate calligraphy: Janice Dryer. "My professional, psychological analysis of Joshua Siconolfi is that he will definitely take the stand."

Thirty-eight minutes later, Judge Cooper says to the jurors, "We are ready to proceed with the closing arguments. And because the state has the burden of proof, you will hear first from prosecutor Milkowski. After which counsel for the defendant will have an opportunity to argue, and then the state will have another chance for rebuttal. Prosecutor Milkowski, are you ready?"

"Yes, I am, Your Honor." He stands, holding a yellow legal tablet, and approaches the jurors, seemingly amused by the whole ordeal. "Ladies and gentlemen of the jury, I would like to extend to you how I feel right now. I am somewhat set aback. I have some kind weird of appreciation for their defense strategy. I do not believe I could conjure up such fantastical stories in my wildest dreams. That was a well-thought-out and well-delivered performance. But it was just that—a performance. So now let us come back to reality because we have important labors ahead." He looks to his notes and begins. "The defendant did *his part* by murdering his girlfriend; I am doing *my part* by proving that to you, and then you will do *your part* by returning a verdict of guilty! So let's get started."

He then takes them step by step for the next hour and forty minutes, leaving not a stone unturned, tying in jealousy, greed, uncontrolled rage, Joshua's disgusting actions, and their blatant disregard for the oath of truth in the court. He dismisses the ridiculous assertion that Kimberly was never real and plays against their own fears, claiming that they may someday read in the paper that Joshua has done it again, and that it could be someone close to them. From previous exploration of the twelve, he knows which jurors have daughters close to Kimberly's age, and he speaks to their heartstrings, propagating their duty to protect them, to shield them from the monsters that prey upon the weak and defenseless.

William stares listlessly, acting as if he is bored, often checking his watch, and smirking along with Joshua.

Finally Milkowski reaches the end of his evidence. He and his yellow legal tablet are exhausted. However, some energy has been reserved for his final assault. He raises his voice and circles dramatically, facing Joshua behind the Plexiglass barrier. "This—this fiend from hell itself brutally murdered Kimberly Wallingsford in cold blood! And he even had the deplorable narcissism to force his evil upon an audience of millions of unsuspecting listeners!" Milkowski's tone amplifies as he charges forward with every word. "He is not a worshiper of God; he is a worshiper of pain, suffering, and hatred! He feeds off others misery. I have never truly hated a man in my life. But he is a plague upon our society that we cannot let loose. He has to be removed from our civilized world. We have to purge this wickedness from our midst. And *you* have to be the ones who remove him. *You* have to do what is right. And *you* have to find justice for Kimberly by delivering a verdict of guilty—guilty of murder in the first degree! That is all; thank you."

Judge Cooper patiently waits until he is seated before surrendering the court over to the defense. And when she does, William springs from his chair, hostile and aggressive, in an effort to outgame the prosecutor's fervor. He cries outs, scorning, "You are an underestimated fat man!"

Judge Cooper slams her gavel. "That'll be enough of that, Mr. Siconolfi!"

He ignores the judge and traverses straight to the jurors, furious. "Fiend from hell? Worshipper of pain and suffering? Plague upon our society? Purge the wickedness from our midst? Now I'm beginning to understand why he wins so much!" William stabs his finger toward him. "How dare he speak to you as if you were fools, as if you would fall for his adolescent antics. Spewing excerpts that only belong in a commercial for an exorcist movie. Shame be upon him for becoming so desperate as to resort to this. Personal attacks. Character assassinations. What about the facts? What...about...the...facts?" He then mumbles his way back to his table. "I can't believe this shit...in all my years...the balls on this effing guy."

There he sits, while the courtroom catches its breath, until everyone, even Joshua, positions back in their seats. Then, from his chair, he begins his prepared summation. He barks out the words *circumstantial evidence*, his tone critical of the phrase itself. He looks to the jurors in disgust. Again he says the words *circumstantial evidence* and asserts, "It is the most dangerous of its kind! How does one defend themselves when there's no proof a crime has even occurred?" He stands searching the jurors and the room for answers. "How can a person get a fair trial when everyone is against him: the police, the media, politically motivated prosecutors, and even you yourselves? Yes, even you. Did you know that studies from acclaimed universities find that nine out of ten jurors believe the defendant to be guilty before they even step into the courtroom? So I need you all to search deep inside and ask yourselves if you can be absolutely confident that you do not hold preconceived ideas of a man who is imprisoned inside a glass box such as this." He presents Joshua. "If a man is accused to be guilty by the police and the prosecutors, do you adhere to the same consideration? Do you say to yourselves he has to be guilty or else why would everyone else think he is? Or do you think to yourselves, he looks guilty; he must be guilty; or just simply do you believe that someone has to pay? Why not him?"

He pauses for a second. "I understand these are tough questions, but why are they tough? It's because deep down inside you know them to be true." William shrugs. "We're only human; we're all susceptible to this. If I tell you a woman is a whore, do you question or believe? If I point out a thief in the neighborhood, do you let him roam free or do you keep a watchful eye? I tell you it is easier to stand with the accuser than to defend the accused!"

Again he pauses for a spell, pacing up and down the jury box. Then he lowers his tone to explain further. "It is hard to oppose a counterfeit accuser, especially when you have a defendant who's an outsider like him." He points to Joshua. "He's an easy target: he has no friends, and the only ones he does have, he makes up in his head; he has no children to consider; he's strange and sometimes creepy, and he doesn't worship the same God as most of you. If he'd lived in Salem during the 1690s he would've been burned alive as a witch. Oh, but you might say, well, those witch trials were hundreds of years ago. Then I would ask you a different way: what if he was a black man from the 1950s? Hits a little closer to home, doesn't it? Oh, then you might say, well, that was another generation. But what if instead of Joshua P. Siconolfi his name was Aazim Namir Muhammad, and he was on trial this day, absent of any evidence, for conspiring an Islamic terrorist plot? Could you? Would you be prudent? Or is it easier to say to ourselves, he most likely did it. The cops think he did it. Besides, I don't like him anyway!

"So, this is about more than just him. It is about *all of you* as well." He shakes a finger at them. "You, you, and you have all done things in your life that you regret. Do not make this one of them. Do not send an innocent man to prison for the rest of his natural life for the wrong reasons!" William stares at them; his facial muscles tremble, and he looks as if he's about to shed tears. He swallows hard and pulls it together, then walks back to his table and thumbs through his notes, allowing a moment for everyone's emotions to settle.

"Okay, now let's get to this so-called evidence. I don't disagree with really any of the circumstantial evidence in this case; I only obviously disagree with the far-fetched interpretation of it. So what are we really dealing with here? My client childishly made a disturbing prank phone call. And personally I do not see the humor in it at all; as I presume neither do you. But just because we agree it's not funny, doesn't mean it wasn't anything more than an unpopular practical joke. Maybe he fits somewhere in the category of a demented Ashton Kutcher, but not a murderer." William sees some consensus from a few of the jurors and surmises, "Okay, so we know he's not a very funny guy...probably doesn't get invited to a lot of parties."

The jurors follow him as he begins roaming aimlessly around the courtroom, still carrying on. "Then there's the blood, but the amount of blood found was miniscule, not life threatening, as you heard Dr. Lutin testify to. Then the prosecution alludes to the assumption that her body was put into the crab trap and tossed into the sea. Well, we've since found the crab trap, so where's the body? It doesn't add up! She couldn't have just floated away; they searched the entire area. Most of this doesn't make *any* sense at all; I've been sitting here for three days now trying to figure out how this prosecutor obtains his extremely high conviction rate. And I tell you: I'm deeply concerned about it; quite frankly it scares the shit out of me! I could be sitting there." He gestures again to Joshua. "*You* could be sitting there someday without any solid proof that you've done any...thing...wrong! And I might add that given the current statistics you would only have a 1.8 percent chance of being vindicated. Nobody—I say, no...body—performs their job with 98.2 percent efficiency. Maybe prosecutor Milkowski is a mad scientist of conviction, or maybe it means this court sometimes sends innocent people to jail!"

He walks over to his notes. "Now, let's talk about this fantasy woman. She has so many diverse identities I can't even keep track myself. Who is she? Kimberly Wallingsford? Kimberly Sharons? Kimberly Siconolfi? Amberly? Are Kimberly and Amberly the very same person? Is she the defendant's wife, or girlfriend? Was she real? And if she was a real person then why doesn't anyone claim her? Doesn't she have a mother, a father, a step-father, a sister, an aunt, a cousin, or a best friend? Did she ever have a teacher or a guidance counselor, a business partner or an employer? Who is she? Where is she? Nobody seems to know. She's just vanished!" He flings his hands in the air. "Disappeared completely from the face of the earth. And I don't mean that she has vanished as of two months ago, but rather she seems to have vanished away from this earth her...entire...life!"

He then walks over to where Joshua sits. There he inspects the enclosed box his son is held captive in; he taps on the glass, dividing some of his time for a brief connection. "You know, I had this friend in college; Buddy we called him. And Buddy wasn't a very attractive man, although he was quite a liar... oh boy, was he ever a liar. He would share with us, in detail I might add, of his numerous sexual escapades. Invented fictions of girlfriends he never had. And I'm going to tell you right now: Buddy never had one single girlfriend. But there were more eye-witness accounts of his dreamed-up girls than there are of this Kimberly. She isn't a real person, people! She never was. Let me make this clear: Kimberly is not a real human being! She's the figment of an overimaginative mind. Now, I could've by all rights spent three more days in here with one... expert...psychological...witness...after...another, explaining all the worlds' minds to you; however, I didn't, because I have confidence in you. I discern that you already know that paranoid schizophrenics fabricate stories and have delusions. Yet I ask of you: what is more insane: a paranoid schizophrenic believing in his delusions or the police believing in his delusions? There's not one shred of proof that any person is missing. The *only* proof in this case is the fact that my client, a person with diagnosed mental problems, was threatened by the police. Wrongly accused; illegally arrested; and tortured into writing a false statement! This we've proved."

A smirk or two from the jury tells him he may have gone too far. As a result he quickly changes the topic away from Joshua being the victim to their personal debt to the court. "You are empowered to do what is right; it is your duty to seek the truth, to attain to the facts."

Then he closes with zeal and passion. "Now, I want you to ask yourselves something. Do you believe that I would do everything possible to make this whole mess easy for you?" He pauses as if one of them might reply. Then he answers for them. "The answer is absolutely not! I want this to be the hardest decision you've ever made. I want you to know with unconditional certainty that you are making the right choice. I wouldn't accept your verdict of not guilty—at this very moment—if you said to me that I created some reasonable doubt. Reasonable doubt is bullshit! It's the politically correct way to say that he probably did it, but some fancy lawyer made a number of arguments, and now I'm not a hundred percent sure. That is not what I demand of you. I demand more—much more! I need you to pore over all the evidence, or lack thereof. I need you to study, use your commonsense, and deliberate and then deliberate some more. I need you to know *why* he's not guilty.

"Now, you may be saying to yourselves, 'Yeah, sure, he wouldn't accept our quick and unstudied not guilty verdict—what difference would it make to him?' But I tell you, it makes a world of difference to me. Because I am not asking you to just say not guilty and be done with it, since that will only be the beginning of a long and tireless journey that lays ahead for each and every one of you. I insist—I demand of you—to fight for what is true! I need you to tell them." He swings his arm over the backdrop of news cameras. "I need you to justify Joshua P. Siconolfi to the world! Thank you."

"Are you done, Mr. Siconolfi?"

"Yes, Your Honor."

"Prosecutor, would you like to rebuttal?"

Milkowski declines, thinking to himself that it was powerful, but it won't matter. I still have Deputy Martinez. Plan B.

Judge Cooper then instructs the jury that they're to stay as long as it takes, and if they are not able to reach a verdict today, then they have to return at eight o'clock tomorrow morning.

Joshua is taken to the visiting room, per the request of his father. William picks up the phone and looks through the glass at his son, who is elated. Joshua hollers through the handset, "You are utterly fucking amazing! I've always wanted to see you in action—not under these circumstances of course—but wow...you are absolutely fucking incredible! You had them eating out of your hands. I almost believed Kimberly isn't real. You were—"

"Josh! Joshua, enough!" Although William appreciates the admiration, he has greater issues pressing. "Josh, listen up. I think we have a very good chance of you walking out of here soon." He tilts his head with self-importance and a matching smile. "And if not, I'm positive I can get you off on appeal. Now, that's as long as you do nothing else. If they convict you, you cannot say *anything*—are we clear?"

"I wouldn't say anything incriminating. I will only teach them of my parables, but still they won't comprehend; they are infantile. We can only allow them to go so far!"

William puts his iron fist to the glass. Joshua does the same. Only a half-inch-thick piece of glass separates them, not enough to part the moment. There William declares a vow; he stares hard at his son, the way he did when he was a child, and says, "No matter what, no son of mine will live out his life in prison!"

Outside the courthouse the media reports all that has happened to a disappointed audience who thrive on Joshua's outbursts. Although his good behavior, combined with his defendant box, has earned him the media proverb of the day: those who defend from glass houses cast no stones.

Chapter Fifty-Eight

Inside Judge Cooper's chambers, Milkowski sits nervously discussing all that has happened. She lets him vent, appreciating his worries and consoling him with her silence. Naturally she's not a good listener and has to make-believe to meet the leve of interest he's in need of as he goes on and on trying to figure out if he's won or lost. Growing frustrated she stands, eyeing the liquor cabinet, and says, "I need a drink. Can I get you one?"

"Yes, please."

She pours two tall glasses of vodka, adding orange juice from a small cardboard box container and a couple of ice cubes. Out of the glass she considers hers, she sneaks a swig and refills it with more alcohol after checking that Milkowski isn't paying any attention. "Here you go," she says, handing him his glass. He stops verbally fretting for a second to take a sip, giving her the chance to change the subject.

"You have to admit William's closing arguments were quite innovative; he throws more curve balls than Randy Johnson." Milkowski is left speechless, and she realizes she might have offended him. Then she adds, "Oh, and you were great too…uhh…I was really impressed with the way you handled yourself in there. And I know it's somewhat taboo to say anything, but I think you got him. I saw conviction in the jurors' eyes." She tells him this convincingly, although she believes in not to be true. She has the rising suspicion that it will be at least a hung jury and that she'll most likely then have to lower his bail to a more attainable amount. It's something she's not looking forward to doing. And to some extent this prospect is responsible for her added alcohol consumption.

Milkowski slurps down half of his drink and replies, "Yeah, you may be right, and I'm almost certain it won't be an acquittal. Worst case scenario, they'll come back deadlocked, and then I will just have to start over." But just to make sure, he thinks, I'm going to have Martinez do his thing.

"I'll tell you one thing right now," she says, "as soon as they come back with the verdict, probably sometime tomorrow, I'm going to sentence his cute little ass right then and there. I want this media circus out of my tent. Did you know that they're talking about me in the press, saying that I've been too lenient, that I've allowed the defense unnecessary concessions to create a spectacle for my *own* recognition?"

"Yeah, I heard some of that on talk radio," he replies, not really interested. "I'm going to ask for, life without."

"And you *will* get it," she replies sharply, holding her drink in the air, toasting Joshua's fate.

He follows suit, posing another question, "What about Detective Cools?"

"What about him? He's done for! He'll be real lucky if he isn't brought up on charges." There's an awkward pause. "You want another drink?"

"Uh, no, actually I'm famished," he says, getting up from his chair. "I think I'm going across the way to Chinese Gardens and get a bite. Would you care to join me?"

"No, I have work to do. I need to be prepared just in case they come back tonight."

Her response is as he expected. He couldn't have her come with him anyway since he needs to be alone to set things in motion. One thing William was absolutely correct about is the fact that prosecutor Andrew Milkowski is an underestimated fat man. And he will do most anything not to lose. "Okay, I will see you when were called back in."

Soon he's hiding in a dark, private corner inside the lounge of the Chinese Gardens, where, across a plate of *mu shu* pork, he stares at his phone, making his final decision. Then he contacts Ghost. And ten minutes later, a secure line is set up between the deputy and himself. "Martinez, this is Milkowski. Are you ready?"

"Yes, are we going to do this then?"

"I need it done, Martinez. So make it happen. I'm counting on you!"

Chapter Fifty-Nine

Right outside the jury room, Hubbard asks Martinez, "Who was that?"

"Ah...jus' my wife. She wants to...she wants to vacation next month back to her homeland, and she jus' bought the tickets. Listen, I'm starving; could you run and get me a Butterfingers?"

"You know I'm not supposed to leave you alone at this post."

"Who cares? No one cares. I got things here; jus' grab me a candy bar real quick and slip back. What's the big deal?"

"All right, all right...Butterfingers?"

"They're the best of all the candy," he replies, waving him on. Hubbard leaves. And Martinez waits until the door at the end of the hallway closes, then moves closer to the jury room door, where he can overhear them deliberating.

"I don't buy any of that bullshit with Joshua and his father discussing the case."

"I believe Kimberly is real and he killed her. But where is she?"

"There's no proof. And it's obvious Detective Cools was out to get him."

"I lied when I said I hadn't heard of this case before, but without a body, I don't think I can convict him."

Martinez turns his phone off and holds it to his ear. Then loudly and animated, he pretends to be speaking into it. "Honey, you're not going to believe what jus' happened; it changes everything! Here's what the jurors don't know!"

Attention inside the jury room is diverted. They still themselves, silently listening.

"Honey, it's her...Yes, Kimberly! The one they found last night with her throat slit in the tree line behind the Kitty Club...Yeah, it's her; they jus' confirmed it...Uh-huh...I know...That's exactly what I'm saying...Uh-huh...And how messed up is it that she's only found now? He might get away with it! He might get away with murder...Uh-huh...I jus' can't believe it...Okay, I'll be home soon, honey...Okay, bye...Love you too."

An hour after the ruse, a cell phone rings inside the bar of the Chinese restaurant. Milkowski answers and receives a message that the jurors have reached a verdict. He throws forty bucks on the table and grabs a handful of mints as he rushes out the door. He chews them up, attempting to mask the few too many he has had, then moves expediently to the courthouse through a gauntlet of reporters.

"Prosecutor Milkowski, what will you be recommending if it comes back guilty?"

"Prosecutor Milkowski, will you be filling charges on Detective Cools?"

"Will you be filing charges for the other missing girls?"

"I am not ready to comment at this time," he says over and over, while pushing his way into the courthouse and down the hall to the courtroom. There he finds everyone waiting for him. He takes a quick look at Team Siconolfi; neither father nor son wears their usual cocky grins, because they both know that a quick verdict is almost always in favor of the prosecution. At the back cameras are dialed in, and the reporters hold dual cell phones, one with the text reading "guilty," the other "not guilty, their spring-loaded thumbs on the send buttons. Blood pressures are high, and the tension is suffocating in the room as Milkowski takes his seat. The second he touches the chair, the court clerk announces, "All rise."

Judge Cooper walks in briskly and immediately asks if both counsels are ready. Then she says to Joshua, with a threatening gavel, "Listen to me carefully, Mr. Siconolfi. I'm allowing you the dignity to stand freely in my court. But be warned: any outburst from you will not help the sentence I may be imposing on you. Do I make myself clear?"

Joshua, seeming uncharacteristically unsure of himself, nods and replies weakly, "Yes, Your Honor, I understand."

Next she orders the jurors back in. Everyone searches their demeanor for insight as they seat themselves solemnly, their expressions revealing nothing. Judge Cooper wastes no time in asking, "Have you reached a verdict?"

The foreman replies that they have and hands a piece of paper to the bailiff, who hands it to Judge Cooper. She reads it and hands it back to the bailiff, who returns it to the foreman. Judge Cooper now knows, but her facade is dense, offering not a clue. Joshua is ordered to stand. William positions close to his side with a comforting arm around his shoulder. And everyone holds their breath as the foreman clears his throat and begins to read. "We, the jury, hereby find the defendant, Joshua P. Siconolfi, guilty of murder in the first degree."

The words briefly pull the life out of the room, and then, like a tsunami, it floods back in. Everybody begins talking among themselves, the murmurings growing louder by the second. Judge Cooper grips her gavel, and the bailiffs coil—all awaiting Joshua's expected eruption. But Joshua appears entranced, as if he didn't hear his verdict; he turns for the cameras, smiling, and leans back, staring into the heavens with the outstretched arms of a martyr. And once more the room becomes silent, ominous.

Judge Cooper interrupts the moment, announcing that she's prepared to sentence him, and asks Milkowski for his recommendation. He responds with a lengthy version of Joshua Siconolfi is the worst of the worst and needs to be removed from society for the rest of his natural life. Then she poses the same question to William, who begs for mercy and leniency. And when he's finished, she asks Joshua if he'd like to say something before being sentenced.

"Yes, Your Honor, I would," he replies, then pauses, swelling everyone's impatience. He faces the cameras, aiming for the spotlight, speaking to them at first as a teacher. "Why is your justice system failing? Because you cannot instruct morality out of corruption! The world machine you have built rests upon a foundation no stronger than the elasticity of water. You believe yourselves too big to fail. Yet, you are sinking, blanketed in bondage, comforted with ignorance. And painfully you will be taught to have respect for the wisdom of our creator." He stalls for a few seconds, receiving opened-mouth stares of mixed sentiments—confusion, sadness, disdain, sympathy. "You are fools! You disgrace yourselves. I know what you have done. I will visit you in—"

"Okay, that's enough of that!" Judge Cooper yells. Joshua stops, unexpectantly. Then she takes in a deep breath and chastises him without response. Stating her reasoning in great detail as to why he is now sentenced to life in prison without the possibility for parole—forever removed from society.

He's then expediently taken away without incident. His temper is stoic and composed as he ponders, for the first time, what it might be like for him in prison, wondering who his friends will be, or more importantly who his enemies will be. Under the fluorescent light, he mulls over his father's whisperings. It's only round one son; I'll have you back in front of this court inside six months on appeal—reassurances of hope that do little for the dark cloud mounting within.

Benson, from the vent, asks what the verdict was. And after Joshua tells him it didn't go well, Benson explains that now it makes no difference, that now he can confess without fearing any further punishment, adding that if he does, it could greatly increase his chances of parole someday.

Joshua replies, "Fuck you, Benson! Or should I call you by your real name, Officer Geoff Ward. I always knew who you were. Tell that to the press, you fucking rat! You tell them I did it, but that they made me do it."

Then all Joshua hears is the door slam shut from inside the adjacent cell.

Chapter Sixty

Five celebrated days later for the powers that be, five agonizing days later, for Cools: out of his car's front seat, he rouses, nuzzling a half-full bottle of Jameson. Empty beer cans, he remembers nothing about, litter the floorboards. And cocaine residue clouds a CD case. His vehicle has been transformed into an anti-rehabilitation center, where he's been practicing the ancient art of alcohol and drug therapies. And with a business-like understanding of "location, location, location," he has parked at the end of a dead-end road—one that leads past remote homes to a locked gate that protects commercial forests from unwanted trespassers. With a push of a button, the window rolls down enough to let in some fresh, cold air. The landscape is unfamiliar to him.

Where the fuck am I?

His only appraisal is that he's secluded far away from the desolation that has become his existence—a world that is full of television broadcasts playing and replaying his journey to rock bottom, and the same that is unwelcoming to insobriety and vigilantism.

Before he can light a crinkled cigarette found in an empty cup holder, his mind recalls the two-hour biography of Joshua on A&E, from his privileged childhood to a life imprisoned. The tag line: "And the devil whispers to him."

He shakes the recollection from his thoughts, swallows some booze, and then through hazy, blurred eyes checks his messages.

Missed calls: Chelsea, three; Michelle, two; Tabatha Sterns, seven.

Chelsea and Michelle want to help him, meaning he'd have to give up the alcohol and drugs. Tabatha Sterns wants to use him, meaning he'd have to give up what little pride he has left and allow her to film another special—this one starring the most dishonest cop in modern times. He adjusts the rearview mirror to inspect the drunken mess he's developed into. His face is older, with a nearly full-grown beard beneath deep, sunken eyes. The youth is long gone. And his head throbs since he's still fairly drunk from last night, when he was drunk from the night before that. Again he tips the bottle to quench the rising anxieties. He holds it to the light, assessing what is left. The level is low; his checklist for the day will begin with a quick stop at the liquor store.

Then reluctantly he looks at his watch for the date. It confirms what he already knows. Today is his big day—his hearing where, mostly due to political pressures by the media that have been calling for his head, he'll be fired, officially. It all churns the undigested alcohol in his stomach. This he remedies with a good-morning line of white powder. The drug burns his nose and drains down his esophagus, waking his wits like twenty cups of Starbucks. He lays his head back, going over the what-ifs.

What if the media attention would've been less?

What if they didn't portray Joshua as the victim just to sensationalize ratings? Putting out half-hour shows under the streamers of "Framed," "Criminal Cops," and "Set-Up?"

What if it could've been explained away under the veil of interrogation tactics, the "getting into the perps head" kind of stuff?

What if the reports would've focused more on the killer instead of me, the man trying to solve the case?

What if Joshua would've been found not guilty, so I could kill him myself?

A new text comes in. Chelsea: Please call. Miss you much. I Love You. Do not let this ruin you ☺

But what she, and even Cools himself, is unaware of is that he's been looking for something to ruin him for a long time. And it is simply the subconscious, natural course for him to assume modest personal responsibility for his actions. Knowing it or not, he directs all of the blame toward his archenemy.

He starts the car, and the news comes on, stating, "Appeals have been filed concerning the Joshua Siconolfi case. And tomorrow he'll be transported to the Washington State Penitentiary in Walla Walla, home to Gary Leon Ridgway (the Green River Killer) and David Lewis Rice, who in 1985 brutally murdered civil rights attorney Charles Goldmark, his wife Annie Goldmark, and two sons.

Also some other infamous men that he'll be living with include Indle G. King Jr. (the Russian-Mail-Order-Bride Killer), who murdered twenty-year-old Anastasia King, Christopher Merrill (the Night Prowler), and Dietfried Eiffel, the German-born pediatrician who in 1977 poisoned his Halloween candy with a homemade concoction of insecticides and cyanide, killing nine trick-or-treaters and sending dozens more to the emergency room. A side note is that while Eiffel is currently serving nine life sentences, he's also attempting to publish his volumes of nursery rhymes, a real *bleeping* sicko, absolutely undeserving of a politically correct psychological diagnosis!"

Good. I hope they become cellmates.

Cools listens to as much as he can withstand before turning it off. Then heads for his apartment, so he can grab a quick shower—he wants to look his best for his official firing. Other than that he could care less. About the only thing keeping him going at this point in his life is the far-off hope that William will win the appeal of the century, a theory he's given much consideration to over the last few days. And within this fantasy, Joshua will be released back to the streets, allowing Cools the opportunity to go down in history as the Lone Wolf of Justice.

Chapter Sixty-One

The prison bus, powered by a roaring diesel engine, labors hard as it crests the Blue Mountains. From there the small community of Walla Walla can be seen sleeping in the valley below. For Joshua, anxiety mounts after each passing mile; his thoughts are overrun by what lurks behind those walls. Soon the vehicle turns off the highway, then slows to a crawl, and cautiously begins navigating through a series of guarded gates. Its passengers, who are growing restless, are those who have affronted or injured humanity so much so that they've been elected to be removed from the world for lengthy periods of time, if not for the rest of their lives. For most it is their deserved consequence. And their journey to this place is nearing its end.

Final destination.

Sitting on the cramped metal seat, Joshua peeks out the slated window at the massive size of the old, brick building that supports lofty gun towers at every corner. Anticipation and fear swirls in his stomach as glimpses of being stabbed or being forced to stab others race through his thoughts. Trying not to think of such things, he averts his attention to the shackles that are cutting into his wrists and ankles, wondering of the man who bled on them beforehand and listening to conversations relating to the history of the penal complex itself.

Three seats back, an African American (a Crip) shares everything he knows for all to hear. Joshua turns briefly to catch a look. He's in his midfifties, with leathery skin covered in facial tattoos. However, his eyes hold truth, knowledge, and the fact that this isn't his first visit here. And seated next to him is a younger recruit, who will in short manner also grow to become a Crip and wear the same symbolic artwork.

The prison's history is told.

"Washington State Penitentiary used to be the old territorial prison, set here because of its geographical location. Basically we're in the middle of a desert. This place is known for two things: its famous Walla Walla sweet onions and the endgame for some of the most notorious criminals in the country. You'll see many walking the yard that you've heard of or read about previously. It originally opened for business shortly after the Civil War. Then in the 1920s, they built a license plate factory, which continues to operate to this day, producing more than two and a half million plates each year." The articulate and seemingly friendly black man pats his apprentice on the leg. "WSP is also known as the Walls, the very location where the executions of death-row inmates are carried out. Two methods are offered. The newest, and the one typically requested, is lethal injection, but still the option of hanging exists. One interesting case was that of Mitchell Rupe who, at the time in 1994, only had the choice of hanging and had his death-penalty overturned on the grounds that it was considered inhumane to hang him due to his obesity, since, being over four hundred pounds, he would've been decapitated during implementation."

The youth listens intently as his teacher raises his voice.

"Pay close attention to my words! Most men *will* die here, either by the hands of another inmate or the gunfire from the guards' M-16 assault rifles. In many cases, men with relatively short sentences, five to ten years, will end up with more charges during their stay—this is the personification of the Walls. Reality is what it is, my brother. Even the address itself leaves all black men who enter without hope: 1313 N. 13th Ave., Walla Walla, WA. This is the white man's ultimate oppression."

"Hey! Watch your mouth, nigger!" A snarling white guy from the rear yells. Right away the back and forth erupts, rage mounting with each bigoted phrase.

"Fuck you, cracker!"

"You're dead, nigger!"

"Home sweet home, huh, *ese?*" says a Latino a few rows ahead, as many stretch to the end of their chains to get to each other.

"I'll make you my bitch!"

"I'm going to cut you!"

"See you in the yard, punk!"

Joshua joins in, defending his kind. And although it's somewhat feeble, he's noticed by others—including the skinny man he's shackled to.

Then the armed guard, standing behind the protective barrier at the front of the bus, hammers the butt of his shotgun on the sheet-metal-lined cab. The sound rings throughout the fuselage. "Settle down, savages, or I will use the other end of my weapon! Settle down now!"

His threat brings an unexpected obedience, and the chaos slows to a halt as quickly as it began. At this very instant, Joshua realizes he might have more to fear from the guards than the inmates.

The bus pulls through the final gateway with only muted mumblings. And then the hard-edged, bony man that Joshua is chained to studies him through narrowing eyes and asks, "Is this your first time?"

"Yeah, it is," he replies, welcoming the conversation and wanting of some experienced advice.

The man says nothing for ten seconds or so. He just stares, reading his face. Then he asks, "You're Joshua...something—the Sickness, right?"

"Yeah, that's right," he answers, amid disapproval for the label, adding, "but I didn't do it. I'm working on my appeal."

"No one cares whether you did or not, so if I were you, I'd just keep that to yourself." Then he leans in closer, locks eyes, and embarks on a series of questions.

"Will you be having money sent in?"

"Well, yeah.... of course, my family is wealthy."

"Good...that's real good." Joshua can see his stock go up in his questioner's gaze. "Are you a snitch?"

"No, absolutely not."

"Good...and it better be true. And what if someone disrespects you—will you fight?"

"If I have to, I will."

"You *always* have to," the man counters. He allows the statement to sink in and then asks ever so bluntly, "And do you hate niggers, Jews, and spics?"

Joshua, knowing that this was going to come up sooner or later, responds without delay and convincingly, "Yeah, can't fucking stand any of them."

His response is scrutinized for a long moment. "You..."The man shakes his head. "You don't seem to me to be the maniac they say you are."

"Uh...well," he stutters, void of any real answer, also realizing others are listening in on their little chat and that his reputation is at stake.

Then suddenly the bus comes to its final stop, diverting the attention of everyone on the bus—all except his strange inquisitor, who coarsely states his rules. "My name is Spider," he says, "and I will tell you this one time, and one time only. If everything you just told me is one hundred percent on the money, I can help you on the inside." Spider shakes his head with cutting eyes. "But if you're not one hundred percent on the money, then you would do best to never speak to me or even glance in my direction. Understand?"

"I'm sure we will speak again," Joshua replies shortly. Then his gut wrenches from the screech of the locks as they are taken off of the metal doors. There's no escape; this is the moment of entrance into a new world, where survival through violence and constant warfare is commonplace. He is about to enter one of the most dangerous prisons in North America.

The Walls. The Walls of Hell.

"Okay, listen up, convicts! You will exit this transport as instructed. You will follow our orders without question. If we have any problems, you will be dealt with swiftly and harshly. If you do not understand this, you're going to have a hard time here. I am not here to teach you. I am here to control you. So get off my transport, convicts, and try not to get yourselves shot."

Shackled in twos they exit the bus. Joshua and Spider work well as a team, stepping carefully so as not to pull on each other's chains. And soon they're standing out in the open, where instantly the hot desert heat hits them. They stand still, watching the others. Angry black men, ugly white guys, tattooed Hispanics—hard-broiled creatures from every ethnicity, all with one thing in common: a diminished value of life. A quick look at the horde tells Joshua to wear an agitated, pissed-off face—an appearance he finds easy to emulate, since this is how he has felt most of his life. All he really needs to do now is concentrate on shrouding his sheer terror.

They're corralled through the thick metal doors of the west wall that has a rusted "Inmate Entry" sign hanging above. Joshua turns against his restraints to catch one last glimpse of what is being left behind. A parking lot full of cars, sparse trees in the desert landscape, a woman wearing a dress, homes and businesses in the valley below—all sights he may never see again.

As he crosses the threshold, a guard whispers, "The Sickness, huh?" It's beginning to be clear; this is going to be his new name.

Then another guard, with red hair and a beer belly, yells, "You two, stand against the wall and face forward!" He and Spider comply, and before long, their cuffs and shackles are removed. It is a relief to have them off, like when blistered feet are slipped out of sweaty roller skates. But their moment of ease is short-lived since they are next instructed to strip for search.

"Lift your ball sack."

"Separate your penis from your scrotum."

"Bend and spread your cheeks."

And so on. All with the prying eyes of creepy prisoners suspiciously watching. Joshua tries not to link himself to their conduct, but human nature is curious. He catches sight of Spider's tattoo. His entire back and shoulder blades depict one giant spiderweb. And when he turns, Joshua sees that he has two lightning bolts down his chest and "White Power" across his abdomen. Spider catches him observing his art and states, "The Aryan Brotherhood will be your only salvation, Sickness."

"Keep quiet, convict!"

Then the guard shoves Joshua into an adjoining room, where he's given clothes, bedding, the official rules, and taken inside the prison. It's bigger than he'd imagined it to be. The cellblocks ascend four stories high, containing seventeen iron-barred cells on each level, the openness of which presents the sounds of loud radios, fighting, and the deafening screaming of bored and caged testosterone. Soon he will learn the noise is never ending. What's more, the air is filled with the smoke of contraband—cigarettes, marijuana, even the burnt plastic of soda bottles as they are melted and reshaped into weapons that can pass through the metal detectors, Wall shanks.

Then they stop in front of his cell. It's smaller than he imagined it to be. It is eight feet by ten feet, the minimum required by law to accommodate four men to live out their lives, furnished with nothing more than a toilet, a sink, one small writing table, two sets of bunk beds, and three curious-looking strangers.

Into the late hours, he gets to know a little of his new cellmates and is made aware of the real rules. Then he lies on the top bunk, thinking to himself that he must either become accustomed to this anxiety-fed environment or find a way to break out of it.

Chapter Sixty-Two

It's after four in the morning at the Shelter; the waitress and bartender left over two hours ago. But due to the fact that Cools had his gun on the table, simply staring at it through wary eyes, no one asked him to leave. Now he is hidden within the darkness, sitting alone in front of a pile of cocaine, snorting, drinking, smoking, plotting. He pictures himself storming into William's home, 21550 Kingsway Drive, gun drawn, crying his name, emptying the clip, calling 911, getting arrested, confessing, arraigned, pleading guilty, sentenced, shipped to WSP, finding Joshua, and choking his fucking life from him. This drug-, alcohol-, and rage-induced scenario plays over and over. And although it involves many dramatic variations, the outcome remains the same.

Chapter Sixty-Three

Over the first week or so, no one approaches or messes with Joshua in the least, but they examine his every move. His cellmates represent a diverse mix: Davidson (the lying loudmouth), Borost (the Russian), and Junkie (the junkie). They are fair with him, even though they ask a lot of questions, never tiring of bringing up many differing situations.

"What would you do if this happened?"

"How do you think we should handle some of our current problems?"

"What are solid codes of ethics a white man should live by?"

It soon becomes crystal clear that all is a test. And he knows it won't be long before they'll want to see if he will stand up for himself and fight. When it's time, I hope its Davidson (the lying loudmouth), the asshole who sleeps below me and never shuts the fuck up. Not even for a minute—always going on and on about nothing and everything. Fucking lying dumbass!

Suddenly it dawns on him that he should initiate the fight. Yeah, I'm getting tired of all this being tested bullshit anyway; it's going to happen sooner or later, besides, I'm dying for some action.

So atop his bunk, he begins stretching and working on his strategy, taking in consideration Davidson's shorter but bulky size. Be quick and wiry, enough to stay free from his grip. Throw many blows, fast and hard, keeping him busy until his fat ass is winded; then when he's lost his energies, move in for the blood and the respect.

It isn't long, just as he expected, for an opportunity to arise. A guard passes by on his hourly rounds. And sure enough, not twenty minutes later, Davidson is disgorging one tall tale about the time he got into a bar fight with five Italian guys. Joshua waits until he reaches a point in the story where he'd cleanly taken out the second guy using a kung-fu move, then breathes out a loud and skeptical, "Hmm!"

Davidson pauses for a second, but says nothing, before continuing, "Okay, so now I'm down to three, right...except this lanky guy to my left has a knife. I take it away from him and—"

"Uh-huh. Whatever, man."

"No, it's true; I'm telling you exactly how it all went down!" Davidson replies, defending himself. Then he steps out of his bunk to reenact the situation.

Joshua let's out an exaggerated sigh, saying, "Okay, let's hear the rest."

"Yeah, you're going to hear the rest!" Davidson blurts out, noticeably agitated.

Borost and Junkie sense an imminent altercation and pay closer attention, given that this is the exact sort of conflict they thrive on. And Davidson, now with their undivided attention, begins to put on a show. He swoops his leg out quick and low, demonstrating how he kicked the feet out from underneath guy number three (the one he took the knife from); then he stomps hard on the floor, showing the way in which he'd incapacitated number four; followed by a foot chase of the fifth guy, who was by this time running for his life.

"Yeah...I...uh...I think I've seen this movie," Joshua wisecracks, setting Borost and Junkie into sharp laughter.

Davidson becomes instantly enraged. "What're you saying? You calling me a liar?" he yells, flailing his arms around.

Joshua constricts his eyes and raises his voice. "I'm saying I'm getting real fucking tired of hearing your bullshit fucking stories all damn day and night!"

"Well, maybe you feel like you need to do something about it," Davidson challenges.

Borost and Junkie shift quietly to the toilet, giving them room.

"All right, bad ass, stand over by the bars. Let me get down and put my shoes on."

"Fuck you!" Davidson yells, grabbing at Joshua's legs and trying to pull him off the top bunk.

Joshua kicks at him barely missing his head as Borost lays down the rules. "No! You let him put shoes on!"

Davidson turns to see that even Junkie agrees. “Okay, put your shoes on, punk! I’m going to destroy your rich pampered ass. And that might not be all I do to your ass, you yuppie bitch. I’m going to make you my bitch. I’m going to butt-fuck your face.”

Joshua keeps his cool, saying nothing. He simply laces up tight and gets into position. And as soon as Davidson starts to say something, he jabs one in flattening his nose. Crunch! Blood spurts out.

Davidson reacts by charging with a deadly haymaker swing. It grazes Joshua’s cheek, knocking him back into the toilet, where he falls into the wall. Borost and Junkie jump out of the way, observing every detail. Davidson rushes in. Joshua, off balance, swings, misses, and gets crushed into the wall. They lock horns and thrash around, knocking books and papers off the writing table. Joshua is cornered, and Davidson smashes him again and again against the concrete. Joshua goes wild, trying to break free. He manages to briefly push Davidson away, then as he lunges in again, Joshua impels a fierce uppercut, catching him under the chin. It hits, fracturing his jaw. Davidson lets out a guttural groan. He staggers backward, trying to catch the edge of the bunk to break his fall. Joshua charges forward, over him, heaving another heavy fist keen on his eye socket. Crack! And Davidson drops to the cement like a weighted tree branch in a windstorm.

“Yeah! Fuck yeah!” Junkie shrieks in a tenor of nervous excitement. Joshua slants a scorching eye at him, and he quiets himself at once. Borost is left thunderstruck.

Then Joshua seizes a moment, inspecting Davidson’s lifeless body carpeting the floor. He hovers above him, mumbling incoherently.

Borost yells, concerned, “Let’s get him up!”

“No!” Joshua snaps. “I’m not finished with this story-telling piece of shit!”

“You fucked him up!” Borost replies. Junkie’s expression agrees.

Joshua ignores their distress. He kneels down and cinches his arm tight around Davidson’s neck, making clear his intentions. “Yeah, but he called me a punk and a bitch, and I’m not giving anyone a chance to do it twice!” Then he begins squeezing just as Davidson regains consciousness and starts to squirm.

“Don’t! No!” Borost and Junkie screech. “He’s one of us!”

Joshua disregards their mercy, wrenching even tighter. Davidson’s legs flail, kicking the air; his face transforms to red, to purple, to fear. “Die...you...motherfucker...die!” Joshua’s own face turns colors under the strain. Davidson’s bulging, bloodshot eyes scream for help before his body goes into a brief seizure. “Die, you fuck.” Then the writhing decreases. “Die!” He slumps. He stops.

Borost and Junkie cannot discern whether he's dead or alive. All they know is Davidson is one of them. And in this split second, they don't care about their rules, which decree to never get involved. At once they spring in unison. They start to pummel Joshua, beating him in the back of his head, booting him in the side. Joshua stoops and tucks under their raining blows, still compressing Davidson's windpipe.

"Stop! Stop it! You're gonna kill him!"

Borost strikes full force, then snatches Joshua's arm, breaks him loose, and drags him off. Junkie leaps in, and together they try to restrain him, but he battles on. "Are you going to stop? Are you done? Stop!" Finally he submits by ceasing to struggle, and Borost ultimately lets him go. Then everything falls silent, only wheezing and gasping for oxygen, while the three of them rise to their feet and look in shock, circled around Davidson, who is lying comatose on the floor. He isn't breathing.

"Hey! Junkie? Borost? What the fuck's going on over there?"

"Don't fucking worry about it," Junkie answers through the bars. His voice is shaking, but his eyes never leave Davidson's limp form. Then, worriedly, he looks to Borost. "What're we gonna do?" Borost stares unknowingly, catching his wind. "Davidson! Davidson!" he yells, jumping up and down, kicking him lightly but repeatedly, calling him a fat piece of shit, anything to rock him back to life.

Borost kneels to check him out. The closer he gets, the more unmoving he is. He slaps his face. Nothing.

"Do the CPR! Do the CPR thing!"

Borost starts compressing his chest as Joshua rests on the lower bunk, assessing the damage. Oh fuck, what if I killed him?

Then suddenly Davidson sucks in a bottomless breath. Borost rears. Junkie jerks, freezes. It scares the shit out of all of them, but at the same time awards relief. Junkie helps, and Davidson is aided to his bunk, where he immediately passes out again, wounded but alive.

Joshua doesn't say a word, just evenly returns to his bunk. If he feels any remorse, Borost and Junkie cannot tell. None of them makes a peep for hours. In Joshua's mind he's assured he won't have any other problems; he's established himself, gained their approval. In his cellmates' minds, he is now thought of as a man to be reckoned with, living up to his media revelations.

Then just before they attempt a restless night, Borost declares an additional law of the house. His voice punctures the dead silence. "You squeezed him so tight both his eyes will blacken; he's too beaten up to go to meals for a week at least. And if his wounds are seen by the guards, we all go to the hole. And we *all* will bring back food until he heals; this is the way we do it!"

Joshua looks down and nods in accord to both of them, then restores to his former position on the thin prison mattress, gaping at the ceiling, secretly smiling. In just a few short and adventurous moments of violence, he's answered all of their questions. He's done proving himself. And now he can focus all his energies on figuring a way out of this hellhole.

Behind the closed doors in his mind, he has a plan. But then, he's always had a plan.

Chapter Sixty-Four

Outside of the Walls, his name has taken on a life of its own. The justice system has given more focus to the missing girls written in his scrolls—bringing forth investigations and press releases. Psychologists list him in their case studies and journals. Teen magazines interview his high school classmates, who claim he carried the traits of a psychopath, and ex-girlfriends cry for the investigative reporters, telling how numb he is within. The mainstream Christian rhetoric asserts he's a sign of the final days. And just to get under their skin, clever pundits refer to him as the second coming of Charles Manson. Rock groups have released new titles like "Murder of the Unknown" and "Playboy Assassin." Lawmakers are advocating a litany of newly needed laws. And he's exploited in comedic routines and late-night monologues. His name is cursed, ostracized, ridiculed, but it's a name that one man is fighting to save—William Siconolfi.

He's been playing every card in the deck, threatening to expose all the dirt he's acquired on his colleagues over the years, resulting in a list of influential members now contributing to his son's freedom agenda, which includes cardinals, politicians, judges, and businessmen—the power players.

He leaves not a solitary sleazy stone unturned, securing at least a retrial. He's also hired a *Fortune* 500 promotion firm to sell the idea to the public that his son is innocent and a security team, former Blackwater militants, to protect his interests and the interests of those with whom he's secretly conducting backdoor dealings. He has to be careful, as it seems the FBI has him under surveillance.

Today, his security team, has set up a meeting with a court of appeals judge. The rendezvous is at a local BMW dealership. The judge will meet him in full disguise. Wearing dark flashy sunglasses, a sporty-gelled man's wig, nametag, and a cheap suit that has salesman written all over it. As the FBI agents sit across the street viewing with their binoculars through the plate glass windows, they'll only see William at the negotiating table, discussing payment options.

When the meeting is over, a text message chimes. It's from his security team, informing him who the mysterious man is (other than the government) who's been following him. The text reads: Former Detective Bradley Cools.

Chapter Sixty-Five

A number of nights after the cell brawl, nerves are calmed, and the men begin to bond as a result of Davidson being mostly healed up and the sharing of the OxyContin pills Joshua scored on the yard. They are now flying high, the best of friends.

Borost and Junkie contribute a few accounts of their past adventures and loves. Then Borost asks Joshua to tell of some personal things about himself.

Joshua quips, "I feel sometimes as if I'm being watched in the chow hall." They all start laughing, picturing the setting of their dining area. Three times a day, they march single file through metal detectors into the large mess hall packed with hardened convicts. Walking among them are many guards carrying pepper spray and nightsticks. And standing above, on the second floor, other guards hold shotguns, teargas, and itchy trigger fingers. Security cameras rotate on their bases, following their every move. The cops are watching, the cons are watching, everyone is watching everyone. There is not one person who lives or works within the entire prison who doesn't already know that Joshua won't eat oatmeal, peppers his French fries, and will trade most anything for chocolate milk.

"Okay, that's pretty funny," Borost says. "But seriously, tell us what you're all about, man."

Joshua shifts his eyes to the wall, thinking for a minute, as the cell plunges into silence. "Well…all right," he replies, and sits up, hanging his feet over the end of the bunk. And then for some unknown reason, he begins speaking freely of something he's held close all his life. "I have dreams...I mean... When I dream, it's different than the way you do. It's called sequential dreaming."

"What the fuck does that shit mean?" Junkie asks.

Joshua starts explaining the best he can, somewhat confused about it himself. "Well, when I dream, it's very vivid, lifelike, and, unlike most men, in full color. And I dream in sequence, complete story lines, some lasting a year or more." He pauses, searching their faces. Their expressions are as expected, suspicious and doubtful. Still he continues, "And the one I've been having lately is of a little boy named Frankie. The story is set in Alabama in the sixties. He lives alone with his mother; her name is Betty, and she is...well, sort of a tramp, a party girl."

"Yeah, I know the kind," Junkie adds.

Joshua smiles, and is encouraged to carry on. "Okay, so one Saturday night, in the middle of a house party, she's called into work. She leaves in a rush, and little Frankie is left with her new boyfriend, Panama-Red. And he's trouble. Big trouble! He ends up taking little Frankie with him to collect some drug money. And in the course of this, he gets killed by the hillbilly husband and wife that are in debt to him. Obviously they figured it was easier to kill him than pay the bill. And what's worse is it all happens right in front of little Frankie."

"Stupid fucking hillbillies," Junkie slips in.

Everyone chuckles and positions themselves to listen more closely.

"So now the situation is, Abe and Sally—that's the hillbilly couple—decide to leave Alabama the Beautiful and abscond to Idaho. And since they believe little Frankie to be Panama-Red's son, and they sure don't want to leave behind any witnesses, they're taking him along."

"What happens next?" Davidson asks.

Joshua answers gently, as these are the first words he's said directly to him since their fight. "Well, that's all I've seen so far...But one thing is that little Frankie is so distressed over seeing Panama being killed he can't hear or even talk."

"So you're saying you'll have another dream tonight?" Borost asks, fascinated.

"Maybe not tonight. Actually I haven't seen him for some time now. But eventually, yes."

"And you're gonna tell us what happens, right?" Junkie asks.

"Yeah, I'll tell you guys." Joshua smiles again, feeling like he's in the company of true friends.

His sharing sparks off an atmosphere of social comfort, and the rest of their evening together is spent joking, laughing, and bad-boy storytelling. Even some hypothetical talk of escape is discussed until they are worn out. Then warm good nights are said, and once again they are buried under thin covers, warding off the cold. For Joshua the talk of little Frankie has opened a doorway that's been closed for a number of nights now. And somewhere in the core hours of darkness, his eyes begin to roll back and forth into REM sleep.

Flashes of radiance shift, imagery twists, and buried emotions emerge—taking form.

Abe, his young wife, Sally, and little Frankie are driving in the old Ford truck down a long gravel driveway. The sun is just rising over a hayfield that ends with a large house surrounded by old-growth forest. It's painted white and across the full width is an open porch, with wicker chairs and potted plants. As they come to a stop, a cedar board can be seen hanging above the entryway. The burned letters in the wood name the home: The Clemsens.

Little Frankie stares out the window into another world. It's a nice and proper homestead bordered by green lawns and fruit trees. There's a playful Labrador retriever running in the yard. And standing on the porch, under wooden wind chimes, is a woman named Mrs. Sue Clemsen. She is a glowing lady with a joy about her that cannot be explained, and she never leaves his sight.

They all go inside, where everything is clean and orderly, and little Frankie is sat down on a davenport sofa. There he appreciates a home that is filled with quietness and the smells of a fireplace and home cooking. Pictures of loved ones adorn the walls. And Mrs. Clemsen shows loving eyes, even as she patiently listens to the tall tales of her wayward brother.

According to Abe they had to leave Alabama because he'd lost his job, and the young boy they have with them is Sally's cousin's kid, who they adopted, since she was using drugs. From there he goes on and on telling of one sad misfortune after another. The only part being the truth is little Frankie's name, which Sally found stitched into the inside of his jacket.

Little Frankie thinks about what Abe is saying before he realizes he can hear again.

Then everything moves in fast forward.

Days go by living with the Clemsens, eating family meals, attending Sunday services, and spending the daylight hours running and playing in the fields with their two children and the dog named Trixter. Their son, Billy, who's close to little Frankie's age, is a lot of fun and always kind to his younger sister, Bobby-Sue. Little Frankie also takes a liking to Jake, Mrs. Clemsen's husband. He's a hardworking man, whose nature is steadfast and gentle. He takes little Frankie around the farm, showing him the animals, teaching him how to feed the chickens and horses, and explains to him the strict rules of the home.

In short manner he begins to adjust into a healthy young boy. And even though he still hasn't uttered a word, no one presses him. The only conflict in him is the notion to hide his mother from them. He misses her greatly but doesn't want anyone to know of her, because he loves it here—he never wants to leave.

Then one day, as they are all sitting down to supper, the phone rings. Jake gets up and talks for a while in the family room. After the call ends, he takes a long time before coming back to the table. And when he does, Mrs. Clemsen asks apprehensively, "Who was that, darling?"

Jake holds a stern hand to her, to which she remains silent. Then he looks to Abe, asking, "Why are the police in Alabama looking for you?"

Abe makes a glance to Sally then replies, "I has no idea 'bout dat, Jake."

"Well, they said something...something about a man being shot," Jake replies harshly.

Abe, with pleading eyes, turns to his sister, who appears as if she might cry. Then he looks down, away from everyone, and says, "Maybe we bet'r leave din." He gets up and walks out of the room with Sally trailing close behind.

Mrs. Clemsen excuses herself properly from the table. She takes her husband by the hand, leaving the room as well. Billy and Bobby-Sue eat in silence with little Frankie as they listen to the grown-ups arguing and moving about the house. Then they hear the fading noises of Abe's truck crackling the gravel in the driveway.

Another twenty minutes or so passes before Jake and Mrs. Clemsen return to the dining room. Together they stand close, consoling arms wrapped around each other. They announce that Abe and Sally have left. And that little Frankie is now the newest member of the Clemsen family.

Joshua loses the association. He tosses and turns the rest of the night, desperately trying to find his way back.

Chapter Sixty-Six

After making it through a two-hour screening process, William waits in the visiting room. It's painted drab, chilly, and deficient of every luxury.

Across the other side of the prison, Joshua's yard time is disrupted by the screeching sound of the loud speaker.

"Joshua Siconolfi, visit!"

Soon he's escorted into the room, looking pale; his skin appears older and loose around the eyes. "Good morning, Josh. How're they treating you here?" William asks, seeming more curious than concerned.

"I'm doing what I have to, and that's all I'm going to say about it," he replies curtly. He then takes his seat and scans the room, getting an eyeful of a young, slutty girl visiting her boyfriend.

"Listen, Josh, I've consulted with some very powerful friends of mine, and we have an excellent shot at securing you an appeal. We are going to get you out of here one way or the other."

"Maybe I like it here."

"Quit talking crazy, Josh. Now, is this why you asked me to come here?"

Joshua removes his gaze from the girl, leans in close so the guards cannot hear, and says, "I want to do another interview with Tabatha Sterns; I need you to set it up."

"I don't think she will, not after what you pulled last time."

"Oh, she'll do it; believe me, she will."

"Okay, I'll see what I can do," he replies, shaking his head, not understanding his son. But then he's never really understood him.

The remainder of the short visit is used up chitchatting of the inner workings of prison life while William quietly wonders if his son is remorseful for what he's done.

Chapter Sixty-Seven

Three days later, Seattle's purple dahlias are beginning to bloom, and blue jays are singing and flying about in the long-awaited sunlight that has returned to the Pacific Northwest. It brings new life to the many shades of green in the city that rests in the heart of glistening waters and snow-capped mountains. Anyone who has ever visited the Puget Sound would agree she is a true beauty this time of year, but Cools hasn't seen any of it. He's been numbing his bitterness in a drugged-out state. Currently he's hiding at his regular table.

Again he's half drunk and sniffling from the line of cocaine he's just done in the bathroom. He takes a long drag off his cigarette while watching the news regarding the upcoming, primetime interview of his old adversary by Tabatha Sterns. In her commercials for the event, she blatantly smears Kimberly's name, presumably trying to incite rage in Joshua beforehand, itemizing the choices she made in life—her vocation as a stripper, her false identities, her promiscuous affair, drug use, heretical religious beliefs, sexually transmitted disease, and her propensity for violence.

The dark side of the deceased.

It all makes him need another drink, another line. "Ahem," he coughs, catching the attention of the new redheaded waitress, and waves her over. As she approaches he pulls out a wad of one-hundred-dollar bills—his recently ill-gotten gains from sales of cocaine to the local riffraff. "Bring me a new bottle of Jameson," he slurs out, "and can you change the channel to anything but this shit?"

"Anything for you, handsome," she replies, with a counterfeit smile. She then turns to fill his request. And when he can no longer see her, she quickly drops her friendly expression. There isn't a great deal known about him. Only what she's gathered from the other girls, who've told her that he's some kind of cop that was given the all clear to be here. But that isn't her concern; all she is thinking is that he's been here almost every night since she started two weeks ago. And he usually leaves absolutely obliterated. It's a story she is all too familiar with. A reoccurrence she's seen time and time again in her many years working in shady cocktail lounges.

Sometimes good men, really good men, drink themselves to their death.

Chapter Sixty-Eight

Final preparations for the audience of her career are underway, and the word on the street is that Tabatha Sterns's employer has already paid $750,000 for the exclusive, maximum security interview. They expect it to set ratings records. Because Joshua, often thought of as a diabolical killer, has gathered a loyal congregation who can't seem to get enough of his arrogance, good looks, or provocative theories of life. And since his exploits have been absent from their screens for almost three weeks now, their imaginations are starving for what outlandish things he might say or do next. Some even hold onto hope that they'll get a genuine confession or hear the fate of the other missing girls.

The elaborate set they plan to erect in the prison's gymnasium is complete with eight-foot-tall, panoramic video panels, completely filling the backdrop from every camera angle. Two of them will be dedicated to digitally enhanced pictures of Joshua and Kimberly, while the others will exhibit alternating clips of the penitentiary itself, depicting where hard men do hard time.

In addition they've arranged to play a variety of juicy videos from Joshua's previous antics and dub in portions of Tabatha's first interview. Up first though will be Officer Geoff Ward, the undercover cop who shared the cell adjacent to Joshua during his trial. Second will be Amberly Carlson, the missing stripper who has recently returned to Seattle, whom William Siconolfi, at trial, alleged was the very same person as Kimberly—the old, "her other personality is the one who is missing" defense, which nobody bought into. Still the accusations from her are going to rock the world.

Third, they'll cue in prerecorded statements from prosecutor Milkowski. And last but not least, a few jabs are going to be tossed in at good old Detective Cools. Although other news outlets have already done his story to death, his very name always seems to infuriate her main guest. Therefore, segments of his audio recordings will be played at intermittent times during the two-hour special.

Of course Tabatha's more personal provisions comprise of her hair, nails, teeth whitening, and the loss of four extra pounds. She and her new stylist have picked out the perfect outfit and jewelry. But her beauty will be deceiving of her cleverness, given that she's also been working diligently in the passing days, among a team of professional criminologists and psychiatrists, building an arsenal of inquiries designed to expose the real Joshua. She plans to conduct a thorough exploration of his mind, to bend and twist his contradictions and play upon his temper and vanities until she unearths his vulnerabilities. Then she'll squeeze every last single drop of truth from his core, exalting herself to the ranks of Diane Sawyer and Katie Couric.

This afternoon her tutoring comes from Jeffery Talmot—her latest coach and advisor. Together they sit on the makeshift set, arranging how her nylon-covered legs will be crossed and going over camera angles, when Tabatha glances across the room to see that her iced toffee mocha has arrived. It's held by a new girl she's never seen before, who's loitering impassively behind camera number two. And although she's very pretty, she is wearing one of the latest and not-so-welcomed fads from the Seattle scene—her head is completely shaven.

Jeffery notices that Tabatha's lips curl smartly as she motions the delivery girl over. And being the professional he is, his concentration is only averted for a second. He quickly ignores the girl and continues explaining the camera positions in a sharpened voice that's telling Tabatha she should remain wholly attentive to his trained guidance.

The girl walks up to them, and Tabatha points to a table, instructing her, "There...just set it down there."

"This is my coffee, lady. I just paid six dollars for it, and I don't feel like giving it to you," the girl replies.

Her curt response is enough even to break Jeffery's concentration. He speaks up, before Tabatha has a chance, saying, "This is a private studio, miss. You're not allowed in here."

She pays no regard to his authority and states, “I came here to see Tabatha Sterns. Are you Tabatha Sterns?”

Tabatha retorts smugly, “Yes, I am. And you are…?”

“I see no reason to be a bitch! I was told to come talk to you. Joshua sent me!”

“Security! Security!” Tabatha yells, thinking to herself that there’s no way she was sent by Joshua. I’ve been in contact with him every day. And if Jeffery wasn’t here, I would scratch this slut’s eyes out for having the nerve to call me a bitch!

The girl reaches hastily into her purse. Tabatha scoots back with a sneer, knowing that any second guards will be dragging her away. And next the puzzling girl says something that changes everything. “Can’t you see that I’m the woman you have on your video screen, or are you blind as well as stupid?”

Tabatha’s expression alters from scorn to confusion as two security guards charge in.

“Here! Over here!” Jeffery yells, pointing her out.

They grab her; she struggles as she screams at Tabatha. “You dumb fucking bitch! You thought I was missing! And in your ignorance my husband’s been sent to prison!”

Perplexed Tabatha looks back and forth from the girl to the eight-foot-tall image on the video display. At first she can’t comprehend what is happening, but the eyes, the cheekbones, lips, teeth—the resemblance is uncanny. “What are you trying to pull? Are you trying to say that you’re Kimberly?”

“Yes, I’m Kimberly…Kimberly Siconolfi!”

Tabatha, seemingly possessed, springs out of her seat. Jeffery is speechless. And the guards immediately let go of her and step away as if they’ve encountered a ghost.

“Oh my fucking God! Where in the hell have you been?” Tabatha asks, circling her, inspecting her more closely as others on the set begin to realize the situation and move nearer.

“It’s Kimberly—she’s alive!” a cameraman yells.

Tabatha’s mind spins considering the implications. This can’t be. I’ll lose my big interview. But wait a minute; this is better…much fucking better! “Tell me where in hell have you been?” Tabatha asks again, accusingly.

Kimberly smiles, taking pleasure in her frustration; she replies softly, “We are…to will to know—to will to be silent.”

Chapter Sixty-Nine

"Fox News alert! Welcome to Studio B. I'm Sheppard Smith, and wow, you're just not going to believe this. We just got word on a story you couldn't believe could get any stranger. But it did! Remember Joshua Siconolfi? Sure you do, the Sickness, as some have called him. You know, the guy we convicted and sent to prison for killing his beautiful stripper wife, but there was never a body. Well, now we've found her body. And get this: she's very much alive! Seems she was simply gone…somewhere. Where? I don't know. She must've fallen off the face of the planet. And once again Joshua bleeds his darkness from the obyss. So now we go live to Tabatha Sterns, in Seattle, who's breaking the story."

Tabatha comes onto the screen with a lively "Good afternoon, Sheppard."

"And a good afternoon to you. Now, tell us where this story has gone?"

"Well, Sheppard, it is all true and substantiated. Here at KUBE Channel 9, we've independently confirmed that Kimberly is very much alive—as well as being a real person, I might add. And her wrongfully convicted husband will be released from prison in upcoming days. I've already talked with the governor, and he's agreed to sign a full pardon sometime later this week."

Sheppard cuts in, asking, "Well, the big question of the day is: where was Kimberly all this time? Has she been hiding under a rock or something?"

Tabatha raises her eyebrows in almost disbelief as to what she is about to report. "Well…she's been living on a ranch somewhere in southern Arizona. It's some sort of cult, the Sisterhood of Mystery and Enlightenment. And, according to her, the ranch consists of approximately sixty-five women who shave their heads, work the land, and live without electricity or any other influences from the outside world—no television, internet, phones, radio, or even newspapers for that matter."

"That's bizarre...But at least, you know, it kinda makes sense—being that, how she could've been unaware of what's been going on all this time...absent of any news and all."

"Yes, and as strange as it is, it all seems to fall into place; she claims that she just simply took off on a whim one day before Joshua's infamous radio call. And as she put it, she was following her guide."

"A whim, huh? And following your guide? Is that what they're calling it these days—when you run off from your, not-husband, in the dark of night, to shave your head and join the Mysterious Sisterhood of Enlightenment? What more do we know about this cabal in the desert?"

Tabatha flashes a quirky look, sneaking a peek at her notes. "She won't tell us much about their beliefs, merely that—and I quote—'We are...to will to know—to will to be silent.'"

Sheppard repeats the phrase to himself, then quips back, "Hmm...sounds more like to will to...not tell us anything." Then he turns, facing across his table to Judge Napolitano. "So where do we go from here, Judge? What, if any, legal actions do the Siconolfi's possess at this juncture?"

"Well, Shep, this case, as you may well know, is far from over. There will no doubt be a lawsuit for wrongful conviction. Most likely the Seattle Police Department will want to settle out of court in attempt to make this all quickly go away, but I assure you it will not! There are a lot of ins and outs here to consider. And I should also add: there may be a lawsuit against Detective Cools, who—to be considerate—grossly mishandled the investigation from its very beginning."

Sheppard shakes his head, saying, "So much has happened so fast. What if...?" He then switches back to Tabatha, who instantly appears on the screen so fast she isn't ready. And as she fiddles with her earpiece, he asks, "Tabatha, is there any proof—other than her summation—that Kimberly ever resided at the sisterhood ranch, unawares as the story goes? Or could she be making the whole thing up?"

"We are currently probing into that very question, but right now we can't even confirm that the ranch exists; there's no listing, no phone number, and nothing comes up on the Internet. But I would like to note that none of that matters at this point; the only thing that really matters is that we have a wrongfully convicted man serving time in a prison for a crime he hasn't committed."

"So it seems." Sheppard turns his attention back to the judge, asking, "What if it turns out that she knew what was going on and let it happen…some kinda revenge, or something along those lines?"

Kimberly's picture pops up.

The judge holds out an open hand. "It's too early to tell at this point, Shep. We just simply don't know."

Sheppard thanks his guests, returns to full screen, and summarizes, "Well, there you have it, folks, for now at least.

"Now, in other news, as if we could top that. President Obama has—"

Click.

The television set in a seedy motel room flashes white then goes off. The remote control is dropped to the floor next to an empty bottle of Jameson. From underneath the pillowcase, a gun is pulled out into the open. The visitor, a redheaded prostitute who calls herself Raspberry, flinches. And the next thing she hears is her coked-out John mumbling to himself, "That's it…now I'm going to kill that son of a bitch!"

Chapter Seventy

Spring winds of bright cold air play upon the afternoon parking lot. Cars and news vans occupy each available space, and every square inch of its asphalt is trampled on by an ambitious gang of reporters. They cluster together waiting impatiently outside the walls of the Washington State Penitentiary for Joshua's emergence. Most of them are already in front of their cameras, doing commentary. What has gathered them all here today is the newly leaked information that he was granted a full pardon by the governor earlier this morning. From there the news spread like a wildfire on a dry and windy oilfield.

Viewership for this event is estimated at over 39 million. Commentators have made the comparison to the all-time record of 111 million held by Super Bowl XLVI, which pitted the New England Patriots against the New York Giants.

Interestingly enough, a daring rock band, Absence of Light, is playing an acoustical version of their new song, titled "To Will to Be Silent." They've cleverly positioned themselves near the center of the lot, performing out of the back of their van in an attempt to get some free publicity. Up front and center, and a mere three days after they'd first met, Tabatha Sterns and Kimberly stand together—superficially as friends. They grip each other's hands, waiting for the door to open. Both are dressed suitably for the occasion in warm coats with matching gloves and knee-high leather boots. In addition Kimberly wears a pink beret over glittery blond extensions. A week ago the two of them could've been thought of as sisters. But now their identities are too well-known to be mistaken for anyone except for who they are.

While dividing the spotlight, Tabatha comforts Kimberly, warming her shoulders from the chill. For Kimberly the congested attention is menacing; for Tabatha it's full of excitement. And part of her wishes to retreat to her camera, with microphone in hand, and share her hyped speculations of appending lawsuits, book and movie deals, and TV reality shows. Nevertheless, temporarily sidelining her aspirations is justified, since she's holding onto the trophy—the Holy Grail. She cleaves to Kimberly, insistently protecting her from the other journalists, while eavesdropping in on a few of them. To her left, a younger curly brunette—skinny bitch, Tabatha thinks—is touting some of the latest gossip, reporting that there's a joint effort by both the FBI and Team Siconolfi to unearth the private interrogation room and expose one of the many tactical abuses of the police that led to this blunder. To her right is a man she's familiar with, John Ahoum, from a competing news station, who is asking his viewers viable questions. "Will Joshua be angry with Kimberly for being gone. Will Kimberly be angry with Joshua for faking their marriage, or will they reunite forgivingly? Will they now marry—for real this time? Could they play themselves in any upcoming movies?" Tabatha listens closely, mindful of what is around her, although completely unaware of who is watching from afar. At the very outskirts of the event, in a Ford Mustang with darkly tinted windows, sits a coked-up, old has-been with a score to settle.

Suddenly the prison gate opens. The crowd's enthusiasm intensifies. Cameras adjust amid flashing lights. And Joshua walks out, larger than life, tall, athletically becoming, and free. Kimberly breaks from Tabatha and runs to meet him. Photographers scramble for the best shot as everyone falls into silence, awaiting the couple's reactions.

It shocks some. They embrace hard. Joshua picks her up and spins her around and around, kissing, whispering to the back of her neck, proving his desire for her. Sentimental goodwill toward the young couple stirs among the crowd. And their shameless groping is overlooked as they lose themselves in the moment, without a care, ignoring the world. They are alone upon a stage and instant celebrities, wanted, loved. And whether one thinks of them as Romeo and Juliet or Bonnie and Clyde, not a soul can deny that Joshua and Kimberly look impressive together, resolute, the perfect fit.

The people hoot and holler for over a minute as Absence of Light plays a nightclub beat in the background. And everyone gets a closer look at Kimberly.

Her coat is now wide open, exposing her short, tight-fitting dress and round cleavage, which is diverting the camera angles. And her eyes are lit up as lightning crackling within ice. She's simply radiant and instantly loved.

Then Joshua seizes one final kiss before composing himself. He makes his way to the podium with wetted eyes and Kimberly entwined under his arm. They seem to possess no will to let go of each other.

The platform is styled as for a press conference, holding numerous microphones, all advertising their respective news outlets. He yanks one of them from the stand—ABC News.

"We love you, Joshua!" teenage girls scream from the back.

Kimberly only smiles at their admiration as Joshua extends his hand in the air, calling for their quiet attention. He displays a demeanor of unreserved significance. The crowd settles at his command. "Ladies and gentlemen, I am here to right the wrongs of a corrupt system!" He pauses, momentarily accepting their affinities, then begins jabbing himself in the chest, his voice growing larger with each word, "I have been harassed by the police, wrongfully arrested, interrogated, and tortured. I have been called a liar. I have been called a killer—a murderer. And I have been sentenced to a life without hope and stripped of every dignity!"

Then he lowers his voice to a more poignant tone. "As you well know, the police set me up. I had to endure the stress of a trial. And in their evident mistreatment of the common man, they convicted me of first degree murder and sent me to this godforsaken place." He pauses again, appearing as if he is about to cry; his eyes gloss over; his voice shudders. Kimberly grips him tighter, supporting her man.

"I am an innocent man. I've done nothing wrong. I...have...done...nothing...wrong!" He pounds his fist on the podium. Everyone senses his pain, his sorrow; their throats begin to swell. Then he steps away from his podium, looking individuals in their souls, building upon their emotions.

"During my time here, I...I have been beaten, sexually assaulted, and forced to join a prison gang!"

With that he pulls up his shirt, flaunting a freshly needled tattoo for all to see.

The crowd wails, staring in amazement at his inked abs. Immediately his bare form is awash with camera flashes, all capturing the large, dual lightning bolts covering his body and the lettering to its sides, rendering a thirteen-word verse: "It descends down upon the Just and the Unjust alike, sayeth our Lord."

"They made me do this! They made me do a lot of things!"

He peers deep into Kimberly, telling her with his eyes more of what they've done. Then he returns to his audience, raising his hands, inciting an uprising.

"I will receive justice! I will see that my wrongs are righted!"

"Yeah!" the crowd yells together.

"*We* will see to it that all our wrongs are righted!"

"Yeah!"

"They will not do this to anyone else, ever!"

"Yeah! Yeah!"

"They are supposed to work *for* us—not *against* us!"

"Yeah!"

"Their days of harassing and lying and torturing are over—finished!"

"Yeah! Yeah!"

Individual voices begin to call out.

"Let's get 'em for what they've done to you, Joshua!"

"We will make them pay, Kimberly!"

"Yeah!"

Joshua throws both hands in the air, accepting their devotion. Then he moves back to Kimberly. They embrace yet again, feeling the energy, feeling each other. The clamoring softens, changing from yells and screams to ohs and ahs. Everyone's eyes are heavy upon them; hence not a single person sees the cool mustang man exit his car.

It is a sweet moment that gets interrupted by an overzealous reporter who yells out, "Mr. Siconolfi, what do you know of the missing girls that were written in your dairy?"

Joshua pivots, spins, and about-faces, peering at him with evil green eyes. His aversion for the question is clear. He looks as if he might leap off the stage and attack at any second. Instead he points a threatening finger, replying with a curse. "Your wife will be unfaithful in passing days, and her joy for the occasion will surpass her guilt!" His words cease, but his glare lengthens as an unseen power seems to be burning out of him. His body starts to tremble, coil. People around the reporter begin stepping away when Joshua flashes his hands open and yells, "Boo!"

The crowd jolts and gasps, followed by a split second of frozen uncertainty, until Joshua forms a light smirk across his lips. Then within the audience a level of nervous giggling and sniggering begins. Somewhat ambivalent at first, quickly it multiplies and grows into roaring laughter.

Kimberly seizes upon the momentum by stepping closer to the microphones and asking the people with a sweet smile, "Don't you think he should marry me...for real this time?"

"Yeah, marry her, Joshua!"

"Yeah! Whoo!"

Next they begin to chant. "Marry her! Marry her! Marry her!"

Joshua circles to Kimberly. She flickers a seductively innocent grin.

"Marry her! Marry her!"

"You want me to marry her? You want me to ask her to be my wife? Right here? Right now?"

The mob goes wild, begging for action.

He kneels down in front of her, taking her hands in his. She quivers with excitement and happiness. And everyone stills until they can hear only breathing through the microphone.

"I believe..." His voice cracks. "Uh-hum...I believe that all love and all lies come into the world through the lips of beautiful women. I love your lips, and I love your lies. You are the most beautiful of all feminine. Your appearance to me is like a white cloud under the snow. You protect me from the invisible shadows of darkness. Before I knew you, I knew nothing. Now all that was hidden is known to me. I want you to be with me throughout all eternity, whether we are troubling the heavens or dancing alone in hell. I love you, Kimmy. Will you be with me forever? Will you be my wife?"

"Yes!"

The crowd explodes as Kimberly jumps on him, kissing him all over. They fall and roll around the platform until Joshua can break free long enough to say good-bye. He shouts over the loudspeakers, "Now I'm going to go home to eat a good meal, get drunk, and fuck my wife!"

He throws the microphone down like a rock star. Then they stride arm in arm to an awaiting limo—the one Tabatha secured for them—and dive into the back. It swiftly pulls away, leaving today's gossip in its wake. The driver is instructed to drive straight to their home in Seattle. It should only take five hours, giving them a chance to make up for lost time. But they are not alone; following from an unnoticeable distance is a black Mustang.

Its only occupant is vengeance.

Chapter Seventy-One

With his new fiancée resting, Joshua takes in the view of the jagged, snow-capped peaks of the Cascade Mountains from the car's window. He feels on top of the world, even welcoming the rain he hasn't seen in weeks and feeling somewhat guilty for being short with her. But he had no choice, since she kept trying to discuss their affairs within earshot of the driver—Tabatha's driver. And he would have none of it. Finally he had to yell at her, demanding that she shut the fuck up and wait until they get home before they talk—something he's been anticipating for a long time now. And home is only an hour away.

He then turns his attention to her, watching while she catnaps on the leather seat. She is mostly covered under her coat, but he can still see her pretty face and slender feet. Her tiny toenails are painted dark purple, and she wears a gold ankle bracelet. I wonder if she's sleeping, or just pretending. I wonder what she's been doing over the last months. Or who? Can I trust her to go forward?

The urge to touch her is irresistible. He snuggles in behind her, resting a curious hand on her thigh. Then he slips it under her coat, finding her as he left her—naked and damp from sweat. "Are you sleeping?" he asks softly, breathing on the nape of her neck. She doesn't respond. "I think it's sexier if you're faking. I like it this way." Slowly and subtly he glides strong fingers to her breast and delicately caresses her still-hard nipples. "Oh, you like that, don't you?" He presses himself against her ass. She wiggles with a light moan. "You want me to do dirty things to you, don't you?"

"Mmm…," she whimpers.

He pinches harder then slithers his playful hand capriciously toward her flower, loving that she still pretends to be asleep. "I want to hear you whisper 'fuck' in your sleep."

"Mmm…fuck…Do you want to fuck me?"

Her eyes remain closed as her flesh warms. "Yes, I'm dying to fuck you more. I'm going to make you beg—"

"Well, if you wanted to fuck me, then you shouldn't have told me to shut the fuck up! Should you have? You fucking asshole!" she says, springing alive and pushing him away.

"Kimmy, listen, we're going to be home in an hour; we can talk then."

"We can speak quietly now," she replies defiantly.

"No, I don't trust this limo. I told you we will talk at home, and that's the end of it!"

She caves and playfully bites her bottom lip. Although she would never admit it, she kind of likes it when he commands control. Neither of them says a word; they just gaze at each other as their smiles grow and the love returns to their eyes.

Then suddenly they're startled by the loud engine of a passing car. The windows are tinted, and Joshua can hear its motor winding down along with the slush of its tires. It isn't passing, simply paralleling them. He looks out the side window, staring at a Mustang as pitch-black as the wet road, its wheelman gunning the engine, lurching the car aggressively forward and side to side.

Kimberly looks out the window next to Joshua. "What the fuck is this guy doing?" Immediately she pushes a button, dropping the divider between them and the driver. "What's this guy doing?" she yells.

"I don't know. I'll see if I can lose him."

"Yeah, step on it," Joshua demands.

The limo accelerates; however, the Mustang remains alongside them, driving erratically. Joshua can see its passenger-side window roll down. His first thought is whether their limo is bulletproof. Then he looks ahead and sees an exit a half mile away. "Go faster! Take the exit at the last second!"

"You got it," the driver replies, pushing the pedal to the floor.

They can all see the Mustang stabilizing its close position as they excel to higher and more dangerous speeds. What none of them can see is the gun aiming at them from inside the blackened car.

Kimberly opens the sun roof and stands out in the open. The Mustang veers slightly at her emergence. She throws a bottle of vodka. It smashes on the door, causing the car to lose control. It swerves off the side of the road at over one hundred miles per hour, chipping rocks and road debris, then squeals back, almost hitting them. Now, angrier than ever, the wheelman steadies his weapon and locks her within his sights.

"Turn!" Joshua screams.

The limo steers off at the very last moment, barely making the off-ramp. They all look back, seeing the Mustang hit the brakes and come to a sliding stop three hundred yards past the exit. Then in a cloud of tire smoke, it begins to spin around on the highway.

"What's going on?" their driver asks frantically.

"Keep going! Go through the intersection and back onto the freeway!" Joshua instructs.

But the light is red. And the 8,200-pound limousine is still traveling at over ninety miles per hour and approaching the intersection fast.

"Go! Go!" Kimberly demands.

Their driver follows orders, accelerating to ninety-five. He grips the wheel tight and reaches under his seat for a special device. Joshua and Kimberly hold on. Then he presses a button, and without a second to spare, their light turns green. They sail through the busy intersection at ninety-seven miles per hour—fast enough that not even the sparks are seen by the man in the Mustang, who'll soon be wondering which way they went.

They all scream out in their excitement as they return to the highway. Joshua yells, "How in the hell did you do that?"

"It doesn't matter...tell me: who was that?"

"Yeah, who is that?" Kimberly asks as well.

"I don't know...I don't have any idea"

Kimberly searches his eyes. They tell her he's lying but that he cannot talk about it now. She covers for him. "Well, whoever it was, he's one crazy fucking maniac. But how did you change the light? Tell me; I have to know."

"I have this," he replies, as he presents the device. "It's not exactly legal, but it sure helps my tips when I can get people to the airport on time."

"That's cool as shit. I want one," Kimberly declares, looking to Joshua for permission.

Forty-five minutes later, the three are parked in the driveway. They've agreed upon a five-hundred-dollar tip and another fifteen hundred dollars for a light changer to be delivered by the end of the week. The limo driver leaves contented, feeling alive with a story to sell. Two blocks away he passes a black Mustang parked beside the road, but travels on, counting his money, deciding it couldn't be the same.

Joshua carries his bride-to-be across the threshold. She's light in his arms. And once they're inside, he sets her down gently and goes to work—locking doors, turning on the television, and facing stereo speakers toward the walls. He's already had his home swept for bugs, but still he doesn't want anyone with an external audio surveillance system to hear any of their conversations. No one can ever know what he's about to say. He grabs Kimberly and pulls her close into him. Their eyes meet as he says to her, "We did it! We fucking pulled it off, Kimmy! Did you have any problems?"

"No, none. I did just like you told me. I just disappeared and stayed on the ranch."

"I could never have imagined this would've gotten so big. They went absolutely fucking crazy over the book with the names of the missing girls—your idea. All those hours researching missing persons on the libraries microfilm machine paid off." He kisses her. "And they published all of my bullshit—ha-ha. And no one ever even suggested that you may still be alive. Kimberly, they've had me on the news every single day. I'm big. We're big. We are big fucking news!"

"I know, I know; I've been watching it all on my iPhone. I had to sneak it into the bathrooms at the ranch; they were very strict. Did they ever find the bloody car we left at the airport?"

"No, but everything else worked. They found your blood on the boat; they asked me a million questions about the car club, just like I said they would. I had them eating out of my fucking hands, and they couldn't get enough of my poems and psychobabble. And can you fucking believe Trace killed himself? I couldn't have planned that better myself." Joshua carries on and on, unaware of her sadness for the loss of Trace. "We're going to be rich. We're going to sell the book deals, movie deals, high-profile interviews, and we're fucking famous. They love us, Kimmy. It's going to be just like I told you it was going to be—and even more."

"I'm scared though... What if they find out? And who was that in the Mustang, Joshua?"

He moves into the kitchen, finding a bottle of scotch and a couple of glasses. "Everything's going to work out. We're fucking famous. And as long as we stick to the plan, they can never prove a thing. You were at the ranch. You had no idea what was going on!"

"And the maniac in the car?"

"It has to be that Detective Cools. I guess he's still mad about losing his job. But they really did torture me; they had me in this room with all these crazy lights, and I felt like my head was going to explode. So fuck 'em! They get what they deserve!" He takes a drink, handing her a glass of scotch.

"Are you sure we're fine?"

"Yes! Absolutely! We couldn't be better…now drink up."

"I love you."

"I love you too, Kimmy. We made it; we're home fucking free. Let's celebrate." They clink their glasses.

"Ha-ha…I can't believe we hatched this entire plan on a meth binge," Kimberly replies, now giggling, loosening in the moment.

"Yeah, I told you it would work. And I missed you, Kimmy; I really fucking missed you."

"Me too," she says, falling into him, kissing, trusting. They enjoy each other late into the night until they are drunk and spent, talking over every detail of their plot—their most beautiful conspiracy.